The ADVENTURES of
JONNY LAW

ISBN: 978-0-615-26342-7

Home Plate Publishing
P.O. Box 18745
Spokane, WA 99228

Printed in the U.S.A.

This book is dedicated to Chris Farley,
who I always envisioned as the character of Frank.

It never ceases to amaze me that whenever I embark upon any creative endeavor, the people I need to assist me in the process seem to magically appear in my life.

Special Thanks to:

Scott Orme, who mentored me through the process of turning my screenplay of this story into book form.

Tom Quinn, my gifted cover artist.

Roman Komarov – graphics.

Diane Merton – editing.

Prologue

"Look at me, Frank!" Jonny yelled.

Frank cracked open the door a few inches and looked at Jonny in disbelief. Man, if I only had the guts, he thought. And at that moment he could feel something welling up inside of himself.

"You can be anything in this life you want to be no matter what anyone says, all you have to do is BELIEVE, just BELIEVE in yourself. That's all I'm asking you to do, Frank." Jonny said standing tall without the appearance of fear while the rat, tat, rap, rap, rap exchange of gunfire rang through the air.

Frank repeated the word to himself, "Believe," he said barely audible, then again, "Believe, believe, believe." As his voice got louder and louder and louder, Jonny sensed a transformation come over Frank from fear to courage.

"On the count of three, Frank, I'm going to run to my Winnebago that's parked just down the street and I want you to follow me."

Frank was panting hard, grunting and groaning as if he was dispelling all the fear that he had put down his throat with every drop of whiskey he had swallowed in the eighteen years since he had graduated from high school. In a matter of moments he remembered a time when he felt like a mountain. That old feeling was coming back.

Chapter 1

The early morning sun shined brightly down upon the dried palm trees that lined the street. J.L. Hoover, alias Jonny Law, parked his home on wheels, a 1989 custom Winnebago somewhere on the east side of Los Angeles.

"Here we are." Jonny said to his black and white feline co-pilot. "Looks a little on the rough side, Boots."

"Meowwww," a hungry Boots responded.

Jonny's agile and hungry companion easily sprang onto the center console. "Meowwww," Boots sounded again.

"In a minute, little one. Hmmnn." He gave a brief scratch under Boots chin, while he studied the terrain. He began to wonder if he was possibly in the wrong location. He felt around under the dash of the behemoth, then pressed a button that popped open an overhead compartment and reached inside for a pair of military green binoculars then scanned the neighborhood – cars on blocks without wheels parked in front of rundown houses with dead lawns, barred windows and graffiti everywhere.

"We're either in Chinatown, or someone needs a serious lesson in spelling. I can't make out one word, Boots." Jonny focused on a streetsign.

"Stonewall. Right street, wrong neighborhood perhaps?" He temporarily placed the binoculars on the center console.

"Meowww."

"I know, you're hungry, let me make one quick call, okay, then we'll get you something to make you happy." Jonny once again scratched the white portion of Boots' chin.

Jonny's six-foot-one lanky frame filled the captain's seat of the home on wheels, a retired F.B.I. surveillance vehicle he had purchased at an auction. It had more bell and whistles and secret gadgets and compartments than Jonny could keep track of, but the thing that really sold him on the yacht-sized vehicle was that it was amphibious. When he heard that tid-bit of information, he knew that it was for him. He gladly paid the seventy-five-hundred-dollars he had been saving his whole life, and drove the high-mile rig off the lot. And since it could sleep six, he figured why pay rent? So, he decided to make it his home on wheels. He had never felt the desire to drive it into the water, but the thought alone made him feel a notch above those who didn't possess such a sophisticated piece of transpo/home/armored vehicle - the perfect solution for his dual lifestyle. The bulletproof windows that came standard gave him an added sense of security.

He could already feel the heat of the morning sun that shined through the front windows. It was going to be another hot day, he thought, as he pulled his cell phone from a piece of Velcro around his belt, flipped it open and hit auto-dial. Just as he did, vibrations from a low rider three blocks down the street could be felt as it turned a corner and approached. Pulsating rap music intruded every weathered looking structure in the neighborhood. Jonny picked up the binoculars once again and got a close up of the four angry looking occupants in the convertible Chevy low-rider that slowly approached.

"Hmnn. Heavy-set, bleached-blond Caucasion female, two black gentlemen and one Latino. The black gentleman in the backseat appears to be wielding a piece of pipe, or perhaps that is a - shotgun? They're a somewhat sour looking bunch, Boots - some recent tattooes, perhaps? I understand they can be painful."

He reached overhead and pressed a button that quickly lowered a sun-shield over the large front windows, which gave the mobile-home sized vehicle a cross-eyed bird look. The numerous antennae and other apparatus that were fastened to the roof of the rig made it appear as if it was also part insect.

He then unsnapped two leather fasteners above his head and pulled down a springy periscope eyepiece and placed the dangling cushioned viewfinder over both his eyes. A quick flip of a switch located on the dash and a softball sized fisheye could be seen on top of the rig as it raised slowly to monitor 360 degrees of the surrounding terrain.

"Locals don't look very friendly, Boots," Jonny casually said with his cell phone in one hand and the periscope eyepiece in the other. The thumping sounds from the low-rider got louder and louder until the frame of the Winnebago pulsated to the heavy beat. A shrill sounding woman's voice at the other end of the phone greeted Jonny.

"Good morning, Stockton Insurance."

"Yeah hi, Gwen, I mean, Ms. Peters," Jonny had to quickly hold the phone away from his ear a moment as the elderly secretary of the large insurance firm scolded him for not properly addressing her.

"Sorry, Ms. Peters, listen, I was wondering?" Jonny pulled the phone away from his ear again, as Ms. Peters fumed about the background noise.

"Umm, I'm not a connoisseur of the latest rap sounds Ms. Peters, but I...I... well, I was simply calling to verify my coordinates over here to see if perhaps there was a mix-up?" he questioned as he spied through his periscope at the car as it slowly approached, then stopped next to the behemoth. The thunderous music abruptly shut off as the occupants of the vehicle pondered the large RV rig with antennas at every corner and, bullhorn loud speakers that decorated the top, along with two satellite dishes, one at each end. Jonny held the phone away from his ear as Ms. Peters, cackled indecipherable scoldings at him for interrupting her paperwork. He paid little mind to her, but watched as a man in the rear seat of the low-rider cracked open the barrel of a sawed off shotgun and loaded a couple shells in the chambers. The driver of the car looked over at the rig and studied what was written on its side.

"If anyone axed, we on vacation," he said slowly reading each word of an airbrushed saying written on the RV.

"Vacation, my ass," the heavyset man with a shotgun replied as he fired the gun into the air.

BAM!!! BAM!!!

"WRarrrrrr!!!" Boots responded, then as if shot from a slingshot, he darted to a safe remote area of the mobile.

"What in Gaaaaaaaawwwwwd's name was that?" Ms Peters howled in Jonny's ear.

Jonny, who continued eyeing the low-rider next to him through his eyepiece, calmly responded.

"Remington 16 gauge double-barreled shotgun with sawed off end. I'd know that sound anywhere. They don't mean it."

"What did you say?" Ms. Peters hollered back.

"Nothing Gwen, I mean, Ms. Peters. Listen, I better get to work over here and you have one lovely day," Jonny flipped shut his cell and continued to study the subjects.

"That boat's gonna be full of holes you don't get it outta here honky, you hear?" The driver yelled out, then once again cranked up the volume of the profane rap song and the deep bass kicked out, vibrating the shell of the towering rig and tested the stress limits on the windows of the shacks in the war-zone-like neighborhood.

Jonny maneuvered the fisheye on top of the rig and watched as the car slowly drove past then turned the corner and drove out of sight. He pulled the viewfinder away from his eyes and jostled the telescope eyepiece back up into position, then got up from his captain's chair, opened a small fridge for some kitty food and poured some into a small bowl, then added some milk.

"Kitty, kitty kitty kitty, come on out Boots, coast is clear. It's got some two-per-cent in it, too."

Magically, Boots appeared from hiding to enjoy some breakfast.

"That's a good kitty," Jonny said and then headed into the back of his home on wheels to change into appropriate work attire, a casual grey suit coat with matching slacks, black soft soled shoes, and white shirt and tie. His attire was embellished with a fake prosthetic arm that he would operate via a levered apparatus in the back of the coat. Numbers were down on sales of the company's dismemberment insurance package and Jonny was the number one and only pick for the special promotion the company was offering. Sign up one customer and get another family member at a ten per cent discount. It wasn't a great deal, but Jonny knew he wasn't just selling insurance, he was guarding America from any and all potential threats, and that made all the difference.

A moment later Jonny was dressed and ready to hit the streets. He looked into a full-length mirror that was adjacent to the side door, took out a pocket comb and ran it through his dark hair so that not a hair was out of place, nor touching his ears.

"Pick your market and work, work, work it, Boots." Jonny tested the motion of his prosthetic extending it outward, up in the air, and then to his cheek to wipe away any tears that he may muster from a repertoire of stories of how he lost his own arm in an effort to evoke the sympathies of his new found customers. It works perfectly he thought. He then pressed a button under a table and looked on as a false wall began to close slowly. Behind it was a full wardrobe of various disguises on one side and a row of miscellaneous warfare-type devices on the other. Included was his old bazooka, that was the centerpiece of his collection, marked with the words - PROPERTY OF THE F.B.I. written on it. His arsenal also included out dated nerve gas canisters, smoke bombs, shock bombs, one parachute, several gas masks, two old Army helmets, bullet proof vests, one life jacket, a WWII bayonet, some rope and an assortment of fireworks, all of which Jonny had accumulated over the years. He also had a wall of surveillance equipment that was not concealed. An outdated but working computer that was custom mounted into the wall, alongside a reel-to-reel tape recorder, and a radar screen that was missing some components. And when that special occasion arose, he had a drawer full of miscellaneous bugging devices that could be planted or mounted in just about any place a person could imagine.

He took several deep breaths to prepare for the day as the slow-moving wall closed. He reached into his top left suit coat pocket and pulled out a small digital recorder and pressed the record button, "This meeting may be recorded for quality assurance," he stated into the device, then dropped the recorder back in his front shirt pocket. He then reached in his front coat pocket for his mirrored sunglasses, put them on and headed for the door.

"Guard the fort, Boots." Jonny opened the side door and stepped down the two steps of the mobile onto the only patch of green grass in the entire neighborhood.

He closed the door then set down his dark leather company issued brief-case with concealed compartments and brass combination latches, and with his right hand patted several pockets, then struggled deep into his left pocket where his keys where located and pulled them out. The keys rang out as they bounced off the curb, then under the beheamoth. "Not a problem," he said as he squatted down and aimed his magnetic prosthetic in the general vicinity of the keys.

BAM!!! A shot rang out.

Jonny quickly stood up and looked around. "Backfire?" His eyes locked onto a passing car a block down. He breathed a sigh of relief. "Yep," he assured himself with a smile, not seeing the indented mark at head level of his thick-shelled rig where he was standing a moment before. He then got down onto his hands and knees where he easily spotted the keys.

"I'm gonna get ya," he playfully said as the keys were quickly sucked up to the magnetic hook-like metal hand of Jonny's third arm.

"There we go." He got back up and attempted to pull the keys from the hand.

"Come on, mnnphh," he struggled. Again, "Come…..on…" he moaned as he pulled with all his might. He took a deep calming breath, shook his head, and tried to reassure himself.

"Don't get mad, get eeeeeeeeeevennnnnn!!!" He grunted and the wrestling match was on, Jonny against a possessed magnetic foe. He grunted and groaned as he fell to the grassy shoulder and rolled about like a man on fire.

On his back, he heard the sound. He tilted his head back to see behind him, while still trying to pry the keys from the steel hook – street cleaner 12' o clock. He let out a cry that could be heard two blocks away. The keys wouldn't budge. The spray from the cleaner got closer and closer until he was immersed in a flood of water and with a herniating tug the keys seemed to magically be released from their pull. Jonny sprung to his feet spitting dirt and debris from his mouth, straightened his sunglasses and brushed off his shirt and tie, then casually locked up the Winnie. He looked around to see if anyone had noticed the event. Not a soul. He pulled out his comb from his back pants pocket, quickly ran it through his hair, then turned and picked up his brief case as if nothing happened and began whistling a tune as he proceeded, dripping wet, down the street.

He slowed his walk to check out the locals as an older model white Camry approached from down the street. Inside were three, somewhat out of place occupants. What first caught his eye were the New York plates.

"Edward, Victor, Libra, six, niner, two, New York." Jonny said, just loud enough to record into his pocket device. "One very large male with goatee driving, another male slight build, either has been getting a lot of free tans, or of middle-eastern descent wearing a white turban, one very attractive woman short, jet black, spiked hair."

The woman and male passenger snarled at Jonny, who returned the gesture with a very warm, "Good-morning there," said with a smile and a friendly wave of his prosthetic as they drove past.

"If looks could kill, I'd be dead," he said to himself as he approached his first home, colorfully marked with gang graffiti. He attempted to open the faded wood front gate that looked as if it might have been painted a quarter century ago. It fell off its hinges and broke to pieces. He quickly scanned the windows that were protected by black steel bars, checking to see if a potentially angry owner might have spied on him during the incident. He discreetly kicked the remnants of the gate off to the side of the cracked cement walkway into some weeds and approached the door of the house. He delivered a good firm knock, then patiently waited. Nothing. He knocked again.

A perspiring, angry looking man, having withdrawals from something and wearing hanging baggies, a muscle shirt, and twenty pounds of gold around his neck, cracked open the door as far as the lock chain would allow.

"Hello there and good morning, could I speak with you regarding a confidential matter, sir?" Jonny inquired with the most hospitable tone of voice he could conjur while he attempted to get a better glimpse of his first potential customer and "his world" through the two inch opening.

The man had many different colored tattoos over the visible portions of his body. He squinted back at Jonny and studied him from head to toe, then struggled to release each word from his mouth.

"Big Dee sent you? Tell him Julio will have the money by six...tonight! No sooner! Just tell him!"

"Julio, that's a nice name," Jonny said smiling trying to warm up to his first potential customer who slammed the door shut.

Jonny looked at the steel door that had some small holes in the upper portion of it, just about the size of a small caliber bullet. He glanced over to the window. Someone had attempted to pry off the bars at some point in time. He stared back to the door and got closer to see through a hole. Covered.

"Hmmnn, Big Dee? He must be mistaking me for," Jonny chuckled. "Take off the glasses for Pete's sake." He set down his brief case, took off his glasses and put them in his suit jacket pocket. "One more time, turn on the charm." He put on an eager smile, the type he had been taught in his sales training classes, then knocked again a little harder.

"Sir?" Jonny pleaded to the man. "Sir?" He called out again to the man inside. "Hmmnn, where did he go?" he wondered. He stepped over to the front window and peeked through the black steel bars and a slit in the curtains. His eyes widened as he saw a woman tied to a chair in the kitchen area with a gag in her mouth. He sounded like a man who had been held under water for twenty minutes as he sucked up a deep breath, then exhaled the word, "Hello," then quickly resumed his position at the front door.

Julio opened the door with a large barreled pistol and put it into Jonny's wide-eyed, frozen face.

"Hey kracker, are you deaf or something?" Julio exclaimed in the same tone of voice as before.

"Yeah, it's funny you mention it, I am a little hard of hearing, what time did you say again?" Jonny sheepishly inquired.

"Six o'clock!"

"Okay, six it is. I heard you loud and clear that time, thanks a lot, I'm really sorry to bother you again, Julio," Jonny said with a rainbow of emotion that spanned from joy to deep sorrow.

"Tell him," the man moaned.

"I sure will. Listen, I gotta run big guy, you take care," Jonny smiled as Julio slammed the door again in his face. He gingerly stepped back away

7

from the door, nearly tripped down the front porch, then quickly turned around and pointed his prosthetic towards the front window in a friendly gesture where Julio's pistol barrel peeked out through the slit in the curtains. He turned around and hurried away from the house.

"Married life, no thank you, not yet anyway." He yanked his cell phone from its Velcro fastener and pressed 911 as he whistled a tune. He paused as he approached the next house, which was charred from fire with boarded up windows. "Hmmn, gone shopping."

"911 operator, state your emergency."

"Ah, I'm not really sure if I'd call it an emergency, but there seems to be a minor domestic spat at 12813 East Stonewall Street."

"Are there weapons involved?"

"Just a hand-gun, maam," Jonny casually stated. "In my professional opinion, they look like newlyweds, and my guess is he's afraid he's gonna lose her - she's tied into a chair in the dining room." Jonny explained.

"Would you state your name, sir?"

"My name is Law, Jonny Law, and you have a nice day, maam."

"Sir, sir?" the operator replied, but Jonny slapped the phone shut.

Heading to the next run-down house, Jonny heard a familiar sound. It was a small kitten's cry for help. He paused, then looked up searching the leafy tree until he spotted the frightened kitten who had wandered out on a thin branch.

"Hey you, you look like you could use a helping hand," he said looking up. He set down his briefcase, then looked around, "Do it when nobody's lookin." With both hands he quickly reached behind his back and pulled the control mechanism for the prosthetic around his waist so he could manipulate the extension features of the mail-order device.

"No need to fear small one," Jonny called up to the kitty. He manipulated a small reel on the device and watched as it extended higher and higher up to the fearfully frozen kitten.

"Come on little Kitty, " he kindly invited. "Come on, I'm not gonna hurt ya," he gently stated as the kitten started to paw at the hooked end. "Just a little closer little one," he softly said, then, "Gotcha!" He maneuvered the device so that he gently pinched the loose fold of skin around the kitten's small neck with the claw portion of the prosthetic, as its mother would do.

Jonny didn't see or hear Emily, the six year old owner of the kitten as she cried out, "kitty, kitty, kitty, kitty, here kitty, kitty, kitty."

Jonny's imagination had taken hold and he was somewhere on the high seas pretending to reel in a killer shark.

"Whoa, she is a big one, come on lil' darlin', I know you wanna fight," he excitedly cried out as he spun the screeching kitten in a full 360 degress while reeling it in to safety.

"Come on baby, come on to daddy, that's my girl. " And just as the kitten was safe on the ground, its owner approached Jonny and grabbed the kitten before Jonny had a chance.

"Fluffy, are you alright?" young Emily, still wearing her pajamas and with bare feet, inquired of her little kitten.

"She's gonna be just fine," Jonny reassuredly replied.

"You're not missing an arm," the little girl sharply responded.

Scowling, Jonny knew he was busted, and didn't say a word. He scratched his head and looked around to see if anyone else witnessed the event as little Emily ran back across the street caressing her little Fluffy in her arms. Jonny adjusted his arm into its normal position of making it appear that he had only one good arm and proceeded on to the next house where he would get the surprise of his life.

Chapter 2

Jonny approached another run-down house spray-painted with numerous, indecipherable, colorful markings. The lawn was overgrown with weeds and cluttered with miscellaneous car parts. He straightened his tie and approached the weathered, wood door that was kicked in at the bottom, then planted a firm knock on it. A moment later the door opened. An unkempt man appeared in dirty sweats. His large belly protruded from the bottom of a t-shirt two sizes too small.

"Good morning sir, and how are you this fine day?" The man quickly shut the door with the exception of a crack of an inch where he could hear what sounded like the man getting violently ill. Then silence.

"Sir?" This wasn't in the sales manual, Jonny thought. A moment later the man re-opened the door.

"Yeah, what do you want?"

Jonny took a second look at the man. "Frank?" he exclaimed with a questioning tone. "Frank Miller is that?...I don't believe this!" Jonny cried out two octaves higher than his normal voice.

"Well believe it pal, it's me in the flesh, who the hell are you?"

Jonny started to chuckle, "Huh, huh, huh. Home economics, ten-thirty, Mrs. Sizemore's class." Jonny removed his mirrored sunglasses and placed them in his shirt pocket.

"Law?" Frank squinted through his hung-over fog.

"It's me, least likely to succeed, page two of the year-book right here," Jonny said, grinning ear-to-ear, eyeing Frank up and down. "You look great!"

Frank nodded in agreement pulling up his sweats around his big belly, "I jog quite a bit, down to the store mostly, twice a day sometimes."

"Mind if I?" Jonny inquired.

"Yeah, sure, come on in." Jonny stepped inside to a disaster area.

He raised a brow as his eyes shifted from the stained, partially ripped up carpet, more car parts that were strewn about, and more jarbled profanity that was spray-painted on every wall, which led him to one three legged chair that faced a TV stand without the TV on it.

"What happened to your arm?" Frank inquired.

Jonny smiled. "Da da. It's a cover." His missing limb magically appeared as he reached for his wallet and pulled out a business card from it and handed it to Frank. "Here's my card."

Frank took the card and gave Jonny a second look. He squinted as he put the card at varying distances for focus and slowly read, "'J.L. Hoover, alias Jonny Law, dismemberment insurance, and other vissisitudes'? Hmnn, what the heck are vissisitudes'?" Frank questioned.

Jonny shrugged it off stating, "Doesn't matter Frank, it's got a good ring to it, don't you think?"

"A little dishonest wouldn't you say, I mean with the phony arm?" Frank handed the card back to Jonny who scowled as he snatched the card back with one swift motion of his wrist and hand.

"It's not my real line of work, okay" Jonny jammed the card back into his wallet in an agitated manner, then quietly added, "lard-ass."

"Four eyes," Frank volleyed.

"Puss ball," Jonny fired.

"Mamma's boy," Frank jeered.

"Shit for brains," Jonny returned barely able to contain his laughter.

"Alright, alright, you win," Frank gave in to Jonny's comebacks. "You were one of those debate team guys if my memory serves me right," he added.

"Could've been if it wasn't for that little miss priss, Janet Posenski. Listen, Frank, I'm on the ground floor of something big, something very big. I started my own agency."

"What kind of agency?" Frank lifted his shirt to scratch his hairy mid section.

"It's called the S.A.A.O.A. Is there someplace we can talk?"

"In the kitchen, I'll be right in." Frank hurried down the hallway of the small two-bedroom house. His feet pounded onto the floor like an elephants'.

Jonny entered the kitchen wincing to the sound of Frank saying his morning prayers to the porcelain God. He scanned the kitchen. Whiskey bottles, wine bottles, and beer bottles decorated the dirty counters, kitchen table, even the filthy stove. The soft rubber soles of his shoes stuck to the dirty floor with each step as he moved over to the window that looked out onto a back yard that matched the front. The fence had a checkerboard appearance with nearly every other slat missing, which gave an easy view into the neighboring backyard directly behind Frank's. It was also weeded and dried up with one full sized lawn chair that sat on a small portion of cracked portions of patio that remained somewhat level. A small fold up table stood next to it.

Jonny eyed a woman with short black hair wearing a white bathrobe as she exited the house. It was the same woman who had snarled at him earlier while driving by in the old model Camry. Her white robe was loosely tied in the front. It was the kind he thought that fancy hotels gave as complimentary tokens to wealthy patrons who could easily afford a semi-truck full of the garments, but gave them away anyway. Jonny, always with an assortment of devices and gadgets on his person, took out a compact set of binoculars to get a closer look.

She untied the cotton belt and took off the robe revealing a shapely figure covered with a scant bikini, then laid it out onto a reclining lawn chair. He focused his binoculars onto a small book and something else with the book she held in one hand, and a small bottle in the other. His view wandered up her long legs, shapely hips, slender waist, "And the upstairs is nicely furnished," he said to himself, but still couldn't make out the title of the book as she set it and the container onto the lounge table, then laid down onto the lawn chair. She reached for the small container and poured some of its contents into her hands and began rubbing the liquid onto her legs and arms. She continued rubbing, rubbing, and rubbing, adding more lotion and more rubbing.

"Okay, enough with the lotion, now pick up the book." The woman set down the container of oil, and as if she could hear him, she immediately picked up the book, and reached for a pair of magnifiers that had a short metal handle attached, held them up and began to read.

"U.S. Secret Service? Hmnn, that's funny, why not People, or The National Inquirer?" Jonny pulled the binoculars away from his face and wondered. Could she be an agent?

Frank's heavy footsteps could be heard as he stomped down the hall.

Jonny continued studying Frank's neighbor. "Nice appliances."

"Yeah," Frank scratched his head looking at the mess. "I was hit pretty hard last October – burglars. Thank God they didn't take everything."

"Uh huh," Jonny agreed.

"New neighbor's a babe," Frank said.

"Healthy too, have you gotten to know her?" Jonny questioned still spying through the binoculars. He watched as she tilted her head up from the book and looked directly towards him.

She raised her eyepiece up from her book and aimed it right at Jonny, spotting him. She held up her middle finger for Jonny to plainly see.

Jonny quickly pulled the binoculars away from his face.

"Hello," he said out loud, knowing he was busted for stealing a look at her. He stepped away from the window and looked to Frank.

"Not exactly, tried to. I went over last week with a case a beer and a tuna casserole, tryin' to make a good impression, you know, welcome 'em to the neighborhood, and some sheik guy answered the door wearin' one of those turbans wrapped around his head, then she stood there behind him, pretended like she didn't speak English, and her name's Debbie if you can believe that," Frank stated.

"A foreigner named Debbie reading a Secret Service booklet, with middle-eastern ties, hmnn," Jonny pondered a moment. "I don't like the smell of it, Frank." He discreetly peered out the back window at the woman who now ignored him as she continued to read.

"You don't?"

"No, I don't. Something in my gut, you know what I bet?"

"What's that," Frank replied.

"I bet they could use some insurance," Jonny said with a smile. His attention was sparked again when the man wearing the turban that had accompanied the woman earlier in the car exited the house to converse with her.

"Uh huh," Frank agreed also sneaking a peek at his neighbor.

Jonny glanced around the filthy kitchen. "How about an early lunch, Frank?"

Frank put his hand under his shirt and rubbed his hand over his upset stomach. "My stomach's feelin' a little upside down," Frank said. "You buyin?" He then quickly inquired.

"You bet I am, big guy," Jonny responded still keeping an eye on the pair.

"Well heck, I suppose. I haven't had any breakfast."

Jonny snapped shut his pocket-sized binoculars just as a voice from a bullhorn could be heard resonating through the neighborhood.

"This is the police. You are surrounded, come out with your hands held high."

"Now what?" Frank casually questioned.

"Two doors down, domestic spat. Julio and his wife appeared to be having some problems. I called it in." Jonny stated.

"That guy ain't married, heck he's the biggest drug dealer on the east side of town, hell, maybe even the whole west coast."

Jonny raised a brow. "Hmnn, kinky neighborhood, Frank, real kinky, let's move." Jonny picked up his brief case and headed for the front door. And just as he opened it, it sounded like World War III had just begun.

Jonny looked outside at the sea of police vehicles on the scene, just like in the movies, cops behind their cars shooting at the bad guy, Julio, who wasn't going down without a fight. Bullets ricocheted wildly through the air as Jonny walked fearlessly out the front door and into Frank's overgrown front yard.

"Danger is my mantra," he called out, then turned to look back at Frank who remained cowering inside the house.

"Are you comin', Frank?"

"Are you crazy Law, or what?" Frank hollered over the spurts of gunfire that could be heard through the door that was open less than the width of the average sized bullet.

Jonny just stood there in the yard and observed the volley of gunfire as strays richochetted off everything in God's creation.

"Just enough to follow a dream," he called back to Frank then turned to face him. "It's two doors down. Frank?"

"Yeah." Frank called back through the slit in the door. His voice quivered.

"Look at me, Frank!"

Frank cracked open the door a few inches and peeked out at Jonny in disbelief that he appeared to have no fear. Man, if I only had the guts, he thought to himself. And at that moment he began to feel the collection of old thoughts, negative feelings and emotions that had remained welled up inside of him, and that had held him back for years.

"You can be anything in this life you want to be no matter what anyone says, all you have to do is BELIEVE, just BELIEVE in yourself. That's all I'm asking you to do, Frank." Jonny stood tall without the appearance of fear or concern of the rat, tat, tat, tat, tat exchange of gunfire that rang through the air.

Frank repeated the word to himself, "Believe," he said barely audible, then again, "Believe, believe, believe." And his voice got louder and louder and louder, until Jonny sensed a transformation was taking place.

14

"On the count of three, Frank, I'm going to run to my Winnebago that's parked just down the street and I want you to follow me."

Frank was panting hard, grunting and groaning as if he was dispelling all the fear that he had put down his throat from every drop of whiskey he had swallowed in the eighteen years since he had graduated from high school. In a matter of moments he remembered a time when he felt like a mountain. He sensed that old feeling coming back.

Jonny yelled out, "One," then paused, "Two," he called out again. He paused one last time then whispered to himself, "Come on, Frank you can do it," and a long drawn out yell exploded from Jonny's lungs, "Threeeeeeeeeeeeee!!!" And at that moment Frank also let out a yell as he threw open the front door and the two charged past the mayhem. They darted parallel to the line of fire. It was the type of incident that felt as if it all happened in slow motion.

An echoed voice from somewhere cried out, "Hold your fire," and even Julio paused and looked on with disbelief at the pair.

"What the?" Julio said to himself as he peeked out from the side of his curtains behind a lead plate. He watched his neighbor and the white dude, who was just at his door, as they ran behind the police vehicles heading down the street. "That sum bitch ain't missin' no arm."

Jonny's prosthetic flailed about as both of his real arms rapidly churned back and forth as they sprinted to safety.

Frank could still run like a jackrabbit and surprised Jonny when he passed him while in a full sprint for his life to the Winnebago. They had made it. And just as they did, the exchange of gunfire erupted again.

In the cockpit, Jonny turned the ignition switch and pumped the gas pedal. A large cloud of black smoke filled the street, which nearly concealed the rig as he fired up the beefy 454 V-8 engine.

Frank looked in the large side mirror at the cloud of smoke that was forming. "I hate to be the bearer of bad news, but I'd say you need a set of rings in this baby, you're blowin' smoke outta this thing like a chimney stack, Jonny," Frank stated still panting from their sprint.

"Smoke shield, Frank." He pumped the gas with a firm steady stomping motion of his foot, "This baby'll sleep six." Jonny said.

Ra tat a tat tat a tat. A large caliber weapon belched out.

"Huh?" Frank questioned still in fear for his life.

"Yeah. It's a retired F.B.I. surveillance vehicle."

"Does it run?" Frank pleaded.

"Gotta hundred gallon water tank." Jonny responded.

Ra tat tat tat tat tat tat...the big gun fired again.

Jonny glanced over to Frank and noticed his eyes to be a bit bugged out from fear.

"Relax, Frank."

"Sound's like one of those guns they shoot planes down with!" Frank cried out.

"Darn near seven-hundred miles, that's with both gas tanks. She's got two you know, oh yeah," Jonny bragged as he continued pumping the gas while twisting hard on the key. His head bobbed up and down in sync with the engine, and then, as if magic occurred, the behemoth started.

"It's tricked out pretty good too, there we go," Jonny revved the engine holding the pedal down for several seconds, then lifted it, then repeated the process.

"Do you really think you need to warm it up, I mean they are still shootin' their guns out there," Frank impatiently said.

Jonny smiled and casually put her in gear, while some strays could be heard ricocheting off the thick shell of the rig. He put on his blinker and slowly drove away, checking his rear-view before pulling from the curb.

"You just don't understand, Frank, it's all about facing your - " and he didn't even finish the statement as the ping of a stray bullet could be heard as it bounced off the rig somewhere, and at that moment, Jonny dramatically clutched his side.

"- Aghhh,!!!" He winced in pain. "Hot... lead....side," Jonny cried out and jerked the rig with a punch of the gas at the instant the bullet struck, then occasional spurts of gas accompanied by a moan to emphasize every pang of pain from the fresh wound as he weaved the rig back and forth like he'd seen so many Nascar drivers do to warm up their tires before the big race.

Frank appeared to lose all color in his face. "Are you shot, Jonny!? "

The pain appeared to be too great and all Jonny could muster was a "agghhhh," and his eyes started going up and down and every which way as if he might slip out of consciousness at any second.

Frank grabbed the wheel to avoid any parked vehicles, "Don't stop, for Godsakes!"

"Would've been great workin' with ya, man!" Jonny eeked out. He winced with each word like they would be the last he would utter in this life.

Frank looked at the road, then back to Jonny to read his condition.

"Don't die on me, Jonny!" he desperately cried out.

Frank momentarily put his face in the hand that wasn't steering the rig, "Oh for love a, my unemployment and now this!" he said now rocking back and forth.

"Haaaaa!!!" Jonny cried out. "I was just kiddin', Frank. A test of fire you might say," Jonny jeered and then back to total health as he straightened out the rig and gave it some gas.

"What the, you mean you're not?"

Jonny shook his head and pointed at Frank. "Ha ha,'fraid not buddy. This baby's got two-inch thick bulletproof glass and armor plating in the walls that a Sherman tank couldn't penetrate! And it's unsinkable!"

"Man oh man, I don't believe you. You haven't changed one bit since high school." Jonny just smiled and shrugged his shoulders as they drove off down the street and headed to Jonny's favorite meeting spot - A Dog To Go, where the menu read, WE SERVE PETS TOO!

Jonny was triple parked for the thirty-foot ride and he had shed his prosthetic before he and Frank enjoyed an early lunch under a dalmation dotted umbrella at one of the outside tables. It was a small and quaint place that was private during off hours, even though bustling L.A. traffic flowed nearby like a never-ending river.

Frank was eating his foot-long hotdog like a man who hadn't seen food in a month. Jonny did most of the talking.

"What I'm talking about Frank is leading a double life."

Frank stopped chewing a moment and looked at Jonny.

"Right," Jonny acknowledged Frank's serious look. "It's big, really big, Frank. There's a couple small formalities, I'd need to get you signed up on the insurance plan and you'd be ready to go, workin' for your country," Jonny stated, then chomped down on his foot-long.

Frank took a sip of his drink and swallowed, "So is this like the C.I.A., and the F.B.I., and A T & T and companies like that?"

"Right."

"So what would I be doin'?"

Jonny chuckled, and thought a moment to tactfully address the question without offending his old friend, "I don't mean to, but it's just, that, well," Jonny stammered, then continued, "Well for starters you'd be taking your life out of the toilet bowl and start living, really living Frank," he stated then took another good sized bite to give Frank a moment to ponder the words he'd said. It didn't take him but a moment before he replied.

"I'll do it."

Jonny stopped chewing almost surprised at Frank's immediate response. He reached for a napkin from the dalmation napkin holder and wiped some catsup from his lip, "I knew you would." He set down his drooping foot-long, wiped his hands with the napkin and reached for his brief case. He placed it flat down in front of himself, then began turning the three rolling combination dials that secured each latch until they were in perfect alignment. He nonchalantly looked around and over each shoulder to see if anyone suspicious was eavesdropping, then opened it.

"That's what my intense training has done for me. I'm an expert in reading body language, Frank, and it was, well, it was pretty obvious that you're a man that has excessive appetites."

At first Frank was taken aback by the comment, wondering if it was an insult to his weight, then Jonny continued, "I meant, for things like danger, Frank." Immediately Frank had a look of pride and confidence as he stuffed the last inch of his hot dog into his mouth.

"So will this involve any surveillance-type work?" Frank mumbled with a mouthful.

Jonny had the insurance forms laid out in front of Frank and held out his pen for Frank's John Henry on the dotted line.

"Right," Jonny replied in agreement. "Just sign here. We'll get you started with our dismemberment plan."

Frank signed his name and handed it back to Jonny. "Just wonderin', Jonny, I've got a ton of photography equipment. It's the only thing the little woman didn't take in the divorce, and that's just because she never liked her picture bein' taken. She's battled her weight for years."

"Right," Jonny eyed Frank's signature and then blew on it for added security and placed it in his briefcase. "You're now officially a member of the S.A.A.O.A. Congratulations agent number?" Jonny paused to glance at the insurance form Frank had just signed, "001752. I'll be in touch, gotta run," Jonny quickly shut his briefcase and latched the gold combination latches, rolled each combination dial several times, then stood up and started to leave. "Oh, and Frank, your first two weeks are free on the S.A.A.O.A. insurance plan, then only eleven dollars per week."

"Hey hold up, I'll need a ride back to my place," Frank stated.

"Right," Jonny halfheartedly agreed. And just as he turned around to head to the RV, a mucky, wet, sloupy-like sound was heard. He looked perplexed down at his dull, black shoes that were surrounded in what looked like brown mud.

"Now that's a Great Dane, gotta be," Frank instantly concluded eyeing the situation.

And just then the foul smell of the feces hit Jonny. He winced and turned his head away. "It ain't no French poo poo, that's for sure."

"There's a hose over there," Frank calmly suggested, then walked over to the side of the small establishment and turned on the hose.

"Sharp eye 001752, let's do it."

Frank squeezed the spray nozzle several times for a quick pressure test. It sprayed a strong blast of water onto the pavement as he walked towards Jonny. And just as he was getting in shooting range the hose got tangled and tugged at Frank. Still squeezing the nozzle with one hand and looking back while wrestling with the knotted hundred-foot snake with the other, Frank nailed Jonny good in the groin area with a strong blast of the water, then the face and body area as well before he violently shook the knot free. He looked at Jonny who wiped his face off and shook his head as he cleared his right ear which had taken a direct hit as he turned his face away from the blast.

"Sorry Jonny," Frank sheepishly said as he walked closer to Jonny to clean him of the foul matter still adhered to his shoe.

"It's okay Frank, I'll live," Jonny reassuredly replied as Frank began spraying away at Jonny's shoe.

Frank started to chuckle. "It kinda looks like you might've had a little accident."

"Very funny, Frank," Jonny said with little emotion.

"So what does this S.A.O.A stand for, just in case my parents or ex-wife ask me what I've been doin'?" Frank inquired to quickly change the subject.

Jonny looked down at his shoe that was free of the foreign matter, then to the other that didn't match the soaked one. "I like that wet look. How 'bout a double, Frank." Jonny suggested.

"You got it," Frank replied and then he sprayed Jonny's other shoe so it would match the other soggy one.

Jonny looked down at the two worn soggy shoes. "Good work, Frank, that's S.A.A.O.A. and it stands for Secret Agent Association of America, let's get out of here."

Jonny trotted to the Winnebago as Frank threw the hose down, then ran over to the rig as Jonny opened it up. The two got in and drove away, once again leaving a trail of black smoke behind them.

Chapter 3

Yellow crime tape was all that remained from the ferocious gun battle at Julios when Jonny drove Frank back to his house. From there, he headed into downtown Los Angeles for a company meeting. He paid no mind to some of the looks he received from his wet, soggy look, as he entered the building and got on the elevator in the high-rise and rode to the twenty-seventh-floor, where the offices of Stockton Insurance were located.

He got off and proceeded past some other offices leaving wet footprints and some remnants of the foreign matter that remained on the under portion of his shoe on the polished, spotless floor. His shoes made a wet soggy scrunching sound with each step as he approached the two thick glass doors with large brass handles that garnered the company name. He pulled open the large heavy door and entered.

He was greeted by the receptionist/secretary, Gwendolyn Peters, who he had spoken to earlier. She was the oldest member of the company and always kept an eagle eye on the clock above the door as members of the firm entered. She also kept a firm mental record of any slackers. Ms. Peters had been with the company since its inception in 1962 and continued working well past her retirement party several years previous. Rumor had it that she was related to the president of the company, Harold Stockton. She was an ornery and cantankerous old maid who reminded anyone who would listen that she was married to the company. She firmly believed in being punctual and despised Jonny for his constant tardiness. But Jonny always managed to keep his sense of humor around those willing to shoot him down with their verbal attacks.

"You're late," Ms Peters said.

"Memory's the second thing to go, Gwen. I'm Jonny, remember?" he said in a carefree manner, then smiled and walked past her. His shoes sounded like two large squeegees with each step, scrunch, scrunch, scrunch, all the way to the back sales office.

Ms. Peters' voice cracked as she angrily spit out, "How many times have I told you that I do not appreciate being called by that name. My name is Miss Peters to you, Mr. Hoover!" She called out to Jonny who approached the sales office door with the nameplate attached, that read, Harold Stockton, President, then turned to give Gwen one last smile before he entered.

Harold Stockton had his back to Jonny putting some sales numbers on a white-board, as Jonny gently and quietly closed the office door then tried to tiptoe to his seat.

The group of eight, neatly groomed, professional looking sales agents took notice of Jonny's wet-look and whispered amongst themselves as he attempted to go unnoticed to his seat. His soggy shoes made the same scrunch, only slower. One foot down onto the marble floor, then another, and another. He paused as Mr. Stockton briefly stopped writing on the board to glance at some sales data, then continued his steps when he began dragging the piece of chalk over the sales board. If he could get to his seat before he finished writing, he could pretend that he had been there all along. Jonny focused on each step trying to set the rubber soul of the shoe onto the floor without that ungodly sound. Every eye was on him as he slowly took each step to the one empty seat that was across the table from the beautiful, Karen Stockton, the bosses daughter, whom Jonny had a crush on.

"Hi, Karen, sorry I'm late, I had an appointment," Jonny whispered loud enough for the others to hear. He then quietly set down his leather briefcase on the table and gently rolled out the leather chair to sit down.

Todd Brighton, a preppy looking type, who thought very highly of himself, also one of the leading sales agent, responded to Jonny's whispers for the group to hear.

"Looks more like an accident, Hoover," he said aloud as the group all had a good laugh noticing Jonny's wet pants.

"Nice to see you could make it, Mr. Hoover," Mr. Stockton announced.

"Sorry Mr. Stockton, I had an appointment," he sheepishly replied, then quickly sat down.

"And how did that go, if I may ask?" Mr. Stockton's voice boomed out.

"Very well, sir, I got the sale," Jonny modestly said.

"You did? Well, good," Mr. Stockton said.

"Is that the first one this month, Hoover?" Todd arrogantly fired off to the group.

Jonny just glared at Todd, who he thought to be the biggest brown-noser, suck-up that ever walked on the face of the earth. After the group quieted down, he opened his brief case and looked across the table and gave the sweetest smile he could muster to the woman of his dreams, Karen. He smiled and gave suave glances to her as he took out pens, rulers, pencils, a box of assorted colored pencils as well, for replicating any graphs that may be shown, erasers and a handful of paper, then closed his brief case and placed it at his feet. He then arranged his things uniformly, rulers at the top of the stack of blank paper, and pens and pencils at each side and erasers stacked on top of one another in front of the rulers. Jonny believed in being prepared.

"Alright, where was I?" Mr. Stockton said breaking up the chatters.

Todd spoke up, "Mr. Stockton, I believe you were just about to unveil the chart revealing the top sales personnel for the quarter, sir."

"Yes, I was and thank you, Todd. And I am very proud to say that those of you who have been giving one hundred and ten percent will be," and at that moment Mr. Stockton paused and stared at Jonny who was trying to communicate something to Karen.

Jonny was unaware of just about any and everything when Karen was around. She appeared perplexed, as she couldn't understand what he was trying to say. He continued, slowly enunciating every syllable so she could read his lips.

"Do you want to go out tonight?"

Karen was bright, and energetic with long, wavy blonde hair. The kind you saw on TV commercials, Jonny thought. She always wore bright red lipstick and always dressed in something that made her appear like something beautiful and lovely.

"What? I can't hear you," she mouthed back flirtatiously to Jonny.

Harold glared at Jonny who continued mouthing something to Karen.

"Do you want to go out to dinner tonight?"

Mr. Stockton had had enough, "Mr. Hoover, do you mind?"

Jonny, startled, glanced up at Mr. Stockton then lowered his head down like a child being scolded, "Sorry sir, " he mumbled.

Mr. Stockton continued, "Our leading sales people will not only be rewarded with a bonus, but will also be invited to a very lavish party that one of our biggest customers, congressman Hyden will be having. A little footnote, the President will be one of the guests."

Jonny quickly raised his arm wildly just he did when he was in elementary, secondary, and high school.

Todd merely shook his head at Jonny's childish inquiry, whatever it might be. He looked down upon any and everything Jonny did, mainly because he had his eye on the boss' daughter as well and felt annoyed at Jonny's butting in on his pursuit.

"Excuse me, I have a question, Haro--" and Jonny stopped himself before using Mr. Stockton's first name, a habit he tried to break, but on occasion slipped. "Mr. Stockton, I mean," Jonny continued.

"What is it, Hoover?" Mr. Stockton impatiently replied while peering down at Jonny.

"That all sounds pretty good, but what's this guy the president of?" Jonny boldly inquired as he glanced to each of the sales people as if he was rallying for them. He sat up tall in his chair relishing in the importance of his own question.

"The United States," Mr. Stockton belted out. "Any other questions?" And he looked directly at Jonny, whose eyes widened before he slipped down into his chair almost like he was trying to hide, then Mr. Stockton, continued, "Okay, let's see who gets the glory." He then removed a cloth covering from another white board that revealed the positions of the salespeople.

Jonny couldn't stomach the fact that his name was at the bottom of the chart with a zero next to it and his bar graph had no color on it indicating no sales. He tried to look away from the chart, but his eyes insisted on wandering back to it. Fed up with the whole ordeal, he took out several colored pencils and began to doodle out his own chart where the graph above his name led up to the moon, which was shaped like a heart that he wrote Karen's name upon, then turned to show Karen, who blushed.

"Congratulations, Todd, and Karen," Mr. Stockton proudly announced. "You two have done it again, it looks like. You'll probably both want to get together and celebrate," he stated.

Jonny appeared nauseous as he looked over at Todd, who basked in the glory of his own presence.

"Oh, and don't let me forget, here are your added bonuses and invitations to the congressman's party," Mr. Stockton stated then held out the envelopes for Karen and Todd to step up and receive.

"Thank you, Sir, and I'd just like to say thank you to all of you for making this another great year at Stockton Insurance, keep up the good work. " Todd proudly held up his envelope like it was a trophy.

Mr. Stockton soaked up the rhetoric from the company's biggest brown noser, while Jonny couldn't help but put his finger in his mouth in a naseous manner.

"Keep up the good work, Todd," Mr. Stockton said as he shook Todd's hand.

"Congratulations, sweetheart," he added to his lovely daughter and gave her a little hug.

"Thank you, daddy," Karen replied in the sweetest sounding voice.

"That's all for now, meeting adjourned and everyone keep up the good work," Mr. Stockton said to the group of sales people who all got up to leave the room.

"I'd like to speak with you, Hoover," Mr. Stockton stated to Jonny who hurried to put his supplies back into his briefcase, hoping he could visit with Karen as they all walked out of the office.

Jonny looked to Karen, who subtly shook her head that made her long blond hair bounce a little, as if she didn't know why her father would want to speak to him, and then left the room with Todd close behind her.

"Hoover, what are we going to do with you?" Mr. Stockton inquired.

Jonny stood there a moment looking like a six-foot-one small child that had just wet his pants.

"Let me go to the party, sir, I'll do better, I promise I will. I'd be so proud to represent the company, sir," he desperately pleaded.

Mr. Stockton just looked at Jonny and subtly shook his head.

"Please, Haro..., I mean, Mr. Stockton, for Godsakes!" Jonny pleaded.

"Hoover, shut up and pull yourself together," Mr. Stockton firmly stated. "Now listen to me," he continued, "I know that you come from a respectable family. I had aquantances that knew your great and famous relative. I understand you sometimes refer to him as your great grandfather. You know who I'm talking about. He was an interesting man. He had his idiosyncrasies, I suppose, but we all do, yourself included, right?"

"I suppose sir." Jonny said with his head down. He didn't dare mention that there was no relation to the famous Hoover his boss referred to for the simple reason that he might be fired on the spot if the truth were known.

"And he had the ability to rise to the top, just as I expect you to do, to live up to that greatness, is that asking too much?"

"No, sir," Jonny shamefully replied. "Does this mean you'll let me attend the congressman's party?" Jonny pleaded.

"No, I'm afraid not," Mr. Stockton replied in a fatherly manner. "But, if you work hard, maybe, just maybe you'll be attending the next event that is offered. That's all, now get back to work," he concluded.

"Yes sir." Jonny felt as dejected as he could ever recall, then he slowly picked up his briefcase and walked out of the office.

And just as quick as his melancholy mood had come upon him, with the sight of the lovely Karen standing by her desk, it was gone in an instant. He approached her in a very suave manner.

"Hi, Karen," Jonny said with a smile.

"Hi, Jonny," she replied.

"How are you?" Jonny said with a hint of anxiety that comes along with asking an attractive person of the opposite sex out on a date.

"Fine, what did daddy want?"

"Not too much, he just told me to basically, ah, to just keep up the good work."

"That's good," she said while organizing some paperwork. "So, did you decide to take a swim this morning?"

"Oh, yeah, that" Jonny chuckled, then squirmed as he looked down at his pants and shoes. "Well, you see, I stepped in some, ah," Jonny stammered and paused to think of something more appealing than simply saying he stepped in a very large pile of dog shit, and hazardous material had such a better, more appealing sound of danger to it, that was almost sexy, so he continued, "ah, well, it was sort of a hazardous material type of substance, I think. It happened when I was meeting with a client, you know, walked right into it, and well, he, ah, he tried to use the hose so it wouldn't go right through and burn down to the skin on my foot, it was on my foot," Jonny nervously rambled, "And the hose just got a little squirrly," Jonny chuckled now feeling more relaxed than before, "And, you know, slipped a little, that's all."

"Well it's probably a good thing you didn't fall in it," Karen added.

"Yeah." Jonny nervously agreed. "Say, congratulations on your bonus and invitation to the party," Jonny glanced down onto Karen's desk to read the invitation that was lying open on her desk, "In Beverly Hills, man oh man."

"Thanks," she replied with such a warm, sexy smile, Jonny thought it could melt the entire Polor ice cap. "What were you trying to tell me in there, anyway?" She prodded him.

"Well," Jonny hemmed with every nervous tick imaginable, "I was," he paused to scratch his head, "Well, I mean, I just wanted to," he took a deep breath, " I just wanted to know if you maybe would like to go out tonight." He exhaled, thankful that he had successfully gotten the message out of his mouth.

"I would, Jonny," and briefly Jonny's eyes filled with a jubilation seen in a child's eyes at Christmas, "But, Todd is taking me out tonight."

And it was as if Jonny's balloon was pierced with a hundred machine guns which made his jubilee fade, replaced by a sick feeling that poured over his entire being.

Todd arrived appearing arrogant and full of sarcasm as usual.

"Seven fifteen okay, Karen?" Todd inquired.

"Sure," Karen replied.

"I won't be late," Todd reassured her. "Clean it up, vacuum man," he said to Jonny before he walked away and approached a group of sales people at the water fountain.

Jonny's eyes zeroed in on Todd like two laser beams. He set down his briefcase and discreetly reached into his pocket for a Bic pen and removed the pen portion from the cylinder holder. Jonny had had years of experience during the course of his education, from pre-school on, and considered himself an expert marksman when it came to spitwads.

"So do you think you'll get to meet the President, Karen?" Jonny nonchalantly inquired as mere small talk as he prepared his weapon.

Karen continued shuffling papers around on her desk, more to appear calm and relaxed than anything.

Jonny reached for a small piece of paper from his pocket and ripped off a portion and put it in his mouth and started chewing.

"I sure hope I do, maybe I can get my picture taken with him," she replied while reading her invitation again.

"Promise me a copy," Jonny said just before he put the Bic to his lips.

"Sure, Jonny," she warmly replied.

Jonny let out a sharp quick breath of air that propelled the spit-filled piece of chewed paper across the room and to a mark on the back of Todd's neck. He then quickly pulled the pen cartridge away from his lips and back into his pocket and pretended to glance over Karen's lovely shoulder to eye her invitation.

"Owww!!!" Todd belted out from the stinging spit wad. He looked immediately at Jonny who had already looked away from his victim and then pretended to cue his concerned look to the sound of pain that rang from a voice from across the office. He appeared wide-eyed and innocent when Todd called out at him.

"I'm telling Harold about this," he pouted.

And Jonny mouthed the words back to him and shrugged his shoulders and looked around and then gave Todd a little wink and smile before his attention went back to Karen.

"Well Karen, I've got some afternoon appointments, wrappin' up a couple big deals, you have a great day, okay? I'll see you later." Jonny said and he began to walk away.

"Say Jonny?" Karen called out as Jonny turned to look back. "I'm not doing anything tomorrow night."

And it was Christmas again for Jonny as he responded glowingly, "Pick you up about eight?"

"Sure," she replied with a smile.

He smiled, then turned and walked away. "Yes!" he said to himself. While exiting, he turned his head and continued looking back at Karen, who stood motionless, smiling at him. Then she was waving both of her hands now. What a glorious and beautiful sight he thought to himself, just before he walked directly into the wall next to the doorway that led to the elevators. As red as a fire alarm, he jokingly shrugged it off and pointed back at Karen who smiled in her usual sexy manner, and that was all that Jonny needed to put him somewhere up in the clouds as he exited the office.

He got on the elevator and pushed the third floor botton and waited for the door to close. He was feeling more than good. It was a feeling he thought that was much better than anything he could ever recall throughout his childhood, which was a time that was marred by being labeled ADD - Attention Deficit Disorder that was accompanied with dyslexia. It was a time when Jonny was extremely rambunctious and easily excited, but he had since learned to control his behaviors. His parents were very proud that he was on his own and working as a professional insurance agent. He couldn't remember feeling so good, even the disco song that emitted from a small speaker in the elevator sounded so good to him that he started to dance and sing along.

"I'm just a love machine and it won't work for nobody but me," he sang as he raised his arms and started gyrating his hips. "A huggin' kiss machine and it won't work for nobody but me." He even threw in some "Owws," and an occasional "oh yeah, baby," into the song to pump it up a level.

"Feelin' good!" he hollered out loud enough to turn heads on whatever floor he passed. He continued to thrust down with his hands and up with his hips, gyrating, pulsating to the beat. The elevator wasn't big enough to try the splits, but if it were, he more than likely would've made an attempt at the manuever. He was so into the music, he didn't hear the tone of the elevator as it slowed to a stop at the third floor and the music stopped, but he continued thrusting down with his hands and up with his hips as if he couldn't stop the electric pulses that ran through his body. It took Jonny a moment to realize the doors had opened and Ms. Peters was standing there, aghast, watching him, still thrusting his hips and waving his arms and with a final move he spun around again and stopped.

"Oh, hi, Gwen, I mean, Miss, -" but before he could even finish saying the old woman's name, she let out a shrieking sound, then "Ohhhhhhhh!" said with total disgust. She appeared as if she was having a brief coronary, her eyes went haywire for a few seconds, and then she stomped over to the stair-well to walk up one flight, then proceed in the elevator without the presence or what she thought to be the disgusting sight of Jonny.

And as Jonny watched as Gwendolyn, or Ms. Peters as she preferred, en-ter the stairwell, he finished his greeting with, " -Shrivel prune."

He headed for the stairwell with the down arrow and headed to the main floor and then out of the building, where he would put back on his prosthetic and "pound the pavement," so to speak, meeting with anyone, age, race or gender, didn't matter, everyone was a potential lead to Jonny. His numbers were flat and he knew it. So, he revamped his opening. He smiled as he passed out some doctored up flyers with a picture of a man missing both of his arms on the front of it, then, he would give an irresistable pitch to them. At one time he used a picture of a man who was missing his head, but real-ized that that might be carrying the example a little too far. He couldn't ever recall of a man in history who had ever survived without a head, so he con-tinued with the man with no arms.

"Can I buy you a cup of coffee, friend, and share with you some very im-portant statistical information thay may surprise you?" Some would take the flyer, many would simply glance at it, wince, and then walk past. But Jonny kept asking anyway. He wasn't a quitter that was for sure. But after about the hundredth hard "No!" the downtown L.A. pavement started to get blistering hot, as did Jonny in his suit coat under the direct mid-day sun. He began thinking that there was something about Frank's new neighbors that puzzled him - Secret Service booklet? What was that about? They sure didn't appear to be the type that would be affiliated with such an elite group. Maybe they could use a little insurance he thought and a little visit at the end of the day. And that was the beauty of his daytime occupation, it gave him the perfect opportunity to stop by and say hello.

Chapter 4

Rushnad Slovak's large six-foot-six 285lbs frame, made the small kitchen of the run-down house on Oleander Street, appear smaller than it was. He was accustomed to the cold climate of northern Russia, not the sweltering heat of East L.A that made every inch of his body feel uncomfortably damp with perspiration. He opened the freezer and felt refreshed as he bent down to get his face near the arctic air. He took in several deep breaths of the freezing cold air, then reached inside a plastic bag for some ice to put in his tall glass. He glanced over at the stove where a pot of okra salsa, a spicy middle-eastern dish was boiling, then stepped over to the doorway and checked the living room, which was empty with the exception of some worn furniture that came with the run down rental. He gave a quick glance down the hallway, then back to the red-hot burner. He shook his head with disgust. It was hot enough without the help of the oven turned on hi. He reached over the hot dish and shut off the burner, then stepped over to the kitchen table and grabbed the half-gallon of Smirnoff's. He poured the clear liquid three quarters to the brim, then reached inside a brown paper sac for a quart sized container of orange juice that was also on the table, opened it and poured a splash of O.J. over his vodka, then took a sip. Perfect. He set the drink down and stepped over to the cupboard, opened it and reached up and pulled out a straw from a box, closed the cupboard and placed the straw in the tall glass and stirred the drink a couple times, then sipped.

"Ahhh," he exhaled, then wiped his brow. It was the perfect drink on a sweltering hot summer day. He looked up and could see out the back window. The fat American neighbor must now be crazy doing jumping jacks in his back yard on a day such as this.

Rhajneed Mamood entered the kitchen in white slacks and matching suit jacket and a dark blue turban on his head with an emerald stone on the front held in place by a gold pin. He took a quick glance at Rushnad, saw the

Vodka bottle and looked away, then stirred the aromatic dish. He took a taste of the dish with a spoon. Luke warm.

"Kaleeb, Kaleeb," he called out. A moment later the scruffy appearing Saudi appeared. Kaleeb Kasir was slight in build, unshaven with messed up black hair, and wore jeans, sandals and a dark colored t-shirt.

Rushnad had seen enough of the fat American and sat down at the kitchen table and ignored the two as they began arguing in Arabic. He sat there and appeared totally carefree while he sipped his mid-day Vodka drink.

Rhajneed questioned him. "Did you turn off the burner?"

"Yes," he slowly answered then looked at the two. "It is too hot in this oven," he added then looked away and sipped on his drink.

Rhajneed directed his anger on the much smaller Kaleeb as the two raised their voices at one another until Rhajneed left the room after turning the burner back on.

Kaleeb scratched his head then stepped over to the kitchen window and looked through the broken slats in the weathered fence where he could see Frank, who was now attempting to jump rope.

"What is that fool doing?" He questioned Rushnad.

Rushnad looked up from his drink, "Cooking like bacon," he replied with a subtle smile.

The doorbell rang. Debbie's voice could be heard from down the hall, "Rushnad!" she cried out.

Rushand, unconcerned, took another long sip from his drink.

The attractive, fit looking woman, sprung from a rear bedroom in the three-bedroom house and entered clad in jeans and a halter-top that revealed, tanned and toned arms. She held a black Glock handgun with a silencer attached at the end of the barrel, "Close that door and quit drinking that, you idiot," she commanded Rushnad, who quickly did as he was told.

"Do you want me to get it?" Kaleeb meekly inquired.

"No," she replied. She glared at Rushnad instead, then gestured at him with a motion of her head to get the door.

In a back bedroom, Rhajneed quickly placed bullets into what he referred to as his Dirty Harry pistol that was also equipped with a silencer at the end of the barrel, which made the gun appear even larger. He loaded the last few bullets as he hurried down the hallway and into the kitchen. He bumped into Debbie with his gun as she stepped back to allow Rushnad to enter the living room to answer the front door.

"Sorry," Rhajneed said, appearing awkward holding the large barreled gun.

Debbie turned her head in disgust, then instructed Kaleeb to watch the back door.

Rushnad opened the front door. He towered over the UPS man who was standing there with his plastic computerized pad.

"What do you want?" Rushnad inquired with his distinct accent.

"Signature," the perspiring deliveryman stated holding out his computerized pad. He nervously looked over his shoulder at his truck that was idling in the poorest, most dangerous part of town.

"Package for a Debbie Black."

Debbie had placed her handgun on a table next to the door and nudged Rushnad back and out of the way as she stepped just outside of the house. She had put on her dark sunglasses to conceal herself.

"Yes, and that would be me," she coldly stated.

"Signature, right here, maam."

She signed her name, then looked at the good sized box.

"I can wheel it inside on the dolly, maam, it's pretty heavy," the driver said.

"No, thank you, I'm in pretty good shape, I can carry it inside," she reassured the man in brown.

"Suit yourself," the driver stated, then removed the box from the dolly and hurried back to his truck. He paused and watched Debbie who struggled trying to pick up the heavy, awkward container in several different ways before she gave up on the idea, then he drove away.

Debbie poked her head inside the house, "Rushnad."

Rushnad rolled his eyes while seated back at the kitchen table and took another sip of his vodka and orange drink.

She stomped over to the doorway of the kitchen. "Get out here and pick this up, you fool," she impatiently fumed.

He slowly got up from the table and did what he was told. He exited the house and easily picked up the box and brought it inside and dropped it down in the center of the living room. Debbie slammed the door shut and removed her dark glasses.

They all looked down at the box.

"Our gift from Vicktor has finally arrived," she stated with a rare smile, studying the box. "Unfortunately we have no key," she announced as the four all looked down at the small lock that was on the front of the box.

"Break it open," she instructed Rushnad.

Rushnad took a deep breath, doubled up his fists, then like a professional wrestler he dropped to one knee and delivered a swift sharp blow with his elbow down onto the top of the box. He winced and grabbed his elbow with his other hand as he only put a slight dent into the hard thick wood top. He looked down angrily at the box as he began to snort like a prized bull as he once again psyched up for the final deathblow that would crush the box to pieces.

This time it would be with his other elbow. His upper lip began to quiver. He paced back and forth as if the box was an opponent he was about to crush. He took one step and dropped to his other knee and delivered the crushing blow once again to the top of the box.

"Uggghhh," he winced again in pain. "Mhhnnn," he moaned. Slowly, he stood up and rubbed his elbow.

"It is obviously reinforced with an impetrible substance," he slowly and painfully stated to the onlookers.

Debbie eyed him from head to toe with an icy glare, "Impenetrable, you idiot," she corrected him. "What are you good for?"

She picked up her gun, aimed carefully, and at the last second closed her eyes as she fired a silenced round at the small lock on the front of the box. Missed. She fired another shot, then another, and another, and another as she missed with each effort. She fumed.

"Agghhh," she painfully cried out through gritted teeth as she unloaded the rest of her clip into the box, missing with each shot. She looked over at Rhajneed who smiled back in a fatherly manner.

"It is a small lock, more than likely Japanese, allow me," he stated then carefully aimed his large weapon at the small lock on the front of the box. The large caliber handgun kicked his arm up, which he wasn't expecting, and sounded like an air pellet gun with its' silencer attachment. A miss. He paused and looked at the others, then smiled to himself, just unlucky he thought as he shrugged it off and attempted again.

Looking down at the lock again he closed one eye and carefully aimed the long barrel.

"Do you feel lucky punk, well do you?" he questioned the box with amusement and with his high-pitched, middle-eastern accent, then emptied his weapon trying to hit the small lock on the front of it.

Debbie shook her head at his childish behavior.

"You're closing both of your eyes when you shoot," Rushnad stated with his deep baritone voice while Rhajneed, perplexed, looked straight up the barrel of his gun for straightness.

"Don't look into the barrel of a loaded gun." Debbie rolled her eyes and did everything in her power to not use the, I word, "idiot" at the other leading member of the team.

Rushnad briefly exited the room to get his ice cold Vodka drink to ease the pain of his bruised ego and aching elbows.

Kaleeb had emerged with a tire iron and excitedly began prying on the front of the box, which opened fairly easily from all the misguided bullet holes in it.

Guns. A collection of modern military semi-automatic rifles rolled onto the floor. Debbie's face glowed at all the weaponry in the box. Just as she reached for the machine gun Rhajneed's hand also found itself on the weapon.

He tugged at the gun with his hand on the barrel portion and Debbie pulled at the stock portion.

"Rhajneed," she pleaded, "this one is lighter, more feminine," she urged. "Take one of the bigger more masculine rifles," she suggested in a sexy manner. And he let go of the weapon. Debbie smiled as she took the weapon to her side and caressed it as if she was firing it. Her vanity had gotten the best of her.

"Get the camera, Kaleeb," she excitedly instructed.

Kaleeb ran into a bedroom and quickly reappeared with a small digital camera. Debbie aimed the weapon directly at the camera and posed appearing sexy and tough looking.

Kaleeb pushed down on the button, but no flash.

Rushnad had reentered the room and sucked down the last of his Vodka, which made a loud sucking sound.

"Do you mind?" she angrily said out of her sexy, stylish, posed look and then the flash went off, which took Debbie totally off guard.

Kaleeb looked at the small digital display on the back of the tiny camera. "Hmn, the battery is dead."

"Enough with the pictures," Rhajneed said. "We have a meeting with Norman," he reminded Debbie, who took several deep breaths in an effort to control her rage that the picture wasn't a success, then childishly stomped out of the room pouting as she headed down the hallway to her back bedroom.

A moment later she reappeared with a scarf over her head and wearing her dark glasses.

"Put those away and stay here," she ordered Rushnad as if he was a child being told to put away his toys. She then flung open the door and walked outside and got inside the car and waited for the others.

Jonny was two blocks down, parked, watching and waiting. He glanced up just as the man he had seen before wearing the turban exited and then a fourth man he hadn't seen before got into the drivers seat. Where is the large one? he wondered as he watched the three get into the old Camry parked in the driveway and then back out and begin to head straight for his RV. He quickly got up from the driver's seat, stepped towards the rear of the vehicle and closed the curtains that separated the cab from the living area of the rig and waited until they drove past. He then popped just his head from the curtains and spoke to Boots who was lazily napping in the passengers seat.

"I think it's getting a little boring just selling insurance, Boots, how 'bout some hot magazines on a hot day, does that sound pretty good to you?" Jonny inquired, then quickly pulled his head back behind the curtains to pick out the perfect disguise. After thumbing through a collection of theatrical disguises, he settled on something not too obtrusive. He was just your average magazine salesman. Dressed for the occasion, he reached up inside a small woodgrain cupboard and pulled down a small box that read - Bugging Transmitters, Property of the FBI. He opened the box and placed several of the dime sized silver transmitters in his front pocket.

Jonny, now clad in an off green leisure suit that had an official looking emblem sewn onto the right front pocket, with a bow-tie, whistled a tune as he walked down the cracked sidewalk carrying a briefcase full of old magazines. He felt comfortable knowing his attire wasn't anywhere near the local gang colors. He put in some large, yellowed false front teeth that attached to the front of his own teeth, which made him talk in a peculiar manner. He also added some wire-rimmed glasses and employed his usual limp for that touch of sympathy that came forth when people saw such a meek and harmless person with a minor physical deformity. It was nowhere to be found in any sales manual, but he felt it was a great tool for selling. He limped up to the front door of the house and knocked on the door with several firm knocks, then stood there and patiently waited. Nothing. Again, he knocked several times.

"Hello? Anybody home?" he called out.

Inside, Rushnad wasn't sure if he was dreaming. After putting the guns away on top of a bed in one of the bedrooms, he had decided to lie down and take a short nap. He was awakened by Jonny's pounding. He opened his eyes and tried to focus. There were two large empty glasses with just a little water in the bottom of each from the melted ice. Two glasses? He closed his eyes and opened them again. That's better, one glass right where I left it, he thought. Empty. He continued lying there, then realized someone was knocking. He lifted his head to listen again. He sat up to listen. There it was again. Somebody knocking. Who was it? He slowly got up, picked up a handgun that was on the bedside table and went into the living room and listened.

"Hello, anybody home?" he heard a voice from outside calling.

Who is that, the authorities perhaps? Had the others been apprehended? Numerous questions darted through his clouded, intoxicated mind as he stood there listening. His head pounded from the heat and the Vodka.

Outside Jonny had set down his brief case and opened it on the front porch. He reached inside and pulled out the top magazine Gash, Swimsuit issue off the pile of old, dated magazines and held it up.

"I know your weakness." He quickly leafed through the pages trying to find the perfect beauty to entice his customer with. "Oh yes, " Jonny said to himself as he stopped on a page. She was the perfect bombshell. He then stepped off the porch and into some weeds that had long ago overtaken any residing flowers and held the bikini clad centerfold up against the front window that had a several inch opening in the curtains.

"Check it out, her name is Ginger," Jonny called out to anyone inside the home listening.

"Mnnn," Rushnad groaned as he caught a partial glimpse of the American beauty centerfold.

"Now that's a little more than what you'd see on Baywatch, and the beauty of this plan is that your first subscription of Gash is seventy-per-cent off. You heard me right," Jonny loudly continued. "That's a seventy percent savings, but - " and Jonny pulled the magazine away from the window and folded the centerfold back inside the magazine, then continued, "- if you're not interested, you can certainly go jump off a bridge, and I'll be back later this evening to settle up with you then," he facetiously said to himself. He paused a moment to listen for any signs of life, then slowly stepped back away from the house as if he might just move on to the next house, which he certainly had no intention of doing. He could hear someone fumbling with the lock on the door and so he quickly turned around as if he was proceeding on to the next house.

"Wait," Rushnad said, "Come inside."

"Well, now we're talking, " Jonny stopped, then turned around and smiled the friendliest smile he could conjure up. His lips stretched over his large false front teeth that protruded jagged and outward.

"Hello there, young man, and how are you this fine day?" he questioned while looking up at the bear of a man through his spectacles. He slowly limped toward the house, then up the front porch steps one by one, milking each step for sympathy with his difficult gait. He smiled warmly into the vacant gaze of the large Rushnad as he walked past him and stepped inside the house.

Once inside Jonny looked around the very drab dirty living room with old, worn out furnishing.

"Oh yes, very nice, very nice. This is quite a lovely home you have here young man," Jonny quipped. "The reason for my call today," Jonny paused then chuckled to himself, "My call, hmm hmm hmm, it just about sounds as if I'm calling you on the telephone, which I can tell you, I certainly do enough of that, too," Jonny chuckled to an intoxicated, stone faced Rushnad.

"But actually sir, my name is Don Brixberry, and you are?" Jonny inquired as he held out his limp hand.

"Rushnad," the large Russian flatly said and didn't extend his hand.

"Rushnad, hmmn," Jonny repeated, then pretended to think a moment. "Is that Yugoslavian?"

"Russian."

"Russian, hmm, I'll be," Jonny said, then looked up at Rushnad. "Is there somewhere we can sit down and chat for a few minutes, so I can share with you some extremely important and exciting information about the savings that we're offering now, and yes I have some pictures too," Jonny smiled, then licked his lips at his potential hot prospect.

"Come, the kitchen." Rushnad gestured for Jonny to follow.

"Certainly," Jonny eagerly replied, then did as he was told and followed Rushnad into the kitchen. Jonny pulled his glasses down his nose and took a quick peek down the hallway to see what appeared to be three bedrooms and a bathroom. One door, besides the bathroom was open. He quickly pushed his glasses back into position as he entered the kitchen.

Jonny strategically set his briefcase on the table so Rushnad would take the seat that placed his back to the hallway. He then sat down and opened up

36

his brief case and took out the same copy of <u>Gash</u> he had held up to the window, and a dated, worn copy of <u>Field and Stream</u> and <u>Sports Illustrated</u> and carefully laid them out on the table like playing cards where you could see each title for Rushnad to consider. The copy of <u>Gash</u> with a beautiful, buxom, bikini clad blond on the front cover was placed on top of the others. Jonny heard the ice falling into glasses and he turned to look behind him to see what Rushnad was doing.

Rushnad had grabbed the bag of ice from the freezer and was preparing two drinks. He began pouring Vodka over the ice in one of the glasses. He turned to look at Jonny.

"Smirnoff?"

Jonny smiled, "I usually wait until the end of the day before getting shit-faced," he answered, then chuckled loudly so Rushnad wouldn't take offense to him not taking him up on the offer.

Rushnad poured Vodka to the brim of the other glass as well, ignoring Jonny, then, a splash of Orange Juice over the top of each drink. He then reached for two straws in the cupboard and finished the drinks with a couple quick stirs, then placed the drink in front of Jonny, who forced a smile.

"Well, if you insist. I'll try and not be a party-pooper as one would say," Jonny chuckled.

Rushnad stared blankly at Jonny. "Cheers," he said with a hint of a smile as he held up his glass.

"Well, I don't see what one little drink would hurt," Jonny reluctantly agreed as he picked up the glass and tapped it against Rushnad's. Jonny put the straw in his mouth and sucked up a good mouthful of the drink, then sprayed it all over the kitchen.

"Mother's milk!" he loudly exclaimed.

Rushnad came to life with a booming belly laugh and he slapped Jonny on the back, which just about knocked him out of his chair.

"You're so tender when you drink," Jonny said under his breath. "I'll just have to learn to not take such big drinks," Jonny smiled, then put the straw to his lips and pretended to take small sips. .

Rushnad was quick to smile and nod in agreement.

"You know, has anyone ever told you that you're a pretty nice fellow," Jonny said buttering up Rushnad.

Rushnad shrugged, then sucked down several good belts of his drink.

"Well, that's my opinion. Inviting me into your lovely home, offering me a cold drink on such a hot, hot day, it is very kind of you, Rushnad."

Rushnad made a sort of grunting sound for a reply, as he was more concerned with the woman on the cover of the magazine than the meanderings of this peculiar man who walked with a limp and with large front teeth that protruded from his mouth.

"Baywatch beauties?" Rushnad questioned. Some of the vodka drink drooled out of his mouth as he started to flip through the pages one by one of the magazine.

"There's a lot more there, than what you'll find on Baywatch, that's for sure, but take your time and see what you think," Jonny said while he studied Rushnad who sat there perspiring as he gawked at the pictures of beautiful women while nursing on his full glass of hundred-proof Vodka.

Jonny took a deep sigh, pretending to savor his drink in the blistering heat as his customer eyed the merchandise.

Rushnad made Neanderthal-like groans as he judged the beauties one by one.

"Excuse me, Rushnad," Jonny dipped his head down as if to look up into Rushnad's focused line of vision. "You know it's been a little while since I checked in with the office, do think I could possibly trouble you to use your telephone to briefly check in? I promise you it won't take more than a minute," Jonny meekly inquired.

"In front room," Rushnad grunted without looking up.

"Thank you so much, I really appreciate that Rushnad, I'll just be but a moment," Jonny got up and stepped into the living room. He gave a quick peek back into the kitchen to see that Rushnad's attention was right where he wanted it, then sat down on the old sofa and reached for the old style phone with the unscrew type mouthpiece. Perfect, he thought as he quickly unscrewed the cap of the mouthpiece, then reached into his pocket for a transmitter. He pulled several from his pocket and one fell onto the floor and rolled somewhere. He quickly got down on his hands and knees and scanned the dusty terrain under the sofa. There it was, too far to reach he thought. He got up and placed another one inside the mouthpiece and screwed it shut, then tiptoed over to the kitchen entrance.

"Typical busy signal," Jonny said to Rushnad who continued thumbing through the pages. "Are you seeing anything that interests you there?" Rushnad ignored Jonny who peeked down the hallway towards the back bedrooms, then back to Rushnad, who had opened up the centerfold and held it up for a full viewing. Jonny seized the moment and quietly stepped down the hallway and opened one of the bedroom doors.

It was a simple room with a double bed that was neatly made and a bedside table with a lamp on it. A closed suitcase was on the floor. Jonny closed the door and peeked into the bathroom - a collection of women's makeup items were cluttered on the counters and toilet. He glanced into another of the bedrooms where the door was opened revealing a messed up bed with clothes strewn about and a mattress on the floor with a sheet covering it and a blanket on top. Jonny glanced back towards the kitchen. Not a sound. He opened the last bedroom door. Bingo! Guns. An arsenal of them lay on top of a bed. He quietly closed the door and just as he did, he could hear Rushnads heavy frame moving back his chair over the kitchen floor.

"Baywatch Beauties," he could hear Rushnad bellow out.

Jonny hurried into the bathroom and quickly flushed the toilet, then exited the bathroom. Rushnad filled the hallway as he glared at Jonny.

"I probably should've mentioned that I have a little bit of an issue with a spastic colon, and I never know when I have to, well, you know," Jonny informed Rushnad who stood there like a large oak tree.

"There are no Baywatch Beauties," Rushnad coldly said with a blank stare.

"Now now, come come, Rushnad, what I meant was, that the women that are in issues of Gash are far more beautiful and sexy than any of your Baywatch girls, I mean there have been actual poles taken, or surveys I should say that have indicated." Jonny could see the growing anger that welled up inside of Rushnad.

"I should break you like a twig," Rushnad said with a frightful blankness in his eyes.

"You know I think it's about time I head back to the office," Jonny said wide-eyed, then limped towards Rushnad as a frightened puppy might that feared its master's wrath. He milked his limp for every ounce of sympathy as he walked past the large man into the kitchen and placed the magazines back into his brief case, then closed it.

"It's really too bad that we couldn't have worked something out, Rushnad," he sympathetically said as he looked into Rushnad's deadpan face, then cautiously limped towards Rushnad and attempted to walk past him to leave.

Rushnad picked Jonny up by the back of his polyester suit jacket and partially lifted him off the ground.

Jonny's feet dangled and skimmed over the floor as Rushnad lifted him to the door.

"Easy big fella, why don't you have another drink to calm those nerves!" Jonny desperately pleaded.

"Out!" Rushnad yelled as he opened the front door. "Get out!" he yelled again and threw Jonny out of the house where he tumbled into the gravel and weeded front yard flat on his face. He heard the door as it slammed shut.

"How 'bout a two out of three," Jonny painfully said. He slowly got up, brushed himself off, then picked up his brief case and walked away as if he was magically healed of his infirmity.

He picked up his stride and headed down the palm tree-lined street and headed back to his Winebago, where he would get ready for a little eves-dropping when Debbie and her cohorts returned that evening.

Chapter 5

Later that evening, Jonny moved his motor home just down the street from the house where he had been ejected from earlier that day. He was lying on his double bed relaxing and had the volume up on his receiver. He found the ideal position to park where the reception from the transmitters he had placed earlier was best. The Jerry Springer re-run that someone inside the home was watching, came in best at just about three quarters of a city block away. It was a good safe distance he thought. He kept a low wattage bedside lamp on inside the back of the mobile to blend into the darkened neighborhood where hardly a light emitted from any of the rundown homes. Jonny was locked down for the night with bullet- proof coverings over all the windows with the exception of a small window next to his bed, kept open for fresh air and any outside sounds.

All kinds of sounds emitted from the neighborhood; speeding cars that raced down the nearby arterial accompanied by the loud bass thumping from beefed up car stereos, people yelling, dogs barking, and what sounded like someone letting off firecrackers. It was hard to tell exactly from where the sounds emitted and it was the same with the continuous stream of sirens that whistled through the warm summer night air. But with bulletproofing on the walls of the rig Jonny felt perfectly safe as he laid down alone on his comfortable bed along with his regular companion, Boots. He slowly petted his very relaxed partner as the reels of his antiquated tape recorder slowly revolved recording any sounds captured from inside the house.

"I asked her out, Boots," Jonny said to his purring, content pet. "You know what she said? Yeeeessss." Jonny stroked Boots soft fur coat. "I like Karen, she's pretty, and the boss's daughter too."

Then from out of nowhere, thump, thump, thump, thump, thump. Someone knocked on the door of the RV. Boots remained unconcerned as Jonny sprung to his feet, his adrenaline pumping. He wondered who would be knocking at 11:40 PM? Jonny was a believer in homeland security. He threw on a bulletproof vest, slipped into some tennis shoes, reached up into a cupboard for a canister of nerve gas and put on an old FBI gas mask that he had rigged with a battery powered light attached to the top, then stepped over to the door and listened.

Thump, thump, thump, thump, thump, again someone pounded hard onto the door.

"Give me a second, I'm just getting out of the shower," Jonny called out. He flipped on the light on the top of the mask so that it would shine down and momentarily blind any possible intruders, then a quick count, one-thousand-one, one-thousand-two, one-thousand-three, he counted, then threw open the door as he held the canister of nerve gas tightly in one hand and his fingers on the pin with the other.

"Jonny?" Frank questioned not recognizing Jonny with the bright light shining in his face and the vague appearance of someone in a weird looking mask.

"Hello, Frank," Jonny said with a sigh of relief, then corrected himself. "I mean 001752."

"Hey, man," Frank said winded from running.

"A little late to be prowling around, don't you think?"

"Yeah, I suppose, mind if I come in?" Frank said with a tone of desperation.

"Why, no," Jonny said standing in the doorway.

Frank lifted his duffle bag filled with all his worldly possessions and stepped up a couple steps into the mobile.

Jonny poked his head outside the doorway to take a quick look around the desolate street for any other suspiscious activity. Nothing. He closed the door and locked it tight.

"I thought you were someone else. It's kind of a tough neighborhood, you know." Jonny said as the two stood nose to nose in the narrow entryway.

"Hey, tell me about it." Frank squinted from the gas mask light.

Jonny switched off the small, attached light apparatus on top of the mask and pulled it off and put it in a cupboard next to the front door.

"Don't tell me, a bag full of DiGiorno's?" Jonny inquired.

"Huh?" Frank questioned.

"Pizzas, I thought maybe you might've brought some pizza, I was kidding, Frank."

"I wish it was pizza," Frank said longingly.

"You seem a little frazzled, fried, fraught, winded, I mean," Jonny quickly said. "What's up Frank? talk to me."

Frank rubbed his hand over his face closing his eyes as if not wanting to think about his life, then shook his head.

"Where to begin, that's the question?"

"Come inside," Jonny began to walk to the rear of the mobile. He ripped the Velcro fasteners from his bulletproof vest and hung it on a hook on the wall.

"Thanks, man," Frank gladly agreed as he followed Jonny carrying his bag to the rear of the RV.

"Take a seat." Jonny pointed to a built in bench chair in the compact bedroom, then laid down on the bed.

"Man, this is quite a setup you got back here," Frank commented eyeing the recording surveillance equipment.

"Oh yes, all the comforts of home," Jonny replied.

"Sounds like the Springer show." Frank said listening to the monitor speakers.

"Right. I'm doing surveillance work, Frank. Your neighbors are all gathered around the set for some quality time, I suppose. Even your low-life scumballs need a little of that every now and then." Jonny said with a serious tone.

"Did you bug 'em?'

"'Fraid so."

"Man," Frank said intrigued and a little in awe of Jonny who was a real, true to life, secret agent at work.

"Yeah. Your neighbors have an arsenal of weapons in one of the back bedrooms, and my guess is they're not the heads of the block watch committee."

"I figured there was somethin' fishy about 'em," Frank replied.

"Could you feel it in your gut, Frank?"

"Damn rights I did, heck they got the lights on over there at all hours of the night, and never see 'em headin' off to work in the mornin', that's for sure."

Jonny nodded in agreement. "Sharp eye, Frank, sharp eye. So tell me, what has you wandering the streets at this hour, insomnia?" Jonny questioned.

"I wish. Somebody trashed my place."

"Again?" Jonny questioned, then added so as not to insult his old friend," I mean, you know with the sprayed up walls."

"Nah, I just went a little bazonkers with that business, was quite awhile back, on the booze you know," Frank explained.

"I see," Jonny gestured with an understanding nod of his head.

"Yeah, and I got a pretty good idea who did it, too."

"Was it a big Russian guy?" Jonny questioned.

"Nah, ex-wife's new boyfriend, who's gotta be the biggest horse's behind on the planet. They probably broke up is why. She always comes runnin' back and then he's all pissed, you know," Frank stated.

"I see," Jonny said. "Listen Frank, you've caught me in the middle of something big, very big, and I'm afraid it involves your lovely neighbors."

"I knew it! If it's one thing I knew, it's those people were scumbags," Frank said with conviction.

"Right," Jonny said. "I've been able to catch some bits and pieces of conversations that they've been carrying on with, and it sounds as if this group, of not-so-friendly foreigners, is planning something with the President of the United States, and it's not a luncheon we're talking about here," Jonny said lowering his voice to nearly a whisper.

"Good gawd almighty," Frank replied in the same hushed manner. "How did you bug their place?"

Jonny gestured shrugging his shoulders as if it was nothing, then explained to Frank. "It's a typical procedure in law enforcement Frank, get your subjects alone, check to see if the stories match."

"Did you get to interview 'ol Debbie?"

"Not yet."

"Who did you talk to?" Frank questioned.

"Rushnad, the big Russian, loves his Vodka. I posed as an innocent magazine salesman. He took the bait, hook, line and sinker," Jonny explained.

"Man, that's sneaky," Frank grinned with excitement.

"Can be dangerous too, Frank," Jonny added with a serious tone.

"Yeah, I bet." Frank agreed. "Do you think they're maybe gonna try and kill him?"

"Good question."

"Hmmnn," Frank pondered.

"Maybe something more devious," Jonny appeared to scour the darkest regions of his own imagination as to what that might entail, then the sound of someone's cell phone ringing from inside the house snapped Jonny back to reality as the tape reels continued spinning, recording every word.

"Phone call," Jonny turned up the volume on the recorder.

"Turn the volume down just a little would you, Kaleeb," Debbie requested.

"So warm and tender," Jonny quietly uttered as they listened in on the call.

"Hello," Debbie answered in the sweetest sounding voice she possessed.

"Now that is a viper," Jonny interjected.

"Yes, Norman?" She paused to listen. "So, tell me, have you made any progress since the last time we spoke?"

"We can't hear the other end?" Frank suggested.

"She's on her cell. I bugged the wall phone." Jonny replied.

"I don't know how they could, we're here, twenty four seven, you know, sweating, waiting to hear from you." Debbie spoke with a tone of boredom as she paused to listen again.

"So, what good news do you have for me?" she inquired.

Jonny and Frank sat motionless listening to every word.

"Just one? A congressman?" She sounded perplexed. "What does he have to offer?" She paused again, "Personal friends with the President, well, isn't he special. And what persuaded him to join our little club?" She paused.

"That's what I'd like to know," Jonny whispered.

"A dice roller, I see." She paused. "Well, we'll just have to sweeten the pot, try five, see if you get any takers with that. Your friends can't be that greedy." She paused again. "Yes, I'm sure, taking him from the inside is the only way," she quickly agreed. "What about him?"

"Wonder who she's talkin' about?" Frank questioned.

Jonny shook his head.

Sounding annoyed, she fired back, "Well, we just don't tell him what the others are getting, Norman." She sounded like an impatient mother talking to her teenaged son.

"Norman," Jonny repeated as the man at the other end quickly hung up the phone and it went to a dial tone.

"That explains it," Jonny said with a twinkle in his eye.

"What?" Frank didn't get it.

"The book she was reading, Secret Service. She mentioned getting him from the inside." Jonny stated.

"What about it?" Frank inquired still not putting the dots together.

Jonny looked at Frank, "I don't know if I would bet all the rice in China, but most of it, taking him from the inside is the only way," Jonny pondered what Debbie had said a moment. "Sounds as if they could be planning on kidnapping the President of The United States with the help of, a very corrupt congressman, and perhaps some very slimy secret servicemen who might be willing to - " and Jonny paused as it was hard to comprehend the thought, then concluded, " - Partake."

"Man!" Frank said with disbelief. "Sounds like I signed on just in the nick of time, huh?"

"Right, 001752," Jonny agreed. "This is a day I've been waiting for, for a long, long time. A chance to do something great, for God, for our country."

"Boy howdy, double-ditto, you said it, Jonny," Frank enthusiastically agreed with a sense of determination and purpose that he hadn't felt in as long as he could remember.

"Time to get some rest, buddy, tomorrow we start living, really living, Frank." Jonny got up from the bed and rounded up some blankets and a small pillow and pulled out the bench seat up in front that doubled as a small bed.

"Here you go, sleeping beauty."

"Thanks, Jonny and thanks for puttin' me up."

"That's what friends are for, buddy."

"Yeah." Frank agreed.

"Get some rest." Jonny shut off the lights so they could sleep.

Chapter 6

Jonny was up at 6 am the next morning outside polishing up his big rig. He wore red polyester pants with a Hawaiian shirt, along with beige sneakers with velcrow straps, a white haired wig, and black bifocals, which gave him a vacationing, senior-citizen look. He had polished nearly every inch of the white and red striped colored RV, and then repolished parts as he kept a close eye on Frank's neighbors Camry that was parked down the street in their driveway. He wanted to appear like a typical retiree who was on an endless vacation, and who had merely stopped on the street to rest over night. He whistled a happy tune as he rubbed on a tiny bit of polish here and there, then wiped it away very slowly while he inconspicuously glanced down the street. He impatiently looked at his gold Timex wristwatch. 9:30 am. He stopped whistling and stood up. He took a deep breath, pulled his bifocals down his nose and wondered to himself, what are they up to?

He was surprised when Rushnad suddenly exited the house and got into the drivers seat of the car. Jonny quickly bent down and pretended to be touching up the big silver rims with more polish. He rubbed an old rag in a slow circular motion while he kept an eye on Rushnad down the street, who sat there a moment waiting in the car, then started it.

Jonny peered down the street as he pretended to apply a sparring amount of the polish onto the rim, then gently rub it off. So what was happening? Was he going the store for more Smirnoff, or? No. The sheik followed, then the lovely, warm hearted, Debbie, and another man.

Jonny quickly grabbed his polish and hurried into the side door of the RV and jumped into the drivers seat. This was it. He turned the key. The tired, old engine turned over slowly.

"Come on," Jonny impatiently said.

The car, carrying all four occupants, backed out of the driveway.

Jonny, frustrated, stomped on the gas hard and held it down, still turning, turning, turning. He gave another hard stomp, then another. Bingo. He revved the engine as thick black smoke poured out the back, then put the big rig in gear and began to follow the deviants. As he did, he glanced into his rearview and eyed Frank who just had awakened and entered the small on-board porta-potty.

"Rise and shine sleeping beauty," Jonny called out to Frank as he turned the corner and stayed a safe distance from his subjects, who picked up speed. He stepped on the gas not to lose them.

The toilet flushed from the onboard restroom and Frank emerged to take the co-pilots chair.

"Ha!" Frank belted out. "What the heck are you dressed like an old man for?"

"Incognito, Frank," Jonny responded. "We're on vacation if anybody asks."

"I can live with that," Frank still appeared to be half asleep.

"We've got a little action. Our little group of friendly foreigners are on the move, buddy," Jonny said with an eagerness and uncertainty as to where their little road trip would lead.

"Man oh man," Frank rubbed his hands through his hair still trying to wake up. "Are you goin' in to work today, Jonny?"

"Nah, I called in sick."

"You do that very often?"

"Whenever there is an e-mer-gen-cy, Frank."

Frank began to crack various parts of his body starting with his knuckles, then his shoulders, his back, and finally his neck. "Don't let 'em get too far ahead of ya, they'll get away."

"Not to worry, Frank," Jonny said as he got onto a freeway on-ramp and immediately took the center lane. The big rig rocked back and forth like a large boat as he corrected from the maneuver.

"I hate to be the bearer of bad news, but I'd say, you not only need rings in this thing, some shocks on this baby too," Frank fired back while he fidgeted in his seat.

"Shocks are fine."

Frank rolled his eyes and shook his head in disagreement. "Maybe you oughta pull right behind 'em and just tap 'em."

"We'd hardly be living up to our God-given titles of Secret Agents, don't you think, Frank?" Jonny gave Frank a good long look.

"It was just an idea, okay." Frank reached up and opened the overhead compartment. His eyes widened as he pulled out a small weapon from the overhead.

"Whoa," Frank excitedly called out. "Too cool, paint ball guns!"

"Frank, now be careful with that thing, it has a hair, - " But before Jonny could finish his statement Frank accidentally shot Jonny with a mound of blue goo.

"Ha ha ha ha ha, sorry, Jonny," Frank laughed out loud from his belly.

" - Trigger," Jonny completed his statement, then wiped the side of his face off. He looked over at Frank and gave him a good long stern look. He didn't realize it but he was coming dangerously close to the vehicle ahead.

"Whoa! Hey, Jonny, better watch what you're doin' there, don't want to hit anybody."

Jonny forced a smile as he backed off the gas, and quickly applied the brakes, then looked over to Frank with a vengeful look.

Frank, still holding the gun, started to giggle, which made Jonny fume even more.

"Hmm hmm...Hey Jonny, are you feeling blue?" Frank inquired while continuing to chuckle. "I'm just kiddin' you man, I didn't mean it, really, I didn't. It was just an accident," Frank gingerly explained still trying to contain himself.

Jonny, who was more focused on getting even with Frank, didn't realize he was now directly behind his Russian drinking buddy, who noticed their overweight jumping-jack neighbor through his rearview mirror.

Frank was trying to spin the gun western style as Jonny repeatedly tried to quickly grab it, swirving the rig wildly as he did. "Very funny, Frank, now give me the gun," he demanded.

"Whoa, be careful Jonny!"

Jonny gritted his teeth, then wiped some of the blue goo from his hair and tossed it at Frank, not realizing he was now doing 90 mph in the beheamoth. Some of the matter got into Franks eye so he was temporarily distracted.

"Sorry, Frank, you understand I had to do that." Jonny, still not finished, released his seat belt and partially got out of his seat. Steering the rig with his left hand and left foot on the gas and stretching as far as he could with his right hand, he reached inside the overhead glove box on Frank's side for the other gun. He unknowingly swirved wildly and nearly lost control of the rig.

The driver of a tricked-out pick-up that was driving along-side, slammed his clenched fist down onto his horn at Jonny's eratic, inattentive driving, then attempted to get on Jonny's other side to pass.

Jonny, consumed by his vengence towards Frank, didn't even hear it. He shot Frank with an orange paint ball. "Ha ha ha!!!" Jonny belted out.

"Why you?!" Frank fired back.

"Okay, now we're even, Frank," Jonny pleaded wanting a truce, but Frank was aiming.

"Frank," Jonny cautioned as he looked at Frank more than the road while driving 20 miles over the speed limit.

Frank was attempting to shoot the gun.

"Hey, what's with this one, man? It doesn't work." Frank jerked the gun about while trying to squeeze the jammed trigger.

The gun unexpectantly went off and blasted another blue paint ball that covered Jonny's front windshield.

"Frank!"

Frank was wide-eyed and speechless.

The macho pickup driver's face contorted into an angry mold as he locked up his tires to miss Jonny, who blindly swirved the RV again, this time over the full five lanes of traffic putting it up on two wheels during the maneuver. It was only by the grace of God he didn't hit anyone as he grabbed a Kleenex from the center console and began to wipe the window, which created nothing but a blind man's blur.

"I'm glad to see that you find risking our lives funny, Frank!" Jonny scolded as he pushed his face closer to the window in an effort to see anything.

"I'm not laughin', man!" Frank cried out.

The now maniacal truck driver smashed the palm of his hand down onto his horn and held it. He leaned over to reach under his seat for his handy gun and threatened Jonny with the weapon, angrily signaling him to pull over.

Frank leaned forward to steal a glance at the madman. "Looks like he's a little pissed, Jonny."

"Yeah, I'd say we've got an angry customer," Jonny casually responded. He looked out his side window to the driver who raised the stakes and began taking shots at Jonny through his opened passenger window.

Jonny continued driving with the clarity of the legally blind, and felt a comfort from the bulletproof glass that surrounded him, so he smiled, put a hand next to his ear as if he was hard of hearing, then mouthed the words, "I can't hear you," which enraged the redneck even more.

"Check it out Frank, this guy's havin' a heart attack."

Frank leaned over, then reflexively ducked at the sound of another gunshot that ricocheted somewhere off the rig. "That sumbitch is pissed, man!"

"An asshole too. I've got the perfect gift for that special asshole to show him that we really care. Would you please take the wheel for me, Frank." Jonny said in a warm tone, then stood up to let Frank take the wheel. "And don't lose our friends up ahead," he instructed, not realizing that they had already disappeared in the sea of vehicles that sped down the busy freeway.

Once again the behemoth swirved wildly and swayed like a large boat as Frank took the pilots seat while Jonny stood up while his foot remained heavy on the gas pedal.

"Hey, where are they?" Frank inquired as to the whereabouts of his neighbor, then quickly attempted to wipe away the blue goo from the windshield with his bare arm.

Jonny was too focused on the emergency at hand, "Just up ahead," he unconsernedly replied. "Listen, see this lever?" He instructed to Frank while he smiled and waved at the maniac like a friendly old codger.

"Yeah," Frank nervously responded eyeing Jonny and then outside at the bobbing and weaving trucker, whose collar size had increased two sizes from his over inflated neck veins.

"When I say pull, let her rip." Jonny left Frank at the wheel and walked towards the back of the rig. Frank swirved the rig wildly at the sound of another gunshot followed by a chorus of honking horns that sounded from every direction.

Meanwhile, Jonny, who always laid the welcome mat out for danger, opened the side door and whistled a tune while he hung with half his body inside the rig, the other half hung outside the speeding whale inches away from the hot asphalt as he connected a long fat hose to a screw on receptacle with small letters above it that read, TOILET.

"That'll do her," he said in the 90 mph breeze. He noticed he had an audience, so he smiled and waved at the two small children in a mini van in the next lane that pointed and waved at him. He gave a friendly smile and nod at their very perplexed looking mother who watched as he began to climb on top of the towering rig carrying a long hose with him. Half way up the side ladder, his white haired wig couldn't withstand the 90mph breeze and blew off his head.

The onlooking children were amused and entertained by Jonny, who looked like a surfer on a wild wave as he struggled to get his footing on top of the rig. He crouched down and threaded the hose around a chrome luggage rack several times so it could be used like a mountain climber's rope for stability, then performed a very brief safety check. Appearing like a skydiver in the ferocious wind, he tugged on the hose. Much better, he thought. He aimed the hose down onto the lunatic trucker.

"Frank! I'm ready when you are!!!!!!!!" But before he could finish his statement, Frank swirled the rig wildly at the sound of a series of rapid gun-shots that sent Jonny flying off the roof of the moving house dangling off its side. Wide eyed, he looked down at the blur of white lines on the road as he hung on for dear life.

"Frank! Help!" He cried out. His feet dangled inches off the hot L.A. freeway in bumper-to-bumper traffic as his body swung about like a rag doll in the battering wind. His legs struggled to catch hold of something so he could climb to safety, but the ladder was just out of reach of his foot.

All he could do was pray. Dear God don't let me be splattered onto this pavement like a bug, he thought. Then, it was as if an angel of mercy had magically appeared. A horn honked. It was the mini van. Is she out of her mind? "Gettin' a little close, sister!" Jonny yelled to the woman, unaware of her intention of saving him. What the hell does she want? Jonny struggled to look over his shoulder. The children were pointing and signaling him. The woman's van was close enough to touch, or step on. She bravely inched the van close enough so Jonny could use it as leverage to reach the ladder.

"Hold her steady, Frank!" Jonny screamed. And for one quick moment the woman's car got close enough for Jonny to step on the side of her front bumper and then reach the side ladder of the rig with one hand, then the other. He was back in business and he started up the ladder again. Half way up it, he paused and looked down at the woman and her children.

"Thank you, maam, you folks have a nice day," He waved at the children and the brave woman who had the courage to help him.

He now felt like a man a mission. He clutched onto dear life step by step as he made his way back on top of the rig once again with the hose in his hand. Once on top, he crouched down as low as he could to stabilize himself better, then when he reached the front of the rig he stood up.

"I should probably introduce myself!" Jonny hollered down to the pickup driver who nervously reloaded his six-shooter.

"My name is Law. Jonny Law! Let her rip, Frank!"

Nothing. Jonny looked over the edge of the racing rig in an attempt to make contact with Frank.

"Frank! Oh Frank," Jonny yelled, "He's shooting his gun at me! Would you please for Godsakes let her rip!!!"

He began to dance around the top of the whale to avoid the pot shots fired at him. It was the sound of Jonny's feet that pounded down onto the hull that signaled Frank, who pulled the lever that released a stream of the foulest matter you could imagine down onto the person that deserved it most. The hose got a little squirley on Jonny and for a moment it went wild like an out of control fire hose, but Jonny wrestled for the end, then watched as the thick brownish, greenish, soupy matter dumped down thick and heavy onto the hood and windshield of the truck.

"Have a nice day, and don't forget to smell the roses along the way!" Jonny yelled to the road-rager "Might want to get her detailed after today, friend," he added as a courtesy, then watched as the truck fell back into traffic as they continued speeding down the freeway.

Jonny breathed a sigh of relief when he reentered the speeding behemoth and slammed the door of the rig shut. Reeking and dripping of the foulest smelling matter imaginable, he casually walked up to the front of the rig to check the whereabouts of the group they were supposed to be tailing.

"Wheeeeeewwww!!!!! Man are you ripe," Frank bellowed out.

"It's called Manly Man, Frank," Jonny leaned toward the large windshield and studied the congested traffic ahead. "Oh Frank?"

"Yeah, Jonny." Frank replied with a hand over his nose.

"Where are our friends?"

"Ah, I'm not sure, man, I guess I might've lost 'em in all the excitement," Frank sheepishly replied, then attemted to wipe more of the blue goo from the blurred windshield.

"Great, take this next exit, I've got a hunch."

"Alright, you're the boss," Frank agreed.

"Sometimes you just have to follow your gut, you know what I'm saying," Jonny scanned the sea of vehicles for an older model Camry, which was nowhere in sight.

"Jonny, that stench is pretty bad and you're drippin' that shit all over the place, do you have another one of those masks like the one you were wearin' last night so I can breath a little bit?" Frank questioned.

"Under the seat. A quick shower for me, Frank," Jonny called out before he turned and stepped to the back of the rig to shower.

Frank reached down under the seat for the mask and quickly put it over his head and face. His voice was muffled from the tight fitting, gas mask and his vision hindered even more from the scratched eyeglass on the fifty-year old device. He squinted through the large ant-like eyes as he quickly approached an overpass that had four different large signs veering into four separate directions.

"Oh for love-a-Pete," he said totally confused as to which exit to take. And he kept speeding along with traffic. He recalled what Jonny had told him – follow your gut. So, in an instant, he jerked the wheel hard right to take the exit less traveled. A blaring horn sounded that quickly faded as a sixteen wheeler sped past.

"Whew, that's better." Frank glanced in his rearview pondering the signage he had just passed under. "Huh? Pier somethin' or other," he rambled as he kept his foot on the gas. He sped past another overhead and missed the sign that read – ROAD CONSTRUCTION FREEWAY ENDS. He thought it a little odd that now all of the traffic had vanished. He looked around for any familiar landmarks.

"Hmnn, the ocean? How did that happen?"

Jonny sprang out from the back of the mobile, his hair still wet and neatly combed as he took the co-pilots seat. He looked out onto the freeway while he fastened his seatbelt. A puzzled look came over his face.

"Ah, where is everybody, Frank?" Jonny looked into the large rearview mirror.

"I don't know, Jonny," Frank took off his mask and tucked it back under the front seat. "I can't see very good in that damn thing."

"Man, what exit did you take?" Jonny chuckled as he looked over to Frank, then back out the window. "We are like way off course. There's the ocean," Jonny said as they crested the top of a hill. Frank was still going 85mph when they saw the large sign up ahead – ROAD ENDS.

"What the heck is this?" Frank said in disbelief.

"Brake!" Jonny said wide-eyed and with a calm firm tone.

"I don't believe this, man!" Frank cried out.

"Brakes, Frank!" Jonny now screamed out, but it was too late.

Frank had hit the brakes only enough to put five feet of rubber onto the roadway, which ended at an unfinished pier that led to the ocean. He plowed right through the sign and the behemoth took to the air.

"Mission Control!" Jonny called out as the huge rig went airborne just long enough to have a slide show of a young man's entire life flash before his eyes. It all felt like slow motion as the three occupants, Jonny, Frank, and Boots, all cried out together, "Ahggggg!....Ahggggg!.....Rarrrrrr!......

Boots, who was comfortably lying on the center consol, floated in mid air. Jonny felt weightless and witnessed his arms rising up slowly. He looked over to Frank with his mouth wide open in disbelief.

"Would've been nice workin' with ya, man!" Frank called out to Jonny, who could not only hear the words, but it was if his brain recorded every inflection of Frank's slow moving lips as he said each word.

The two turned and looked out the large front windshield just before they hit the water. It seemed surreal, and somewhat like an episode of Jaque Cousteau where the camera goes underwater. And that's just what they did. It seemed like forever that the rig plunged down, down, down, into the dark water before it changed direction. And then, like a huge cork, the whale-sized rig popped up to the surface.

Frank shook his head in an effort to regain his senses. He had hit his nose and broken it on the steering wheel and could feel a small trickle of blood dripping from it. He put his hand up to his face in a reaction to the numb wet feeling. He felt numb at the sight of the blood that covered his hand, which he quickly wiped onto his jeans.

"Aghhh, broken nose," He moaned as he came to his senses. The seaweed that covered the windshield nearly startled him at first.

"What the?" he mumbled to himself. Slowly, he became more conscious. Still dazed, he looked over to Jonny who was slumped over in his seat, and who appeared to be unconscious. It didn't really register. His eyes gazed through the seaweed that had wrapped over the windshield, and through it - water. Endless water that began dripping down over his head. His pulse began to pound at a rapid pace. He snapped out of it and looked back over to Jonny. Was he dead? He unfastened his seatbelt.

"Jonny, wake up, Jonny, for Godsakes would you wake up!" He said nearly gasping in desperation looking into Jonny's lifeless face wondering how long the big rig would stay afloat.

"Water, need some water," Frank thought. He looked about the cab of the rig, then was startled when he looked out the window at the vast Pacific. "Yikes," he said to himself. "Hold on Jonny," he cried out. He felt rubbery legged as he hurried back to a small sink in the kitchen area. He pounded his head with his hands, "Aghhh!!!" he groaned in frustration. "Why didn't I take those swimmin' lessons!" He scolded himself as his hands shook uncontrollably, "Aghhh," he moaned again as if to release his fear and he grabbed a small paper cup and turned on the faucet. Thank God it still worked, he thought to himself. His hands shook while he filled it up and tried not to spill a drop of it as he hurried back to his friend.

He poured a little of the water into his hand and then splashed it onto Jonny's face. A groan. That was good, that was very good, he thought.

"That's my boy, wake up, that's good," Frank loudly said still in a total state of panic.

"Aggghh?" Jonny moaned again, almost like someone who suffered with a severe case of mental retardation, Frank thought.

"Huh, that doesn't sound good." Frank looked closely into Jonny's eyes that drifted open, then shut, then open as he stared directly into Jonny's face like a doctor who was examining his patient.

"Snap out of it!" Frank demanded as he snapped his fingers in Jonny's face. "Jonny, is there a life-raft on this baby?" Frank pleaded to a groggy, disoriented Jonny, who just opened his mouth and drooled down his chin.

"Oh man, brain dead," Frank loudly said as he studied Jonny's droopy face. He scratched his head, thinking. "Insurance papers," he wondered aloud. He darted towards the back of the rig. His mind raced in desperation. Maybe he could leave something other than his large unpaid credit card bills to his ex-wife, he compassionately thought to himself in what he figured to be his last moments on earth.

Jonny opened one eye and turned his head just a little to listen in amusement to Frank who appeared more desperate than a woman in labor rummaging through every cupboard, under tables, under the bed, and even the refrigerator.

"Aghhh," Jonny moaned with a little life. "Where am I?" he slurred.

Frank, hearing Jonny's voice, scurried back up to the cab and bent over with excitement that his friend was coming back to life.

"We're in the ocean and the ship is sinkin' now where's your briefcase?" Frank stuttered.

"Who are you?" Jonny questioned looking at Frank.

"Who am I? Oh for love a..." Frank cried in frustration. "Frank! 'Member! We're in the ocean about to sink, Jonny! I need to find your briefcase to get some extra coverage before we die here. We're goin' down with the ship, I'm afraid to say. Hopefully somebody'll find 'em when they fish us out of this mess." Frank pleaded as he bent down and studied Jonny's vacant demeanor.

"Are you saying you're unhappy with your present policy, Frank?" Jonny questioned in a near comical delerium.

All Frank could say was, "Huh?"

"Huh, ha, ha," Jonny chuckled as he miraculously snapped out of his self-induced stupor. "Oh Frank," Jonny clearly enunciated.

Frank squinted his eyes at Jonny.Was it a miracle? Jonny appeared to have flown back to consciousness in a hurry.

"Would you relax, man. Geeez. You better calm down, because you are as white as a ghost," Jonny chuckled in between each word spoken. "I told you it was unsinkable, man! You are thick," Jonny laughed out loud.

Frank's expression grew sour as he caught on to the gag Jonny had just put him through.

"It's got a diesel powered prop in the rear, it's an advanced prototype of the first amphibious vehicle designed by the FBI after the cold war," Jonny stated in a matter of fact voice. He unfastened his seat belt and got out of his seat. "Take a seat, Frank. You can be the first mate," he said as Frank looked back distrustingly at him. "Really," Jonny reaffirmed his statement to Frank after noticing his distrustful demeanor. "You're not going to die, Frank," Jonny took the drivers seat then switched on the windshield wipers momentarily to remove the seaweed from the windshield. He got most of it brushed back to the sides of the large window, which made it appear that they were looking out a large pair of glasses with green frames.

"I'm not?" Frank felt embarrassed at his frantic behavior.

"'Fraid not, buddy," Jonny casually stated, then smiled as he reached overhead and slid back a small compartment door that had another concealed ignition switch. He primed the engine for the prop with several quick pushes of a rubber-coated button with the word, "choke," written on it, then turned the engine over. It sputtered and coughed. Jonny primed it again, then turned the key again and held it. Turning. Turning. Turning. And just as he appeared to have an ounce of worry that they just might drift out into the open seas and end up at God knows where, the engine started up. Jonny exhaled.

"What beach do you want to pull up to, Frank?"

He looked back at Jonny, "You really had me goin'. Heck, I thought you was brain dead."

Jonny laughed. "Not yet, buddy. Is that nose okay?"

"One of many. I'll live. I'll owe you for that one, ol' buddy," Frank said as he looked over at Jonny. And just as soon as his distrustful tone of voice came over him, it left him. "Let's hit Santa Monica, there's a lotta babes over there."

"You got it," Jonny replied. "Kitty, kitty, kitty, kitty," Jonny called out. And magically Boots appeared from his hiding.

"Hey Boots, you okay?" Jonny looked down at Boots who then sprang up onto the center console.

"Meeoowww," Boots replied and Jonny gave him a little scratch under the chin. "Sorry Boots, it wasn't me, it was him," Jonny pointed to Frank as the culprit of the plunge into the ocean waters, then petted Boots.

"Santa Monica it is," Jonny said with a lively tone to his voice as they slowly began to trudge forward in the somewhat calm waters.

"You know, I should probably tell ya, Jonny, and I hope you're not mad at me. I had kind of a hard time sleepin' last night, without a fifth a booze in me, so I took a little walk last night when you were sawin' logs, and put one of those FBI transmitters you showed me, and tucked it under the wheelwell of that piece of crap they drive," Frank stated.

"Oh realy?" Jonny looked over at Frank and smiled. "Hmmnn, hmmnn, hmmnn," Jonny chuckled. "You are good, 001752, oh yeah."

Frank nodded in agreement, then put his feet up on the square, out of date looking, tan dash and looked out at the rolling waves of the beautiful Pacific and relaxed as they slowly plodded through the waters enroute to Santa Monica beach.

Chapter 7

Later that same day, after a quick stop at a Wash'n Go on Santa Monica Boulevard to remove strands of seaweed and the corrosive salt water from the motorized home, they got back to task of tracking down what Jonny thought to be some very dangerous, ruthless characters. His first objective was to get some pictures of them and run checks on each of them to see if any were being sought by any law enforcement agencies, other than his own, and do the same to the other slime balls they were partnered with. Since Frank had planted a transmitter all they had to do was follow the beep heard on Jonny's receiver, which was a relic of a device probably manufactured in the fifties that rested on top of the engine console between the driver and passenger's seat. The unit had a brown metal casing with one good-sized V.U. meter on the front. It was much larger than today's palm-sized equipment and stamped with "Property of the FBI" on its side. It had an old, worn, cloth type brown cord with a male receptacle that plugged into the cigarette lighter for power. The headset for the unit had the same aged look about it, with old, brown, cracked, padded leather earphones, that Frank had over his ears to monitor the signal. But even though the device was a museum piece, and very worn looking, it still worked like a charm.

"Nice neighborhood. I think I'd like to settle down here, Frank." Jonny eyed all the Beverly Hills mansions with perfectly manicured grounds, while Frank kept an eye on the V.U. as he monitored the beep from the planted bug.

"Nah, turn around, Jonny, signal's gettin' weaker," Frank loudly instructed his pilot, oblivious to Jonny's comment, and who now appeared like a raccoon with two good shiners from the accident.

"Frank, I've been up and down this street ten times. There's got to be something a little out of - " and before he could finish his statement his eyes locked onto something that caught his attention, " - place."

"I know, I know." Frank spoke louder than normal due to the headphones that muffled his own voice. "But, I'm tellin' ya, it's right around here, gotta be Jonny, signal is beepin' like a banshee, man."

Jonny slowed down his large out of place clunker and pulled into a driveway of one of the estates and stopped inches before his bumper touched the two, large, closed security gates at the entrance.

"Oh, and look what we have here. I believe we do have a Bingo, ladies and gentlemen." Jonny stated.

"What?"

"Do you see what I see, Frank?"

"Well, I see a pretty house that'd be one heck of a party pad," Frank replied.

"Something else, buddy."

"What are you lookin' at?"

"Well, for starters, a ten million dollar mansion and the ass end of a, 1995 Toyota Camry. Something about that picture just doesn't work for me. And it just so happens to be the same kind of piece of shit that our little friends were riding in earlier today," Jonny smiled.

"Man, you got a good eye, Jonny, looks like they've got some rich friends."

"Oh yes, partners in crime is probably a more accurate description."

"I wonder who they are?" Frank inquired.

"Only one way to find out, 001752," Jonny slid open his side window, reached out and pressed a button on a shiny brass intercom and spoke into it in his most childlike voice.

"Hi, Aunt Lucy, it's me, little Timmy from Kansas. We made it, a little tired, but we're here." They sat a moment and waited until a very distinguished voice responded.

"Excuse me sir, what was the name?"

"Timmy Wayne, Ned and Betty's boy, 'member? Gramma said a butler would probably answer."

"Sir, there is no Lucy at this residence." The distinguished sounding voice stated.

"What?" Jonny responded as if heartbroken to hear the news. "If my Aunt Lucy doesn't live here, who does?"

"This is Mr. Hyden's estate."

"You mean, as in Congressman Hyden?" Jonny inquired.

"Precisely," the man answered.

"Sorry bucko, wrong house." Jonny slid his window shut and put the rig in reverse and backed out of the driveway.

"Isn't he the one I've seen on TV with the flaming lisp," Frank inquired?

"You said it," Jonny answered with a lisp. "His friends call him big Jim."

"No kiddin'?"

"Sheeeeeeeeerrr speculation 001752," Jonny answered using his best Sammy Davis Jr. impersonation. "Are you up for a photo shoot, Frank?"

"Sure, what do you got in mind?"

"You'll see," Jonny pulled the RV up to the curb behind a large brick wall a short distance from the house, then went to the back to change into something a little more chic.

Meanwhile, inside the Congressman's lavish mansion, Debbie tapped her black painted nails on the wood handles of an antique chair in an upstairs den. The chair faced the entrance so the congressman's eyes would immediately see her first. She had a pouty, irritated look on her face, put out that the congressman was making them wait.

An impeccably dressed butler entered the room. "The congressman will be in shortly," he announced.

"Tell him we don't have all day," Debbie stated not looking the man in the eyes until she had finished her statement, then, punctuated it with a disdainful look.

"I will tell him, Ms." He politely stated, then exited the room.

Rushnad appeared oblivious to the man and continued with several practice swings with the congressman's putter. He smiled with excitement as he hit the golf ball towards the ball catch and looked on with child-like anticipation of making a shot.

Kaleeb stood back and acted as ball return each time Rushnad missed. Each time he would shake his head as he rolled the ball back to him across the floor.

Rhajneed ignored the two and sat stonefaced while they continued to wait.

"What is that sound?" Debbie questioned the others.

They all stopped to listen. Music was playing from somewhere. Outside?

"Elvis?" Kaleeb stated, then walked in front of Debbie and stared out the window.

Rhajneed got up from his chair and looked over Kaleeb's shoulder down to the grounds below. "Someone is shooting photos," he stated.

"It is Elvis," Kaleeb proudly stated correctly guessing the artist. "Jailhouse Rock?" he attempted to guess the song that played.

"No," Rhajneed firmly stated. "'It is, 'Love Me Tender.'"

"Ha! Ha! It is not 'Love Me Tender.' 'Love Me Tender' is slow," Kaleeb argued. Then Debbie got out of her chair and looked out the window. Her eyes locked onto Frank, who she immediately recognized in his usual attire of sweats and a t-shirt.

"No, you idiots, it's that pig of a neighbor and his friend." She seethed at the two of them while Frank stood next to a ghetto blaster and took pictures of Jonny who hammed it up to, 'Caught In A Trap.' Jonny appeared in a complete Elvis attire, with the gold tinted glasses, black wig and sideburns, white studded waste-length suit coat, and white bellbottoms. The pants had a fake buttless-look to the rear that he had picked up somewhere to add to his repertoire of disguises. He did a montage of Elvis moves from his early hip gyrations, the head moves that Jonny had recalled from all the old Elvis movies and he also threw in a deadly karate move whenever he felt it to accentuate the beat of the music. He had a scarf in every pocket that he periodically threw up in the air to all the imaginary fans and a white towel around his neck to dab away perspiration.

Frank's lens wandered to the second level window and he fired off a rapid succession of four to six quick shots with the press of a finger.

"Are you getting some good shots, Frank?" Jonny inquired while having what appeared to be a controlled epileptic seizure to the music.

"You're lookin' great, keep it up, man," Frank continued at various angles. He zoomed in tight on the trigger happy Debbie just as she aimed her weapon, then closed her eyes as she fired it.

"Come on, gimmie one with your eyes open," Frank said.

"My eyes are open, Frank," Jonny stated.

"Yeah, yeah, feel the music Jonny, feel it in your bones, man," Frank instructed Jonny as he continued getting shots of the others who all gathered around Debbie to get a glimpse of the show and to hear the music better.

"I think we better think about concluding the show, Jonny," Frank announced just as Debbie fired off a wild round that hit a cement fountain at the other side of the meticulously groomed grounds.

A Tour of The Stars bus happened to be driving by as shots were being fired, which caught the attention of the passengers on the bus and the tourguide.

"And over here to my left, we have Congressman Hyden's estate," the flashy dressed tour guide announced to his awestruck passengers who could see what appeared to be an out of control Elvis ham it up while a photographer shot stills.

"My goodness, they must be shooting a movie, either that or somebody's trying to kill Elvis," the guide said as gunshots echoed through the otherwise quiet neighborhood. He chuckled along with the group who continued to point and stare, thinking they were watching a movie being filmed.

A loud gunshot rang through the neighborhood from one of the guns that blew the corner off the boom box. The speed of the song began to waiver, speeding up, then slowing.

Jonny threw the white towel that was draped around his neck up into the air for the show finale, which caught a wild bullet.

"Frank?"

"It's a Kodak moment, Jonny."

In Frank's lens, it looked like the group of misfits had gathered for a family portrait at the window as he fired off a rapid succession of portrait-like close ups of Rhajneed, Kaleeb, Rushnad, and Debbie as they stood huddled together at an upstairs window all firing their weapons in an attempt to kill the two bothersome pests.

Perspiration rolled off Jonny's forehead as he emulated various Elvis poses, oblivious to the increasing number of bullets that were penetrating, the well-manicured lawn. "How we doin', Frank?"

"Throw 'em a scarf and let's hightail it, Jonny!" Frank threw his camera in a small bag, picked it up and sprinted to the wall they had scaled earlier.

"Ten-four big buddy," Jonny tossed another scarf into the air and reached down and latched onto the ghetto blaster and followed Frank, who zigzagged the 40 yards to the six foot brick wall as Elvis sang, "Warden threw a party in the county jail, gathered round a cell they began to wail..." and the music played accompanied by loud blasts that echoed through the neighborhood as bullets ricocheted off the brick wall they sprinted towards.

"Did you get some good shots?" Jonny hollered to Frank.

"Oh yeah." Frank grunted as he tossed his camera bag high up into the air and over the wall, then jumped up and put a leg on the top for leverage, then rolled over the wall landing face first into shrubs on the other side. He then made a beeline for the RV.

Jonny, close behind, tossed the blaster over the wall, which killed the music, then sprang up and used his hands to push himself up and rolled himself over the wall and landed on his feet. He stumbled through the same shrubs, then as he started to follow Frank, paused, turned around, reached for Frank's camera bag that dangled from a low hanging limb of a tree, grabbed it, then sprinted to the rig.

"I don't think they liked the show," Frank said panting from the sprint as Jonny caught up to him at the RV.

"Probably headbangers." Jonny replied. "I think you forgot this, Frank," Jonny handed the camera bag to Frank.

"Sorry, I guess I didn't want to get shot, Jonny."

"Understandable, 001752." Jonny searched through his key chain for the key, then unlocked the door and opened it.

"I hope you don't mind that I only got you from about the waist up, but I threw in a couple head shots I think you'll be happy with," Frank facetiously mentioned.

"Frank?!" Jonny cringed as he entered the rig and pulled off his wig still leaving his large black sideburns attached to his face.

"Did you think to maybe take one or two of those kind hearted people that were shooting at us? That was the objective of our mission!"

"Yeah, yeah, don't get so worked up, I'z just messin' with you. Heck, you didn't even know your name a little while ago, member?" Frank said as he closed the side door and locked it.

Jonny got into the driver's seat, pumped the gas pedal hard several times, then paused and looked over to Frank with a raised brow, then cracked a smile. "Not bad 001752, hm hm hm." Jonny chuckled.

"Just checkin' to see if you can take it as well as dish it out," Frank said.

"Indeed, Frank. I want you to take the film, work with it see what we've got." Jonny turned the key and started up the large 454 cubic inch engine.

"I've got a computer in the back, Frank, see what you can find on any Secret Service agents named Norman. I've got a hunch about him, and it's not pretty," Jonny put on his blinker, looked in his side mirror, then started to drive away from the mansion.

"Who's Norman?" Frank questioned.

"Debbie's friend, on the phone last night?"

"Oh yeah, that dirtbag," Frank recalled.

"I have a very important client that I'm going to brief this evening."

"You signin' up more members, Jonny?" Frank inquired.

"Something like that, Frank."

"Man, you've got this secret agent business down," Frank said.

"Right."

"Hey, Jonny."

"Yeah."

"You know back there, when we was bein' shot at, and runnin' for our lives in the line of duty."

"Right. What is it, Frank?"

"Well, I felt like I just about pissed my pants if you know what I mean. Has that ever happened to you before?"

"Hmnn," Jonny reflected, a moment then smiled over to Frank. "When I first got started, I jumped in with both feet, probably in over my head for a rookie. I had to wear Depends on probably twenty of my first cases, you know, until I built up my nerve," Jonny revealed.

"No kiddin'?" Frank stifled a giggle.

Jonny turned to laugh along with Frank. "Just kidding ya, Frank," he said, then pulled off his Elvis sideburns and set them on the center console.

"But, it's nothing to be ashamed of," Jonny replied as they slowly drove through the ritzy neighborhood. "Looks like I'll be crashing a party tomorrow night."

"Oh yeah? Whose party?" Frank questioned.

"The congressman's." Frank looked back at him surprised.

"You gonna print up your own invitation, Jonny?"

"Not exactly." Jonny sounded like he still pondered the idea of how he would crash the party. "I'll think of something. In the meantime maybe we can at least find out some more about these characters we're dealing with. I have a computer program that links to a large F.B.I. data base of what you might call your low-life scum balls that are wanted for serious crimes, devious behavior, Frank."

"Man oh man, sounds pretty high techie," Frank said with awe at the fancy gadgets Jonny had at his disposal.

"Just tricks of the trade. We've got work to do 001752," Jonny said as the RV turned a corner and drove out of sight.

Chapter 8

It was a warm summer evening when Jonny escorted Karen to Luigis, a small Italian Restaurant located in walking distance of her apartment. He was feeling just a smidge nervous, for this was his very first date with the prettiest, most eligible young bachelorette in their office who appeared stunning in a light floral dress with spaghetti shoulder straps. She was dressed like a glamorous movie star, Jonny thought, which made him feel even more nervous and made him want to impress her more.

He smiled over at her, even though he could hardly swallow his mouth felt so dry, and his palms so sweaty. The well-groomed waiter, who walked with a stiff leg introduced himself as "Tony," then seated them at a center table, which made him feel even more uncomfortable. He would've much preferred a corner table, but the dark, wavy haired waiter said they were reserved. There was only one other couple in the place, which soured Jonny's opinion of the waiter who he thought was pretending to be more Italian than he actually was.

It was a very romantic setting with candles on the tables that embellished the low romantic lighting, and ceiling fans that stirred the warm evening air. Light background music with an Italian feel added to the ambiance that created the perfect atmosphere for love to blossom Jonny thought as he gazed into Karen's beautiful eyes.

Karen smiled back at Jonny who looked up, annoyed, at Tony who approached them at just the wrong moment and poured some water, then left some menus.

"I will a be a right a back when you are a ready," he smiled at Karen and then gave a more serious look to Jonny, which Jonny matched and then raised his eyes accompanied with a nod of his head as if he were brushing the underling off like an annoying fly that bothered him.

Karen picked up her menu.

Jonny thought it would be a good opportunity to take a drink. His mouth felt as dry as a desert. The waiter didn't fill his glass very full, mainly ice, and Jonny had to tip the large glass back, and then the ice came unstuck and dumped the dammed up water over his chin, shirt and pants. He coughed to take the attention away from his dribble, then wiped his best satin shirt off with the white cloth napkin. Karen just smiled pretending not to notice the incident. Jonny smiled back and shrugged his shoulders as if it were no big deal, then he wiped himself down with his napkin. The water made the light blue shirt appear dark and stained over the portion it had fallen, which was mainly over the entire front of his shirt.

Tony quickly came back carrying a tray with two bowls of soup on it.

"What's this?" Jonny snapped at the intrusion as they hadn't had two seconds to look at their menus and he was already back.

Again, in a very thick Italian accent, Tony replied with a joyful smile. "It's a complimentary-a tomato soup." And then he tapped his heels together with a loud clap, like two blocks of wood being struck together, smiled, then said, "en-a-joy."

Jonny looked down at the waiter's shoes, then up to his face.

"Complimentary huh?" he said distrustingly as if he was very unimpressed with the display of showmanship, and still miffed at not getting the corner booth.

The waiter smiled and nodded.

Jonny motioned with his eyes and head once again that it was okay for the waiter to depart, and he thought it wise not to argue with anything free and Tony left the table, but not before saying, "I will a be back."

"Great," Jonny leaned over to smell the aromatic soup, then put his cloth napkin into the collar of his shirt to protect himself from any further accidents.

"Daddy was pretty mad at you today for not showing up for work. He said he was thinking about firing you," Karen said half looking at her menu, and half at Jonny.

"He doesn't understand what kind of life I lead," Jonny said nonchalantly, then took a sip of his soup that dribbled down his chin and put a long red dribble mark down the front of his white cloth napkin. Once again, perturbed at his difficulty that stemmed from nervousness, he held up his spoon to the candlelight to check for any holes or possible imperfections. None.

Karen sounded a little reluctant when she inquired, "So what kind of life do you lead?"

"Promise you won't laugh."

"Promise."

"I lead a double life. You see, Karen, I'm not just an insurance agent, I'm another kind of an agent as well," Jonny said then slurped half of his soup from his spoon and the other half went again down onto his napkin.

Karen pretended not to notice Jonny's nervousness. "Do you have a product line or something?" she inquired.

Jonny, tired of beating around the bush, told her as simply as he could, "Karen, I'm a secret agent."

Karen politely sipped her soup just as Jonny delivered his declaration, then coughed, almost choking as she looked up smiling as if it was a joke.

"As in secret agent?" she inquired.

"Right," Jonny matter of factly replied, then glanced around the small establishment to see if anyone had heard his revelation. "FBI wouldn't take me, a little physical ailment. I formed my own agency and I'm working on the biggest, most dangerous case of my life. I might even need your help, Karen," he said then picked up his fork to prepare for the next entre. He held it up for inspection. Water spot. He discreetly tucked it under the table onto his lap and began polishing it with the tablecloth.

"I could probably help a little after work," Karen offered so sweetly Jonny thought as he smiled back to her. And just as he did, his fork slipped out of his hand and landed on the floor next to the table just as Tony returned to collect the soup.

He stood right on top of Jonny's fork. Jonny inconspicuously looked down at the fork that was now concealed by the waiter's large foot, then up to scowl at the pest as he opened his little tray that he'd placed next to the table. His leg must be wooden, Jonny thought, otherwise he would be able to feel the fork under his shoe. He picked up Jonny's soup and set it onto the tray, then picked up Jonny's soggy napkin and rung it into Jonny's soup bowl. Jonny scowled at him again for the embarrassment as a stream of soup collected into his bowl. The waiter let Karen have one more sip, then gave a slight gesture with all four fingers as his palm remained steady. It was as if he was using sign language. Come on, give it up, he gestured. She lifted up the bowl, and he snatched it from her hands before she had a chance to even put her spoon back into it.

"Are you a ready to order?" The waiter inquired with what Jonny thought to be a very phony smile directed at him.

Jonny snarled and gave a slight nod, which brought his gaze back down to the end of his fork that stuck out from under the waiter's polished black shoe. In an effort to maintain his total coolness, Jonny pretended nothing was amiss. And the waiter lifted one foot and grinded down on the other with his wooden leg in a quarter spin to ask Karen the same question.

"And-a are you-a ready to order?" He amused himself as he asked Karen the same question.

"I'll have the spaghetti," Karen softly said with a very pleasing and most polite voice.

And the waiter did the same move again, lifting his weight from one foot, then grinding down with the prosthetic to mangle the fork even more as he turned to face Jonny.

Jonny glanced down to the floor again, then back up to the waiter.

"And-a you-a sir?"

"Spaghetti," Jonny said with a concealed seethe, and gritted teeth while not looking at the waiter.

"Two-a spaghettis a-comin' up," Tony enthusiastically called out for all the occupants including the cook in the restaurant to hear. And he clicked his heels together again that made a loud clap, then, in a stiff legged manner hurried away from the table.

Jonny inconspicuously looked down to the floor. He struggled to swallow as he saw the fork was twisted and mangled. Normally he would've simply asked for another fork, but due to his nervousness and wanting to appear smooth and sure of himself to the girl of his dreams, he didn't let on anything was wrong. He wanted this to be the perfect night, so he just sat there and his eyes wandered around the restaurant and then back to Karen. What could he do? He thought a moment, then, almost automatically he said, looking out the window, "What is that?"

And Karen turned around to look at whatever it was Jonny was supposed to be looking at, but nothing caught her attention. And Jonny seized the moment and quickly bent down to pick up what used to be his fork and concealed it in his lap.

"What?" she questioned.

"What?" Jonny said back. "Nothing," he quickly added, then continued to look up and around the establishment while his hands paused motionless, under the table until the moment had passed and he could start to un-mangle what was once a fork.

"You were saying the FBI wouldn't take you because of what kind of ailment?" Karen inquired.

"It's kind of private," Jonny nervously scratched his head appearing ill at ease at the idea of revealing his weakness.

"Ah, you can tell me," Karen said with such sexiness that Jonny immediately divulged the private information.

He said it as he coughed, "Spastic colon," and then he looked up and away and every-which way from his embarrassment.

Karen, started to smile, but paused, "Really?" she questioned.

Jonny coughed again, gave a quick nod, then said with great discomfort, "Yeah."

"Oh," Karen replied, pondering what Jonny had said and appeared as if it was no big deal. "Well, I think you should be really proud of yourself that you didn't let it hold you back from pursuing your dream," she then said, and Jonny looked back at Karen, his embarrassment had dissipated and a thought flashed through his mind that if he was an ice cream cone he would have melted onto the floor into a little creamy puddle right before her eyes. He smiled thinking that was probably the sweetest thing anyone had ever said to him in his entire life. Karen was so beautiful and romantic he thought as he looked up and into her sympathetic eyes.

"It's still kind of painful to think about – still." He took a drink and once again the ice held back the water and when he tipped it back just enough all the remaining water came out gushing all over him again. This time, he simply pretended it didn't happen as water dripped from his chin while he continued manipulating the bent fork to make it appear normal.

Once again, Tony appeared with his small tray. He had two small bowls of vegetables, peas, carrots, and bits of corn mixed in to add more color than anything. "Here are-a you're-a vegetables," he proudly stated.

Jonny looked down at the vegetables in disbelief, then up at Tony.

"I'm afraid we ordered spaghetti, remember?" Jonny firmly, but politely reminded the waiter, then looked over to Karen, shook his head in disgust and raised a brow as if the waiter was a total lunatic.

"It's a complimentary," the waiter proudly stated. "You must-a have-a your vegetables to-a stay-a healthy." He told them with a smile while emphasizing his comment with his hands.

Once again Jonny shrugged his shoulders and smiled at Karen as to say, what can it hurt if they're free, he then nodded at the waiter and blinked as to imply, you can go now. And the waiter acknowledged Jonny's look with a returned nod and walked away, but not before clicking his heals together loudly.

Jonny once again pretended to be looking at something outside the window of the establishment until Karen turned and looked.

"What is it?" she questioned. And as she turned Jonny placed his fork back on the table thinking it was straightened enough to be useable.

"Oh nothing," he replied pretending to be more relaxed than he was. He continued looking at Karen as he suavely picked up his fork that he had just quickly placed next to his vegetable bowl. His eyes took a double take at the fork that he thought was nearly straightened, but was still mangled and twisted. He looked at Karen and smiled and pretended nothing was amiss as he attempted to eat some of his vegetables. He placed his fork into the vegetables and attempted to gather them up. Each time he tried to get some of the vegetables to his mouth they would all fall off his twisted piece of metal. He casually set down the utensil, smiled and paused in a relaxed manner to take a small sip of water, which he only touched to his lips for fear of the ice becoming unstuck again and gushing over the front of him. He set the glass down, took a deep breath, picked up his fork, looked down at the tiny vegetables more determined, then tried again as most of the peas and small carrot portions landed around his little bowl, or into his lap, or on the floor.

Growing more frustrated, he tried again, this time he leaned over and got his head closer to the bowl in an effort to scoop up some of the veggies, but even that wasn't working. He looked over at Karen who was, once again, gracefully and effortlessly enjoying her vegetables that she easily nudged onto her fork with her butter knife. He smiled at her and then leaned over again, farther this time, as he tried tossing up some of the peas in an attempt to catch them into his mouth. He made a chomping sound, like someone's pet would do each time he landed one or two of the small bits of food into his mouth.

"Vegetables okay?" Karen inquired. She could tell Jonny was having a hard time.

"Yeah, it's this fork that's giving me kind of a hard time. I don't know where they purchase their silverware around here," he commented to focus the attention on the utensil that he held up to the light, rather than himself.

"Hmnn," Karen winced as she looked at Jonny's twisted fork. "My guess is they probably have some more of those," she said and just then the waiter arrived.

"Two a spaghettis a-nice and-a hot," Tony said with a smile and in full deep voice.

"Could we get some other utensils?" Karen inquired as she handed over her empty vegetable bowl and fork to the waiter. Jonny placed his fork into his bowl and also handed it over to Tony, who immediately took notice of the fork and the vegetables that he'd stepped in and that were strewn about the vicinity of Jonny's placemat and he gave Jonny a distrusting look.

"Hmnn," the waiter said. He picked up Jonny's fork and he held it up to the light for an inspection, then back to Jonny. "Did you-a damage this-a fork?" he questioned Jonny while studying him for any signs of guilt.

"No, I didn't damage the fork," Jonny challenged the waiter as if that was the most preposterous thing he had ever heard in his entire life.

"Hmnn," Tony said, then he smiled to Karen, "Sometimes-a the dish-washer, it-a get-a little hungry-a too, ha ha ha," he chuckled to his own joke, then gave a stirn look to Jonny, who appeared naseous as Tony left the table, then quickly returned with fresh utensils wrapped in white linen napkins.

"En-a-joy," He said with vigor, then walked away.

Jonny breathed a sigh of relief as he unfolded his napkin and held up his new utensils for a quick inspection, nice and straight he thought. Once again, he placed his napkin into his shirt and they began to enjoy their spaghetti.

"So tell me, what kind of case are you working on now?" Karen innocently inquired.

"Are you sure you want to know?" he forewarned her.

"Yeah, I'm sure." Karen replied, intrigued as she took a drink of her water.

Jonny looked into Karen's eyes. He knew that she was sensitive and sweet and kind and everything that these ruthless characters he'd crossed paths with weren't. Would she even comprehend it? He was about to find out. "I stumbled across a small group of people, who I believe are planning on kidnapping the President of The United States," he stated, which made Karen start to choke and cough profusely.

"You okay?" he inquired with concern as Karen nodded back, still unable to answer. "Wrong pipe?" He questioned to ease her embarrassment. She nodded.

"And - " Jonny paused to look around the room to make sure no one was eavesdropping on their conversation and gave a moment for Karen to fully recover, then said in a hushed voice as he leaned closer, " - I believe this Congressman Hyden is in on it too, if you can believe that," he added.

Karen coughed a moment longer before she composed herself.

"That's impossible."

Jonny sucked up several foot long strands of spaghetti into his mouth.

"Is it? I'd say he's probably the most valuable man in America. They could demand billions for his release and who would refuse them?"

She shook her head. "It just sounds so, so crazy."

"Yeah, it's a crazy world. I may need you, Karen. Will you help me?"

She almost surprised herself for jumping in so readily. "Yeah, sure, I'll help you." Deep down, she thought Jonny was merely fabricating the situation to impress her. Her father had always taught her to be very thorough and careful to analyze every bit of data before committing to something. She partially agreed with her father's philosophy, but also thought that you had to follow your instincts and what your heart was saying too. And that's what she did, and it made her feel good inside that she was learning to trust her own intuition. And even though Jonny was a little, "different," there was something charming about him and his dedication to pursue his dream with passion, even though others had tried to extinguish that dream, and it was that, that attracted her to him and made her believe in him.

"I knew I could count on you, Karen," Jonny said with a total belief in her. And that made her feel good inside that somebody, even though it was only Jonny, the worst salesperson in the history of the company who had an unquestioning belief in her. Everyone else at the company, including her own father, doubted her at the first hint of faltering on her sales performance. And most would stab her in the back at the first chance just to get ahead. She knew that that thought would not even enter Jonny's mind. And she smiled back at him with the sweetest smile. And they enjoyed a wonderful meal and talked about each other and really nothing in particular. Even the big case that Jonny had brought up had taken a back seat to their unfolding romance as they shared small talk and gazed romantically into each other's eyes as the candles flickered and the ceiling fans moved the warm summer air and the music that played in their hearts drowned out the soft background music that played in the small neighborhood restaurant where romances flourished.

Jonny decided to leave a tip, more to impress Karen than to reward the annoying waiter for his continual checking on them. He forced a smile and raised a hand up when they walked out the door and Tony called out to them.

"Thank you-a very much, and you-a folks have a wonderful evening." And they left the restaurant and took the short stroll back to Karen's apartment.

Jonny realized Karen was doing most of the talking. On their short walk he felt like he knew every detail of her entire life. And the one thing she made sure he would remember was that she wanted to have a family. That was very important to her. Her voice sounded so lovely as she spoke. He felt at the doorstep of a blossoming love. As they got closer to her apartment, his mind was thinking all kinds of things. What would he say when he said goodnight? A kiss? Should I kiss her? he questioned himself. His heart began beating faster and faster at the thought and his palms got clammy and with each step he knew the inevitable would be upon him. He would have to do something. And then, they were there almost instantaneously.

"Well, here we are," Karen said with a hint of remorse that the lovely evening was about to end.

"Is this it?" Jonny asked in a somewhat surprised tone of voice.

"Yeah, 'fraid so," she replied.

"Huh," Jonny chuckled to himself. "I don't know what I was thinking, I thought it was another block down," he said then looked into Karen's eyes. Karen just shook her head.

"Nope, it hasn't moved," she said.

"Well," Jonny hem-hawed. "I usually don't kiss on the first date," but when he looked into her sweet eyes and she looked up at him with the warmest, most tender look he could ever recall receiving, something came over him, which felt like a bolt of lightning.

"You're the exception," he said with a dreamy tone and felt like he was taken away by her beauty and he embraced her fully and kissed her a good long kiss. Several moments passed and Jonny pulled back to come up for air, then Karen surprised him with a barrage of kisses on the cheeks, lips, and neck, and as quickly as she performed the maneuver, the moment had passed and he stood there and watched as she appeared to float up the steps of her apartment and turned back around to give a little wave.

"Karen?" Jonny questioned.

"Yeah," she softly replied.

"Todd kiss you?"

Her mouth was slightly open as she answered, "Ah, not like that," she answered with a subtle sexy smile. "Goodnight."

"Goodnight," he answered and felt as if his body started to ascend to some heavenly plane.

She blew him a little kiss just before she headed up the steps that led to her apartment door. He stood there a moment savoring the feelings of love he had for her. I did it, he thought to himself and he smiled back at Karen as he watched her enter her apartment. He had the courage to kiss her and she liked it. He turned around and, feeling as light as a feather on a breeze, began to walk down the street and headed for the Winnebago.

It was past midnight when Jonny returned. The hours flew by while he had been with Karen. He quietly entered his home on wheels and snuck up on Frank.

"I must say Frank, you do take a good picture."

"Gimmie a heart attack would ya!"

Jonny took a seat next to Frank and was impressed by the pictures he had taken earlier. They appeared to be portrait-like, studio shots; close ups, two shots, and complete group shots of the wincing deviants as they stood in the open window of the congressman's mansion with smoke and flash emitting from their guns.

"Yeah, I was head photographer for K-Mart for nine years when I was married. The lighting was pretty good out there today, and heck, you can make even a dirtbag look good, Jonny if the lighting is right," Frank modestly stated.

"We should really try to find the addresses of their parents and send them some shots, they're just great," Jonny facetiously said.

"You think we should?" Frank eagerly responded.

"Negative Frank, just kidding. Did you run 'em through the program?"

"You bet I did, Jonny. That's the best part." Frank jostled the mouse to open up the identifier program, that had all four shots loaded onto the page. He placed the icon over Debbie's photo and pressed down on it.

"Check it out." The screen came to life with a moving geometric sphere.

"Interesting, but what is it?" Jonny inquired.

"Give it a second, it's your FBI site. It's just like you said, they got the dirt on some people that's for sure," Frank said. "Did you have to hack into it?"

"Well?" Jonny wavered. "Promise you won't tell?"

"That's a yes, and my lips are sealed."

Jonny moved a little closer to the monitor to read the page.

"Sphere – World Organization founded in 2001 by former members of the KGB who have recruited additional members throughout the world. Members of Sphere are considered to be heavily armed and extremely dangerous. Involved in organized crime - illegal drugs, prostitution, gambling, kidnapping, extortion and selling illegal weapons to dictator regimes around the globe."

Frank guided the mouse to an icon that read, Members and clicked. "And now ladies and germs, the stars of our show, at least a couple of 'em." An angry picture of Debbie appeared on the monitor.

"There she is, my lovely neighbor as a blond," Frank said as they studied the photo of Debbie who appeared to be walking down a street somewhere with a handbag strapped over her shoulder.

"They do have more fun, Frank, that's common knowledge."

"Sure. Now that was taken with a telephoto, probably two blocks away, and check this out," Frank shook the mouse and placed it over a section of the same photo, put a square around it and hit zoom.

"Our sheik?" Jonny said.

"Yeah. Rhajneed, is his name."

"Really? Man I'm gonna nick-name you the dirt collector," Jonny said.

"They don't seem to have any dirt on him, other than his name, but check this out," Frank zoomed back out, then placed the cursor over Debbie's photo and pressed on it. Another photo appeared. It was a black and white FBI wanted poster.

"Personally, I think I take a better photo than your buddies at the bureau," Frank said.

"Oh yes. I like your pictures much better, Frank," Jonny looked at the photo and what was printed below it.

"Yeah, she looks like somebody beat her up before they took that picture," Frank added.

"Maybe somebody did," Jonny agreed, then read aloud from the screen. "Nadia Kieg a.k.a. Debbie Black, is wanted for questioning. Questioning? That's no fun. Where is the meat and potatoes, Frank?"

"Well, now, hold your horses. Scrolling down just a little farther and we see that my sweet, little, innocent neighbor's wanted for questioning in a kidnapping, and... "

Jonny finished the sentence. "And for the murders of two FBI agents. I don't think she's for you, Frank."

"Damn."

Jonny continued reading, "Believed to be second in command of Sphere, a group of deviants that have been linked to disruptive activities around the globe. Hmmn, doesn't tell me a lot, Frank," Jonny surmised.

"I bet it's not loud block parties they're talkin' about, Jonny," Frank said.

"I'd say your right 001752," Jonny agreed. "Sphere headquarters are believed to be located on a nuclear powered Soviet submarine, location is unknown, hmmn," Jonny pondered to think. "Well, if she's second in command, I wonder who the big cheese is?"

"Head of Sphere is unknown at this time." Frank read from the computer screen.

"Great. You're no fun, Frank. I thought I was going to see some quality entertainment and you can't even," and Jonny stopped as another picture appeared.

"Let's check the friendly folks of Sphere again, you might find this interesting?" Frank suggested as he jostled the mouse and clicked on another icon.

"And what do we have here? known members," Jonny read.

Frank highlighted an empty box where there was no picture.

"N.F."

"There's no picture, Frank. You know how I like to look at the pictures."

"Hold the phone. I did a quick little Google search and let's see what we find when we enter – Norman F., Secret Service," Frank stated, then glanced up to Jonny who had a more serious look on his face.

"Oh Frank, you are the man." Jonny said as Frank clicked open another pre-selected page.

"Norman Felder, N.F., is a thirty year member of the Secret Service with a distinguished record of service in the United States and abroad, who is looking forward to retirement," Frank read.

"Connections overseas. She said, Norman." Jonny said referring to the taped phone conversation.

"You know what I think, Jonny?"

"What's that?"

"I think our buddy Norman is renewing his membership, and it's not with the good ol' boys."

"That's it," Jonny casually agreed.

"I'd bet money on it," Frank added.

"Looks like somebody's been keeping a discreet eye on ol' Norman. He's a dirtbag."

"Pusball came to my mind."

"It's good to vent, Frank." Jonny said as if his mind was elsewhere.

"Looks like we better get out the bullet proof vests, huh?" Frank suggested.

"A vest for you, party attire for me, after a very short trip to the office in the morning," Jonny patted Frank on the shoulder for his good work.

"Party attire?"

"Congressman Hyden is one of our most popular, and well respected customers and golf buddies with my boss." Jonny said thinking aloud.

"And?"

"And he's throwing a party tomorrow night. A couple of the top sales people were invited along with Mr. Stockton," Jonny said.

"Are you a top sales people, Jonny?"

"'Fraid not, Frank, but I'm gonna pretend I am for one night, promise you won't tell anyone?"

"Oh, I won't tell a soul. You got some kind of disguise you're gonna dress up in?" Frank questioned.

"You said it," Jonny said with a flare.

"Man, oh man," Frank said with a growing excitement.

"Better get some rest, we've got people to meet and places to go, buddy."

"Isn't it places to go and people to meet, Jonny? Frank questioned.

"Right you are, 001752," Jonny agreed and sounded again like his thoughts were elsewhere as the two stared at the computer screen.

"Time to hit the hay," Jonny then said.

"Oh yeah. Dibs on the sofa."

"You got it big guy. Good work." Jonny said and Frank closed the window on the computer screen and the two went to bed.

Chapter 9

The next morning Jonny drifted into the offices of Stockton Insurance at his usual 9:00 am time, give or take fifteen to twenty minutes, as opposed to the other workers 8:30 sharp arrival time. He immediately felt something wasn't quite right when Ms. Peters greeted him in a very friendly manner.

"Good morning, Mr. Hoover," she said with a subtle smile that resembled that of a blood thirsty assassin's as her eyes followed and burrowed into him as he walked past. The unusually warm behavior caught Jonny off guard, because Gwendolyn never greeted him in the morning, the afternoon, or any-time for that matter. His gut told him something was up and he was right. There was a note on his desk to see Mr. Stockton.

Mr. Stockton remained seated in his brown leather chair and glanced up briefly from some documents.

"We've decided to let you go, Mr. Hoover," he began with and then the rest of what he said didn't even register. It's the kind of thing that makes you numb, in a state of disbelief and perhaps a dash of shock to make the experi-ence memorable.

What just happened? Jonny could hear the voice in his head asking as he slowly walked out of Mr. Stockton's office and back to his desk. It was a cold feeling being fired, even if it's at a place he didn't like and where he didn't feel he fit. He felt like hiding under a table or anything for that matter. It was the worst feeling in the world being told you're not wanted anymore.

Where was everybody? Namely Karen. She wasn't at her desk, and no Todd. Sick maybe? Jonny thought a second, no, the person he hated the most in the company was never sick. He's one guy I won't miss. Oh well, chalk it up to experience, and don't waste your time in the future doing something that you have no interest in whatsoever. Selling insurance was not his bag and he knew it. It was the longest Jonny had held the same job, eleven months and a handful of days, almost one year, he thought. Jonny looked at the small Stockton Insurance calendar as he placed it into a small box that had magically appeared on his desk to put all of the junk that he had acquired.

What's the date? He pulled the company calendar from the box. Is it the twelfth? he pondered as he counted the days. Nope, it's the thirteenth, unlucky thirteenth, and on a Friday too. He placed the calendar back into the small box, more as a momentum of a time in his life, if he ever cared to look back at his time spent at a company and job he had little concern for. He pulled down the one document of recognition from the corkboard that was in his cubicle. It read: Perfect Attendance, July. The one month, he had successfully made it to work every day.

He heard some commotion, a small group of people entering the office. He looked over his cubicle wall. There was Karen, and Todd too, along with several of the other sales people. They all had coffee in their hands. Probably sent out so the dirty work of firing some poor sucker like himself could get done with and out of the way, and then back to business as usual. It was not a good feeling, not a good feeling at all.

Karen surprised him when she snuck away from the group and poked her head into his small cubicle. Her voice sounded like the most understanding and compassionate, and sweetest he had ever heard in his entire life.

"I'm so sorry, Jonny."

Jonny appeared startled for a brief moment, then nodded in agreement that he felt sorry too, even though he didn't like the job, he did like some of the people, namely Karen - especially Karen.

"Maybe I can talk to him," she said in a very sympathetic tone of voice. "He'll change his mind."

"Don't. I appreciate it, but don't, Karen. I was never meant to be in this business." Jonny glanced down at a small stuffed monkey that held a small sign that said - Congratulations on your 1st Sale! He picked it up and tossed it into his cardboard box. "I have a name to live up to."

Karen nodded. And from out of the blue Todd appeared along with a couple of his brown-nosing admirers who sucked up to him like leeches who are hungry for anything, even if it's ridiculing someone.

"Did vacuum man get fired? Aww, that's too bad, now we won't have anyone to poke fun at," Todd said with a biting sarcasm as the trio had a good laugh at Jonny's expense.

"Todd, one of these days," Jonny said leaving the conclusion open ended.

Todd looked at his fellow co-workers and chuckled, "One of these days what, vacuum man?" He said wide-eyed pretending that the comment instilled great fear. He then snorted from his unbridled laughter as he looked to his cohorts for support towards his endeavor of belittling Jonny.

"That's what I thought," he answered with a sickening arrogance. "Lunch Karen?" he then added to his insult.

"Not now, Todd," she replied.

She didn't even say no, Jonny thought as he glanced at Karen, then back to his small box where he placed the rest of his things.

"You know I hear the company needs a night janitor, Hoover," Todd said that roused himself and his followers into another bout of laughter. Then Mr. Stockton came out of his office for something and that scattered Todd, and what Jonny thought to be his little cockroach buddies into their little holes to do their duties at the Insurance agency.

"My day will come," Jonny reminded himself, then looked at Karen who stood there not knowing what to say. "You'll see." He looked at her, as if it was a solemn promise, then proceeded to pack one last eraser into the box.

"This is weird." His eyes welled up just enough to notice. "As much as I hated this place I think I'm really gonna miss it."

"You've got my number," Karen said, then reached for Jonny's hand and squeezed it a moment.

"Yeah," Jonny said then exhaled. "Well, time for a celebration." He smiled at Karen who appeared puzzled by what he meant. "Big party's tonight, remember?"

"Oh yeah, that," she said.

Jonny picked up his box and started to walk away, as he did he turned around and mouthed the words, "See you there," then smiled at Karen who appeared puzzled by the comment.

Jonny walked through the reception area and past Ms. Peters, who had her head down pretending to be extremely focused on whatever important task she had at hand, so focused that she wouldn't have noticed if the man on the moon were to walk by, let alone the person she despised the most, Jonny.

"Gwen?" Jonny stood at the two thick glass doors until Ms. Peters looked up and gave her usual look, which appeared to be somewhat of a glaring look. "It's been really great workin' with ya," he said with the friendliest tone of voice and the warmest, most genuine smile he possessed.

And if looks could kill, Jonny would've been a goner. Ms. Peters raised her head enough to look over the top of her old fashioned wire-framed bifoculs, and her eyes appeared to emit smoke and flames as she threw every degrading, demoralizing, dehumanizing, demeaning and humiliating comment at Jonny she could retrieve from her old brain, in an attempt to diminish him to the lowest form of life she possibly could.

"I wish I could return the compliment Mr. Hoover, but I just can't." She took her glasses off and gave Jonny both barrels.

"You have been the most unprofessional, uncooperative, untidy, unscrupulous form of a misfit," she ranted as Jonny interjected.

"Tardy too, Gwen," Jonny cordially added another one of his faults for her to sink her old false teeth into as she continued.

"Yes, and that too," she agreed. "And disorganized, and your flagrant disregard for those in authority has certainly not won you any awards around here, and your rudeness that you display when you attempt to win some sort of 'being cute award' with those little childish pranks that you seem to love to play on people has been enough to make me literally sick. And your performance has been the worst I have ever seen in the forty-seven years I have been at this company, and if I were you, I would also see a doctor about your flatulence problem," she paused to catch her breath.

It was just a gag, he thought to himself. He looked away from the old woman and decided it would be a good idea to walk out the door during her performance to spare her from having a heart attack, which he did. He pushed open the heavy glass door for the last time and left behind the old company. He could hear her continue with her venting as he stood outside the door. He paused to reflect a brief moment and thought to himself - it was the perfect time to leave. Even though he would miss not seeing Karen every day, he had bigger fish to fry and he felt lighter than he had felt in a long time.

He walked down the marble floored hallway to the elevator and took his last ride down to the main floor. Mindless Musak played in the slow moving elevator as Jonny stood there with a blank stare, still feeling a little numb from what just had occurred.

The little jingle that played from his cell phone startled him when it began to chime. He pulled it from its' Velcro fastener, opened it up and placed it to his ear. "Yeah, talk to me," he said sounding a little down.

"Hey Jonny, how ya doin?" Frank inquired.

"Oh…" He paused before continuing, "Not bad, what's up, Frank?"

"I've been buggin' our new friends if you catch my drift and they're having a meeting today at the beach, with guess who?"

"Ah…Don Rickles?"

"Not exactly. Norman." Frank said.

"Norman Foreman, ah, Freedman, no, Fronhausen? " Jonny humorously rattled off.

"Try Feldman."

"Ah yes, but I was darn close."

"Yeah, do you think you can break away from work and we can do a little spy work?" Frank enthusiastically questioned.

"Oh, I don't see a problem with that good buddy, since I'm no longer working at the company, I mean." Jonny said.

"Ah-oh, what the heck happened?"

"Doesn't matter, it's a beautiful thing. Listen Frank, they've made us, so we'll have to go incognito."

"Well, sure." Frank agreed. "I'm about two blocks away do you think you can be out front in a few minutes?"

"Perfectomundo," Jonny said. "I'll be waiting,...Oh, Frank," Jonny said just before closing his phone.

"Yeah, Jonny?"

"Do you like ZZ Top?"

"They're one of my favorites, them and Zepplin, why?"

"Ohhhh, you'll see," he said then slapped his phone shut and paused a moment as he waited for the doors to open, then exited the elevator and walked outside and onto the bustling downtown street, where all the people hurried about like busy worker ants walking in every direction. He held a hand up to shield the sweltering sun - another summer scorcher. He looked up and down the street for Frank, and it wasn't a moment later that he spotted the big rig heading his way.

Frank pulled the motorcoach up to the curb and Jonny opened the side door and got inside. He took a front seat and leaned over and kept his face next to the AC/vent on the dash. "Ah, that's better."

Frank looked over to Jonny sizing him up after the firing. "Well, don't feel bad, there's probably a gazillion insurance places you could find to work at if you really wanted to." Frank reasurred.

"Yeah, I suppose," Jonny said.

"It never feels good when the ax comes down though, and I can say that it has happened to me too, a lot. You're not alone, Jonny, not by a long shot. Heck, I been fired so many times, I can't count 'em all," Frank said.

"Really?" Jonny questioned. He couldn't figure if he felt lonely because he knew he would miss not seeing Karen each and every day, or that he thought he was the only person on the planet that had been fired, because that's how it felt.

"Heck yeah, nothin' to be ashamed of that's for sure. I don't think a person can say he's really lived unless he's been fired from someplace. It's just a part of livin' man. You get a job, you get fired, no big deal."

Jonny looked over at him and chuckled as Frank looked back with his two glowing raccoon-like shiners.

"Now what's this business about ZZ Top you were askin' me about?"

"You'll see. To the beach, James." Jonny cried out as Frank put on his blinker and pulled onto the freeway entrance and blew a cloud of black smoke after he stomped on the gas and they headed south towards Santa Monica Beach.

People strolled along in every direction around the bustling beach area as Frank, incognito, wore a wig and matching ZZ Top beard that hung down over his Hawaiian shirt, along with a cowboy hat and dark sunglasses. He and Jonny, weighted down with beach necessities, walked across the hot asphalt as they approached the sprawling Santa Monica beach area.

"What is so funny, Frank?" Jonny asked disguised as a blond pregnant woman whose large false-belly protruded from his one-piece woman's swimsuit. The large belly bulge was apparent as it stuck out from the loose shirt that blew in the warm sea breeze.

"Take a look in a mirror pal, ha, ha," Frank chuckled.

"Don't you know that beauty comes from the inside, Frank." Jonny answered as the two hurried across the boulevard. Their thongs flopped as they lugged a cooler, blanket, handbags, and a good-sized umbrella onto the miles of hot, white sand, where thousands of people had come to relax upon, and soak up the sun and cool off in the gently rolling waves of the Pacific.

Jonny stopped to scan the area and to see if he could spot Debbie and her comrades.

Frank relished in the attention he received from his new look. His wandering eyes darted from one beautiful bikini clad woman to the next who passed them, followed by the scent of Cocoa Butter. He then glanced over to Jonny.

"You might've thought to shave your legs and under your arms, honey, they don't really match your blond hair. And take a little more time with your make up too, that red lipstick's on a little thick and sloppy. I'll think twice 'fore I take you out here again, baby, ha, ha," Frank chuckled.

"I'm a nature chick, man. Haven't you ever seen one of those?" Jonny replied as he searched the large crowd of sunbathers.

"Yeah, I try to look away as quick as I can," Frank acknowledged.

"You're so old fashioned, Frank."

And they trudged through the crowded beach area where every age, size, and color of man, woman, and child, came and paid no mind to them and their objective.

"I gotta hand it to you though, Jonny, all kidding aside," Frank said as they walked through the gathering of people closer to the water, "These disguises are really somethin', man. Heck, they wouldn't even recognize us if we were to kick sand right in their faces," Frank said.

"Right, that's the beauty, hold up a second, Frank, I think I felt the baby kick," Jonny set down the cooler and pulled down his large pink sunglasses to study the terrain.

Frank, who had become blind from the rock star attention he received, bumped into him.

"Ha, the baby kick, yeah right," Frank laughed.

A light pacific breeze with the scent of the sea felt good under the direct sun. The sound of hungry, yapping seagulls had a relaxing effect as did the slight waves that restlessly rolled over the miles of white sand. Jonny looked up and down the vast beach, then adjusted his large straw hat with a pink satin tie around it, and looked out from under his sunglasses at Frank, who continued smiling at all the beautiful women who walked past. Where are they? He wondered.

"See anything, Frank?"

"Oh, I see a lotta things, Jonny," Frank tipped his coyboy hat to three gorgeous, freshly oiled women who all smiled back at him.

"Let's set up camp," Jonny said and they quickly seized a small portion of unoccupied sand near by, and laid out the blanket and placed their things on top of it. Jonny reached into the military green cooler and took out the only two drinks from inside it and handed one to Frank, who gladly accepted it.

They both patiently sat there a while pretending to be your average sun bather/vacationers as they eyed the terrain. Jonny brushed the hair from his blond haired wig off his shoulder, then casually reached into his handbag for a pair of stylish opera glasses that had a long handle attached to them and held them up to his eyes and began scanning the throngs of big people; fat people, short people, tall people, skinny people, hairy people, old people, tiny people, light people, dark people, fully dressed people, nearly naked people, naked people?

"Hello."

"What do you see?"

He stopped. "Don't look now, Frank," Jonny said as he lifted his eyes from the dainty glasses, then placed them back into position.

"Holy guacamole, I see 'em too, Jonny, could spot that big idiot a mile away," Frank also eyed the foursome and pulled out his camera from the cooler.

"'Your innocent neighbor appears a little incognito too with her scarf and dark glasses."

"Yeah, you don't see too many snakes on the beach, Jonny, not in these parts anyway," Frank agreed.

"Pre-ceptive, Frank. Looks like our sheik forgot his beachball. You think maybe he's wearin' his swimsuit under that neatly pressed suit, or maybe he's just got it stuffed under his turban?"

"That'd be my guess," Frank said as he focused on them through his tele-photo. He clicked off several rapid shots, then scanned over to Kaleeb and Rhushnad who seemed unconcerned and like the rest of the people who came to simply enjoy the scenery and the water, and got some shots of them as well.

"Your neighbor has kind of a, Jackie O look," Jonny said eyeing Debbie from a distance.

"You think?"

"Oh yes."

"She tries to be glamorous, Jonny, but, it sort a don't work, though, with a hardened criminal, scum-ball like her."

"Sharp eye, 001752," Jonny peeked through the binoculars. "Say, Frank?"

"Yeah."

"Do you want to get our umbrella in place and aim it in the direction of our subjects, please?" Jonny opened the cooler and quickly reached for the small inconspicuous earpiece and placed it into his ear, consealed by his long blond hair.

"You betcha, honey, ha ha, I'm just kiddin' you, man," Frank ribbed Jonny as he set up the umbrella and angled it down the crowded beack to-wards Debbie and company. He pressed down hard with his thumb on a rusted metal button three-quarters up the long pole, and pushed up on the contraption that stretched out the old, faded, unstylish aqua colored, vinyl material until it blossomed into an umbrella. At its top there was a small parabolic dish that acted as a receiver, which Frank aimed down the beach as Jonny listened.

"No signal."

"Huh, what did I do?"

"Nothing Frank, simply an operator error," Jonny quickly reached for an old weathered cord that dangled from the base of the umbrella pole and plugged it into a female jack from an extension inside the cooler that connected to a tape recorder.

"That's what I like to hear, little to the left, buddy," Jonny instructed as Frank adjusted the umbrella to aim it more directly in line with the sound.

"Perfectomundo," Jonny said focusing on the sound. "Frank, let's get 'em at every angle, huh? And save some pictures for the kids that are coming to the party later," Jonny innocently suggested as if it was a birthday party for some very scummy secret servicemen.

"Yes my love," Frank said snickering at Jonny while he played the role of the doting husband.

He aimed his lens out to the ocean as he made some quick adjustments, then, once again pointed his lens in the direction of Debbie, and Rhajneed, who stood next to her. The two appeared to scour the area like two cats on a hunt.

Kaleeb tossed a beach ball around with some small children, while Rushnad got his feet wet in the incoming tide.

"Can you hear anything, Jonny?" Frank inquired as he balanced his camera on his knee while keeping an eye on the group.

"There not talking, no wait," Jonny paused. "He asked her, where is he?" Jonny replied.

Frank studied Debbie through his telephoto.

"She is pretty, I'll give her that. You think Debbie and 'ol turban head are married?"

"Negative," Jonny answered. "My guess is he's probably not a lot of fun, Frank. I'd bet you still might have a crack at 'ol Debbie."

"Don't look now, but I'd say we got some company comin'." Frank focused his lens on a man, who also appeared out of place wearing a three-piece-suit who walked towards the two.

Jonny darted about the vicinity via his opera glasses.

"Guy in a grey suit, approachin' 'em?" Frank said as he fired off a couple quick shots. "I could be wrong, but it looks like a Norman to me."

"Oh yes. I see him. We're watchin' ya buddy. Looks like he's walking right past them," Jonny followed the man who stopped a short distance from them, then stood there. Jonny lifted the lid off of the cooler and pressed the record button on the battery-operated old-style Nagra tape recorder, then proceeded to relay the story to Frank.

"She asked him what time it was. Half past six? I don't think so, friend. He just made them, and they just made him, he's our boy, Frank, do your magic." Jonny said as he set his binoculars down. Inconspicuously, he looked out at the ocean as he continued listening in on their conversation.

Frank's motor drive sprang to life, cranking out several shots at a time, pausing, then another succession of quick shots of the malicious group as they made arrangements.

"Our sheik's a little pissed he's late."

"Oh really," Frank replied while composing shots and firing away getting close-ups of the trio.

Kaleeb and Rhushnad continued to be unconcerned about the whole affair as they continued enjoying themselves like lost children that got their feet wet by the incoming tide.

"Oh my God," Jonny exclaimed.

"What? What'd they say?"

Jonny paused, still listening, "Six takers on at five million a man."

"Good Gawd almighty," Frank said in disbelief still studying the group in his viewfinder, then his motor drive fired off another series of shots.

"He just handed her a manila envelope, Jonny."

"Bio's." Jonny said still listening. "He gave her bio's on the agents. Quick meeting. And there he goes." Jonny said as the man walked away from them. "Did you get him?"

"Oh yeah. I was tight on him, perfect focus too."

"Great. She said she wants to meet them tonight at the party."

"What party, Jonny?" Frank inquired with interest.

"Our lovely Congressman's of course." Jonny replied.

"Man, what a scumball."

"You mean the Congressman?"

"Take your pick."

"You said it, 001752, great granddad's probably turning over in his grave."

"Country's headed for hell in a hand basket, Jonny, with douche-bags like that runnin' around."

"Right," Jonny agreed. "I'm tired of being pregnant, Frank, what do you say we make like waves and roll on out of here, develop some film?"

"Bye bye, Billy Gibbons," Frank said and the two quickly packed up their things and walked over the hot sand and through the crowd to leave.

"That's either the same Norman we looked at or a very, very close relative," Jonny said.

"Boy howdy, you said it, Jonny."

"Looks like it'll be a vest for you and party attire for me," Jonny said as they zigzagged their way through the crowd.

"A vest. What kind of a vest? What are we talkin' about, here, Jonny?" Frank reluctantly inquired a couple steps behind Jonny.

"Oh, simply the kind of vest that'll stop a bullet, Frank," Jonny casually responded.

"Holy hot tomoley, this is gettin' heated up isn't it?"

"Right you are 001752. I want every piece of dirt on this Norman character imaginable, Frank. I mean if he has so much as even jay-walked I want to know where, and I want to know when, read me?"

"Ah yeah, I suppose," Frank replied, unsure where to look for any outstanding jaywalking infractions.

"Double duty on the night shift tonight, buddy and don't' forget to look both ways," Jonny instructed as they crossed the busy street and headed to the parked Winnebago.

There, the two would develop some film, attempt to find anything out of the ordinary on their new found friend, Norman, play some video games, which Jonny knew would put Frank in a relaxed state of mind and at that time he would brief Frank on his new job as an information gatherer - one who works alone at night when no one is home. He would be doing the same in disguise, while crashing the Congressman's party.

Chapter 10

That evening, new stretch limos with tinted glass, an assortment of BMW's, Mercedes, and Jags lined both sides of the street of Congressman Hyden's mansion.

Another long line of limos led up to the open gated entrance and waited to enter as Secret Service agents carefully checked each individual and invitations before anyone entered the gala event.

Inside, politicians, including Govenor Swarzeneggar, Maria Shriver, entertainers, and friends of the congressman were in attendance and who all eagerly awaited the arrival of the President of the United States.

Jonny, dressed in a tight, hot pink, satin suit that was temporarily covered by a black jump suit with black stocking cap, hid in some shrubs a short ways down and across the street from the mansion where there was very little illumination. He carried a small black zip bag that contained a red wig, stick-on mustache, pink-rimmed glasses, and some make-up to embellish his disguise. Since most knew, including the secret service, that the congressman was gay, he figured that adopting a flamboyant and audacious presence, along with a definitive Capote-like accent, would be his ticket to moving about freely and unencumbered during the evening. He would wait until the Presidential limo pulled up to the well-lit gated entrance, which would draw just enough attention for him to cross the street, and then jump the wall without being spotted. He would then proceed to the southeast corner of the grounds, which was the shortest distance from the surrounding six-foot brick wall to the house, and when the moment was right he would make a quick sprint to the house and enter through a basement window.

In the meantime, he had instructed Frank, who proudly wore his bullet proof vest under his AC/DC t-shirt, to enter his neighbors' house any way he could, and retrieve anything that might help them foil what this group of misfits had in mind.

Jonny continued waiting, waiting, and waiting in the darkness. He began to wonder if the President would make it. Finally at around, nine-forty-five, when everyone had entered and there was no congestion at the gated entrance, the President's limo appeared. And sure enough, just as he expected, the secret servicemen on duty gathered around the entrance area, which gave him the brief moment he'd expected to make his move.

When every eye was trying to catch a glimpse of the President, Jonny shot across the darkened street and jumped the wall. He landed in some shrubs on the other side, unnoticed. He crouched down, and followed the wall to the spot he recalled earlier that was the shortest point to the house.

The grounds were more well lit than he had anticipated. He spied on some of the late arrivals whose invitations were being checked again as they entered the mansion. He could feel his pulse start to race, knowing that secret service agents would be wandering around the grounds and would spot him if he didn't do something and do it quick. Should he make a run for it? Some of the people at the entrance would easily see him if he did, not to mention the handful of agents who milled around the entrance of the mansion and carefully scrutinized the late arrivals. He felt like a guy up against a brick wall. He couldn't just jump back over the wall. What would he tell Frank. No, he wouldn't do that, he couldn't. He recalled a passage from one of the many F.B.I. manuals he had read when he studied for their entrance exam. When an agent is on a mission and the situation appears to be dire, the agent must wait for an opportunity. Opportunity, what opportunity? He thought as a bead of sweat dripped from his brow. He wiped his forehead with the back of his hand and pondered the situation, there's me, and twenty yards of well-lit green grass between this wall and that mansion and no opportunity as far as he could tell.

And then, out of the blue and when he least expected, opportunity found him. It came in the form of a small ball of well-groomed fur. A stray poodle with its leash still attached had wandered out onto the grass. Unbelievable Jonny thought, and he knew he had to act, and act quick. He stripped off the black jump suit and stocking cap, unzipped his small bag and put on his red wig and pencil thin mustache, then a smidge of light pink lipstick to highlight his pink suit, and some red rimmed glasses as a final touch. He then gave a quick high-pitched whistle to the wandering poodle.

The toy looked up.

Jonny made a kissy sound and the little white, cotton ball of a pet slowly wandered over towards him.

"Come on little fella," he gingerly said as the small dog got closer. "What's your name?" Jonny innocently inquired just before he latched onto the leash and rustled up the small dog back into the bushes. "Gotcha! You little pooper," he whispered. He looked around the grounds as he stroked the head of the little furball. "The moment is golden, don't you think little one?" He inquired in the ear of his newfound friend. He felt a metal tag on the dogs diamond studded collar. "And what do we have here? My name is Puddles." Jonny read from the ID tag.

"Ruff!"

"Shhhhh! You be a good little doggie and keep your yapper shut! Okay?"

"Mmnn," the tiny dog moaned sympathetically.

Jonny set Puddles down, then turned around with his back to any potential onlookers, and while bent over, he backed out of the shrubs as if he had just reached in and picked up the little wandering stray. He pointed a stirn finger at the presumed disobediant pup as if he was giving it a brief scolding, then pretended to be casually and inconspicuously led back towards the mansion by the little prancer.

Jonny scanned the landscape while he occasionally jerked on the dainty neck of the dog to keep it on task. So far so good he thought as his eyes darted around the grounds for any onlookers who wore suits with earpieces.

"Come on you little fart," he quietly said to the curious, little pooch. And just as he thought he was home free into the darkness of the backside of the estate, a voice called out.

"Hold it."

Jonny stopped in his tracks and felt his heart shoot up into his throat. He had to become the world's greatest actor in an instant, or he might find him-self in a jail-cell, rather than undermining a plot that threatened the life and safety of the president.

He casually turned around and saw the two secret servicemen, who ap-peared just like they do in the movies, clad in dark suits. A thin wire, barely visible, came out from under their collars that led to a small communication device discreetly tucked into an ear.

"What are you doing out here?" One of the young men firmly inquired.

Jonny quickly conjured up one of his many impersonations, "What does it look like I'm doing out here? I'm letting my little friend relieve herself, do you have a problem with that or something?" he confidently stated with the stately arrogance of a world-renowned figure.

"Do you have an invitation?" the other agent inquired with a respectful tone.

"Invitation? I live here most of the time, and I am Jerry's guest and I do not need an invitation for your information," Jonny said as if it was the most preposterous thing to assume.

"Jerry who?" the first agent inquired.

The other agent whispered in his ear, "Jerry's the congressman."

"Yes, he right, Jerry's the congressman. It's good to see that at least some of you boys do your homework." Jonny said, then subtly shook his head in disgust. His attention was quickly drawn to the poodle, who appeared to be onto a scent of perhaps its owner and wanted to make a break. He picked up the rambunctious pet and cuddled it.

"It's alright, Puddles, it's gonna be okay," Jonny said in the most tender voice he could conjure. He kissed and doted on the newfound companion and continued with the act of giving out more information that would hopefully convert the two agents into believeing he was who he said he was. "When you're someone's special friend you don't need an invitation, do you, Puddles? No you don't baby, you sure don't. That's my little girl. Kisses, kisses, give me some kisses, that's my sweet baby, that's my girl." Jonny elongated each word and hammed it up with the dog with a baby-like voice as he kissed and rubbed noses with it. The poodle licked the side of Jonny's face as one of the agents looked to the other and shook his head.

"Head back around the house and don't come back around here," the agent instructed.

"I certainly won't," Jonny said as if disgusted for the intrusion and he set the dog down and slowly strutted around the house. A short distance away, he casually glanced back over his shoulder to see no one was looking, then, quickly snatched up Puddles and snuck behind some shrubs that lined the large stately home. A moment later, he peeked out to see if the agents had continued around the house, which they had.

Jonny tucked his head back into the thick shrubs, then crouched down low and made his way back in the direction he had just come. He peeked out periodically from the lush growth that surrounded the mansion to see that the coast was still clear, until he came upon a basement window. The window was tucked back into a thick-bricked foundation of the historic mansion.

"Hope there's no creepy crawlers," Jonny said as he pushed on the window. The window didn't budge, so he pushed on its edges.

"What did they super glue the damn thing?" he quietly said to his small companion. "When the hands don't work, Puddles, we try the legs, which are considerably stronger."

"Mmnph," he moaned as he pushed again, this time leaning back. The window fell out and onto something. Jonny had closed his eyes with the anticipation of breaking glass, but nothing.

"Thank You, Jesus," he whispered looking up, then turned to grab Puddles. He clutched the delicate pup tightly and they entered through the window and eased down upon a bed where the window had fallen. He fumbled through the darkness and set Puddles onto the bed.

The room smelled musty like it hadn't been inhabited in a very long time. He carefully picked up the window and put it back into place as if nothing had happened. He eased himself off the bed and felt his way over to the door. He slowly turned the doorknob and peeked out to see the coast was clear, then exited.

A dim light revealed a fully stocked wine cellar with hundreds of bottles of wine that lined the concrete walls. Jonny looked up the old steep, wooden stairs and slowy made his way up them. At the top, he cracked open the door, which viewed the kitchen, and could see a busy chef with his back to him. He tipped-toed over to the swinging door entrance to the kitchen, pushed it opened and pretended to enter. The chef turned around to see who had entered.

"I am so sorry, I thought this was the restroom, would please excuse me?" Jonny said just as sweetly as you could imagine as if the statement was coated with the same powdered sugar the chef was applying to his decorative desserts.

The chef turned back around to get back to his desserts and mumbled something in French. Jonny thought he could make out one of the words the chef rattled off, which sounded a little like, "cockroach."

"Merr-c-bou-coup to you, too," Jonny returned with a contentious look. "Now in about one second there'll be a guy with a full tray of glasses coming through that door," he boisterously called out to the arrogant chef, who briefly turned to give a quick glance at Jonny, then turned his attention back again to what he was doing. A waiter with a full tray of champagne glasses pushed his way through the swinging door.

"Ha!" Jonny called out. "What did I tell you?" He paused and looked over at the chef. "One more," he loudly called out again. The chef ignored him as another waiter with a full tray of champagne glasses plowed through the entrance and entered the kitchen.

"I am good! I am great, and I wasn't born yesterday either, pal," Jonny loudly stated totally out of his original sweet-talking character. He then swaggered towards the swinging door to join the party and crashed into a waiter with a full tray of dirty dishes that shattered all around him onto the kitchen floor, which made the chef erupt in what sounded like an accident victim screaming in French with the two English words he knew.

"Get out! Get out! Get out!"

"Curve ball," Jonny meekly said. He brushed himself off, which left his tight pink suit stained not only in the front from food and red wine, but also in the rear from the damp brown soil he had previously sat in. He glanced in a mirror by the doorway, licked a finger to make some adjustments to his hairpiece, pressed down onto his stick-on mustache, and then made his way into the main room where the impeccably dressed group of high-society party attendees had gathered.

Some light jazz played from a trio of musicians cramped into a corner of the room as the scent of cigar smoke and expensive perfume filled the air inside the spacious, and lavish setting that was embellished with expensive antiques.

Jonny immediately sensed that he looked a little out of place in his stained, pink, satin outfit amidst the sea of tuxes from the looks he received from some of the guests. But, he carried himself in such a sexual and aristocratic manner that he simply raised his chin and sneered at anyone staring, then looked away from the person as if they were nothing more than a speck of dirt. He made his way into the midst of the elegant group and looked around the room. He spotted Governor Swarzeneggar across the room mingling with some guests. He raised a hand up over the crowd and gave an excited wave to the Governor with his right little pinky.

The Governor appeared at a loss as to who this peculiar looking man was. He forced a half-smile, then quickly looked away.

Jonny eased his way through the gathering to see if he could find Karen. He was taken totally off guard when he came face to face with Debbie and Rhajneed, who stood in the center of the room holding champagne glasses, which they didn't drink from, but were more for show and blending into the high society gathering.

"Good evening," Jonny said in a surprised tone of voice to a stone faced Debbie, who stood there next to Rhajneed, and Kaleeb. "It's a lovely party isn't it," Jonny added as an icebreaker, thinking that she certainly couldn't recognize him in his attire.

"Yes, quite lovely," she replied eyeing him from head to toe with ice-cold eyes.

Jonny turned his attention to Rhajneed. "That's lovely what you're wearing on your head," he said. "It has a very elegant look. It's kind of sexy too," Jonny flirtatiously said to Rhajneed with an inviting smile and chuckle as if he was amusing himself. Rhajneed also stood there, stone-faced and without a word to say. He glanced back to Debbie who appeared to be searing holes into him with her eyes. He smiled back at her. Kaleeb said something to Rhajneed in Arabic, then smirked at Jonny, who glanced briefly at the smaller man as if he was an insignificant morron, then, placed a hand under his chin and turned his gaze back to Debbie.

"You know I'm just dying to meet the President, have you folks seen him?" He tilted his head down to look above his flamboyant eyewear, then creased the corners of his mouth upward to form a smile.

"No," Debbie coldly replied.

"Hmnn," Jonny raised his head and quickly turned his glance away to look through the crowd, and then back to Debbie who continued to give him, what appeared to be a death look. He partially looked away again, then looked back to her to see her cold, empty eyes staring back at him.

"Well, it's been lovely chatting. That's a beautiful dress too, by the way," Jonny now eyed Debbie from head-to-toe in a manner that made it hard to discern if it was a compliment or an insult directed at her plain black dress with matching black high heels and nails amidst an array of beautiful evening gowns and precious gems. He then smiled warmly at the three. "You folks have a wonderful evening, I'm going to mingle," he said, then gave a pinky finger wave goodbye, before he sauntered off into the crowd. "Most definitely a close relative of Satin," he muttered.

He found a spot in a corner where he pretended to be getting into the music while he sized up the crowd. He wondered where the President was, and Karen and Mr. Stockton. They've got to be here somewhere. He stood on his tiptoes and raised his head to see over the large group. No familiar faces from this vantage point, he surmised. He discreetly pressed down on his mustache making sure it was still in place, while unaware that Debbie was still keeping an eye on him through the crowd.

She had put two and two together and recognized Jonny. She didn't know or care what he was up to all she knew was that she was not going to let any charlatan get in her way. She handed Rhajneed her champagne glass, then discreetly reached inside her small black purse that hung from her arm and pulled out a small pill in capsule form, looked around to see that no one was looking, opened it, then dumped the lethal contents into her champagne glass, and placed the empty capsule back into her purse, closed it, and then reached for her glass. She then innocently called out to a waiter who passed by them. When he approached, she pointed to a very beautiful woman who appeared to be alone, then explained that the woman had instructed her to have the drink sent over to the interesting looking single gentleman in the pink satin suit that she assumed the woman was dying to meet. She explained the circumstance with such a tone of tender compassion that could cause one to think she may be have been a nun who had recently been released from a convent.

The young waiter instantly agreed.

She politely thanked him and then watched as the waiter headed over and handed the drink to Jonny, who appeared befuddled. She and her cohorts watched in amusement as his eyes searched about the room until they witnessed the waiter point directly over to the ravishing beauty that finally caught Jonny's eye. She stood alone near the group of musicians who were entertaining.

"You're saying she wanted to give the drink to me?" Jonny inquired of the waiter in disbelief as he accepted the drink gleefully with his little pinky held upright.

"Yes sir," the waiter enthusiastically replied, then hurried away.

"Hmmn, how sweet of her," Jonny said with honey dripping from his voice. Maybe she's into strange looking, flamboyant, gay men, he thought. He pushed through the crowded room and headed over to the woman to at least thank her for the warm gesture. It's the least he could do for a woman who was probably accompanied by armed guards to protect what looked like the queen's collection of jewels around her neck, on her ears, and in the bracelet she wore. He wondered what the woman was looking up at as he approached.

"Good evening and thank you for the drink. It was very kind of you." Jonny brightly said as he spoke over the music.

"Excuse me?" the beautiful woman questioned looking off into space.

"The drink, thank you," Jonny sweetly reiterated with a glowing smile.

"I don't drink," the woman said as her eyes wondered aimlessly around the room. Jonny tried to look around the room to figure out what she was looking at, old paintings? the ceiling? a large moose head at the top of a stairway? Or perhaps nothing in particular he thought as he looked back at the woman who wore what appeared to be a very expensive, low cut evening gown that revealed a very shapely figure.

"Has anyone ever told you that you're quite beautiful," Jonny loudly stated just as the jazz selection ended.

A good-sized, older gentleman, wearing a white Stetson and western style suit approached Jonny from behind and surprised him.

"I tell her all the time," the tall Texan announced to Jonny, who turned around surprised as he looked up to the man who stood at least six-foot-five inches tall.

"Butch, is that you?" the woman inquired as she felt his face with her hands. She was obviously blind.

"Yes, sweetheart," the man replied.

"I am so sorry, I just thought that," Jonny tried to explain as the man interrupted.

"Whatever you thought, she's with me, and in just about two seconds I'm gonna rip your head off and use you for an outhouse on one of my ranches in Texas if you don't move your frilly little ass."

"I see," Jonny said. He placed a palm under his chin and sized the man up from head to toe. "It appears to me that you have a little problem with your anger. I certainly hope you can control that, and you have a nice evening, maam, " Jonny gave a warm smile to the woman, then raised his head in defiance towards the man and appeared to be carried away by the music as the musicians began another number.

He set his drink on a nearby table and disappeared into the crowd. Just as he did, a waiter, ending his shift, picked up Jonny's drink and set it on his full tray of mostly empty glasses and headed for the kitchen. He downed the drink just before he stepped through the swinging door and by the time he entered the kitchen, he fell over dead, accompanied by a loud crash.

"I never drink on the job," Jonny said not realizing the close call he had just escaped. "Where was I?"

He looked about the room. Through the crowd, he spotted the Congressman who was having a private conversation with a heavy-set man in a corner of the room. His hair was black and slicked back and he puffed on a long fat cigar. His expensive looking suit stood out from the room full of tuxedos.

"A new cast member of the Sopranos perhaps? I think not," Jonny said under his breath. "Just a smidge suspicious looking, I'd say." He took out a miniature camera from his pants pocket, discreetly glanced around the room, everyone appeared to be distracted while enjoying the party. The moment was golden.

"Smile for the camera." Jonny said as he took a few pictures of the congressman, who also looked about the room to make sure his conversation with the man was going unnoticed. His lens then focused on two other men who were as wide as they were tall and stood near by. They also wore their hair greased back. He pushed down the tiny button that briefly flicked open the tiny shutter. A few pictures would suffice for now he thought. He scanned the lively room of wealthy people having a grand evening. And there was Todd, Mr. Stockton, and Karen, who appeared radiant as ever in a long flowing evening gown. He had never seen her look so beautiful as she stood with the group of admirers who had gathered around the President and his wife.

Jonny quickly grabbed a glass of Champagne from a passing waiter, took a sip of the bubbly that intentionally dribbled down his chin and all over the front of his evening attire, tilted his bow-tie slightly, un-tucked a portion of his yellow shirt, then, as he came up behind Todd, reached into his jacket pocket and squeezed his farting toy. He placed a hand on Todd's shoulder as a reasurring gesture.

Todd appeared appalled and speechless at the flatulent sound, and also from this peculiar man who rudely pushed his way into the circle of people.

"Hey, don't feel bad young man, you're not alone," Jonny said pretending to be intoxicated. He squeezed the toy again that made it sound as if he farted, then brushed his hand across his nose.

"Whewwww…I've got it too," he said as he squinched his face at the foul imaginary odor, then smiled with contentment at his release. "Flag down a waiter for a double shot of Preparation-H. Ha ha," Jonny chuckled as several of the bystanders, including the President and his wife, gave upsetting looks to the drunken humor, which stifled the conversation.

"I'm going to talk to that chef about my burning ring of fire," Jonny stated just as nonchalantly as if asking for the time. The group fell silent, disgusted at the comment. Jonny stood there with an inebriated smile. He pretended to struggle with his balance and casually glanced at the others, then to Todd who looked sourly at him.

"Lord that food was spicey they served, wasn't' it?" He looked around to the other members of the group for acknowledgment as he pretended not to notice the President. Most glared back, some looked as though they thought he was crazy. His eyes wandered past the President then back to him.

"Silly me, I am so sorry." Jonny corrected himself for overlooking the presence of the President. "I'm so glad to see you could make it, Mr. President," he then blurted out.

"Oh I made it just fine, thank you," the President replied. "Sounds to me like you oughta make your way to the men's room," the President added.

Jonny smiled back at the President. "Yes, you're probably right." he sweetly agreed, then slowly looked around the admirers until his eyes landed upon Todd again, whom he gave a flirtatious smile and a wink to, then discreetly pinched his butt, which made Todd turn as close to the color purple that's possible for someone still breathing.

"Has anyone seen Jerry?" Jonny innocently inquired as his eyes scoured the room.

"You mean the congressman?" Mr. Stockton firmly interjected.

"Well, unless there's anyone else here named Jerry, yes that's who I'm referring to." Jonny's eyes continued to wander aimlessly around the room.

"He's here, I've seen him. Why don't you go find him," the President suggested, which got a couple chuckles from the bystanders.

"Yes I suppose I should. I also want to find that Governor Swarzenneggar and squeeze those big arms of his." he added, then smiled at the onlookers in a drunken manner. Once again, he gave Todd an inviting, flirtatious smile and a subtle wink, then made his exit to mingle.

"You folks have a lovely evening, oh and miss?" Jonny gently pulled on Karen's arm. "Could I speak with you a moment, please?" He insisted quietly into Karen's ear.

"What?" Karen impatiently questioned, not recognizing Jonny in his outfit and very different sounding voice.

"Karen, it's me," Jonny said in his own voice.

"Jonny?" She gasped.

"Right."

"What are you doing here?"

"No time to explain, other than it involves National security. You said you'd help." He discreetly said, half looking at Karen and also keeping his eyes on those that may be watching, namely the secret service agents present, and Debbie and Rhajneed, who appeared to be nowhere in sight.

"Yeah," Karen reluctantly replied.

"Did you bring your little camera?" Jonny questioned.

"In my purse."

"Get it. I want to pose for you." Jonny said.

Karen smiled, "Alright, give me a minute." She said as she went to get it. Several moments had passed, and Karen was back with her small disposable camera. She searched the crowd for Jonny, then heard a high-pitched voice.

"How's this, sweetheart?" Jonny called out halfway up the staircase for the whole room to hear. Karen smiled back, then looked into the small view-finder and flashed a picture.

"Should I go a little higher?" he called down to Karen, in a brazen and daring tone as if he was climbing Everest. She was obviously amused by his tone and manner as he daintily trotted up a few more steps.

"All the way to the top? My goodness!" He declared, and without waiting for any reply he pranced up the lush carpeted stairs. He paused briefly to pose, extending his chin, puckering his lips, then rolling his eyes upwards so only the whites showed, which made him appear like a total lunatic. He then called to Karen again. "Under the Moose head!?" he cried out in a state of jubilation, then sauntered over and put a hand on one hip and the other under the chin of the big Moose. "Well alright, how 'bout another quickie," he called out while looking down upon the sea of tuxes and world class designer evening gowns. He then dished out varying poses of flamboyant eroticism down onto the crowd below as if he was the owner of the mansion and host of the gala event.

"How's this?" He said as he glanced down to Karen who continued play-ing along and motioned him to get directly under the head of the great Moose. But, he didn't follow her commands, instead, his eyes darted around the room to each of the Secret Service agents who were strategically posi-tioned around the room, who seemed bored with his audacious posing, and from one, to another, to another, each one appeared to have their attention occupied by something other than himself. And at that moment, after Karen had flashed a dozen or so shots, when she looked up from her viewfinder to give him the thumbs up, he was gone.

He entered the room at the end of the hall where he and Frank had ob-tained pictures of Debbie and company earlier, and figured it was the Con-gressman's meeting office. He tapped lightly on the door then opened it. He peeked inside. Nobody. He quickly entered and went directly to the phone that was on the Congressman's desk. It was an antique, probably original from the time the mansion was built. The hand piece was heavy. As Jonny unscrewed the mouthpiece, his eyes widened. Somebody had already placed a bug inside of it. He pocketed it then reached into his other pocket where he had two of his own bugs. He placed one into the mouthpiece of the phone

and screwed it back together, then looked around the room for an inconspicuous place for another bug. The frosted shade of an art deco light that
hung down from a cord mounted in the ceiling looked as good of a place as
any. It was too high for someone to reach up and check, so he tossed the bug
up into it, then quickly went to the door and peeked outside. The coast was
clear. He quietly exited and just as he had closed the door and was about to
turn around, a man's voice called out.

"Hey, what are you doing?" A man wearing a dark suit and tie with a receiver in his ear, inquired.

Jonny had his hand in his pocket and started to squirm a little. He
squeezed his farting toy and winced and struggled as he spoke.

"I'm about to let go of the mother load in about two seconds if I don't get
a seat, if you catch my drift," Jonny pleaded to the agent with a contorted
expression.

"That's not the bathroom," the agent informed him.

"It's not?"

"Second door down on the left," the agent instructed.

"Thank you, young man," Jonny tenderly said as he lightly placed a hand
on the man's chest. "I can't tell you how much I appreciate that," Jonny
slurred to the agent, then squirmed his way slowly down the hall heading
towards the washroom. He squeezed the farter just as he approached the
washroom door. The agent winced and shook his head in disgust as he could
see the back of Jonny's pink satin suit was stained with a foul brown color.

Just as Jonny placed a hand on the doorknob the door abruptly opened. He
was surprised by, soon-to-be retired Secret Serviceman, Norman Felder, who
exited the room. He also couldn't help but notice that his white dress shirt
appeared wet with a red smear on the front of it and his lip was swollen.

"Excuse me," he said with a warm smile, then entered the restroom and
closed the door behind him. He cracked open the door and watched as Norman entered the den, leaving the door open. A moment later several other
agents followed him into the den, and then the door closed.

"Somethin's brewin'," he quietly surmised as he shut the door and turned
the bolt lock. He pulled out his wafer thin cell phone and pushed the auto dial
button as he stood in front of the mirror and made sure his disguise was still
in place.

"Oh, Frank, where are you?" He pushed down on his stick-on mustache as
he looked in the oval mirror above the sink. The phone continued ringing.
"No answer. Not a good sign." He closed the phone and pocketed it, then

reached into his back pants pocket and took out the bug he had found in the congressman's phone earlier, held it out as he reached for his farter and squeezed it several times for anyone who was listening, then placed it inside the toilet paper dispenser.

"Listen up, people, get out your notebooks, this is where all the big shit comes down. The plan is this," Jonny said in a deep voice to anyone that may be eavesdropping, then abruptly flushed the toilet. He stifled his own laughter at the joke he played on whoever it was that was keeping tabs on the Congressman. He stepped over to the mirror, straightened his bow-tie, applied some fresh, light-pink lipstick, reached for one of the nicely wrapped linen hand towels, folded it and pressed his lips down onto it making a perfect lip imprint, tossed it into an antique metal receptacle, then exited the room.

As he headed down the stairs to the main room, a hair-raising scream could be heard that reverberated against the walls of the old, well-kept mansion. Jonny hurried through the crowd to see what the commotion was. As he did, a man in a tuxedo opened the French doors that led out back to the swimming pool area, which was closed off for the event and yelled into the gathering.

"Somebody call the police! There's a dead man in the pool!"

And by that time Jonny had made his way down stairs and over to the French doors to witness the spectacle himself. The lights in the pool were turned on and a man in a dark suit could be seen floating face down in the water. He appeared to have been bludgeoned, as the water near the man's head was a murky red.

Jonny shook his head, then announced to the crowd, "Cramps, remember people, it's one hour after you eat!"

There was brief bit of pandemonium as the Secret Servicemen hustled the President and his wife out of the mansion and away from the area in the event there was something more sinister underlying the tragedy. An eerie silence quickly fell over the once lively group.

Some prepared to leave, others reached for drinks from the waiters who passed by with full trays of champagne, and some, not realizing the severity of what had transpired, began to dance as the Congressman, who was summoned from his upstairs office, instructed the band to resume playing.

Jonny searched the crowd until he found Karen, who was standing next to Todd. She appeared shocked as she looked out at the group of men who were attempting to fish the limp, lifeless body from the pool.

Jonny tugged at her arm through the gathering and she briefly slipped away from Todd, who continued looking out the window.

"Things are starting to get ugly," Jonny said in her ear. "The Congressman was just upstairs meeting with some members of Sphere, and some low-life secret servicemen, who I believe are planning on joining the other team, if you know what I mean."

"Sphere? What's that?" she inquired.

"A group of people who do very bad things," Jonny said.

"And you think they're going to try and kidnap the President?"

"That's my guess. This isn't just a coincidence." He paused and looked around the group of people who all appeared stunned. "Still want to help?" He asked her as he looked into her big, beautiful blue eyes.

"Yes," she said with conviction. "Earlier the Congressman gave the President Laker tickets."

"Really?" Jonny said with a growing interest. "That could be something. I've planted a bug that should tell us more. Time to sneak out of here, I'll call you."

"Alright," she said, then tilted her head up and closed her eyes, preparing to be kissed, but there was no kiss. Jonny had vanished into the dwindling crowd.

Todd was surprised, and probably a little frightened if the truth be known, when he looked around and Karen was nowhere in sight. He stepped through the crowd, then came upon her.

"Karen, why did you walk off?" He said in a scolding manner. "Do you realize what's just happened?"

"I've been right here, Todd, and would you please not speak to me like that." She said and then walked away.

"Karen?" He called out, then stood there stunned, wondering what he did wrong.

In the meantime, Jonny had stepped behind the pool house, and slipped over the brick wall that surrounded the estate, unnoticed, while bystanders milled about wondering what might have happened. He had stuck around long enough to see that the limp and lifeless person they pulled out of the pool had the same attire as the other Secret Service agents. Perhaps he was one of the few who didn't want to throw his life and career down the drain for a large bank account. Time would tell, he figured.

He had taken off his jacket and bowtie, and stuffed his wig, glasses, and mustache in his back pocket. He hurried down the shadowy side street several blocks until he reached the Winnebago, safe and sound. His hands shook from nerves as he reached for his keys, opened the door to the Winnebago, and entered. He exhaled when inside and turned on a light next to the doorway. He could see Boots asleep on his bed.

"Good kitty," Jonny said to Boots who, as usual, ignored him. He stood there a brief moment leaning against the door he had just entered staring at the wood paneled wall, drained, while he reflected on his numerous close calls at being apprehended.

"You can be anything you want to be in this life no matter what anyone says." He reminded himself of the comment his mother had told him a long time ago when he was just a boy. He felt a great sense of pride knowing he had just outwitted and outsmarted everyone, even the Secret Service at the well-guarded mansion. And then a sound caught his attention. He had almost forgotten. His receiver was on and the slow moving reels on his tape recorder were still recording everything from the bugs he had planted earlier. The sound of a phone number being dialed could be heard. He stepped into the bedroom and sat on the bed next to the recorder and turned up the volume on the ancient amplifier and listened.

The number rang a couple times, then a deep, gruff sounding voice answered, "This is Theo Califano, leave a message."

"Mr. Califano, Jerry Hyden. I had the meeting. Our friends are willing to pay a lot for the package. If we did a little maneuvering it could be very lucrative. Let's meet. You have my number."

The Congressman was brief and to the point, then hung up the phone. Jonny turned down the volume. He thought a moment. It sounds as if somebody's about to get double-crossed. He stared blankly at the slow turning reels of tape.

"Frank." The word seemed to fall out of his mouth. Where was he? He reached for his cell phone and auto dialed Frank's cell number, again, no answer. "Where are you buddy?" He quickly realized that he still had work to do. Rescue Frank.

Chapter 11

The 405 Freeway was still fairly busy at 12:40 am and traffic sped along at a brisk 80 mph. Jonny's mind raced too with lots of questions and concerns. He hoped and prayed that Frank hadn't gotten caught inside his neighbors' house, or even worse, hurt, or possibly even killed.

"Please, Dear God, not that." he said to himself, "I'm not going there. He didn't get killed." He figured, if anything, Frank was a good bull-shitter, and could weave a tall tale quicker than a Chinese dressmaker and talk his way out of about anything. He would've come up with some kind of story if they caught him burglarizing their house. Burglarizing their house? That didn't have a very good ring to it either. They wouldn't call the police with the weapons they had in their possession. No. Rough him up a little, perhaps. He could feel the fear start to flow through his veins. He silently prayed he hadn't made the biggest mistake of his life.

Jonny had gotten off the freeway and his headlights now illuminated the dark, run down side streets of East L.A., a sharp contrast from where he had just been. He felt as if he was being watched from the shadows as he pulled up to the curb and stopped at Frank's house. It was completely dark, which was not a good sign. He stepped into the back of the rig and changed.

Dressed in black from head to toe, and with a charcoaled face, Jonny appeared as black as the night. He grabbed a pocket-sized canister of tear-gas for protection. FBI issue – 1948 was the production date. Did it work? He didn't want to think about it. He stuffed it into his pocket and figured he would find out if and when the time came to use it.

He got out of the Winnebago and locked it, and went to the front door and lightly knocked. No answer. The front door was locked. He stood there a moment, and thought. Their house is right behind Frank's. He decided to leave the Winnebago where it was at, then, after he looked around, he quietly snuck around the side of the house and into the back yard.

He slowly opened the creeking, old gate and entered the yard. He could see the outline of Debbie's house through the rickety back fence and saw it was completely dark too. He listened; crickets, distant sirens, dogs barking, sporadic gunfire popping, and roving Rap music that emitted from speeding low riders permeated the neighborhood. It wasn't the safest place to be and Jonny knew it. He figured, to calm himself, that this would be nothing compared to where he had just come from. Secret Service everywhere that could've cuffed him up in a minute, if they wanted, and threw him in a cell and dealt with him when they damn well felt like it. This would be a cakewalk compared to that, he reassured himself. Trying to be as quiet as a church mouse, he tiptoed through the yard. He didn't see the over-turned reclining lawn chair. It felt like something had a hold of his foot, which caused a knee jerk reaction that he attributed to his fall.

"Frank!" Jonny angrily whispered, "Why don't you clean your damn yard!"

He got up and brushed himself off, nothing broken, thank God, he thought to himself. He paused then looked around to the nearby houses. Not a light, not a soul – nothing.

Frank was an alcoholic. Peculiar rumblings were probably commonplace from the Miller residence, he thought. He cautiously proceeded to the back fence. His eyes had now grown accustomed to the darkness and he could see some of the open spots in the fence, where broken slats had been removed. He carefully crawled through one of them and entered Debbie's backyard. The house was totally blackened with curtains drawn. That was okay he thought. How should he do this? He pondered a moment in the darkness. Knock on the front door and say he lost his pet. It's an option, he thought. He gingerly walked around the side of the house to the front. What about the charcoal on his face? I'll say I was workin' on my car. Yeah. That's believable, maybe, he thought.

"Relax," he whispered to himself, what to do would come to him he thought, it always did in the past. This was a serious game to be played by feel, intuition and quick witts. That's what he surmised it to be after watching every James Bond movie umpteen thousand times.

From the side of the house he could see a porch light that was on across the street and two doors down, which gave a hint of illumination to the house and the area. The coast appeared to be clear. He tiptoed into the front yard.

The front was no different than the back. Blackness emitted from every curtain drawn window. No cars in front, or in the driveway. Three of the four were at the party, so, if anyone were in the house, it would be the largest man of the group. The one who loved his Smirinoff and the Baywatch-beauties.

He reached for the tear gas canister from his pocket and held it in his left hand, then slowly proceeded up the front steps of the rancher/stucco style house.

He stood there a moment and listened. Nothing could be heard coming from inside, no TV, no music, no talking – nothing, just the typical night sounds that emitted from the street/jungle of East L.A.

He thought a moment, here goes nothin', he slowly and quietly opened the flimsy screen door, then placed a hand on the doorknob and turned it. It kept turning, turning and turning. It was unlocked. Unlocked? He could hardly believe it. As quietly as he could, he slowly pushed open the door. He peeked inside. Not a sound emitted from inside the pitch-black house. His pulse raced up where it could be felt in his neck. It pounded harder from his chest as his adrenalin shot up. He looked up and down the block, and across the street, nothing but darkened houses where most people slept and tried to stay safe in their barred up American dreams. The coast appeared to be as clear as it was going to get, so he cautiously, and as quietly as he could, entered the house, then closed the door behind himself.

Inside, again he listened, not a peep. With the curtains drawn it was darker inside than out. He couldn't see his hand in front of his face. Great, he thought. "Why didn't I buy those stupid flashlight batteries at the store the other day?" he whispered to himself. "Damn-it. Maybe it's because you're damn near broke, that's why?" he argued with himself to calm his nerves. He started to feel his way through the house.

"Ughhh," He grunted as his foot hit something, which made him lose his balance and start to fall. His hands automatically reached out for anything to break his fall. He crashed down onto something, unsure of what it was. He slowly got up, listened, still nothing.

"Hmmn," Jonny said to himself, wondering what he broke. The crunching of broken glass could be heard as he proceeded with extreme caution. Well, if anyone were here they certainly would've heard that, he thought to himself, unless they were shitfaced out of their gord, he debated.

He held his hands in front of himself to feel his way through the darkened house and once again it felt like a lamp cord or something had gotten tangled onto his foot. He turned and raised his leg in the darkness, and again his equilibrium was lost in the pool of blackness. His arms flailed as he reached out with his hands in desperation to break another fall. A flash thought of the blind woman at the party, who reached for the angry cowboy's face shot through his mind. He could hear things as they crashed to the floor and shattered to pieces. More Broken glass, be careful, he thought to himself as he once again slowly moved his limbs, making sure there were no broken bones. He raised his upper torso and started to get up, then heard a sound. Mumbling. He held his breath and listened. There it was again, a sound from down the hall coming from a bedroom. He got up once again, now more determined, he made it to where he figured was the hallway. He listened.

"Frank?" He said in a quiet, cautious manner. Then the moaning continued. It sounded more desperate. "Frank, buddy is that you?" He called out with less reluctance into the darkness.

"Mmnnn….mnnmmn…mnnnn…mnnn," Jonny could hear. The hallway was a clear path as he felt the walls that led towards the back bedroom. He opened the bedroom door and felt for the light switch and flipped it on. There was Frank, tied up to the bedposts with a gag stuffed into his mouth.

"001752!"

Frank grunted and moaned. "Right," Jonny quickly came to Frank's aid and untied him. He started with his feet.

"Mnnn…mnnmm," Frank groaned.

"Gag first, you got it, buddy," Jonny said and he untied the leather strap, that was tied in the back of his head by a leather string and that held what appeared to be a torn part of a t-shirt in Frank's mouth.

Drenched in sweat, Frank dispelled a large breath, and took a couple more. "Thanks Jonny. Get my hands, then I'll help ya with my feet," he panted from the ordeal.

"Is it my imagination, or did somebody add some tint to those shiners?"

"That damn Russian, giant. He surprised me, Jonny."

"You must mean the Bay Watch fanatic," Jonny humorously replied. He untied Frank's right hand, so he could get his other hand by himself and then began to undo his feet.

"Holy boloney, did you just hear that?" Frank inquired.

"What's that?"

"Car just pulled up outside, Jonny."

Jonny's eyes widened and he hurried to untie the knot on Frank's right foot as Frank got the left. The sound of someone revving an engine from a close proximity could be heard. It shut off. Time was of the essence and he knew it.

"Time to party," Jonny said as Frank got up from the bed.

"Sounds like the big boy's back," Frank said.

"You must mean my drinking buddy," Jonny started to pace back and forth to gather his thoughts, then a plan came to him. "I would say that the moment is golden, to – hide! Frank!"

"That's a can do, but I've got to find my gun first." Frank quickly started crawling around the floor.

"Gun? What gun?" Jonny inquired. He peeked out the bedroom door down the hallway. The front door was pushed open hard and slammed into the wall. Heavy footsteps crunched down upon the broken glass on the hard wood living room floor. There was a pause as if the visitor immediately sensed something was awry, then silence. An indecipherable moan could be heard that erupted from the large Russian.

Jonny held his breath as he listened. A slow Crunch, crunch, crunch of broken glass could be heard - somebody was coming. Jonny quietly closed the bedroom door, then quickly pulled out the dresser that was pushed up against the far wall, grabbed a ceramic lamp from the top of it, ripped the cord from the socket, then took a position in the closet.

"Frank! What are you doin?" he desperately whispered to Frank who was still down on his hands and knees looking under the bed.

"My gun, found it." Frank retrieved the weapon he had when he entered, which Rushnad had taken from him at gunpoint and tossed to the floor, then kicked it under the bed in a mocking manner, before pistol-whipping Frank.

"Do you want to get the light switch too, Frank," Jonny casually said from inside the closet before he slid the closet door shut.

"Ten-four," Frank whispered, then shut off the light.

Jonny and Frank waited and listened in darkness. They could hear the heavy, looming footsteps of the big Russian who proceeded slowly down the hallway.

"Where are you fat man?" He called out in an errie tone of voice, then, his footsteps stopped. He had stopped just outside the bedroom door. The door-knob turned slowly, then the door was gently pushed open. The hall light partially illuminated the bedroom. His subject was not in his bed where he'd left him, bound. He could see that the dresser was pulled away from the wall.

He filled the doorway as he spoke, slurring his words with a thick accent. "Come out from behind there." He paused a moment, then fired off five si-lenced rounds into the dresser. He flipped on the light switch and stepped inside the bedroom and walked over to the dresser to view his kill.

Frank, who was squatted down, concealed next to another dresser in the opposite corner of the room, stood up. "You're no ballerina yourself, now drop it," he ordered the large man as he held his gun on him.

Rushnad turned around slowly and appeared stunned for an instant. He stared at Frank with a drunken stare, then jogged his foggy memory of the gun he had taken from him earlier. His vacant eyes moved slowly down to Frank's gun. He started to chuckle. The same gun he thought.

"Ha ha ha ha ha…plastic, hmn hmn hmn," He chuckled.

"Jonny?" Frank cried out in desperation just before Rushnad unloaded his weapon into his chest. Frank reflexively fired a psychedelic paint ball into the large man's face.

"Blaaaahhhhh," Rushnad cried out as he spit paintball matter from his mouth.

Jonny, with perfect timing, quietly slid open the closet door and swung the heavy lamp. It shattered along side of Rushnad's head. The mountain of a man stood there a moment, dazed, not knowing what hit him.

"He swings," Jonny waited wide-eyed for a reaction.

Rushnad slowly toppled down onto the floor unconscious.

"That baby's out of here!" He said. While in the closet, Jonny had taken the large lampshade off of the lamp so he could swing the weighted end of it like a baseball bat. He quickly looked over at Frank who was slumped over in the corner.

"Frank!" He hurried over to his friends' aid. "Frank? Can you hear me?" He pleaded.

Frank's eyes opened slowly. He winced in pain, then rubbed the back of his head with his hand.

"Mnnn," he moaned.

"Frank?" Jonny looked down at Frank's mid section for blood.

"Oww, my head."

"Your head? Looks okay, Frank." Jonny continued searching Frank for bullet holes.

"Man am I hungry, Jonny."

Jonny smiled. "Appetite's back, that's a good sign, buddy. Where are you hit?"

"I hit my head on the wall. That gun of his kicked my ass."

"I don't see any blood, man," Jonny assessed.

Frank knocked on his bulletproof vest. "Yeah, thanks to this baby."

Jonny gasped. In all the excitement he had totally forgotten about the vest he had given Frank to wear. He started to get giddy, chuckling to himself. "The vest," Jonny laughed to himself. "Ha ha ha ha ha. You wore the vest. I forgot in all the…" Jonny was too ecstatic to finish his statement. "Ha ha ha ha…Good work 001756243," Jonny said nearly in tears that his friend was alright.

"Hey, Jonny?"

"Yeah Frank," Jonny replied.

"Looks like our buddy's comin' round. We better give him the double-beef-deluxe wrap, don't you think?"

"I think that would be a very nice and thoughtful gesture, Frank," Jonny agreed, then the two tended to the task.

They struggled as they attempted to lift the large, heavy man onto the bed, but were unable.

"Forget it, Frank. He's dead weight."

"How 'bout a hog tie?"

"Is that okay with you, big fella?" Jonny questioned the motionless giant. "I'd have to say that was a yes, Frank, work your magic."

"Jonny, do you think he'll mind if I use the same gag he used on me, I mean the one that was in my mouth?" Frank inquired.

"Of course not, Frank," Jonny warmly said with a chuckle. "We're all friends here, aren't we, I mean when all is said and done."

"Course we are," Frank agreed. "Open up big boy," Frank squeezed open the mouth of the semi-conscious Russian, then stuffed the gag into his mouth, then tied the same leather strap around his head which held the gag in place.

"It's too bad we don't have some tape too, Jonny. I was in shipping and receiving for a while at the Mart. I can work magic with a roll of tape, I must say." Frank quickly wrapped the rope around Rushnad's feet, then proceeded up to the hands.

"I think he's tucked in pretty good, you know, with the rope. He looks like he's enjoying the gag too, ha! No pun intended, ha ha ha ha," Jonny said as the two enjoyed a laugh.

"Yeah, that's a good one. Sweat dreams you big idiot."

"Well, let's turn out the lights and let the big boy get a little shut-eye," Jonny suggested."

"He'll probably wake up in the morning and not remember a thing, until he tries to get up that is." Frank humorously said.

"Yeah," Jonny shut out the light and they exited the bedroom and headed into the living room.

"Whoa, what the heck happened in here?" Frank questioned in astonishment at the totally demolished living room.

"It was dark, okay, man," Jonny shrugged off the comment.

"I guess it was," Frank chuckled briefly, then headed for the kitchen as Jonny examined the ruin. "Sad thing of it is, I bet they have little to no coverage," Jonny surmised.

"Yeah, I bet you're right." Frank called out from the kitchen. He opened the fridge and grabbed the one remaining can of Pepsi and placed it onto the counter, then reached for some bread and bologna and mayonnaise. He found a butter knife in a kitchen drawer and prepared himself a quick sandwich.

A moment later, he glanced into the living room with his sandwich and Pepsi, then headed down the hall to a rear bedroom where the door was open and the light was on.

Jonny sat in front of a computer in the bedroom and stared at the screen.

Frank entered and stood behind him and looked over his shoulder at the screen. "Invalid entry, please try again," Frank mumbled with a quarter of the sandwich in his mouth.

Jonny seeing that Frank was enjoying a sandwich, presumed he had brought the drink for him, so he casually reached for it. Frank quickly pulled it back.

"Hey, what are you doin', that's mine," Frank said trying to quickly swallow down his sandwich. "They only had one," he contested.

"I just want one drink," Jonny argued.

"I'll need it to wash down this sandwich, man," Frank countered.

"Frank?" Jonny tugged at the drink again and the two started to have a vigorous tug of war with the drink. "One drink I said is all I want," Jonny firmly declared. Frank finally gave in and released the drink.

"Alright, if it'll make you happy have your one drink," Frank said to appease Jonny.

"Thank you, Frank." Jonny said with a harsh look to Frank. "I'm just a little stressed trying to break this computer code to find some information that will save the President and probably the whole world," Jonny scolded.

Jonny pulled back the flip top on the shakened can of Pepsi and appeared helpless as it sprayed a shower of liquid over the computer monitor and keyboard. In a frantic attempt to not get any more of the sugary substance onto the keyboard and monitor, he held the can off to the side where the drink also rushed down over the computer tower in what seemed like an unending gusher of the softdrink. The first overflow had made its' way to the back portion of the monitor and through the venting slits. A foul smell, typical with anything electronic that is about to fry, filled the small room.

"Hey, what's that smell?" Frank inquired. Jonny raised his head up to take a whiff.

"I don't smell anything."

Then came the smoke and then a few little pops, followed by a couple brief spark flashes from the back of the monitor and the screen went black.

"Great, can you believe this?" Jonny stared at the dead computer screen.

"Well, it looks like you broke it," Frank facetiously said as the two continued listening to an assortment of sizzling sounds followed by some little pops.

Jonny scratched his head. "I once put a computer monitor in our bathtub, when I was still livin' at home, filled it up with water, let it soak, took it out and dried it off, let it sit for a few minutes, you know for the guts to dry, then plugged it back in," he explained.

"And?" Frank questioned wanting to hear the rest of the tail.

"It still worked, not like this piece of shit," Jonny replied frustrated.

"For how long?" Frank inquired.

Jonny hem-hawed a moment, glanced up at Frank annoyed at his inquiry. "A few minutes," Jonny quietly answered, then, it was as if someone had popped a paper bag. The screen imploded.

"Holy shit!" Frank cried out. "Give me a heart attack would ya!"

"Well then, what else do we have?" Jonny casually said as he looked around the computer area. He reached for a manilla-envelope on the computer desk. "And what do have here?" He opened the envelope and pulled out numerous eight-by-ten glossys. "Graduation photos perhaps? I think not."

"I'd say that those are your basic secret-service scumballs," Frank eyed the photos over Jonny's shoulder, then something caught his eye. "I don't think they'll be needing this," he said as he pocketed a computer disc that was on the desk.

"Mnn hmnn.." Jonny agreed preoccupied with the photos. "And some personal information too," Jonny quickly scanned over the personal information Debbie had attained on the agents. "I'd say we really hit the jackpot here, Frank. Check this out, Bob Cramer - Weakness, bondage? Likes to be bound by ex-wife, wearing under garments and lightly whipped. Hmnn...and where is her lovely photo?" Jonny quickly thumbed through the small stack of photos not seeing any female shots.

A sound from outside could be heard and Jonny looked up to Frank, who just swallowed the last bite of his sandwich.

"Car, Jonny."

"I do believe this party could be over. You want to check on that, Frank." Jonny quickly placed the photos and bios back into the envelope as Frank scurried across the hallway into another bedroom that viewed the front of the house and peeked out the window.

"It's them," he called out.

"The neon in my mind is flashing, window!" Jonny cried out to Frank, who quickly reentered the room. The big Russian could be heard in the next room, grunting and moaning.

"Sounds like our buddy's wakin' up," Frank said as Jonny pulled the curtains back from the bedroom window.

"That big cowboy's gonna be in some deep doo-doo in just a few minutes." Jonny said. He struggled with the window that wouldn't budge.

"He can tell 'em all about the party," Frank added.

"Yep. Let's do it, Frank," Jonny grunted. He gave it every thing he had to pry the window free. "Mnnmnph, appears to be stuck."

"Here, let me try," Frank lifted as hard as he could on the handle at the base of the window. He grunted and groaned while he strained to break it free from the countless layers of old paint that secured it. "You're right, Jonny, damn thing's stuck."

"Frank! This room is going to be painted red in about ten seconds, and I don't mean with paint, now would you please try it again!" Jonny frantically spat out the words in desperation, then looked over his shoulder at the closed door.

"Mnnmnnnphhhhh...." Frank lifted as hard as he could, but the window simply wasn't going to open.

A screeching voice could be heard from the living room as Debbie entered the house. "Ahhhhh!!!!"

"Frank, are you up to doing something really crazy!?"

"Rushnad!!!" Debbie screamed from the living room.

Frank appeared wide-eyed and speechless.

"Follow me, buddy, and don't look back."

Frank watched as Jonny took several steps away from the window, then dove through it head first, shattering the window into a million pieces and landing into the backyard. Frank followed him and landed on top of Jonny, which protected him from the broken shards of glass.

Jonny quickly sprung to his feet and hurled himself over the next-door neighbors six-foot fence. Frank followed. He surprised himself that he flew over it with such ease. He fell and rolled onto the other side as Jonny was already through the yard and to the next fence.

"Stay low, Frank!" Jonny whispered while in full sprint so he wouldn't wake any neighbors and also not catch a bullet.

"Doberman, Jonny," Frank cried out as a cautionary note, knowing there was a large dog that resided at one of the neighbors houses in the vicinity.

Another shrill scream could be heard four doors down the block which emitted from Debbie, whom Jonny figured had just set eyes on her computer.

The two continued running and jumping fences as they heard the whoosh of silenced bullets that nearly missed them as Rhajneed unloaded his weapon in their general direction. They raced through yard after yard through the darkness until they felt they had finally gotten away.

"Hold up, Frank," Jonny said out of breath. They paused near the end of the block to listen and catch their breath. The two stood there a moment, perspiring and panting from the hundred-yard hurdle race they had just run. Debbie's screams of profanity continued to echo through the neighborhood, more than likely, they figured, at the big idiot who let his guard down by being drunk.

"Definitely a Kodak moment," Frank whispered in the darkness.

"Beautiful memories, Frank."

"Doesn't sound like anyone's followin' us," Frank whispered.

"No." Jonny whispered back as he listened. "What's that sound, Frank?" The two simultanesously looked across the yard and saw two, small, glowing lights.

"Holy bee-Jesus, Doberman, Jonny, don't make any quick moves," Frank whispered in a slow, calm voice as the two stood frozen.

"I won't," Jonny nervously said focused on the two, beady eyes of the doberman that glowed in the darkness.

"I thought he lived a few houses back." Frank whispered without moving a muscle.

"Doesn't look like it, Frank."

"He's a mean one too, Jonny, bit a bunch of kids in the neighborhood - thought they had to put him down."

"Doesn't look like it, Frank. They must really love him, huh." Jonny squeaked out as the dog took a cautious step towards them with a deep continuous growl.

"No. Guy's a gangmember, he treats him like shit, that's why he's mean," Frank said.

"Nice puppy, good boy," Jonny said in the calmest, most soothing, lullabye-like voice he could muster, in an attempt to win favor with the hungry, poised beast. "On the count of three, sprint to the fence. Ready?"

"Born ready," Frank agreed.

"One," Jonny paused as the Doberman stood there frozen like a statue focused on its' prey. "Two," he paused again, then, "Three!!!" Jonny yelled. Frank hollered and raised his hands up into the air to startle the dog and then the two sprinted to the fence and hurled themselves over it. The dog's vicious barking was right at their heels as they raced to the fence and over it into the next yard. The dog jumped up and nipped at Frank's jeans and ripped the pocket on them, but was choked back from its' leash, as they made it out of the yard alive.

Safe, in another yard, Jonny stopped as Frank picked himself up from the ground. The dog could be heard choking and coughing from the leash that yanked hard on its windpipe as it attempted to lunge over the fence. A moment later it resumed growling at the two through the fence.

"You okay, Frank?"

"Yeah, barely. I think I've had enough fun for one night, Jonny, let's get the hell out of here." The two quietly snuck in between the houses and down the street to the Winnebago, then drove to a secluded, quiet spot to sleep for the night.

Chapter 12

The next morning Frank was awakened by the early morning sun as it shined through the partially opened curtains on the side window of the Winnebago and over his small bed, which doubled as a bench seat. His hair appeared lopsided and clown-like from sleeping with a pillow under and over his head. He raised his head up and peeked out the window and saw the large letters written above the sprawling storefront – WALMART. He attempted to rub his eyes when the sharp pain he felt quickly reminded him of the large fist that collided with his face the previous night. He closed his sore, swollen eyes and reopened them.

"Walmart?" Squinting, he eyed the store with one eye, then leaned over and glanced towards the back of the motorhome and could see Jonny's bare feet that stuck out from the blankets of his bed. No, he wasn't dreaming he thought to himself. He looked out the side window at the one other car that was in the large lot. He wondered if the driver had slept there all night too. Probably just waiting for the store to open in about three hours, he surmised. He placed his head back down onto the pillow and immediately placed the other one over his face and drifted back to sleep.

In what seemed like an instant later, he was awake.

Jonny made enough racket to wake the dead as he searched for just the right cooking utensils to prepare a quick breakfast. "Morning, sunshine," he said with a smile as Frank slowly awoke.

"Uggghh," Frank groaned.

"How do you like your eggs, Frank?"

"Grrrrrmmph," Frank sounded again as if he was dreaming.

"Did you say scrambled?" Jonny loudly questioned with an added bit of enthusiasm, in an effort to rouse him. "Because that is just the way I love to prepare them," he loudly declared.

Frank didn't budge. He pulled the small pillow away from his face. "Hey, do you mind?"

"Looks like your shiner bloomed out overnight, I just thought you'd like to know that."

"What else is new?" Frank mumbled.

"Coffee, Frank?" Jonny inquired.

"Yeah, I reckon," Frank slowly lifted himself upright and sat on the long, vinyl, bench seat.

Jonny poured a cup from his coffe maker and handed it to Frank, who remained seated while he sipped the hot drink.

"Is there a big sale today, Jonny?" Frank facetiously inquired as he glanced out the window.

"That's right, mister," Jonny eagerly agreed. He lifted several slices of the hot greasy bacon out of the frying pan with a fork and placed them onto a plate with a paper towel laid out over it to absorb the grease.

"Good. Why don't you go in and do your shoppin' and I'll just stay inside today and rest this ol' tired eye of mine," Frank wearily said.

"Nay, nay, nay. We've got work to do, big boy," Jonny placed bacon and scrambled eggs onto a plate for Frank and set it on a small table that he had pulled out from the wall that was the kitchen table.

"You stay at the Walmart parking lot often, Jonny?"

"Whenever I get the urge to. You see, I feel that Walmart is not only a great place to shop, it's a great place to live as well, Frank, oh yes. I'm hoping to be their poster boy," he humorously said then scraped out the remaining scrambled eggs onto a plate for himself, reached for several slices of bacon and set them onto his plate, then sat down at the table.

"Come and get it while it's hot." Jonny had to breath through his mouth to cool the mouthful of hot crisp bacon and eggs he tossed into his mouth. "This is so tasty, Frank, I think I could go for seconds." Jonny's eyes began to wander over to Frank's plate of food.

Frank noticed the gesture and didn't have much trouble getting up from his resting area. "Man, am I hungry," he said as he tossed his bed blanket to the side, got up and placed his coffee in front of his plate, then sat down and began to eat.

Jonny quickly scooped up the rest of his egg into his mouth, along with the last piece of bacon, then licked the bacon grease from his fingers. He peeked through the side window curtains outside and could see more cars had arrived and parked, waiting for the store to open.

"When they start comin' is when we start goin," Jonny said like a crusty old codger. He set his fork and plate into the stainless steel sink, then walked to the front of the rig, got into the captains chair and turned the key on the big rig and got the Winnie running.

"Where are we headed, oh mighty captain?" Frank inquired with a mouthful of food.

"Congressman's place." Jonny replied as he put the rig in gear and pulled her out of the lot and onto the road.

"What's over there?"

"Transmitters. I have this bad habit of leaving them wherever I go."

"Did ya bug the bastard, Jonny?"

"Yes, I'm afraid I did," Jonny confessed pretending to tear up with regret.

"What do you think we'll find?"

"It's a surprise." Jonny smiled with a glimmer in his eye. "It's always a surprise, Frank." It was easy to see that this is what Jonny loved about doing his job - The excitement of not knowing what would happen next and where it would take him.

Twenty minutes later they were inconspicuously parked a short distance down the street from the congressman's mansion. Marked and unmarked L.A.P.D. police cars lined the street and driveway of the Congressman's estate. Tape reels on Jonny's old Sony tape recorder spun at slow speed picking up sounds from the transmitters inside the mansion, while Jonny and Frank played video games to entertain themselves.

Brrrrrrrrrrrrrrrr.....brrrrrrrrrrrr....brrrrrrrrrr emitted from the tiny speaker on the small tv that was mounted on the wall next to Jonny's unmade bed as the race car reved through gears as it winded around curves and corners and slow moving vehicles on the track.

Frank's face winced and contorted as if he was in a real racecar maneuvering around corners and curves, then BAM!

"Oh come on. I can't believe this thing!" Frank cried out. "Get out of there, come on, we're losin' time!" He shook the small hand control and crunched down with his thumb on the button that gave the car gas to peel out of his spin out, then, once again – brrrrrrr...brrrrrrrrrr....brrrrrrrr...... brrrrrrr....through the gears as the car sped faster and faster down the winding track.

"So, who do you think the dead guy was?" Frank asked.

"Wasn't the Lone Ranger, that's for sure. I could tell because the guy wasn't wearin' a mask." Jonny replied while he peered through the curtains eyeing the L.A.P.D., and other suited men, who were either detectives, or possibly Secret Service, as they scoured over the grounds looking for possible clues.

"You think it could've been a Secret Service guy?" Frank questioned as his eyes followed his racecar as it buzzed around the winding track.

"That was my second guess, after the Lone Ranger. He was probably the only good one in the bunch who didn't want to go along with the new program of throwing his life away for a little wad of cash."

"I won," Frank declared as his racecar sped past the finish line.

"What do you mean, you won?" Jonny challenged.

"I mean I won, I beat your time."

"No, Frank. I hold the record. My time was just a hair better than that." Jonny glanced at the screen then quickly looked away.

"What was your time, and why did you erase it?" Frank emphatically continued.

"It was just a little bit better than your time," Jonny reiterated.

"You little cheater," Frank said.

"Man, you're so serious. It's just a game, Frank. Does it matter that much that I'm just a little better than you are at it." Jonny chuckled as he looked out the window.

"In your dreams," Frank fired back, then a phone could be heard through Jonny's monitor speakers as it rang from inside the Congressman's mansion, which took the two off the subject.

"Hear we go," Frank said as they both eyed the slow spinning tape reels and listened to what was being recorded. The phone was answered.

"This is Congressman Hyden."

"It's a machine, Jonny," Frank quickly interjected.

"I'm sorry that I am unable to accept your call at this time, but please leave a detailed message and I will get back to you as soon as possible. Thank you." The message said.

A woman's voice left a message. "Your laundry will be done at twelve o'clock - building number seventeen."

Jonny looked down at his Radio Shack wristwatch that calculated everything but the movement of the planets. "Twelve-thirty now, must mean tonight," Jonny said.

"Debbie must've got the house all cleaned up," Frank added.

"Yeah, she's quite a gal," Jonny agreed smiling, then put a hand to his chin. "Building seventeen?" Jonny questioned with a puzzled look in his eye, then looked to Frank.

"The only place I know of where the buildings are numbered, Jonny, is down at the pier. Those buildings all have numbers on 'em," Frank stated.

Jonny's eyes lit up. "Good work 001752. You're buckin' for a promotion, dude," Jonny said with a twinkle in his eye. "Midnight you say?" He said with a flare. "Well....weeeeee'll be there, ha, ha, ha, ha," Jonny chuckled as he rubbed his hands together, then hit the stop button on the reel to reel.

"What do you say we take a little drive, Frank, you can show me where these numbered buildings are," Jonny suggested.

"Well, I'll have to check my appointment book and see if I have some free time," Frank eyed the palms of his hands. "Nothing scheduled today, Jonny."

Jonny noticed Frank checking the palms of his hands. "You used to write everything on your hands back in high school, even in junior high if memory serves me."

"Yeah, did that used to bother you or something?" Frank inquired.

"No, I did think it was a little quirky though, to be perfectly honest," Jonny said in a challenging manner.

"Quirky huh? Well, I'd say livin' in a Winnebago at the local Walmart is a little quirky in my book, so there," Frank countered.

"I see," Jonny replied raising a brow at Frank. "I guess I'll have to try a little harder next time to find a more suitable place for you to pass out."

"Sounds like you're getting a little testy this morning," Frank said.

"Afternoon, Frank, and I am not," Jonny countered as he walked up to the drivers seat and started up the engine, after he stomped on the pedal a dozen or so times.

"Are too," Frank replied.

"Am not," Jonny fired back.

"Are too."

"Am not," Jonny continued.

"Yeah, yeah, okay, whatever you say," Frank agreed as he stepped up to the front of the cab and sat down in the passengers seat.

Jonny pulled away from the curb and proceeded slowly down the street, which was narrowed by police vehicles parked on both sides of the street. He slowed the rig to a crawl to catch a look of the investigative team at work as they drove past the congressman's large, iron front gates.

"I wonder if they're findin' anything?" Frank inquired looking out his passenger window.

"If they are, it probably won't lead to the congressman," Jonny said.

"Why do you say that?"

"Congressman didn't have a reason. In fact my guess is that he probably doesn't even know who all is on board with this thing." Jonny momentarily stopped the rig to spy on the investigative personell. Several wore white gloves, while others appeared to stand around and do nothing.

"Check it out, Frank, guy's holding up a bloody glove!"

"Where, what are you lookin' at?" Frank eagerly prodded.

"Gotcha."

"Ha ha," Frank replied as Jonny proceeded driving.

"It's a twisted world when the good guy is the drowned rat. Our job, Frank, if we choose to accept it, is to untwist it. Are ya with me, brother?"

"Boy howdy, you know it," Frank said.

"Well, then – to the pier we go." Jonny said in a stately manner.

"To the pier we go, " Frank agreed as Jonny proceeded slowly through the wealthy neighborhood so they could both check out all of the million dollar mansions. Many had expensive European cars that lined the driveways like added jewelry that embellished something of refined taste and beauty.

"You know this is quite a life you lead, Jonny, out of one mess and dippin' our toes right into another one."

"That's right, Frank. Feel okay? Are you up for it?" Jonny questioned.

Frank's imagination got the best of him as he sat in the co-pilot's seat and looked out the window and imagined himself living in one of the estates with a butler waiting on him hand and foot as they drove through the ritzy neighborhood.

"Frank?"

"Yeah, what'd you say, Jonny?"

"I asked you if you were up for it?"

"Heck yeah," Frank said as he paused to think. "You know Jonny, you and I are alike in a lot of ways."

"Oh yeah? How's that?"

"Well, I think we've both been considered to be kind of the worthless down 'n outers that'd never amount to a hill a beans. Heck, you were considered least likely to succeed in the yearbook, did that ever bother you?"

"Not really. I guess I've always figured I'd prove them all wrong some day," Jonny said.

"And me, for what I did for the football team and they didn't even mention my name in the yearbook," Frank sourly noted.

"What did you do for the football team?" Jonny glanced out the corner of his eye, knowing perfectly well what Frank had done for the football team.

"You don't remember!?" Frank exclaimed in disbelief.

"Something about the last game of the season, senior year. We won on kind of a fluke if memory serves me." Jonny said edging Frank on to tell the story again.

"A fluke!?" Frank loudly exclaimed.

"Yeah, wasn't it?"

"Hardly! Hell, that coach didn't like me from the get go, and the only reason I got put in the last game of the season was because Brian Mitchell broke his thumb, if you can believe that. Coach had figured we'd lost the game anyway, there was about fifteen seconds left to play, we were down three points, three measly points and their team, the Bobcats, were on our four yard line getting' ready to win by nine and take home the championship and the trophy. They had that great big running back nobody could stop.

"Yeah, I remember, guy was a monster, six-four, two-hundred-and thirty some odd pounds of solid rock," Jonny said intrigued by the story.

"Well, you know Jonny, that idiot we had as a coach always thought I was slow. See, I went on kind of a bender at the beginning of the season and the first day of practice we had sprints to see who was fastest and who would get to start. Well, I finished last, just because I was up the whole night before sayin' my prayers to the porcelin god, if ya know what I mean."

"Not good, Frank."

"Tell me about it. So anyway, I'm on the bench darn near the whole season until this last game. We had a great team and it all came down to this last championship game that we were about to lose, and who gets put in the game as kind of a fluke, that's right, yours truly."

"Okay, okay, refresh my memory, Frank, I don't recall all the details," Jonny impatiently prodded with growing enthusiasm.

"Well, sure enough, they give the ball to this big sumbitch halfback, who'd been runnin' over kids half his size all season, and who's comin' around my side. I was outside linebacker. His front guy, I think it was his fullback, picked off our end pretty easy, knocked him right on his butt, then it was just me and him. He was comin' right at me Jonny like a big chargin' bull, and I was not backin' down. I stuck him with my helmet right into the ball and that thing sprung out of his hands like a greased, pig, I swear a good ten feet up into the air."

124

"Oh really, you got him good, okay, then what, Frank, don't leave me in suspense," Jonny prodded.

"Okay, okay, well anyway, people told me he was turnin' in circles wonderin' where the ball was! It was hilarious. It was all in slow motion to me, Jonny. I was so focused on that ball I didn't see anything or hear anything. My eyes were on that ball until that thing landed right into my hands, and I showed that dumb-ass coach of ours, Brook Myer, who was fast. I outran their whole damn team as I ran down the length of that field, ninety-six yards with everyone one of 'em chasin' me, including their big star running back, who was supposed to be the fastest guy in the league. They all told me he was ten yards behind me when I reached the endzone. We stole the game from 'em that night, Jonny and the championship," Frank concluded.

"You did, Frank, nobody else." Jonny looked away as his eyes had watered up from the memory of the story.

"Damn rights I did. I'z pissed for sittin' on that cold bench the whole season."

"I nearly had a heart attack just trying to keep up with you following down the field on the sidelines," Jonny said as he glanced over to Frank.

"You were there?" Frank asked in a surprised tone.

"Oh yes. I'll never forget it as long as I live, watchin' my buddy win the championship for our team. It was a beautiful thing, Frank."

"Man, why didn't you ever say anything?" Frank questioned.

"I didn't want you to get a big head. And, it just goes to show, you can be anything you want to be in this life no matter what anyone says, or doesn't say, even a hero. You just have to believe it. You did that day." Jonny put on his blinker just before he got onto the freeway, then punched the pedal to the floor as the big rig spewed exhaust out the back as they merged with traffic in the fast lane of just another busy L.A. freeway that headed southwest.

"Ain't that the truth, Jonny, ain't that the truth," Frank added.

"Oh yes." Jonny agreed, then his cell phone rang. "Law here," he said as Frank evesdropped. "Hi, Karen," he softly said oblivious to the world. "Oh not much, just driving, heading out to the beach." he said dreamy eyed.

"Jonny, Jonny! Getting' a little close there," Frank cried out as Jonny nearly rear-ended a compact.

"It's just Frank, he's an old friend of mine," he said as he casually made an abrupt lane change.

Another driver blasted his horn continuously until it faded away. Jonny, either pretended not to hear the extended honk, or didn't, due to his condition of love he was experiencing.

"Tonight? Sweetheart, I don't think that's good, you see, it's this case I'm working on."

"Sweetheart?" Frank questioned.

"Would it be okay if I called you a little later? Don't worry, I'll be fine, I've got Frank as a backup. I will cupcake, bye bye." Jonny said, then slapped his cell phone shut and fastened it back onto the velcro holder on his belt.

"Cupcake, and sweetheart, you sounded like a married man, there."

"I'm married to my work, Frank, you know that," he countered as Frank gave him a second look and dropped the issue.

"Say, you think after we scope out this pier building, we could maybe kill a little time down at the beach? I mean they're not meeting until midnight," Frank inquired.

"Yeah. We'll need to develop some party pictures. I got some lovely shots of some select guests, but after that, yeah, sounds like a plan to me," Jonny agreed as they sped down the busy L.A. freeway. Neither spoke a word as they pondered the good memories of the past they had shared together, and what might lie ahead as they made their way to the pier to check out building number seventeen, then wait for the cover of darkness to make their move.

Chapter 13

Headlights from the Winnebago cast a short beam through the thick fog down at the pier. Foghorns belched from invisible ships that arrived from various parts of the world and remained moored in the harbor waiting until morning to unload their contents.

Jonny proceeded slowly and cautiously, then parked the rig between two large train transport containers several buildings away from number seventeen, and where it couldn't be seen from anyone arriving or departing. He pressed a button on his wristwatch and glanced down at its lit up dial.

"Ten-forty-seven," he said to Frank who sat quietly in the passenger's seat. He turned off the ignition and looked over at Frank who was dressed in the same attire he was, all black clothing and with a charcoal painted face and black stocking cap.

"Well, here we are."

"Yeah, that was easy enough," Frank quietly said as they sat in the darkness.

Lights from the numbered buildings peeked through the thick fog, which gave them a sense of direction.

"Arriving always is," Jonny replied.

"Man, it feels like we're in a Bond movie or somethin' like that. You gonna issue me a weapon on this one, Jonny?" Frank asked hoping for something fancy that held a good-sized clip with a lot of rounds. Since he had never fired a gun, he assumed he would need some practice rounds to get the feel.

"No," Jonny flatly replied. "No weapons."

"Huh? No weapons? I must say that that sounds a little on the, what is the correct word I'm lookin' for? Dumb, if you don't mind me saying."

Jonny looked over at Frank, unsure if he should confide with Frank on the matter. They were best friends, but Jonny had an image to uphold and it was a prideful matter and a somewhat embarrassing predicament that he had no weapons.

"They'll probably all have uzis. They do in the movies, man," Frank reminded Jonny.

"You don't think I know that."

"Well, let's bring it on, man. You must have some sort of a pea-shooter don't ya?" Frank prodded.

"If you want to know the truth," Jonny gave in. "I had a small arsenal."

"Well? Don't you think I can handle a weapon?" Frank insisted.

"No, it's not that. The truth is I had to hock 'em," Jonny reluctantly confided as he stared into the darkness.

"You hocked the guns?" Frank groaned, disappointed he wouldn't get to fully immerse himself into the James Bond role where women would bow down before him in awe as he clutched onto the implement of power.

"We're sittin' in one big fat gas hog, buddy," Jonny sympathetically confessed, which snapped Frank out of his mental picture of himself on a large movie billboard.

"I suppose, but your guns?" Frank replied in disbelief.

"So, you want to pack it up? I'll take you home right now if you want." Jonny looked directly at Frank.

Frank just stared out the window as he imagined the bigger than life billboard image of himself, dissipate like the fog, then stated, "Nah, I don't think so, man. I came on board to start livin', really livin', isn't that what you said, member? " He reminded Jonny.

"That's the beauty, Frank." Jonny smiled. He looked out the large windshield into the tranquil blackness where nothing moved and all was quiet. "Now if I'm right, building seventeen should be three down, let's do it," he said and the two got out of the rig and Frank slammed the door shut behind them.

"Frank!" Jonny hissed.

"What?"

"You wanna know why they call guys like us secret agents?" Jonny whispered.

"Why?"

"Because we're quiet."

"Alright, alright," Frank said.

Due to the darkness and soupy fog, Frank stepped on Jonny's heels as they proceeded cautiously between large storage containers until they came upon a dimly lit building with the number seventeen on it.

"Do you mind?" Jonny said.

"Sorry. I'm just a little nervous, okay," Frank whispered.

"Alright. Nerves are your friend, they're your God-given instincts to protect yourself in the event of danger." Jonny sounded like he had committed the saying to memory to be performed when needed.

"Listen," he instructed Frank as his eyes searched every corner of the thick fog.

"What?"

"Dead quiet out here," Jonny whispered.

"Yeah," Frank agreed.

"What was that!?"

"What?"

"Nothin,' Frank, ha ha ha, just tryin' to break the tension, that's all," Jonny whispered.

"Don't give me a heart attack tryin' to break no damn tension. I got all the tension I need, thank you."

Jonny chuckled to himself. "I know, I know. Are you ready?"

Frank farted. "Ooops."

"Oh for Pete sake, this is serious business, mister, and there will be absolutely no farting on this mission, is that understood?"

"I'll do my best, and that's all I can do. That take-out isn't sittin' too well with me."

"There it is." An overhead light cast a soft beam of light down upon a weathered wooden door with the faded number seventeen barely visible above it. It appeared to be the perfect location for evil to manifest itself - under the veil of darkness, where all such deeds are born.

"Let's do it," Jonny whispered.

They cautiously crept out from behind one of the large storage containers and approached the door. Jonny peered into an office window into blackness.

"Looks like nobody home to me."

"Are you gonna check the door, Frank?"

Frank turned the knob, then tried it again. "They must've locked it," he whispered.

"Huh?" Jonny said, then checked the door himself.

"Well, if they're like most people they probably keep a key close by the door," Frank suggested.

Jonny rolled his eyes. "Yeah right, Frank, wishful thinking won't get you very far in this business. Let me get you straight on something, in this game nothing is that easy."

Jonny folded his arms as Frank searched the immediate area, around the windowsill, next to a large anchor that was next to the window, inside and under a bucket that was a short distance away from the door.

"I hate to say I told you so, Frank, but, I told you so."

"Gimmie a second here." Frank's gaze went upward to the top of the door frame. He reached his hand up over the door, felt around for a moment, and sure enough his hand landed onto something metal.

"What's this?" Frank held a key out to Jonny.

"It's not the key to the door, Frank, I can assure you of that," he said in a nonchalant manner, then shook his head at Frank's amateurish approach.

Frank put the key into the lock and turned the knob and opened the door. Jonny looked away and chuckled.

"I don't believe you, man! You are buckin' for a promotion mister, you realize that, don't you?" Jonny excitedly whispered as the two entered the large, old, faded wharehouse and closed the door behind them. A moment later Jonny opened the door, peeked around outside, then put the key back into its original position above the door.

Inside the sparse warehouse the two headed up a flight of old wooden stairs to the upper level. Jonny checked the door to the office that overlooked the main floor below.

"Locked." Jonny said, then paused as a car could be heard pulling up to the building.

"We got company," Frank said.

"Right." Jonny looked up. The hinged window above the door had a slight slant to it. He stood on his tiptoes and pushed in on it. "Oh yes, sweet Jesus, the river has parted."

Jonny quickly instructed Frank to crease his body at the waist and put his shoulder, head, and hands against the wall as he put a foot on Frank's thigh, put one foot on his back, then mounted his shoulders.

Frank grunted as he raised his torso and lifted Jonny high enough for him to push open the upper window and crawl through it into the office. He eased himself down inside the office then turned the lock on the door and opened it for Frank who entered the office then closed the door. Just as Jonny closed the overhead window, Debbie and her three partners in crime entered the warehouse. The heels of Debbie's military boots echoed through the old structure as the group approached the collection of tables set up in the center of the building that formed a U-shape. Additional lights sprung on that illuminated the area below.

"That was close, man," Frank whispered.

Jonny nodded. He pressed a button on his wristwatch that lit up the dial. "Eleven-thirty-seven. The rest of the scumballs should be arriving anytime."

Jonny peered through the blinds and secretly spied down upon Debbie and her cohorts as they prepared for their meeting. Silently they waited in the darkened office. It wasn't long before several cars pulled up to the building.

"Speak of the devil, sounds like the guests are arriving, Jonny." Frank spied out the back window that viewed a parking area below.

"How many?"

"Well, three cars, brand new Crown Victorias. I know the model 'cause my parents owned the same car a couple years ago. They haven't changed much in their design."

"Gimmie a head count, Frank."

"Six, two per car. You think they would've car-pooled. It would've saved 'em a ton on gas, anyway," Frank quietly replied.

The group of agents sounded like a raucous bunch as they entered the building. Their voices echoed throughout the large empty building as they talked and joked amongst one another like members of some sort of team who were feeling good after just finishing the big game, or perhaps having a few drinks, Jonny thought.

"Frank?"

"Right here, Jonny," Frank whispered back.

"Open the window above the door for me very slowly and just a couple inches. I need to put a receiver out there to hear what they're saying."

"Are you gonna tape record 'em, Jonny?" Frank whispered as he got on his tiptoes and reached up to the window and pulled it open a couple inches, while Jonny continued to look down on the group as they all took seats around the good-sized table.

"Yes I was. Do you think they'll mind?"

"I wouldn't think so," Frank said as he started giggling.

"Frank, quiet."

"Sorry, Jonny, it just seems kind of funny." Frank stifled another fit of laughter.

"Oh Frank, when you contain yourself would you please hold this receiver just on the windowsill of the door, so I can make out what they're saying."

"Sure, where is it?"

"Right here in my hand," Jonny replied.

"Got it," Frank felt about as Jonny handed him the Dixie-cup-sized receiver that had a wire attached to it that led to a pocket recorder. Jonny pulled the tiny earpiece from his front pants pocket and put it into his ear.

"Pretty cool set up, man. Where'd you get this stuff?"

"Radio Shack. Oh and Frank?"

"Yeah?"

"Whatever you do, don't drop it, buddy, okay?" Jonny instructed.

"Don't worry, I won't drop it," Frank assured Jonny. He then stretched out his arm as far as he could and held the receiver on the ledge of the door.

Jonny, feeling a little more comfortable that Debbie now had an audience, lifted up the blind a little farther and spied out the window with his opera glasses, doing close-ups on the individual agents, several of whom he had seen the previous night at the congressman's party. He wondered how they could all be so foolish to throw their lives and careers down the drain. The word "greed" popped into his mind.

"Beautiful, Frank, comin' in loud and clear."

"What do you see?" Frank asked still standing on his tiptoes with the receiver balanced on the doorframe.

Jonny described the setting in detail of the six agents, who all appeared professionally dressed in suits, seated around several tables that were joined together. Debbie was standing in front and center dressed in camoflage fatigues and a holstered revolver under her left breast. The big Russian, who looked like he had recently been in a boxing match, stood to her left and the Sheik was seated to her right and the other slender, wiry guy was seated next to him. A large map of the world with the word, "SPHERE," written over the entire map was angled off to the side of the gathering where it could easily be seen by everyone present. Debbie put on a pair of slender, fashionable reading glasses, then began her presentation.

"Alright, let me just call some names before we begin to see who's here, Thomas Randolf?" she said, then looked up at the young agent who raised his hand. "David Banks?" she said and another middle-aged agent raised his hand. "Norman," she said as she gave an acknowledging look to Norman, the oldest member of the group, whom she had already had several encounters. "Bob Grossman?"

Bob gave a subtle nod.

"Bob Cramer?" she said and looked out at a very handsome middle-aged man, who raised his hand up in acknowledgment along with a seductive wink.

"Hello, gorgeous," Bob flirtatiously replied.

Debbie gave Bob a second glance. "Two, Bob's how 'bout that," she said with some nervousness and a forced smile. "And Herbert Dryers?" she said. She looked around the group until the last remaining agent raised his hand.

"You're not related to the ice cream family are you?" she inquired with a warm smile and dollar signs in her eyes.

"No, I'm afraid not, if I was, I probably wouldn't be here," the overweight out of shape Dryers replied.

"We seem to be shy one member, ah," Debbie adjusted her glasses and nervously scratched her head, wondering what to do to kill some time.

"Maybe each of you would like to share a comment or two about yourself with the group, and give our last member a chance to arrive," Debbie suggested with a subtle quiver to her voice.

Mr. Dryers sounded agitated at the suggestion. "I'm not willing to share anything until I know a little more about what the hell is going on with this deal," he said. The other agents joined in in agreement.

"Aren't you going to introduce yourself?" Bob Cramer inquired.

"Yes," she said with reluctance, "I'm known as Starfield," she proudly announced to the members of the group, who briefly chattered and chuckled amongst one another at the introduction.

"Alright, - " she firmly announced. " - why don't we get underway. I laid out some handouts in front of you that tells you a little bit about our organization, ah, well,...take a look at that...and, ah, I suppose we'll just begin with our presentation and we can update our late arriver some other time," she stated with as much warmth as she could muster.

Debbie was startled at the sound of a door being closed that echoed through the warehouse. The Congressman had arrived. She glared at him like an angry teacher for his tardy arrival.

"Congressman, Hyden, glad to see you could make it," she seered holes into him with her penetrating eyes as he approached the group.

"Good evening," he politely said to the group with a cordial smile before he sat down in the seat next to Bob Cramer and unbuttoned his overcoat.

"Alright, let us begin." She placed a headset microphone on as she nervously thumbed through her papers briefly, then glanced over to Rhajneed, who gave her a fatherly supportive nod.

"Tell me if I'm too loud or not loud enough," she instructed the group as she started to pace in front of them. "Thank you all for coming, and I, along with my colleagues." She paused as her mic began to ring with feedback. "Rushnad would you turn my level down?"

Rushnad got up and walked over to a portable mixer that had a confusing collection of knobs on it and attempted to find the one to adjust the level. "Testing, one, two," she said into the mic that faded to nothing.

Bob Cramer leaned over to converse with the Congressman. "I wonder what the hell happened to him?" he inquired, referring to Rushnad's taped up nose.

"Probably got sassy with someone. He certainly is strong looking," the Congressman effeminately replied.

Bob raised a brow at the comment, then, brushed it off as nothing.

Debbie had walked over to where Rushnad was and scolded him about not reading the manual on the mixer and how to operate it.

"I sure wouldn't kick her out of bed if she had a small whip in her hands," Bob discreetly said to the congressman.

"Ewwwww...I think she's repulsive," the congressman fired back.

"Repulsive? What are you talking about?" Bob said leaning over to confide in the congressman's ear. "She's built like a brick shit house," he countered while eyeing the sleek and shapely Starfield.

"So is he." The congressman leaned back in his chair and winked at Rushnad.

Rushnad, oblivious to the gesture, looked out at the group of agents to study their reactions to the sound level. He ignored Debbie's harsh looks while she paced the floor spitting out, "one, two, test, one, two," over and over giving him jerky hand signals, signaling for more volume. Rushnad nervously fished for the right knob on the portable, rented mixer. Then a loud shrill sound of mic feedback filled the large warehouse as he found it.

The agents winced and some put their hands over their ears.

Bob Cramer shook his head, then took out a small bag of bubblegum and dumped a few onto the table in front of him. He unwrapped a couple pieces and put them in his mouth and began chewing.

"Candy ass, huh?" he said to the congressman with a sour look. "Pass this down to some of the men in the group, would you?" He moved his chair away from the congressman.

The congressman returned a pouty look to Bob and also moved his chair away from him, but obliged and passed the brown bag of gum and candy down the table.

"Down you fool, not up!" Starfield shouted.

Bob Grossman, who was seated down from the congressman, gladly accepted the candy bag, then shook his head at Bob Cramer who also acknowledged the amateurishness of the presentation. He unwrapped a couple pieces of the gum and also began chomping away, then passed the bag to the next agent, until all of them looked like a group of major league ball players chomping on a large wad of gum in their mouths.

"Yes, there, Rushnad. Do not touch it!" She fumed at Rushnad who took a seat in front of the group.

"Alright, were was I? Can you hear me now?" She questioned the obviously bored group who all nodded in agreement. Some had begun blowing bubbles with their gum as they sat there with eyes on the sexy and attractive Debbie, a.k.a. Starfield.

"And now, what I would like to do is introduce the leader of Sphere, whom I've mentioned in your handouts, if you haven't already looked at them, I suggest you do so." She typed in some quick commands on her laptop that was opened on the table in front of her, then looked over to her left and watched a good sized screen come up from the floor, then retract again.

"Aggrrrrrr…" she scowled and moaned to herself as Rhajneed came over and placed a hand on her shoulder to consol her a moment. "If you would please excuse me a moment," she instructed the group. Once again, she frantically typed the command on her laptop then looked over at the screen that bobbed up, then back down.

Kaleeb, who had set up the screen earlier, hurried over to a cluster of colored cables that ran across the floor and disappeared behind an electrical box that hid the connections that operated the large screen.

"Kaleeb, no Kaleeb, try the blue cable!" She fumed, then, in an attempt to appear more professional, she forced a calm tone of voice and said, "I believe it is twisted." She subtly rolled her eyes in disgust.

"I don't think it is the blue one," Kaleeb said hunched over the tangled mound of cables that ran along the floor to the large screen.

"Well, then try the red one!" she angrily said. She sounded as if she was about to boil over as she frantically reentered the command again in an attempt to raise the screen. She glared at the inattentive group of agents who were now all competing to see who could blow the biggest bubble.

Jonny was amused at the childishness of the agents and the fact that Debbie was boiling over. He had to stifle the urge to laugh out loud.

"Jonny, my arm is startin' to get a little tired," Frank confessed.

"Hang in there, buddy. She's about to introduce the leader of Sphere, but she's losin' her crowd - technical difficulties, screen won't raise."

"I'm gonna change hands," Frank said.

"Go for it, just be careful not to drop it," Jonny whispered.

"I'm not gonna drop it," Frank reassured him.

Jonny spied through his binoculars down on the agents who continued blowing bubbles with their gum. He scanned over to the screen. "The head cahuenga looks like he's on a submarine! - A little oriental guy. He's talking to the group."

"What's he sayin'?" Frank asked.

"He's congratulating them for deflecting, deflecting? deflecting from the Secret Service. Guy doesn't even know how to speak English for Pete sake,... and having been sworn in as members of Sphere, he's telling them they'll be brieved, come on dude get your words right,... on the upcoming project, blah, blah, blah." Jonny paraphrased.

"Holy bologne! I don't even believe this!" Frank said aghast.

"Believe it, Frank. Okay, her partner is going speak. He just thanked the guy on the sub."

"What's he sayin'?" Frank eagerly questioned.

"Oh, just that the goal of their project is to raise eight-hundred million dollars, so they can expand their operations throughout the world and release prisoners who are being held indefinitely. And to reach their goal they're demanding the eight-hundred mill for the ransom of.....," and Jonny paused to listen, "The ransom of the President of the United States of America." Jonny reiterated in disbelief.

"Eight-hundred million bucks, President of the United States! who in the hell do they think they are, good Gawd Almighty!?" Frank whispered aghast at the plea.

Jonny continued listening as Starfield shared more information on the plan that was in their handout packets they had received. She explained that there was a number in the packet that represented their Swiss bank account. The number they see will be in their account when the mission is completed."

"Swiss bank accounts," Jonny whispered to Frank.

"Wonder what they're gettin' for sellin' out?" Frank said.

"Don't know. She's telling them to stop blowing bubbles with their gum, incessant childish popping," Jonny attempted to stifle his laughter.

"That might piss a couple of 'em off," Frank added.

"Yeah. Congressman's whispering something to the guy next to him, looks like he's trying to compare their numbers." Jonny paused. "He looks a little pissed," Jonny focused his binoculars on Bob Grossman who politely raised his hand. "One of the agents is suggesting they try to have some fun with the project," Jonny reiterated in disbelief.

"Fun? Is he out of his mind for cryin' out loud?"

"Probably, he says it's a great idea, but the plan doesn't give a lot of detail. The abduction will occur at the Laker game tomorrow, and he's asking her what they're supposed to do," Jonny relayed to Frank.

Jonny's earpiece went dead. "Frank, no sound, what happened?"

"Ooops," Frank sheepishly replied as Jonny's earpiece went dead. It was as if time momentarily stood still as the small, plastic, dish-like receiver bounced a couple times on the cement floor outside the office door, then sprung over the edge of the upper tier tumbling end over end until it shattered onto the main floor.

"Uh oh, sorry Jonny."

"We're in deep do-do now, Frank!" Jonny frantically exclaimed. He held his binoculars on Debbie, who abruptly turned around and stared upwards directly at the upper offices.

Frank held out the thin wire that had a pin plug at the end of it.

"She's looking up at the ceiling," Jonny whispered.

"There's not a back door in here Jonny, just thought you might like to know."

"Oh I know, Frank. Listen, grab that mop and the bucket and follow me buddy, and play along. If we get to the main floor without being shot, make a beeline out the back," Jonny quietly said with a hint of desperation.

"Did you say shot?" Frank inquired.

"Yes, Frank. Shot."

"Got it."

Frank picked up the mop and placed it in the bucket and rolled it over to the door. Jonny threw open the door and like a chameleon turned himself into a raging lunatic. He sounded like a man on the verge of going completely out of his mind that was remniscent of Mr. Hitler himself as he spewed his message at Frank.

"I vant you to use more soap! Do you understand you idyeeeat!!! Vesion, heisen-housen-dieb-logen housen!!!!" Jonny screamed as his arms flailed in an uncontrolled manner as he scorned Frank in what sounded like German, even though Jonny's vocabulary of the language consisted of only a handful of words.

Frank followed him to the stairs that proceeded down as Jonny pretended to swat him in the head.

"Pick up ze bucket!!! Vhat don't you understand! Vhen I say soap, I mean soap!!! You idyeeat!!!," Jonny screamed at Frank, who held his head down and took his swats to the head, as the group appeared stunned and shocked at the audacity of Jonny's performance, which was the idea.

"Excuse me?" A shrill sounding voice addressed them over the speakers that echoed through the building.

Jonny and Frank kept their eyes turned down and away from the group to conceal their blackened faces as long as they could until they were at the bottom of the stairs.

"This is a private meeting."

Jonny ignored the comment. "Now dump za vater onto the main floor and ve vill get ze hell out!!! Do you understand?!!! Jonny screamed, then glanced over his shoulder to see Debbie's laser-like eyes that locked onto his. She immediately drew her gun.

"Agggrrrr!!!! Them!!! Kill them!!!!" Her screeching voice once again rang out from the loudspeakers and echoed throughout the high-ceiling structure.

"Come on Frank!" Jonny ran to the back door and opened it and then high-tailed it out of the building.

Frank dumped the bucket of water onto the floor and sprinted to follow Jonny out the door followed by a succession of bullets that richochetted off the steel beams and pierced the walls of the old structure.

"Thank God she's a horrible shot!" Jonny called out to Frank, who was right on his heels as the six Secret Servicemen and Rushnad followed in hot pursuit.

"What the heck happened to the fog, Jonny?!" Frank cried out to Jonny.

"Must've lifted! Let's get the hell out of here!!!"

"Ten four, buddy," Frank said as they sprinted around the building, then weaved through a maze of large cargo containers in an attempt to lose the blood hungry group. Gunshots echoed through the darkness and ricochetted off the large metal cargo containers as agents unleashed a flurry of deadly lead.

Jonny gasped for air as they arrived at the Winnebago. His hands trembled as he attempted to find the keyhole.

Frank, never having taken karate, stood poised in a master's stance as cover.

Jonny flung open the door, which knocked Frank off his feet, then raced to get inside and behind the wheel.

"Lock that door, Frank!" Jonny called out.

Frank scrambled up the steps and slammed the door shut, locking it, then made a beeline to the passengers seat.

"Man, if my ex-wife could see me now, she'd be crawlin' back to me, " Frank said basking in the moment.

"Yes!!!" Jonny cried out as the rig started. He turned on the headlights.

"Whoa!!!" Frank yelled as Rushnad came out of nowhere and jumped onto the front bumper with one hand holding onto a wiper, the other clutching his gun at Jonny.

He attempted to say something as he waved his gun towards Jonny's face.

Jonny pretended he didn't understand. He shook his head and mouthed, "What?" At the same time he put the rig into gear, then held his hands up in the air like someone being held up at gun point, then he put the pedal to the metal and drove the length of the cargo container before smashing his bumper into one of the agents Crown Victorias, that popped out from nowhere to block their path.

"Hello," Jonny casually said as the crash ejected Rushnad off of the Winnebago and onto the hood of the agent's car, which spewed steam from the heavy blow to the car's radiator.

"Man! You nailed his ass, Jonny! Take that you big gorilla!" Frank cried out in a vengeful tone.

"A short, but sweet flight," Jonny casually replied.

"Rushnad was laid out on top of the hood of the Victoria unable to move as steam spewed forth from the radiator of the car.

"Now that's a <u>Time</u> cover photo right there, Jonny. The background lighting is perfect and the tiny bit a fog acts as a softner to your headlights," Frank said to Jonny as they eyed a semi-conscious Rushnad and two dazed Secret Service agents who were slow to exit their wrecked car.

"You think so?" Jonny inquired. He paused to notice what did in fact appear to be the perfect magazine cover shot. "You know, I hate to leave the scene of an accident, but in this case, I think it is a very good idea," Jonny said, then quickly dumped the rig in reverse and looked into his rearview mirrors.

"Ha ha ha, you said it man!" Frank hollered enjoying the excitement.

"Coast appears to be clear," Jonny said not paying much mind to what was behind him. He backed away from the damage done, then proceeded to put the rig in Drive and sped down another row of cargo containers.

Another one of the agent's cars waited for them and with arms held out their windows they began emptying their weapons into the front windshield.

"Come on, is that all you've got, you bunch of little woosies?" Jonny yelled at the agents who let lose every bit of firepower they had, from their pistols, shotguns, and even a machine gun that riddled the front of the rig as they drove straight into harms way. "Oh, and I should probably share a tid-bit of information about the windshield and the front of this baby - it's, oh what is the word I'm looking for, Frank?"

"Ah, let me see, bulletproof?"

"We have a winner to tonight's contest and his name is Frank!" Jonny emphasized Frank's name as they k-oed another one of the shiny new cars. "Ooops. Oh, and my goodness, I am so sorry for hitting your car, I just can't tell you," Jonny said aghast and with the sincerity of a person that would lend one to think he attended church services regularly. He glanced over to Frank.

"I'd say you nailed his ass to the wall, Jonny!"

"Oh yes." Jonny looked into the rearview and dumped the rig into reverse to once again leave the scene of the wreckage.

"Say, how 'bout a little mood music?" Frank suggested.

"Indeeed, Frank. How about something with a little pazzaz!"

"How 'bout a little "'Highway To Hell'" Frank said as he inserted the cassette and AC/DC began to play.

Jonny punched down onto the gas and looked both ways as they proceeded through the maze of cargo containers.

"Don't look now, Jonny, but somebody's ridin' right up your ass, and it sounds like he's firin' with a repeater or machine gun at us," Frank said looking through the rearview.

"Not good, Frank, lower your head." Jonny lowered his head down as a line of bullets riddled the upper portion of the cab.

"Uh oh?" Frank desperately cried instantly realizing the back of the rig didn't have the same bulletproofing as the front.

"Stay low," Jonny instructed as he swerved the rig wildly. "Have I ever told you how I hate tailgaters, Frank," Jonny said in a high-pitched voice, shooting looks into his rearview mirror.

"I don't remember if ya did, man! " Frank shrieked out.

"Well, I do!" He weaved the big rig back and forth to make for a difficult target. "I could stop the vehicle and have a polite conversation with him, but I think I'm gonna give him a little heat-seeking-missile right in the ol' bread basket, instead." Jonny chuckled as he opened a small panel that revealed a row of red push switches – Rear Missile Launcher. He firmly pressed down onto the red rubber button that had probably never been used. Nothing. His eyes widened with fear as he could still see the headlights of the ensuing vehicle in his rearview. "What is the matter with this stupid thing?!" Jonny cried out hitting just above the switch as bullets shot through the hull of the whaler.

"Here let me help, Jonny!" Frank delivered marshal art like blows to the dash just above the switch. "Uh-yah! ....yah!"

"It's okay, Frank! Plan B, how 'bout a little ten-forty." Jonny reached overhead to another switch that released a large stream of oil behind them.

"They're still on us, man!" Frank cried out.

"Say your prayers, Frank!" Jonny weaved the rig erratically, then a loud - WHOOOOOSSHHHH...sound could be heard from the top of the rig.

"What was that?" Frank hollered as the switch for a heat-seeking missile made connection and fired a heat seaking rocket that arced upwards briefly, then straight down and onto the engine of the tailing vehicle that created a huge fireball. The driver, blinded by the blast, zigzagged out of control before he crashed the vehicle into a cargo container.

"Whoa!!! You blew his ass right out of the water, man!" Frank cried out looking at the ball of fire behind them through his rearview mirror.

"That was close." Jonny wiped his forehead with the back of his hand.

"Gimmie some skin, baby, right there!" Frank hollered with excitement as he held his hand up for Jonny to slap, which he did. A moment later another loud explosion from the car could be felt as the gas tank exploded.

"Gas, when accompanied by spark or extreme heat as from a fire, can be very combustionable," Jonny said mimicking a crusty scientist.

"Boy howdy you said it, would you take a look at that," Frank eyed the ball of flames in his rearview as they escaped the group of misfits unharmed.

"There gonna have a bit of explainin' to do, I'd say," Jonny said chuckling.

"You know Jonny, we're gonna need a place to hide out after this wake of destruction. We'll be sittin' ducks in that huge Walmart lot."

"Know just the spot, and it's spelled, K A R E N," Jonny said as they exited the pier area and sped down the sparsely driven road.

Chapter 14

Both Jonny and Frank were unusually quiet on the forty-minute drive to Karen's apartment in West Hollywood. There was hardly any traffic in the early moring hour, just an endless row of streetlights on the artial they traveled down. They both felt relieved that they had made it out alive and not seriously wounded from the hail of bullets that were directed at them. And both now fully realized the seriousness of who and what they were dealing with - people that will kill you if you get in their way and not think too much about it after the fact. Jonny didn't want to think about it. He knew of a spot behind Karen's building that was a no parking zone, but at this hour it wouldn't matter, and you couldn't see the home on wheels driving by the front of the building. It was nearly 3 A.M. when they pulled up and paused to glance up at Karen's apartment window where a dim light could be seen.

"Kind of late, Jonny, you think she's still up?"

"Only one way to find out." Jonny pulled the rig around to the back of the building to park.

"I think she's been wanting me to come over late for quite some time, she just hasn't said anything. It's just a gut feeling." Jonny turned off the engine and glanced over at Frank. "Let's wash this black crap off our faces, then we'll head upstairs." Jonny sounded excited to see his true love after their recent ordeal.

"Okay, you're the boss," Frank said with some reluctance in his voice, due to the late hour, but he did what his friend suggested and they washed the charcoal from their faces, then proceeded around to the front of the building, and then up the stairs to the second floor to Karen's apartment number 217.

They approached the door. Jonny knocked. They stood there a moment in silence and waited. Jonny fidgeted by picking at his teeth, and quickly groomed his hair with his hands.

"Do I look okay?"

"Yeah, you look fine, just be yourself, man," Frank said.

"I always am, what can I say." Jonny shrugged his shoulders like a nervous comedian, then smiled and waited.

"Just a minute," a deep voice called out through the door.

Frank looked over to Jonny and Jonny back at Frank.

"Sounded like a man, are you sure this is the right place?" Frank put his ear to the door and tried to hear anything else coming from inside, then shook his head.

"Yes it's the right place. I think she has a sore throat," Jonny said.

"I hope you're right," Frank said with some reluctance, then, the door popped open. It was Todd. His hair was messed up like he had just gotten out of bed. He stood there in what appeared to be a woman's bathrobe, and since it was Karen's apartment, it was easy to conclude that it was her robe.

"Vacuum man? What are you doing here?"

Jonny looked like he had swallowed something large like a whale and totally lost his color in his face as Todd stood there.

Jonny was speechless and hurt. He glanced down at Todd's bare legs and bare feet, then back up at his ugly face and messed up hair.

"Karen and I were just taking a little break. She's a wild one," Todd said mockingly.

Jonny just stood there, cold and with a blank deadpanned look. "Let's go Frank," he said with a flat, almost lifeless tone as if the life was just ripped out of him.

Frank followed Jonny as they headed down the stairs and around the building in silence. Frank didn't dare to say a word. He was speechless too, knowing how much Jonny thought of Karen, and the feeling of hurt and rejection that you feel when the one that is special in your heart is with someone else. He knew the experience too, and could see it was very hard and painful on his best buddy.

They got in the Winnebago and slowly drove out of the parking lot and down the well-lit arterial without saying a word. Frank broke the ice.

"Man, sorry, Jonny. I've been there too, in the ol' dumpster so to speak." Frank looked over to Jonny to see how he was looking.

"Yeah," was all Jonny said as they continued driving under streetlight after streetlight after streetlight, which seemed like about a million of them before Jonny took a quick turn onto Beverly Boulevard.

"We gonna bed down on the rich side of the tracks tonight, Jonny?"

"Why not." Jonny blankly stared out through the chipped up windshield. He had already forgotten about all the bullets that had recently richochetted off the thick glass that otherwise would've killed both, himself and Frank.

"Where do you have in mind?" Frank inquired.

"Congressman's place," Jonny flatly replied.

"Hey, that sound's good to me." Frank agreed as they began to drive past more upscale homes in the area of Beverly Hills.

Jonny stopped and parked the rig in the same spot they were at the night before, a short ways down the street from the Congressman's estate.

"Let's get some rest." Jonny sounded totally depleted, dejected, and depressed as he shut off the small cabin light and headed to the back of the darkened rig.

"Yeah, I'm pooped, Jonny," Frank called out to Jonny who had already made his way to the back of the Winnebago as he struggled to release his seatbelt.

Jonny turned on a small bed side lamp then flipped on his receiver and tape recorder, hoping to obtain any other tid-bits of information from the receiver he had previously planted that might help them tomorrow. The recorder could run on slow speed until morning. At that time he could check for any sound bites. He shut the bedside light off, preferring just the light from the TV, which he turned on.

From the dim light of a street light that shined in through a side window, Frank pulled out the side bench seat that doubled as a bed, removed a blanket and pillow from an overhead cupboard, then, unfolded them over the cushion and layed down. He could hear the TV next to Jonny's bed. It sounded like a Psychic Love Connection.

"Having love problems, financial difficulties? Psychic Hotline has the answers. Our psychics are waiting for your call. Pick up that phone and call me. I'll be here all night, just do it," a seductive voice said.

Frank listened while Jonny channel surfed until he paused on a news station.

"An investigation is still under way in the mysterious drowning death of Secret Service Agent, Thomas Brown. Brown was an avid swimmer who drowned in Congressman Hyden's swimming pool last night in Beverly Hills at a party where the President was a guest. Some sources say that Brown was depressed and believe the death to be a possible suicide. We'll have more details on the death of Thomas Brown as the investigation unfolds." Jonny shut off the TV.

"I'm havin' a hard time sleepin' thinkin' about tomorrow, Jonny." Frank called out from his makeshift bed trying to divert Jonny's attention to something other than his broken, bleeding heart.

"Yeah, me too," Jonny replied in the darkness.

"Women are pretty hard to figure sometimes," Frank said, then waited for a reply.

"Yeah, I haven't had much luck with 'em."

"Me either."

"My eyes were crossed in grade school and junior high, then I got those corrective lenses in high school, you probably remember. It wasn't pretty." Jonny confessed.

"Yeah, I remember," Frank said. "And if you recall, I had a bit of a weight problem back then, all the girls just poked fun at me, then I met Becky. Things went pretty good for a while. I'll probably see her tomorrow at the game. My ex is a big Laker fan."

"I'm sure Karen will be there, more than likely with the idiot," Jonny said with disdain.

"Well, try not to think about her, Jonny, that's what I do with my ex. It seems to work for me, most of the time, anyway,"

"Thanks 001752, better get some rest," Jonny flatly said growing more tired by the minute.

"Yeah, tomorrow's gonna be a pretty big day for us, huh?" Frank sounded a little reluctant and tired too.

"Yeah, buddy, we'll have to be on our game tomorrow," Jonny said.

Frank remained silent as Jonny also pondered the next day and what he would do to stop a group of ruthless kidnappers who planned on abducting the President of the United States. All sorts of thoughts ran through his mind. This congressman was a very unsavory character as well, and what was he doing brushing shoulders with what appeared to be organized crime figures? That's what they looked like anyway. This was a do or die mission, unlike anything he had ever encountered in the past. He wasn't spying on somebody's cheating spouse, this was bigger, much bigger, and the stakes higher than anything he had ever undertaken. He'd already risked his life, and his friend's, and had been shot at twice, nearly killed twice. How would this story play out, he wondered, a double funeral for him and his old high school buddy, where old classmates would gather to pay their respects, and have kind of a reunion and reminis on the two biggest losers they had ever known – or as heroes? Where their old friends would read about them in the papers and be proud and say to themselves, "Hey, I remember those guys, wow! What happened? And they would erase from their memories that he and Frank were always referred to as the class clowns, or more accurate, class losers, and least likely to succeed.

Who knew, maybe he should call the FBI in the morning, request some aid and backup. Even though he resented them for all the times he had attempted to get hired, coming back each year with his application, until he became a running joke at the hiring office.

"Aren't you the guy with the spastic colon," one of the interviewers would say, then they would all have a good laugh at his expense. It was painful to think about, but not as painful as the pain he felt now. He tried to push the thought of Karen from his mind. His eyelids grew heavier by the minute. He decided to sleep on the matter of contacting the FBI. In the morning he would have a fresh and rested perspective. Maybe the wound to his heart from being dumped would also lessen after a good nights sleep, but probably not, he thought. A moment later he could hear Frank snoring.

"Night, Frank," he said and he also quickly drifted into slumber.

The next morning felt as if it arrived too early for Frank. It seemed like he had just closed his eyes and in an instant it was morning. He squinted his eyes at the bright sunlight that shined through a slit in the curtains of a side window.

He moaned, then rolled over away from the light. Flap, flap, flap, flap, flap. What was that sound he wondered? He lifted his head. He wasn't dreaming, he thought, then the sound stopped. He tossed back his blanket and slowly got up from his narrow bed and proceeded to the back of the Winnebago.

"Jonny?" He called out. Jonny's bed was empty. The old reel-to-reel tape recorder with ten-inch reels that had been running on slow speed all night had just run out of tape. That was the flapping sound. The lights on the VU meters remained on. He didn't want to touch the machine. I'll let Jonny take care of that little toy. He turned up the volume knob on the receiver to see if anything was going on inside the congressman's house.

Footsteps could be heard approaching, then a door closing. Somebody was there. Frank sat down on Jonny's double bed to listen. Somebody picked up the phone, and dialed a number from the phone, the same phone Jonny had bugged. The number rang.

A man at the other end picked up. A deep and gruff, "Hello."

Another voice spoke into the phone, softer, and with a distinctive effeminate manner.

"Theo Califano, please," the man politely requested.

"Speaking."

Frank immediately thought, pen, paper, write this down, I'll forget, but no pen and paper, listen carefully he told himself, to every word.

"Mr. Califano, Jerry Hyden."

"Hyden, I was wondering when you were going to call, are we still on?" Califano questioned.

"Yes, everything is on as planned," the congressman now stated in a near whisper as if he was trying to keep a deep, dark, shameful secret.

"Good. Say that was a hell of a nice party you threw the other night," Califano said.

"Thank you," the Congressman meekly responded.

"So let's cut to the bullshit, where are we meeting?"

"Nothing's changed," the congressman said, then paused, "I sure hope those Lakers win today," he then added, discreetly revealing the meeting location.

"Yeah, me too." Califano agreed, then paused. "Listen, my breakfast is getting cold here as we speak, so we'll take care of business as we discussed. This'll be a piece of cake, we do this sort of thing all the time, and I promise you we'll treat you a hell of a lot better than those third world bastards were going to, okay?" There was a moment of silence. "Are you still there?" Califano inquired.

"Yes, I'm still here," the congressman said with some reluctance at what treating him better meant exactly, but was afraid to ask. It was like trusting the devil, and he knew it, but he went along anyway. "I'll look forward to it. Thank you, Mr. Califano," he said then hung the phone up.

"Man oh man, sounds like somebody's gonna get double crossed," Frank said to himself just as Jonny sprang through the door and entered.

"Frank?" he called out.

"Back here, Jonny."

"Hey," Jonny greeted.

"Hey, where ya been?"

"Took a short jog, just to sort of, clear my brain out a little."

"Your tape recorder kind of woke me up when the tape ran out," Frank said.

"Not much activity through the night, didn't hear anything, anyway."

"Well, I just heard some stuff," Frank confessed.

"Oh really? Like what?"

"Oh just that your congressman buddy sounds like he's teamin' up with a rough soundin' guy named Califano, said they'll pay him more than those third world bastards will. Those were his exact words, Jonny."

"Califano? As in Theo Califano?" Jonny asked.

"Yep, he asked for Theo Califano."

Jonny reached to the side of the recorder and picked up a photo mart envelope. "There he is, Mr. Theo Califano in the flesh, and some of his partners in crime." Jonny pulled out the photos he had taken at the congressman's party and handed them to Frank who skimmed through them. "F.B.I.'s been tryin' to nab his ass for a long time, but he's one slimy dude," Jonny said.

"Looks like it." Frank stared at the photo. "Who are the other guys?"

"Box Deadman, Domonique Crook - Dom for short, Imus Steel, and I'm not sure about the other two." Jonny said pointing to the men.

"They look as hard as nails, Jonny."

"Mob men usually are."

"Congressman said he hoped those Lakers would win, right after the other guy asked him where they would be meeting," Frank stated.

"Looks like we're still goin' to see our favorite team."

"Boy howdy, you said it," Frank agreed, then handed the photos back to Jonny who placed the pictures back in the envelope and set them next to the recorder.

"I was having sort of a hard time sleeping last night, and with the information you've just given to me Frank, it makes my decision a little easier. I think this one time," Jonny paused.

"This one time, what?" Frank questioned.

"I think I'm gonna request a little back-up," Jonny pulled his cell phone from his belt and auto-dialed a number.

"Who you got in mind?"

"Friends over at the Bureau," Jonny said as if he was almost embarrassed to seek anyone's assistance from the organization that had labeled him a reject.

"F.B.I.?" Frank sounded as if Jonny had lost his marbles. Jonny nodded then turned away as Frank shook his head.

"Edward Goodman please," Jonny flatly said to someone at the other end.

"J.L. Hoover, tell him it's urgent."

Jonny listened as some classical music began to play briefly on the phone, then it stopped as if the "on hold" button didn't catch, and he could hear Goodman's secretary speaking directly to the head of the F.B.I.

"Mr.Goodman, a J.L. Hoover is on line two, he say's it's urgent," he heard the woman say. He continued to listen. It was like a dull knife piercing his heart as he overheard Goodman telling his secretary that he was a screwball – a nut, and to tell him he was busy. He listened for a brief moment longer until he had heard enough. He hung up the phone before Goodman's secretary had a chance to give him some phony excuse that he was unavailable. It had become the standard routine whenever Jonny called in an attempt to chat with Goodman about activities in the bureau that he thought questionable.

"Not in," Jonny looked away as he told Frank a white lie and felt more determined than ever to show the F.B.I., C.I.A, and whoever else doubted his abilities that he had what it took to rise to the occasion, whatever that occasion might be.

"It's for the better anyway, Jonny. Heck, we can do this, man." Frank said with enough conviction that Jonny just about believed it.

"You think so, huh?"

"I know so, man. I tell ya Jonny, with no booze in me, I feel like a new man. I mean I still feel a little jittery." Frank held out his hand to check for steadiness. He tried to hold it steady, but it shook and he quickly put it down.

"Not bad, Frank, not bad, a little nerves are to be expected." Jonny pondered the situation.

"My only fear is my ex. That woman makes me crazy, Jonny."

"Try not to think about her, isn't that what you told me?"

"That I did. It works ninety-nine percent of the time, man."

"Alright then, we're gonna do this thing on our own," Jonny agreed.

"Now we're talkin'. Shoot, we don't want to give those hosebags any of the credit, 'cause they'll take every bit of it. We want to be the ones that go down in the anals of history, where my buddy, Jonny Law, becomes a common household word as common as the kitchen sink, and who is pictured right beside him in the Encyclopedia Britanica or whatever issue they have out? - that's right, your's truly, Frank Archibald Miller, " Frank proudly said with a fire in his belly and he held out his hand to Jonny who reached out and followed Frank's numerous hand moves that began with a hand shake then twisted around and locked and unlocked, tapped on top, on bottom then tapped knuckles together.

"High school handshake seals the deal." Jonny said smiling.

"Boy howdy, you said it," Frank agreed.

"Seems like a million years ago."

"Fifteen years, huh?" Frank asked.

"Try eighteen." Jonny said.

"Good Gawd almighty time flies when you're havin' fun, I reckon."

"Right." Jonny's thoughts were elsewhere. "Game's at four o'clock. That'll give us time to get there early, develop a battle plan."

"I'm up for whatever you have in mind," Frank agreed.

"Let's do it," Jonny walked up to the front of the rig and got in the driver's seat and they proceeded to head to the Great Western Forum in Englewood, where L.A. would battle the Chicago Bulls, and he and his old high school friend would do whatever was necessary to thwart the efforts of a misguided group of ruthless misfits.

Chapter 15

Jonny and Frank arrived several hours early to the game. While parked in the forum parking lot, which was empty of cars with the exception of forum employees and team staff, they painted their faces Laker yellow and blue. Jonny had a large blue L painted on his face, and Frank a large blue A, both over a yellow base. Then, they sat and waited as cars trickled into the large lot. Like a team that was about to show the world and themselves what they were really made of, they sat unusually quiet inside the comfortably cool Winnebago that baked in the mid day sun. Jonny gave Frank some bullet deflecting pens to put in his front and back pockets and simply told Frank to hold the pens for him rather than explain their nature. He wasn't sure if Frank was pulling his hair out due to what was about to transpire with the President, or the possibility that he might see his ex. It didn't matter at this point, they were there and they were going to do everything they could to thwart any possible abductions and that was that.

"Doors are open." Frank said peering out a slit through the curtains from the kitchen area of the rig.

"Let's do it," Jonny said.

Once inside, they roamed the upper corridors of the forum in their Laker sweatshirts over bulletproof vests, against the flow of throngs of people doing the same thing, searching for the entrance nearest their seat. Frank appeared to be hyperventilating, taking deep breaths in an attempt to calm himself down.

"Nervous, Frank?"

Frank figideted. "They're gonna kidnap the President, man!" he said with desperation in Jonny's ear.

"Well, we'll just see about that." Jonny pretended to be calmer than he was, hoping it would rub off onto Frank. It didn't.

"Man, I could sure use a drink about now," Frank said as they arrived at the entrance to their mid-level seats.

"Don't go there, Frank, hold up," Jonny said. He walked over to the large upper floor window that over looked a sea of vehicles and stopped. He thought a moment, then pulled out his cell phone and dialed a number. He reached for his binoculars that were hung around his neck and checked out the view below.

"Who you callin'?" Frank pleaded.

Jonny pulled the binoculars away from his eyes and smiled at Frank, then spoke into his cell, "Could you kindly page Secret Service agent Bob Cramer, it is an E-mer-gen-cy. Thank you." Jonny covered the mouthpiece of the phone. "Time to even up the playing field, buddy."

Frank paid no mind to the comment as he continued taking deep breaths in an effort to calm himself.

"Try and relax, Frank," Jonny said.

"I'm tryin', I'm tryin'. My knees are shakin', Jonny." Frank put his hands on his knees to steady them and also lowered his head to ease his light-headedness.

"Frank, if it'll ease your mind a little, those pens I gave you?"

"Yeah, what about 'em?"

"They're made of the strongest substance known to man and they have a magnetic field powerful enough to catch a bullet." Jonny said.

"No kiddin'?"

"That's right." Jonny agreed.

"You're always thinkin', Jonny," Frank gasped.

"Bob?" Jonny warmly said into his cell as he spoke to agent Bob Cramer. "Big Dick, bartender at the Surf'n Turf in Santa Monica, how are you today? Good, say listen, your ex-wife is down here practically naked in a pretty skimpy bikini, ah….yeah, I'm afraid so, ah, what color? Let me see, it's kind of a pinkish-maroon, real sexy, got a small whip in her hands too. I don't know what the handcuffs and rope are for Bob, but, well, she's been a little abusive to some of the customers, you know in sort of a playful way, and she's been calling your name, wanted me to give you a call." Jonny paused to listen. "Tell her your busy? hmnn, that's too bad," Jonny pretended to think a moment before he continued. "Well listen, I can probably just take her over to my place, relax a little, if you know what I mean. I mean, she is your ex, right, Bob? " He chuckled a loud and obnoxious laughter into the phone. "What's that?" He paused again, "Well sure, of course I can," he said in a soothing and reasurring tone. "See you in few, thanks, Bob. Yes, I'll make sure she doesn't go anywhere too, bye bye." Jonny cordially said, then slapped the small phone shut.

"Man! Pretty slick, Jonny, I'd hate to be that bartender when 'ol Bob arrives good 'n hot." Frank said.

"Right," Jonny agreed. "Five to two, Frank, ready to play some ball?"

Frank eyed the concession stand then looked to Jonny. "A couple dogs and a coke would sure help ease these nerves of mine, Jonny," Frank suggested.

"Yeah, let's do it." The two stocked up on a couple hot dogs and Cokes, then proceeded to their seats.

The National Anthem had just concluded and every seat in the forum, with the exception of two were filled as Jonny and Frank inched by people who moved their legs to the side so they could make it through to their seats.

Announcer, John Gary addressed the excited crowd. Jonny paid not much mind to what he was saying until he heard Gary saying something about a warm L.A. welcome. Did he just say warm L.A. welcome? He quickly stopped chewing and reached for his pocket-sized binoculars that hung around his neck and scanned the crowd below. It was hard to hear with all the crowd noise and echoed boominess of the loud speakers. Warm L.A. welcome to who? He appeared like an eagle on the hunt with a flexible neck that could rotate 360 degrees. Where is he? A small boy several rows in front of him was pointing at something. He focused his binoculars. Bingo. There was the President, who was accompanied by several Secret Servicemen in the box seat section on the upper level. He waved to the crowd.

"Hello, Mr. President," Jonny said.

"Ya see him, Jonny?" Frank inquired.

"Right," Jonny replied.

The loud boomy sound of the announcer continued as Gary extended a warm welcome to Congressman Hyden, and commissioner of the NBA, Mr. David Stern. Jonny's eyes darted in every direction. Where? Where are they? Just as the thought crossed his mind, he might be seated with the President, he noticed the same small boy, seated several rows in front of him, looking into the box seats again. Congressman Hyden.

"Can ya see Starfield, Jonny?" Frank inquired in Jonny's ear.

"Ah, let me see, little miss tender heart where are you?" Jonny continued to scan the area for any other suspicious characters. "Don't see her. Looks like the F.B.I. made it." He focused on two suited men who stood tucked inside one of the corridors, then shuffled through the crowd for anyone else suspicious. "And what do we have here? I see little Theo Califano with some of his mob friends, too," Jonny confided to Frank.

Frank seemed to have calmed down somewhat, mainly from what distracted him down at courtside. Roughly a dozen, beautiful cheerleaders playfully danced about as they rallied the large crowd. He opened his second hot dog, then stuffed half of it into his mouth.

"Check out those cheerleaders, Jonny," Frank mumbled as if his brain had completely tuned out the whole idea and purpose of why they were there, as sort of a coping mechanism, rather than go on total overload and have a full-blown anxiety attack, that's what Jonny surmised anyway, but didn't say anything.

"Hot mammas, that's for sure," Jonny agreed.

"Man, this is gonna be a great game," he said.

Jonny nodded as he thought that everything was okay for the moment and that's what mattered. He wanted to do a little investigating, see if anything was out of the ordinary. He knew he had a little time, not much though, so he gave Frank an excuse to get up and take a quick stroll.

"This dog needs some more catsup, Frank, be right back." Jonny got up from his seat and proceeded out into the main corridor, then up one flight of stairs to the upper level where the box seats were. A handful of people milled about in the corridors just before game-time. He could see a Secret Service-man standing outside the box seat area. He didn't recognize him. Then two others came out from a corridor that led to seating that he recognized from the meeting Starfield held. They immediately entered the box seat area. He proceeded through the short tunnel that led to the arena seating area, then momentarily stood between two unrecognizable, suited men with earpieces that he knew were agents, each one looked at him. F.B.I.? He wasn't sure.

"Ooops, wrong floor," he said to the two, then turned around and headed back into the corridor, then back down a flight of stairs back to the level he and Frank were seated. What's with that? He noticed a men's washroom that was taped off with yellow tape and a sign on the door with the words NOT IN SERVICE written on it, and a yellow sawhorse with a sign that read DO NOT ENTER. He looked around.

"Not in service?" That's funny, he thought that on game day they would have a restroom out of service. He placed his hot dog in a side, leg pocket in his pants, looked around, and when the coast was clear, he stepped around the sawhorse, then ducked under the taped off doorway and entered.

He casually approached the mirror, pretended to check for food particles in his teeth, bent down to see if anyone's feet could be seen in any of the stalls, then entered one of the stalls. As he closed the door behind himself, he noticed an adult sized pink rabbit's outfit hanging on the stall door.

"A rabbit suit?" He pondered. "That's funny and a little strange." He began to relieve himself and with the word "strange" still in his mind, and to ease some tension, he began singing. "Strangers in the night, exchanging glances, wondering in the night, what were the chances, we'd be sharing love, German version," he quickly said changing the words, "Bevor die Nacht vorbei war..." and just as he sang several words in German, he stopped. He thought he heard someone enter the washroom.

One of the defecting Secret Servicemen, Bob Grossman, who was at last night's meeting, entered the room.

Jonny finished with a trickle.

"Hey, you?"

"Who me?" Jonny replied.

"Yeah, you, can't you read? This room is out of service," he called out to Jonny who zipped up, then exited the stall.

"Sorry, I had to go really, really bad," he explained and was surprised that the agent had his gun drawn.

"Cool gun, you must be with either the F.B.I., or the secret service. Since the President's here, I'd put my money on Secret Service, am I right? am I?" Jonny inquired with a gentle prod, like a child who wanted information from a reluctant parent.

Bob, showed a hint of a smile, then gave a modest nod, like he thought he was the coolest guy on the planet to be in the "Secret Service."

"I knew it! I knew it! How long have you been on the force, I mean, I don't mean force, I mean with the bureau, or the agency I mean, geez, get it right, sorry, man."

"Longer than I care to think about," Grossman modestly said as he looked down at Jonny's lower side pants pocket at what appeared to be something shiny and aluminum-like sticking out. "What's in your pocket?" He questioned.

"Just a hot dog, needed a little more catsup."

"Alright, you're gonna have to get out of here," Bob said, lightening up.

"You know I bet your parents are so proud of you." Jonny rubbed it in, figuring that there might an ounce of reservation left inside of him that might force him to think for a brief moment that this stupid, un-thought-out action he was about to take would surely ruin his life and any good feelings that anyone might ever have for him in the future.

"Yeah, I suppose."

"Man, I bet you have some stories to tell come turkey day with the fam, or no, that stuff's probably all top secret, right?"

"Yeah, I'm afraid so, come on let's go," Grossman holstered his gun in a relaxed manner.

"Alright," Jonny smiled warmly at Bob, "But not before I give you one big hug, man." He walked over to Bob, wrapped his arms around him and gave him a hug.

"Thanks," Jonny passionately said pretending to well over with emotion giving Bob a firm hug, then one more emotion filled, "Thanks," before he left. Bob just stood there a moment, somewhat stunned. He glanced into the mirror, saw his own face, then quickly looked away in shame.

Jonny had only taken several steps out of the washroom when he heard Grossman, who called out, "Hold up," he said.

Jonny froze, then slowly turned around. "Yeah?"

"What's on under the shirt?"

Jonny tapped on his chest, which made a hard thud-like sound.

"This?" Jonny smiled innocently, then lifted up his shirt that revealed a painted-on man's hairy chest with the words L.A. SCORES, written on its front. Bob just smiled and said, "Get out of here."

Jonny pointed both index fingers at Bob, six-gun style, and smiled. "Take care -" He turned around and headed towards the concession stand. As he did, he completed his statement, " - low-life."

As he walked past the entrance to the main arena area, he could hear the roar of the crowd. He hurried to the concession stand and stood behind a woman whose back was facing him who waited for her order. He was unrecognizable with his face painted and felt his heart nearly stop when he overheard the woman. It was Karen, who had just paid for a hamburger and drink and was about to walk away. Before he had a chance to think what to say, a "Hi Karen" seemed to pop out of his mouth. He slowly turned around to face her. She appeared stunned.

"Jonny?"

"Yeah," he reluctantly replied. "How are you feeling today?" he continued in a monotone sounding voice, still hurt from last night's revelation.

"Fine, why?" she innocently replied.

"Oh, I just thought that after a wild night with Todd that you might be feeling a little under the weather, or something like that," he prodded.

"Under the weather?"

"Yeah," Jonny whipped back.

"Oh, I get it. It was you last night," she said. "Jonny, Todd dropped over last night and said his car broke down and he wanted to call a tow truck. I said okay and went back to bed. I was in bed when you came to the door, then when you left, he tried to get a little fresh, so I put him in his place."

"You did?"

"Yeah, I did," she stated.

And before Jonny could finish, "What did you?" Todd approached with a good shiner that immediately explained what Karen did.

"Karen, we need to talk," Todd demanded.

Jonny glared at him. "Tidd," he said.

"Butt out freak show." Todd said to Jonny. "Karen, please," he then whined.

"I don't have anything to say to you, Todd," she said and started to walk away.

Todd didn't seem to know when to leave something alone and he continued pushing as he reached for Karen's shoulder and spun her around.

"Karen, you will not walk away from me, do you understand?" Todd scolded her in a furious manner, which ignited something of a fire inside of Jonny that had been brewing for a long time. He surprised himself when he reached for Todd's shoulder and spun him around and looked him directly in the eye.

"There's something wrong with this picture," he said. And Todd didn't know how to react to a guy who had been taking his arrogant, belittling comments served up daily for months on end, so he appeared stunned by this new behavior, and all he could say was, "Huh?"

And that's when Jonny gave him a sharp left hook that knocked him to the floor and blackened his other eye. Todd sat there a moment and held a hand over his eye.

Jonny quickly came to grips with what was still at hand. The President of the United States was about to be kidnapped if somebody didn't do something to try and stop it. He reached for Karen's hand and looked her in the eye, "Karen, whatever you do, don't leave your seat until the end of the game. Something very bad is about to happen, and I don't have time to explain." he said with an urgency that made her believe it.

"It's the President, isn't it," she said.

"Just promise me."

"I promise," she agreed and that's when Jonny kissed her. Before she could open her eyes and tell him to not do anything foolish, he was gone.

Jonny hurried back upstairs to his seat and was shocked when he looked down his aisle to see an empty seat where Frank had been sitting. The crowd let out a group roar after a long ball put three on the board for L.A., who trailed by four points. His heart began to race.

"Frank, don't do this to me," he desperately said to himself as his eyes darted around the immediate area. Did he take the wrong entrance? He spotted the elderly couple seated next to them and immediately recognized the woman wearing an L.A. jersey. "Frank, where are you?" He reached for his binoculars and searched the lively crowd. He scanned the immediate area. No Frank. He then looked over to the expensive private box seats where the President and congressman were seated. The congressman was getting out of his seat.

"Oh Frank," he said as he scanned about the lively crowd. "Where in God's name," and then something caught his eye. Hello. There they are. At the far end of the arena, he focused on Rhajneed's white turban, which stood out when he got up. It appeared that he was taking a break at the same time the congressman was. What for? And he was seated next to Debbie - little miss Starfield. Why didn't I see her before? He wondered. She wore a bright red outfit with dark sunglasses and was looking through binoculars - at what? What is she looking at? Jonny zoomed around the crowd. The plot was getting thick as molasses and he could sense that everything was about to hit the fan. He knew from experience that when things like this began their forward motion you had to be ready for anything at a moment's notice. He scanned the crowd. The President hadn't moved and neither had the Secret Servicemen, nor had Theo and his boys, and the Cheerleaders are doing a great job and so is? Who is that not wearing a shirt and on the court? "Frank?" He said out loud, aghast and in disbelief as he pulled the binoculars from his eyes. Then he looked through them again. He focused on Debbie.

"001752, I think you just blew your cover, buddy." He realized that Frank was what Debbie had her binoculars on. He cringed, then refocused his binoculars back down to courtside, where a short, squatty woman fed beers to Frank. He had a beer titled upward and quickly chugged it. She handed him another, which he also chugged. Half the beer went down his throat, the other half down his chin and over his hairy front. He was getting an audience, who cheered him to chug the alcohol faster. Each time he finished one of the beers, the woman fed him another. He paused to swing his shirt around as he ranted and hollered at the L.A. team, then turned and waved his arms wildly and yelled to rally the crowd.

Jonny focused on the woman next to Frank, who also chugged the beer. "Becky," he concluded. He instantly recalled what Frank had said about his ex who drove him crazy and that's just how he looked. He needed to do something to snap Frank out of his very brief relapse and do it quick. He hurried through the crowd, then ran as fast as he could down a flight of stairs to the courtside level where he entered the corridor he thought was closest to Frank, then pushed and shoved his way through the crowd towards courtside.

In the time it took for Jonny to sprint down the stairs and get in the vicinity of where Frank was standing, Chicago had made two three pointers and was up by ten. He could hear Frank, who continued to scream at the L.A. team as he approached him.

"Come on L.A.! You can do it! You gotta fight to win you bunch of lazy bums!" he yelled at the team, then chugged the rest of his beer and threw his empty cup onto the court.

Frank's ex, remained by his side egging him on, "That's tellin' 'em Frank!" she spewed out as an official called time to clear the court of the debris. The sound of boos echoed through the arena, which provoked Frank even more as he raised his hands up to the crowd for more.

The official quickly approached him and had to shout at him to be heard over the deafening, riled up crowd.

Jonny arrived to overhear the yelling match that ensued.

"You throw something out on this court again and you're out of here! You understand?" the official hollered directly into Frank's face.

"Yeah, yeah, yeah, tell me about it. I wouldn't be missin' much the way these L.A. bums are playin," Frank said directing his last comment to the L.A. bench.

"Hey, we paid our money! Are you gonna let him talk to you that way, Frank?" Becky said.

Little did Jonny realize the ball had begun to move and it wasn't the ball on the court.

Earlier, agent Norman Felder, had slipped into the restroom in the Presidential box seat area, plugged up one of the sinks and the floor drain and let water overflow onto the floor. A short while later, when he excused himself, an inch of water had accumulated onto the floor. He explained the news to the President, then instructed agents Randolf and Banks to secure a restroom for the President, which had already been done. However, they played along and made their exit and proceeded down one level to a restroom they had already marked OUT OF SERVICE, then they all patiently waited. The President would give the cue for his own abduction when he needed to use the restroom. Then, with a discreet push of a button on his cell phone, Felder would send a message to Randolf, who would then text message Debbie and the others that the President needed to use the washroom.

The President got up from his seat and the plan slipped into action as planned.

The youngest agent, Richard Reed, who stood outside the door to the box seat area, was unaware of what was about to take place and simply followed orders he was given.

As agents Grossman, Dryers, and Banks, who had returned from supposedly securing a restroom, escorted the President to the designated restroom, Felder instructed agent Reed to also accompany the President and he would keep the area secure.

A handful of Laker fans walked through the corriders as the President walked past.

Felder immediately dialed Randolf. "There on their way. Where in the hell is Cramer?"

Agent Randolf could sense the contained rage in Felder's voice. "Ah, Norm, Bob had to take off, said it was an emergency, something involving his wife."

"He what? He's not married!"

"His ex, Norm." Randolf replied.

"That son of a bitch! " Felder ended the call. He stood there a moment wondering about Cramer and their plan.

Two F.B.I. agents were assigned to monitor activities at the corridor nearest to the President's location and act as backup to any emergencies that may occur. They had spotted Califano and several of his mob partners, who were all on the F.B.I.'s wanted list, so their attention was diverted on them. They mistakingly trusted the group of Secret Service agents to guard the President.

One of the F.B.I. men had noticed the movement in the box seat as the President got up from his seat. He looked over at his partner to get his attention, then glanced to the empty box seat.

"Taking a leak," his partner said.

The agent nodded in agreement and the two continued keeping an eye on Califano and his closest partner and bodyguard, who ironically had the last name of Crook. He wasn't very bright, but he was tough and loyal to Califano.

If it weren't for Crooks obvious attention directed to the President's seat, the two F.B.I. men might have called for assistance to make a collar on the gangsters, then followed the President. But their actions were just suspicious enough for them to be considered a threat, and any and all potential dangers directed towards the President would be dealt with in a swift manner.

Califano also appeared to be antsy as he elbowed Dom in the ribs each time he looked back towards the President's seat. Like a child, the slower man still didn't get it. He did catch on, however, when over the roar of the crowd, he heard Califano mentioning something in his ear about "doing that again, and, broken legs," it was then he got the message to keep his eyes on the game and on the beautiful dancing cheerleaders.

The crowd continued to roar as L.A. appeared to show some signs of life, and the quarter was near its end. The excitement of the game was like a blindfold to the audience who were oblivious to what was about to unfold. Even Jonny had his hands full with his now intoxicated partner, Frank.

Little did game announcer John Gary realize, he wasn't just calling the game on the court, but another game that was much bigger and with significantly higher stakes than a mere basketball game. It was a game that could hold the fate of the world in its outcome. The seconds on the clock ticked away one by one, while excited fans continued to be held captive with all eyes on the ball. Cheerleaders danced to upbeat music as each team charged from one end of the court and then to the other.

A time out was called and the crowd began to chant, L.A., L.A., L.A., L.A! as the most powerful man in the world was about to be taken hostage right before their eyes if something drastic wasn't done to prevent it.

Chapter 16

Norman Felder stood alone in the pricey Presidential box seat. He kept away from the window so he wouldn't be seen. As he contemplated what was about to take place, he started to experience a shortness of breath, along with a heavy chest. It felt like a truck was parked on it. Heart attack? The only thing he had was asprin. He walked over and opened the private restroom door and looked at the inch of water that had flooded over the floor. He wasn't about to get his feet wet. Instead, he walked over to the bar and poured a shot of whiskey, tossed the asprin in his mouth then downed the shot. He looked into the mirror behind the bar, grabbed a napkin to wipe the perspiration from his forehead, then exited. He made sure to lock the door behind himself.

In the meantime, the Secret Servicemen led the President down to the second level.

"Isn't there a washroom on this level?" the President inquired.

"F.B.I. suggested a private restroom down a level sir," agent Banks stated.

"Very well, I suppose I could use a little exercise." The President replied.

On the second level, they approached a men's restroom that had tape across the door that read, NOT IN SERVICE. One of the agents moved the sawhorse that blocked the entrance and had a metal sign that hung down from it with the words, DO NOT ENTER written on it, and the President and group of agents entered. The President stood at a urinal and casually chatted with his secret service escorts.

"I think it's about time that L.A. team put on the full court press or they're gonna be hanging their heads pretty low after this game," the President said.

All the agents agreed with some small talk and then Debbie entered the restroom followed by Norman and Rhajneed, who had just taken care of business with the congressman in a janitors office after learning from a bug they had planted the previous evening that he had attempted to double cross them.

Agent Reed appeared stunned at the presence of the woman who had just casually entered the men's room. He immediately placed his hand under his suit coat and on his revolver and addressed her as she approached the sinks with her back to him.

"Maam, you are in the wrong wash room and I want you to leave now," he ordered. The other agents looked at one another pretending to be amused and shrugged their shoulders at each other as if it was an honest mistake.

"Yes, but I really have to go," she pleaded with her back still to them. And as he drew his pistol, Norman hit him from behind knocking him unconscious. His service revolver fell to the floor next to him.

"Tie him up," she ordered and Norman picked up the revolver and agents Dryers and Banks proceeded to tie Reed up with some rope they obtained from a trash receptacle that had been placed there previously.

"What in God's name!" the President cried out stunned at the reactions of the agents. "What are you doing?" he said in disbelief.

Each of the agents had drawn their service revolvers, and remained silent while they waited for a command.

"Get him into the suit," Debbie coldly stated.

"Quickly," Rhajneed said.

"Some of us thought it would be nice to have an early retirement party, and it was an offer we just couldn't refuse," Norman said to the President with his gun aimed at him.

"You're all out of your minds if you think you'll get away with this," the President glared at the group of traitors.

Debbie stepped up to the President and got in his face, "Well, we'll just see about that." She eyed him up and down.

"If you would be so kind to take off your shoes, Mr. President," Grossman kindly said. And the President had no choice but to comply.

"Your costume has got the cute little feet already sewn in," Banks added, then laughed out loud and presented the pink rabbit suit to the President.

"Coat, take it off," agent Grossman demanded, then assisted the President and helped him remove his coat then stuffed it into the trashcan.

"You're pitiful," the President said to him, then looked to the rest of them and added, "All of you."

"Shut up! And do what your told," Debbie demanded to the President. "We don't have all day!" she yelled to the group, who hurried and got the President into the pink rabbit suit. They placed the unconscious agent Reed into a stall and sat him upright on one of the toilets and handcuffed him to the toilet paper dispenser.

In the meantime, Jonny had settled the dispute between the ref and Frank for throwing debris onto the court, then drug him away from his very intoxicated ex-wife, who managed to lower Frank to the lowest form of life she could by screaming every four letter word that popped into her inebriated brain.

Jonny pulled Frank through the group of dancing cheerleaders, then up several flights of stairs, while Frank struggled to redress himself. They stopped. Winded and perspiring, Jonny peeked around the corner to eye a men's washroom where he thought the President to be.

"Hold up 001456," Jonny nervously said while he caught his breath.

"Isn't my number double-0-one-seven-five-three?" Frank questioned panting like a racehorse.

"Right," Jonny said not paying any mind to Frank's number. He eyed the washroom door, then looked to Frank and smiled as he put a hand on his shoulder. This was it.

"It's a sacred moment, Frank, we're about to make history," Jonny gasped. The cement corridor appeared vacant and eerie Jonny thought. He looked up and down it each way. "Looks like they even eliminated the concession stand guy."

"Huh?" Frank inquired.

"Nothin'. Time to get out the bullet-deflecting pens." Jonny reached into his back pocket and pulled out a handful of the silver metal pens.

Frank pulled some of the silver pens from his pockets and studied them. "Do these things really deflect bullets, Jonny?" Frank inquired in a squeaky voice he'd just lost at courtside.

"They're supposed to Frank," Jonny said as he was now the one who took deep breaths in an attempt to calm himself.

"You okay?" Frank asked.

"Yeah. We've come a long way buddy." Jonny felt elated that they were about to become the biggest heroes the world had ever known.

"Where did you get these things anyway?"

"Army surplus. 1955 test equipment for the F.B.I." Jonny said.

The crowd's noise inside the forum echoed through the halls of the upper corridor.

"Looks like they took down the Out of Service sign, the tape too, but they're in there, you can rest assured of that fact." Jonny spoke in a hurried manner while he eyed the men's room door. "Okay, hold one high, one low." Jonny held the pens out as a brief tutorial to Frank. "One over the family jewels, Frank and one over your heart." He then took several deep calming breaths and looked at Frank who mimicked the maneuver with him. They breathed in and out together like two anxious bulls, pitted for battle.

"Ready?" Jonny stated like a man about to jump out of a plane without a chute.

"Yeah," Frank squeaked.

"Let's do it!" Jonny belted out like a S.W.A.T. commander and the two charged into the washroom.

They entered and pointed their pens in every direction, like cops who aimed their weapons to the left, the right, high and low searching for a dangerous armed assailant.

Frank sounded like an ailing horse, "Freeze, maggots," he hollered as Jonny kicked open each and every stall door.

The only person in the restroom was an old, blind man, wearing a crumpled suit coat with a Lakers t-shirt underneath it and dark sunglasses. His tall, thin, white cane leaned against the wall as he stood in front of one of the urinals.

"Who's there? What you boys up to?" He inquired as Jonny looked to Frank and Frank to Jonny.

"Oh not too much, we're just here enjoyin' the game," Jonny nonchalantly said to the man, then looked to Frank and shrugged his shoulders.

"Yeah, we're just enjoyin' the game, sir."

"I don't have any money on me, if that's what you're about," the old man said, then quickly zipped up and reached for his cane and turned around. "But if you boys are lookin' for trouble, you come to the right place, mmmnn hmmnn," he said as he held the cane up into the air and started to swing it wildly. Whooosh, whoosh, whoosh the cane sounded as it cut through the air.

"You think I'm some sort of maggot, do ya? I'll show you boys a thing or two, try'n rob me!" the man vehemently said as he sliced the cane through the air again and again looking upwards towards every portion of the ceiling as he performed the self-defense maneuver.

Jonny casually motioned with his head for Frank to follow him out of the room and the two quietly exited the washroom. They stood outside the door a moment and could hear the old man still wrestling with them.

"I may be blind, but I'll kick your asses anyway," the man fervently belted out. "That's right, the both of you! You hear me! Take that! You little whipper-snappers!" And they could hear the whoosh of the old man's cane as it continued to be swung wildly through the air. "Come on, is that all the fight you got in ya!? You little, young sissy asses, come on!" He cried out. "Some of those chicken feathers comin' off you boys, hmmnn?!!!" the man ranted.

"You think it's another washroom?" Frank questioned perplexed.

Jonny appeared stunned for a moment, then looked to Frank, "What floor is this?"

"If memory serves me, we went up three flights, I do believe Jonny," Frank stated.

"Hmmnn," Jonny chuckled to himself. "Wrong floor." Jonny smiled and shook his head.

"It's an honest mistake, man," Frank said in a consoling tone.

"Geeez, nerves." Jonny chuckled. "Come on, let's head down," he breathed a sigh of relief to Frank and they proceeded down a floor.

Just as Jonny and Frank headed down a level, Debbie and her Secret Service entourage escorted a large pink rabbit out of the men's room and then down a flight of stairs down to the main floor.

Jonny peeked his head around the corner of the stairwell and just missed the group of misfits as they slithered around a corner and out of sight.

"Oh yes, now this is it, Frank," Jonny could see the same Out of Service sign that was still in place.

"I'm ready whenever you are, man," a determined Frank said to Jonny.

"Okay, are you feelin' okay? How many fingers, Frank?" Jonny said as he fanned some fingers in front of Frank's face.

"Very funny. I only had a couple Jonny, really, I'm okay," Frank reassured him.

"Alright then, we just had the dress rehearsal, man, this is the real McCoy," Jonny, once again started to take deep breaths, as did Frank, to get pumped up for whatever they might encounter.

"A moment of silence," Jonny paused to bow his head and closed his eyes, and Frank did too, honoring the moment. "Ready, Frank?" Jonny said as if snapped out of the momentary self induced meditative trance.

"Born ready!" Frank squeaked out two octaves higher than his normal voice.

"Let's do it!" Jonny cried out like a military commander leading his troop into battle.

Their tennis shoes screeched over the floor as they charged into the washroom like before with bullet deflecting pens held high and low and directing them in every direction.

"Freeze, dirtbags!" Jonny shouted. His voice echoed through the near empty washroom. They heard a moaning sound that came from one of the stalls. Jonny looked to Frank, who was in a martial arts stance, and Frank to Jonny. The two slowly stepped over and cautiously opened the door. Agent Reed was still out of it, but alive and handcuffed to the toilet paper dispenser.

"Secret service guy?" Frank questioned.

"Right," Jonny agreed.

"What do you think?"

"I think we missed 'em, and my guess is he's one of the good guys," Jonny, agitated, slammed the stall door and it bounced opened and closed several times, then before they had a moment to think, a loud popping sound along with a chorus of screams erupted in the main corridor.

"Holy bee-Jesus, what in God's name is that?" Frank questioned.

"Good question," Jonny peeked out the door.

"Give it up, Califano," the F.B.I. called out as intermittent gunshots echoed through the corridor.

"F.B.I.'s tryin' to put a collar on Califano and his friends," Jonny said as he closed the door.

"Great. What timing. You think we should hang tight for a minute?" Frank suggested.

"Negative, time is of the essence. My guess is they're probably heading out the door as we speak," Jonny peeked out the door again.

"Why don't we use the concession stand for cover, I'll grab a couple burgers for us, then the stairwell is only about twenty feet away, " Frank suggested.

"Sometimes your brilliance amazes me." Jonny pulled out his wallet and reached for a five-dollar bill.

"Wanna leave a whole five?" Frank inquired as the screaming and mayhem continued in the corridor.

"There's no way out, Califano," an F.B.I. agent called out.

"Yeah, it's all I've got," Jonny searched every hiding spot inside his wallet.

"Catsup and mustard?" Frank questioned.

"Right." Jonny casually agreed. "Get your pens out and stick to the wall, Frank."

"Got it," Frank agreed and the two exited the washroom and side-stepped down the corridor holding their bullet deflecting pens out as bullets ricocheted off the cement walls, then ducked behind the concession stand where they grabbed several burgers. Frank reached a hand up onto the counter of the stand and felt around for some condiments that were stuffed into paper cup containers. Jonny peaked out to see if the coast was clear, then placed a five-dollar bill in the attendants tip cup.

"Sounds like a reload to me," Jonny said during a moment free from the popping sound. "Let's do it, Frank." They sprinted to the stairwell and down to safety.

In the meantime, Debbie and her entourage, now accompanied by one large pink rabbit, were roaming through the nearly vacant corridor on the main floor. They had gotten somewhat turned around with their directions and Debbie was too filled with pride to ask the Secret Servicemen for directions to the back of the building, so she quietly addressed Rhajneed.

"Rhajneed, I believe we are going in the wrong direction. Rushnad has the car parked behind us in the opposite direction." She nervously stated with some doubt.

"No," Rhajneed, stubbornly insisted. They continued walking, "We are going right."

"Everyone stop!" she insisted and pulled out a drawing from her slender red purse and opened it up and showed it to Rhajneed to explain her position.

"You see, we are here and Rushnad is back that way," she discreetly pointed to her drawing, "behind us," she insisited.

"No," Rhajneed defended his position again. "He is up in this direction, this way, I am certain of it. You have the drawing wrong," he insisted. He continued walking in the same direction as the group followed.

"No!" Debbie fumed and stopped dead in her tracks. "I drew it from the blueprint. It is not wrong," she demanded like a pouty child. And finally the President who was standing next to her addressed the issue.

"Where in the hell is he parked?" he asked.

"He is outside the back exit," she explained in a sweeter more diplomatic disposition.

"Well, little lady, I think your friend there is right. I think we're heading towards the back of the building right now," the President explained. Then the Secret Servicemen got into the discussion, some agreeing with the President and Rhajneed, while others insisted that they were heading in the wrong direction.

"Would everyone just shut up! Let's get the hell out of here! If we're wrong we can all just walk around the building," she fumed as the Secret Servicemen whispered to one another still debating the matter. They proceeded walking through the handful of people who milled about using restrooms or getting refreshments and who were oblivious to the mayhem that the F.B.I. was involved with on the other side of the building, and to the kidnapping of the President of The United States.

A moment later they arrived at the front of the building. Debbie immediately seethed. She was right. "What did I tell you! Now we must walk around!" She fumed.

"I knew we were going wrong," said the President as he slid his large pink feet with white toes over the cement floor as they approached the entrance.

"Hmnn, your drawing was right," Rhajneed casually stated.

"My drawing was right," Debbie reiterated in a disgusted tone.

"It felt to me that we were going in the wrong direction too," Norman said trying to win points with Debbie, who shot him a look that could kill, then led the group like an angry school teacher out the front door of the arena.

Bob Cramer, who had left earlier to find his ex, trotted over to the group as they exited the arena. He had been blowing bubbles with his gum while he waited outside for the group to emerge from the crowd. He popped a good-sized one, which caught their attention as he approached them from behind.

"Hi you guys," he said like a boy who knew he had done something very bad and looked at each member like a lost puppy who wanted acceptance back into the group. They all scorned him with their looks, especially Debbie's, whose sharp look could easily have melted him where he stood.

"Had kind of an emergency with the ex, false alarm," he stated in a sympathetic, yet relieved manner, then tagged behind the silent bunch, who dared not say a word for fear of what might happen if Debbie fully erupted. Norman looked over at Bob behind Debbie's back and put a finger up to his lips to shush him. She startled all of them when she stopped abruptly and turned around and stepped close to Bob's face.

"If I could, I would kill you right here," she slowly stated emphasizing each word.

Bob, being the slut he was, gave her the same soft, subtle, sexy smile he had given so many women in bars. "Sorry," he said in the most caring and romantic tone of voice he could muster. "I promise," He paused to milk it for more, "It won't happen again." And he looked into her dark sunglasses as sexy as he could, then he gave her one of his favorite looks from his deceptive repertoire that included a subtle wink of both eyes accompanied with a reassuring nod, concluding with a smile. She shook her head in disgust, knowing their fate, then turned around and proceeded to stomp to the back of the building where Kaleeb and Rushnad waited, parked in a limo they had stolen.

Jonny and Frank approached the front of the building from the opposite side and had just missed the group again, who proceeded towards the back of the arena. The two looked around in every direction. There was nothing resembling a group of scumballs, escorting a large pink rabbit anywhere in sight.

"What do you think, Jonny, you think they might've left already?" Frank inquired as he swallowed the last bite of his burger and threw his wrapper in the trash.

"Negative," Jonny took a bite of his burger. "I can still smell a pack of rats. Let's head outside," he said, and the two exited the building and stepped back from it to get a look at the upper floors.

"I don't see any pink rabbits, Jonny," Frank said as the two stopped outside the forum and looked high, low, and in every direction.

Jonny reached for his binoculars and looked out over the large lot. "There must be a million cars in this lot." He skimmed over the sea of cars that were magnified larger than life. "Hello," he paused on two lovers making out in a sedan.

"The only thing I see, Jonny, is a speeding limo 12 o 'clock!"

"Huh?" Jonny pulled the binoculars away from his eyes just in time to see a long stretch limo that sped towards them at a high rate of speed. It all seemed like slow motion, even Frank's voice.

"Look out, Jonny!"

Instinctively Jonny tossed up his hamburger and dove out of the way. Frank was sure he'd never in his life witnessed such a close call. The limo hit Jonny's hamburger before it had a chance to hit the ground.

"Man!" Frank cried out as the limo sped off. "You okay?"

Jonny quickly got up, and before he had a chance to brush himself off, the tires from the limo screeched to a stop.

"A little shakin' not stirred, Frank." The two wondered what was up with the limo.

"What the heck is with them?" Frank questioned as the two stood there stunned.

"Don't know." Jonny said. They both immediately knew as Debbie stepped out of the limo and starred at them a moment.

"Guess who? My lovely neighbor," Frank said.

"Indeed. Maybe she forgot her purse, you think?" Jonny questioned.

She appeared to look around a moment for any potential witnesses, then bent over and reached inside the limo and pulled out an automatic weapon. All of the secret servicemen turned and watched to see what Debbie was capable of doing with the weapon.

"Holy bologna, duck Jonny!" Frank screamed and the two dove to the asphalt. A barrage of wild stray bullets ricocheted off everything under the sun, but nowhere near them.

"Ahhhh!!!!" She cried out then quickly got back inside the limo and it sped away.

"Thank God, she's one lousy shot, Jonny," Frank said.

"You said it brother. Let's go catch a rabbit!"

"Ten-four, buddy," Frank replied.

They sprinted to the Winnebago in an attempt to rescue the freshly abducted President.

Chpater 17

Frank stood on the bumper of the Winnebago with his head under the hood, spraying starter fluid into the carburetor while Jonny desperately stomped on the gas.

"Keep sprayin', Frank." Jonny's right leg appeared to keep time, raising up then back down in a rhythm as the big stubborn engine turned, but refused to fire.

"I'm sprayin', I'm sprayin'," Frank shot back. And then magically the behemoth started. Jonny revved and revved the engine so there was no doubt it wouldn't die on him.

"Yes!" Jonny cried out as thick black smoke bellowed from the tail pipe. "Close the hood and get in!" he yelled to Frank, who stepped down from the bumper and slammed the hood shut, then got in. Jonny drove as quickly as was safe through the parking lot. Little did he realize that another similar looking black limo had just exited the arena in the opposite direction as the President's limo. He slid open his side window as he pulled up to a booth where an attendant sat inside looking at a magazine.

Jonny held out his VIP parking pass.

"Okay," the man said, then gave a hand signal to proceed.

"Say, did you happen to see a black stretch limo just leave the area?" he inquired.

"Which one?" the man questioned.

"Jonny, look! There they are!" Frank excitedly cried out.

Jonny's eyes locked onto a black limo that had just sped away from the lot. "Nevermind," he said to the man and he put his foot onto the gas and began to follow them.

"Okay, this is it, man. We got 'em!" Jonny was ecstatic.

"Yeah, just don't lose 'em," Frank said.

"Oh, I'm not gonna be that stupid and lose 'em, no sir-e-Bobby." The words sprang forth from his lips. He held up his hand for Frank to slap a high-five.

"Good," Frank said and he slapped Jonny's hand.

"This feels too good, man!" Jonny bubbled over with childlike giddiness.

"Yeah, we're stuck on 'em like glue and they don't even know it," Frank said.

"Do you realize that we are about to crack the biggest case in the history of this great nation of ours?" Jonny felt elated and patriotic at that noble thought.

"Yeah, we're gonna be famous heroes, Jonny." Frank paid no mind to the freeway traffic, instead, he visualized himself pictured alongside Jonny on billboards all across America with something catchy and very patriotic written underneath them in large bold print so that every American, young and old would know who they were.

"Ain't that the truth, one more for luck." You couldn't pry the ear-to-ear grin from Jonny's face. He held up his hand again and Frank slapped it again, then chuckles of laughter sprang forth from him like that of a small boy at Christmas, who had just received that favorite toy that made quivers run up and down his spine.

"Right on, man, right on," Frank said as they continued following the limo down the freeway.

Several hours had passed and both Jonny and Frank's elation had faded. Jonny's fingers tapped on the large thin steering wheel. His frustration was beginning to show from what seemed like an endless ride heading north.

"Man, where do you think they're headed?" Frank impatiently inquired.

"Don't know, but I sure hope they don't drive all day. We're on tank number two." Jonny said.

"Heck, maybe you oughta just ram 'em into the ditch, you know like they do on cops."

"And what if the President isn't wearing his seatbelt and he gets thrown from the vehicle as it rolls fifteen dozen times and is killed, and we get to spend the rest of our lives in a friendly little state prison. Does that sound good to you, Frank?"

"Nah, I'm a little claustrophobic in confined spaces, particularily with large, angry men. Is there an airport out this way, Jonny?"

"Not that I'm aware of," Jonny replied trying to not show too much concern at that thought as he wondered what they would do if there was an airport.

"That does it," Jonny said.

"What?" Frank replied.

Jonny didn't respond immediately, but took out his cell phone and dialed a number.

"Who you callin'?" Frank prodded.

"F.B.I."

"Man?" Frank pleaded. "They're just gonna take the credit for this caper buddy, then no chicks'll be beggin' to meet us, no endorsement deals, no press, and we'll be hung out to dry," Frank pondered out loud their futures as Jonny spoke on the phone.

"Eddie Goodman's office, please," Jonny said to a receptionist at the main F.B.I. office in Washington D.C.

"Isn't he the top dog, Jonny?" Frank inquired.

Jonny nodded as he listened to the woman at the other end.

"Mr. Goodman is in Los Angeles meeting with the President. Can I take a message?" The woman inquired.

"Uh," Jonny stammered unsure how to properly address the matter. "Tell him Jonny Law called, and uh,…" Jonny paused thinking Frank might be right in the fact that the F.B.I. would probably take the credit for their work.

"Will he know what this is regarding?" the woman inquired.

Jonny paused again, then looked over at Frank who shook his head in dis-approval for what Jonny was doing. He put the phone down on his leg cover-ing the mouthpiece. "We'll video tape it, Frank, so they can't take the credit. We'll have proof," Jonny said waiting for his buddy's approval.

Frank continued looking out the window, then looked over at Jonny, "Do it," he said.

"Are you still there?" Jonny spoke into the phone. "Tell him the Presi-dent," and Jonny paused a moment wanting to choose his words carefully so there was no misunderstanding. "The President of the United States of Amer-ica has been kidnapped, and we're following the kidnappers on the 405 north-east. They're driving a newer model black stretch limo." Jonny looked over to Frank who nodded with approval at Jonny's statement.

"My number?" Jonny questioned in a surprised tone that anyone at the F.B.I. would want his number, then gave a cordial smile. He realized he was not only holding all the good cards, but the entire deck. "Sure, no problem, three-one-zero, nine, nine, zero, seven-two, seven-nine."

He wondered if the woman at the other end had fully comprehended what he had just told her. Her demeanor remained as calm and flat throughout the call as if it related to the President's dry cleaning as she stated that she would make sure he got the message.

Jonny replied with an enthusiastic, "Thank you," and he slapped his phone shut. "She's gonna make sure he gets the message. Sounded like it was no big deal to her."

"Well, my guess is that when the chunky do-do hits the fan, and they find out what's goin' on, that cell phone of yours will be ringin' off the hook," Frank said.

"Yeah," Jonny agreed as they continued following the limo and maintained a safe distance as it took an exit.

"Exit two-fifty-seven," Frank said. "Where are we, Jonny?"

"Not sure, north east somewhere."

"Kind of secluded out here," Frank said.

"Yeah."

"You think there could be an airstrip out here?"

"My exact thoughts Frank, an old airstrip that hasn't been used since World War II, probably that's not even on the map."

They rounded a corner and tucked back in a remote area was not an old abandoned airstrip, but rather an old gas station, where the limo had pulled up and stopped at one of the old 1950's style pumps.

"Jonny, Jonny, pull over right here!" Frank said.

"A gas station," Jonny pondered wide-eyed as he obliged Frank and pulled over and stopped on the shoulder of the secluded road.

"Man, looks like an old one, must still be in use," Frank said as they eyeballed the limo from a distance.

"Right. There's a little ravine off the shoulder we can use for cover. It's perfect. We got 'em, man! This is it!" Jonny sounded as if he had just been resuscitated back to life.

"Yeah," Frank agreed also savoring the moment. "Our pictures'll be in every paper in the world. Chicks'll be beggin' to meet us!"

"Right you are, Frank." Jonny agreed in near tears as if they had already won the World Cup or something on that level. He reached under the seat for a towel and attempted to clean off his game face paint wiping the colors that smeared into one yellowish blue color that now appeared to be of an alien nature.

"Better wipe off, Frank, we'll want to look good for the press. CNN'll be out here in just a little bit," Jonny smiled in a cocky manner, then handed the towel to Frank.

Frank wiped his face too and smeared his colors so they both looked sickly. But, they were both too elated from their big score to be too worried about their appearance.

"You think we could win a Noble Peace prize for this, Jonny?"

"Oh, I'd say probably, more than likely. It's a pretty noble thing we're doin', I'd say."

"I think I'm gonna put on my vest, man," Frank casually stated as if he'd been through the drill a million times.

"Good idea, grab mine too, would you."

"No problemo," Frank responded.

"Boots kitty, where are you? Get in your box," Jonny said to Boots, who had been trained to enter his custom lead-lined box in emergency situations. Boots immediately jumped from Jonny's bed to a small opening underneath it, then pawed a small door shut.

Jonny pulled out an old video camera that was mounted on a flimsy metal tripod from an overhead cupboard. He then stepped over to the side door where Frank held out a vest for him.

"I picked these vests 'cause of the big letters. They see that F.B.I. logo, they'll be shakin' in their boots."

"Right you are, Frank." Jonny set down the video camera on top of the stovetop and they put on their vests. He then opened up another cupboard and took out two old, oversized, chipped up army helmuts, handed one to Frank who put it on, then put on his own.

"How do I look, Jonny?"

"Like a Rambo, buddy, let's do it." Jonny picked up the video camera and they exited the rig.

"What do you think they're up to?" Frank inquired standing in plain sight as Jonny set up the video camera that faced them so they could record the capture of the ruthless criminals.

"I don't know, maybe they're taking a collection for gas. Camera's ready to go," Jonny said, then eyed the limo through the viewfinder as it sat there. "I got a little surprise, Frank." Jonny stepped over to the rig and opened up a side luggage compartment and pulled out a long, military green bazooka.

"Bazooka! Good Gawd almighty, Jonny. I thought you had to hock the guns?"

"I did. They had a little problem with this one." Jonny said as he drew an imaginary line under a white spray painted logo that read – PROPERTY OF THE FBI.

"Jonny, don't look now, but somebody just opened the driver's door of the vehicle, probably gonna pump some gas," Frank observed.

"The more gas they pump, the bigger the explosion," Jonny said.

"Yeah, I reckon. Have you ever fired it?" Frank asked.

Jonny ignored the question.

"Hold this, Frank," he said as he handed the bazooka to Frank, then hurried back into the Winnebago. A moment later, he exited the motor home with a hand held mic that had a long curly cord that ran from a cupboard inside the rig. He spat into the mic to give it a subtle check. "Still works, man," he said smiling.

"What are you gonna say?" Frank inquired.

Jonny looked at Frank as if to say, you've got to be kidding. "I have watched "Top Cops" a couple times, Frank," he chuckled. "I'm sure something will come to me," he raised an eyebrow and shook his head at such a ludicrous comment.

"Give me the bazooka." Frank handed Jonny the weapon. "Would you go turn the camera so it faces me, Frank, and how about a close up of me when I first tell them that the party's over," Jonny suggested.

"Yes sir, Mr. Spellberg, ha ha." Frank commented, then zoomed in tight on Jonny, who crouched down on one knee holding the bazooka with one hand and the mic in the other. He appeared a fleshy green in the viewfinder.

"How do I look, Frank?"

"I think the color might need to be adjusted on this thing, but it looks pretty darn good and tape is rolling, whenever you're ready, Jonny." Frank gave Jonny a finger countdown to his talent like it was a major news production.

"Hold up, Frank. Can you see the bazooka, too?" Jonny inquired.

"Ah, let me zoom out just a little, there ya be, Newsweek cover shot right there, Jonny."

"Okay, here goes nothin,'" Jonny put the microphone next to his mouth and pressed the button on the side of it.

"Testing one, two," he said and then his cell phone rang.

"Oh brother, now what?" Frank said.

"Stop the tape, Frank." Jonny set down the bazooka and answered the call.

"Hello. Hi, Eddie," Jonny said like a guy who held the Hope Diamond in his hands with an excited glow, then grinned at Frank and mouthed, "It's him." "Yeah, no, it's no joke, I know, yeah, I know, I was just a stupid kid when I did that," Jonny said smiling. "Well," he said, then paused as he nervously made a mark in the dirt with the toe of his sneaker. "We're not really following them anymore. I've got a bazooka aimed right at them. What are they doing? Oh, they're getting some gas," he nonchallantly explained. "Do you think that maybe I could get a job with your company if I were to help you guys out of this, 'little jam?'" Jonny looked at Frank and nearly busted a gut before giving in, "Okay," he continued more composed. "They're stopped at an old gas station about fifty miles northeast of the Englewood Forum. 405 North, exit two-fifty seven," he instructed. "Don't worry, we're sittin' on some pretty good fire power over here, they won't be going anywhere. And yes I promise I won't kill the President, geeezzeee, Eddie, I wasn't born yesterday," Jonny reassured Goodman with a chuckle. "Yeah, right, make it snappy, we'll be here, see ya soon. Bye bye." Jonny slapped his phone shut.

"F.B.I. comin'?" Frank inquired.

"Yeah, man," Jonny quivered with such elation that he felt he could jump up and touch the moon if it was in sight. "I don't believe this, man! This is too good to be true!" Jonny picked up the bazooka and aimed it towards the limo.

"I better turn the camera back on," Frank stepped over and hit record on the camera. "You think we oughta have 'em line up outside the car?" he suggested.

"Yeah," Jonny said with a sigh, grinning ear to ear and not knowing if he should laugh hysterically or cry at this grand victory that was happening right before his eyes.

Jonny placed the hand mic up to his mouth, pressed a button to activate it and took in a breath to address the deviants. He paused, shook his head, and released the push button then casually held it in his hand at his side.

"Listen Frank, do you want to do the honors?" Jonny said in a kindly gesture of honor.

"You mean it?"

"Course I mean it, just let the camera roll and step over here so you're in the picture too," Jonny said.

"Oh yeah, gimmie that thing, Jonny. I've watched a few episodes of "Top Cops" myself." Frank stepped over and reached for the mic and cleared his throat before he spat into it several times to check it.

The limo driver was now checking the oil in the limo and bumped his head on the hood when he heard Frank's voice over the loudspeakers located on top of the Winnebago.

"Okay, dirtbags in the limo! You! That's right, you, you know who I'm talkin' to, get out of your vehicle, and get on your knees, now!" Frank commanded.

"Beeeeautiful, Frank!" Jonny applauded Frank for a well addressed forceful message.

"Was that pretty good, Jonny?"

"It was great, Frank," Jonny gave Frank the ol' thumbs up, then looked towards the limo. A peculiar, quizzicle look slowly came over his face.

Jonny had a queasy feeling in his stomach when he saw the Laker's oldest fan looking out her back window snarling at them. He quickly set down the bazooka and stepped over to the video camera and quickly aimed it towards the limo and zoomed close on her. His heart felt like it might pop right out of his chest as he wondered, who is that? He could read her lips as she spoke.

"Are you talkin' to me?" The elderly woman asked, then looked to her driver, who also appeared surprised and shrugged his shoulders at the loud intrusion.

"Frank?" Jonny felt faint.

"Yeah."

"Who is that?" Jonny appeared nauseous as he popped his head up from the viewfinder.

"Ummm, I'm not sure," Frank said eyeing the two.

Jonny looked to Frank, and Frank to Jonny, both perplexed. "And who's the dude, man?" Jonny wondered.

"Ah, that is a good question, Jonny," Frank replied.

"Let's pack up the gear, do a drive by, see what's goin' on, huh?" Jonny nervously said to Frank.

"Yeah," Frank agreed and they quickly grabbed the bazooka and video camera and carried them to the rig and got inside and drove over to the limo.

Jonny slid open his driver's side window. "Hi there," he said to the driver, who was wiping off the front windshield. "We were just doing some military maneuvers, hope we didn't frighten you folks," Jonny peered inside the window of the limo. He looked down at the little old woman who sat alone in the back seat.

"I'm too pissed off at those damn Lakers to be frightened of anyone, sonny-boy."

180

"Right," Jonny agreed wide-eyed, then looked over at Frank with a pale look on his face. He slid the window shut.

"What happened, Frank?" Jonny appeared like a desperate man who had just received news he was headed for the gallows. "Where'd we go wrong?" he whimpered.

"Be a month to Sunday before I can figure," Frank scratched his head.

"We better get the hell out of here. Eddie's gonna be pissed." Jonny waived a hand up at the old woman, then punched the pedal to the floor as they sped away from the scene.

Jonny proceeded down the same narrow two-laned, rough road they drove in on. The Winnebago nearly got up on two wheels as he sped around corners to quickly get back on the main road to make a discreet departure.

"I'll never get into the F.B.I. now, Frank, ever." Jonny flatly stated.

"Ah, forget about them, heck you've got your own agency anyway," Frank said to cheer up Jonny.

"Yeah, it's not the same though," he replied as they got onto a highway and headed south and fled the scene as quickly as the big rig would allow. The two sat there silent as they sped off into the sunset. Jonny's fists clutched the wheel tightly. "Damn," he hollered, then hit the steering wheel with both hands, which made Frank jump. Dark thoughts clouded his mind as six military choppers flew overhead close enough to touch. Jonny looked over at Frank, who glanced back without saying a word. Then came numerous State patrol vehicles that appeared to be going a hundred miles an hour plus, then several military transport vehicles filled with military personnel sped past, all en route to an old gas station to find an innocent old lady and her driver, who would probably be checking the tires by the time all hell would break loose.

"Say Jonny, I don't think we're on the main highway we came in on," Frank stated.

"Yeah, this is the old highway, less traffic," Jonny flatly said still depressed from feeling like he had let down the world.

"That's an understatement," Frank said not seeing another car on the old road.

"I don't feel too good, Frank," Jonny sounded ill.

"Ah, don't feel bad, shit happens, man," Frank said.

"I feel like crawlin' under a rock," Jonny's voice squeeked as he choked back emotion.

Frank had never heard Jonny sound so despondent, but what could he do. He didn't have the words or couldn't find them. And that's when the thought popped into his brain. It was like magic.

"Hey.....hey.....hey, man," Frank said elongating each word and in a higher pitch than normal. When he said it again is when it caught Jonny's attention. "Man, I almost forgot!"

"Forgot what?" Jonny said like he had just woke up and was in a grumpy mood.

"That computer disc that was in my pocket," Frank said.

"What computer disc?" Jonny's eyes widened with interest.

"The one I took from Debbie's the other night."

"What?" Jonny said showing a little sign of life. "You took a disc from their place?"

"Yeah, man, I took it when you were openin' up the envelope with the pictures in it. But, I do believe, when I jumped that fence runnin' from that rabid-assed dog, who ripped my pocket, it fell out." Jonny looked over and saw Frank's large side pocket was ripped open.

"Ah huh," Jonny said with a tinge of hope and a reborn spark in his eye.

"And I'd bet ya all the rice in China, Jonny, that that disc is somewhere in that yard. It just might have some answers," Frank stated.

"Buddy, you know what the beauty is?"

"What's that?"

"When ya got nothin', you got nothin' to lose," Jonny pressed his foot down on the gas and picked up some speed.

"The guy that lives in that house, "Melio," isn't a very nice fellow either. He's got a gang – The Peronas. Him and some of his amigos came over to the house one day, asked me if I wanted to join up with 'em," Frank said.

"And?" Jonny questioned.

"Well, I was a little hung over that day and still kind of out of it, so I said, well maybe, but what do you have to do to get in? is there some sort of initiation or monthly dues or anything like that?"

"And he said?"

"He says, no, no monthly dues, notheen like that bro, you keell someone and then you in, so easy. He said it like it was as easy as fishin' you can be a gangbanger," Frank explained.

"Sounds like a warm, friendly bunch. Well, we'll just have to wait till it gets good'n dark, then do a little investigative work. " Jonny said.

"There ya go. Ya never know, there could be somethin' on that disc that might save our hides after all Jonny, cause you know what they say?" Frank questioned Jonny who looked over at his buddy.

"Tell me, Frank what do they say?"

"It ain't over till the fat lady sings."

And that sparked Jonny's attention and he looked, in an instant, like a man who had just been shocked back to life. The sun had just started to set and he smiled at Frank as they headed back to East L.A.

Chapter 18

It was ten-forty-five p.m. when Jonny and Frank arrived at Frank's house. From there, they could spy on Debbie's house and see if there was a remote possibility that her and her partners in crime could be held up over there, and then make their way down the street to search for the computer disc. Dressed in black from head to toe, they crouched down on their hands and knees on the kitchen floor and peeked out the back window. Through a slit in the curtains, they could see Debbie's house was as black as the night.

"I'd say they flew the coup, Jonny," Frank said in a hushed manner.

"That's what cowards do when the heat gets turned up a few notches. Let's take a walk, Frank." Jonny pointed to the front door like a military officer would do in the thickets of some jungle, fighting a battle with an unseen enemy. They got up from the sticky kitchen floor, felt their way through the darkened house and stopped at the front door. It was the preparation before the battle.

"Quick check, Frank. Firecracker strip?"

"Check." Frank stated as he checked his pockets.

"Smoke screen canister?"

Frank felt the canister bulging out from a pocket on his thigh. "Check."

"Bullet deflecting pens?"

"Check."

"Let's do it," Jonny somberly said and they quietly exited the house. They casually headed down the vacant street, dressed in traditional all black robbery attire. Getting towards the end of the block, Jonny gave the arm signal to stop.

"Frank?" Jonny whispered.

"What?" Frank bumped into Jonny.

"That was the signal to stop. We're here," Jonny whispered in an agitated manner.

"Sorry," Frank whispered back.

They paused a brief moment and with the exception of the lively sounds of the street jungle; distant sirens, low end thumping, hollering coming from somewhere, yapping dogs, screeching tires from a nearby artial, and occasional pops, there appeared to be not a soul in sight. Jonny gave a nod and military hand signal to proceed. They gingerly walked in between two run down houses, where no signs of life emitted, then stopped at a chest high wooden gate, which led into the backyard that was behind the house where the disc was lost.

Jonny, still feeling every bit the military commander of a top secret, covert mission, gave some unusual, confusing hand gestures to Frank, who thought he might be initiating some break dance moves as a relaxation maneuver, so he started to mimmick the movements then embellished them with something of his own added to each command motion. The two could have been viewed as a mime team if only they had painted their faces white instead of black.

Jonny, growing more frustrated at the behavior, initiated his hand signals once again in a more forceful manner expecting Frank to carry out his orders.

But Frank merely continued making his arms appear wave like as one arm went down, then up as if the wave rolled over his shoulders and down onto the other arm which did the same motion.

"Frank!" Jonny whispered.

"Yeah?"

"What are you doin'?"

"I'm loosenin' up man, isn't that what you're doin?'"

"No! Now, are you gonna open that gate, or are we gonna stand here until somebody shoots us?" Jonny seethed in a hushed manner.

"I didn't know what you were sayin', man!" Frank whispered loudly defending himself.

"Shhhhh!"

"Alright," Frank said, then reached his hand over and unlocked the wooden gate.

"Slowly, Frank," Jonny said at a barely audible level with more breath and mouth movement than volume.

Frank pushed open the gate as slowly as he could, but it's rusted hinges eaked out like fingernails on a chalkboard. He opened it just enough for them to get through and they entered the backyard that was shrouded in darkness. There was an eerie quiet as they tiptoed into the fenced backyard. Frank began to slowly close the rusted gate. Jonny tapped him on the shoulder. "Leave it open, just in case," he whispered. Frank nodded.

Jonny gave a hand signal to hold up.

"Umph, sorry Jonny." Frank bumped into Jonny in the darkness. What sounded like several cars and a raucous group had just arrived at the house they were about to visit.

"Great, Melio and his gang just pulled up," Frank whispered in Jonny's ear.

"Wonderful. You think they'll head inside and sip some tea and listen to old rock records?" Jonny suggested.

"Hell no, they'll sip on their tequila and whip up a batch of crystal-meth, then dole it out to the neighborhood kids," Frank replied.

"A group that shares, they sound like a fine bunch. Let's find that disc and get the hell out of here."

They slowly approached the cracked and weathered, six-foot, back fence that hadn't seen paint in twenty years and stood in the darkness where not even a cricket dared make a sound. Some yelling began to erupt from the gang members. They were all masters at the fine art of profanity. F'n this and F'n that, and bitch this and bitch that, the group of about six continued with their banter from the side of the neighboring house in the driveway until Frank and Jonny heard what sounded like a gun pop, then another and another. It sounded like a firecracker followed by some ooh's and ahh's mixed in with some other profane gruntings. "Man you wasted him," was heard coming from someone.

"That bitch had it comin', take him out back," Melio instructed his fellow gang members.

Jonny and Frank listened in shock as the group struggled to lift the now dead weight.

"Just drag the bitch," one of the gang members suggested.

They could hear grunts and groans as someone opened the gate, then they proceeded to drag the corpse into the yard.

"Bitch weighs a ton," someone complained.

They listened as the gate to the adjoining backyard closed and the group entered the house.

"Aren't you sad you didn't join the group," Jonny whispered to Frank.

"Oh yeah," Frank whispered back.

"Let's pull a couple of these boards out, we can crawl through," Jonny quietly suggested. Frank followed Jonny's instructions and the two squatted

186

down and reached from the bottom and slowly pulled out one of the eight-inch wide boards from the bottom. The old rusted nails, that had seen years of sun and rain, belched out a wretched sound as they pried it away from the lower two-by-four and let it hang by the upper nails. Then, a sound that made the two freeze. A porch light from Melio's house came on and somebody exited the back door. Jonny and Frank peeked through the slit from the pryed off fence board and watched as Melio and another gang member, who carried a fifth of something, emerged. Melio had his hand under his Doberman's collar, then opened the back gate and let the dog free in the yard.

They peeked through slits in the fence and watched as Melio spoke to his friend who chugged from the bottle of either based substance to numb himself of wretchedness.

"We won't have to bury him," Melio said with a tinge of delight as he and his fellow gang member watched the dog as it went right for the fresh blood from the bullet wounds on the corpse. "Give me that." Melio yanked the bottle away from the other gang member then chugged from the fifth. After several large gulps he pulled the bottle away from his mouth. "Killer will eat him, you watch," he wiped off the cheap whiskey that dribbled down his chin, then reached for his gun again and yelled at the dog.

"Get back, Killer, stupid mutt," he said then fired several more shots into the corpse to make it a more inviting, juicy meal for the animal.

The two stood there and passed the whiskey bottle back and forth while they watched the dog go for the blood, then they laughed a sick laughter and went back inside. The porchlight shut off and with the exception of the animals' eyes that appeared to glow in the night, there was only darkness.

Jonny and Frank just stood still a moment and listened as the dog made unusual sounds that nearly made them sick.

"Remind me to get sick later, would you," Jonny whispered to Frank, who just nodded in silence and reached for another board to slowly pull out and away from the fence. Once again the old fence groaned a wretched sound as they pried another one of its boards free. They paused a moment to make sure their sound went undetected. Killer growled at the intruding sound, but resumed tearing into the ex gang member who lie dead in the dirt.

The two boards were now loose and hung there so they could easily be pulled back, then slip into the backyard unnoticed.

Earlier, they had stopped to pick up a juicy t-bone to be served very rare to occupy the hungry, vicious pet, while they searched for the computer disc.

Frank pulled the goodsized steak out from under his shirt that was wrapped in a plastic bag and handed it to Jonny.

Jonny reached inside the bag with three fingers and pulled the bloody piece of meat from the bag, poked his head through the fence to take a peek, then tossed the meat as close to Killer as he could. The dog paused a moment to give a brief growl at the slab of meat that hit the dirt close by, but ignored it to the larger meal before it.

"Here goes nothin'," Jonny entered through the fence while he kept an eye on the dog to see his reaction to him entering. All he could see was two beady glowing eyes as the dog glanced up and paused a moment, then immediately resumed its task. Jonny, on hands and knees, started to search around the fence for the computer disc. Frank proceeded through the fence right behind him and the both of them sifted through the dirt and other obstacles for the disc.

"Oh, Frank? Watch out for the..." And before Jonny could finish his statement, Frank gasped as his hand sunk into a fragrant, soft goo.

"Oh, shit," Frank moaned.

"It's a mine field, buddy. Where 'bouts were you when you jumped over?" Jonny inquired barely loud enough for even Killer to hear.

"Kind of right in the middle, I think," Frank whispered while he attempted to hold his breath from the foul odor.

"You mean over here?" Jonny crawled over on all fours to a different spot in the yard that was grown over with weeds and wild growth.

"Yeah," Frank agreed.

"I don't see it, Frank," Jonny whispered with a tone of desperation. Then a light came on from the backyard they arrived by and someone stepped outside and lifted a trash can lid, disposed some garbage, then dropped the lid back onto the metal can and went back inside.

Both held their breath in the darkness until all was quiet.

"You think I should go over and tell him he forgot to shut the light off," Frank suggested.

"Find the disc first, then you can tell him." Jonny continued scouring his fingers through the dirt and weeds next to the fence.

"Nothin," Frank whispered in a discouraging tone, then, a noise came from the side door of Melio's house as it opened. Both Jonny and Frank perked up like a couple of bird dogs. Jonny gave one of his military hand signals to Frank, but before he completed it, Frank was already through the slats in the fence where the chances of being shot decreased by twenty percent. Jonny scurried on his hands and knees over to the open slat and kicked up a small cloud of dust as he also shot through the fence like a rock from a slingshot to the other side, then ever so gently pushed the boards back as close to their original position as he could, but far enough to still get a glimpse into Melio's yard. The two were like sitting ducks under the flood-light that remained on in the yard they had entered by, but they had no choice but to stay put. They listened as the gang of thugs emerged from the house with flashlights to be entertained by Killer, who enjoyed his midnight snack. They laughed it up as they passed the whiskey bottle from member to member and practiced their cursing as they enjoyed the show. Then a beam of light from one of the flashlights landed on something in the dirt, which caught one of the member's attention.

"Hey, man, what the hell is that?" one of them questioned.

Jonny peeked through a crack in one of the boards and could see that he had his flashlight aimed at the steak.

"He saw the steak," Jonny mouthed to Frank, who appeared to have stopped breathing, then glanced over the backyard to see if there were any obstacles if they had to high-tail it. And at that brief moment, Frank's eye caught onto something shiny lying in the grass and he kept low to the ground and crawled on his belly over to the object like someone who was on a top secret, covert, military mission.

"Frank!" Jonny desperately whispered.

And Frank picked up the computer disc and gave it a little kiss, then turned around and held it up for Jonny to see. Jonny's eyes lit up like two sparklers on the fourth of July and he held the thumbs up to Frank and smiled. It was the disc.

Jonny's smile faded as he thought it peculiar that the rowdy group had silenced their banter. There was a thump on the fence as if someone had kicked it. He held his breath to listen, then a hand reached over the fence and fired off a couple wild rounds that sounded like an innocent little pop and then recoiled itself like a deadly snake. Then another popping sound, and another and Jonny cried out for the whole neighborhood to hear it, "Run, Frank! Run!" then buried his face in the weeds up against the fence.

Frank sprang from his belly like a darting Jack rabbit caught in a blind fleeing a deadly predator.

Jonny frantically fumbled through several pockets until he pulled out a string of firing caps that were used as a diversion tactic in the military. He pulled a string from the packet and tossed it into an adjacent yard to Melio's to give the enemy the impression they were being fired upon from another direction. He then reached for a smoke canister and unfastened it from his belt and tossed it into the yard.

"This is the police, you're surrounded," he called out to the thugs. And it worked. Jonny could hear the group yelling F'n mother F'n this, and mother F'n that, and you're ass is dead you mother F'n bitch. And they fired their guns in every direction under the stars but at Jonny as he made a quick path and followed in the direction right behind Frank and back to the Winnebago.

Out of breath and panting hard, he arrived at the Winnebago parked down the street. He stopped at the side door of the rig and in the darkness reached into his pocket for his keys.

"Oh, Frank," Jonny called out, his voice shaking like his knees. And immediately Frank popped out from under the Winnebago.

"Where ya been?" Frank said.

"Oh, I thought I'd stay behind and mingle a little, you know." Jonny said as he attempted to steady his hand to open the door.

"I'm not sprayin' starter fluid in that carburetor, Jonny, and get my butt shot off by Melio or his trigger happy amigos," Frank reminded him.

"I realize that Frank. It should start, I hope to God!" He unlocked the door and Frank followed Jonny up the steps and into the Winnebago, then slammed the door behind them.

"Make sure that's locked, would you Frank!" Jonny said like a man who had just run for his life.

"Oh, you know it," Frank locked the door securely behind him, then hurried up to the passenger's seat where he sat there while Jonny anxiously attempted to start the rig. In a continuous effort he stomped down on the pedal hard enough each time to put a hole in the floorboard.

Jonny slid open his side window and listened as the popping sounds continued like from some grand holiday celebration in the distance. He pulled out his cell phone and opened it to dial a number while he continued to stomp on the pedal repeatedly.

"Who ya callin'?" Frank inquired.

"Thought I'd wake the block watch commander, Frank, let him know that World War III is in full swing."

"Good luck," Frank said knowing there was no such thing in this neighborhood.

"911 operator, state your emergency," a woman on the other end of the phone stated. And at just that moment the engine started and Jonny put the rig in gear and slowly proceeded down the narrow darkened street as he spoke to the operator.

"I'd like to report that, well, there's a little gun battle that's ensuing over at around the twelve-thousand block of east Oleander street," Jonny stated. "And you might want to wake those SWAT boys up and get 'em over here, pronto. Oh and a guy that goes by the name, Melio, just killed a guy," Jonny paused to listen before responding, "Shot him, and then fed him to his dog in the backyard," Jonny casually said while he continued driving slowly down the street so not to arouse any suspicions. "His last name? Ah," Jonny looked over to Frank.

"Vohas or Johas, something like that."

Jonny fed the information Frank gave back to the 911 operator, who found the whole ordeal a little hard to believe.

"You think we'd joke about somebody killing someone? Oh, just the feeding them to their dog part. I see, yeah, I know it sounds pretty gross. Maam?" Jonny said to the woman, "Maam," he said again, but the operator must've thought it was a prank call and began to scold him, and at that point he had just about had it, "Maam, would you just shut up and listen!" He sprayed his words onto the windshield, then pounded his foot down onto the brake pedal to halt the beheamoth in the street. He held the cell phone out his side window for the woman to hear for herself. And the gang was still shooting as the long string of timed firing caps continued popping intermittently and the return fire continued popping in reply and the whole neighborhood sounded as if the tanks could roll in at any moment.

"Did you hear that? Those aren't firecrackers lady!" Jonny enunciated each word in an attempt to power drill the message into the woman's brain.

He took a breath to calm himself. "My name? My name is Law, Jonny Law, gotta run," Jonny slapped the phone shut and they drove out of harms way.

Just as they did, Melio and one of his partners in evil got wise to the fire cap pops and searched the neighborhood thirsty for blood. They ran from between the houses and into the street and under a lone streetlight just as Jonny's Winnebago was driving away. Melio's fellow gang member held his gun out sideways and was about to shoot at the back of Jonny's home on wheels.

"No!" Melio said in a manner that halted the thug from firing. "It's not them," he said in a ridiculing manner, then recited a dictionary of profanity as they stood there looking in every direction for something that was right in front of them. All of their false gold jewelry and their stylish hanging baggies, and muscle shirts that showed off a collection of tattoos, couldn't ease their dis-ease of being duped. They looked around a moment longer until sirens could be heard approaching, then quickly disappeared and slithered into the darkness of the night.

A short while later and miles away, sheltered by some large elms at a secluded park, Jonny and Frank hovered over Jonny's computer trying to figure out the password of the newly found disc they obtained from the kidnappers.

An hour and a half had passed and they were growing weary as it approached 3:00 am. They had entered every imaginable password they could think of that might be the key to viewing the contents on the disc.

"Starfield, Starfield," Jonny pondered to himself as Frank held his head in his hands from exhaustion.

"Pluto!" Jonny exclaimed to rouse Frank.

"You already entered every planet in the solar system, Jonny. That's not it," Frank wearily stated.

"Damn!" Jonny said in frustraton. "I just don't get it." His eyes had become bloodshot and tired. He typed in anything that popped into his mind as rapidly as he could then popped a middle finger down hard on the enter button.

"Invalid entry, invalid entry, invalid entry! I am sick of seeing that stupid message." Jonny shouted revealing his growing frustration.

"Say, maybe it has something to do with the word Sphere." Frank momentarily showed a morsel of life.

Jonny's eyes grew wide with excitement. "Yes, 001752, I love you man, because?" Jonny frantically typed the word as Frank watched. "Because," Jonny typed the word in every format possible, small case, all caps, first letter capped, first letter small case, spaces in between, space between first letter, capped followed by the remainder of the word. "Because," he continued, "You are amazingly wrong," he said with a deflated tone of voice.

"Wait a second," Jonny said then sounded like he was dreaming when he repeated the phrase, "Wait a second."

"What?" Frank sounded as if he might fall over unconscious at any moment.

Jonny's eyes lit up as if he had seen a precious gem. "He is Viktor," Jonny turned to look at Frank.

"Huh?" Frank flatly responded as he watched Jonny type.

"You didn't hear it, Frank, I was the one wearing the earpiece, remember?"

Frank just shook his head not knowing what Jonny was talking about.

"When their leader, when she introduced their leader, that's what she called him." Jonny hit the enter button.

"Holy toledo! You did it! That was it, man!" Frank lit up coming back to life.

"Ahhhhhhh!!!!!!!!!!!!!" Jonny sang out the highest note in his range. "Yes, yes, slap me on the back yes! And that was my impersonation of a heavenly choir, by the way, Mr. Miller." They waited a moment as a percentage graph indicated the information was being loaded. "She's loadin' up Frank, looks like a lotta pages. " Jonny said with a smile.

"Boy howdy, you said it," Frank said as they studied the screen.

"Hmnn?" Jonny appeared a little perplexed as a picture of a beach appeared.

"Man, I hope this is the right disc, Jonny, cause that looks like waterfront property or some damn thing," Frank said as the two looked at the screen.

"Zane Grey, Cat, Is?" Frank uttered with a question in his voice as he read the caption below the picture.

"Zane Grey, Cat Is?" Jonny repeated, then looked blankly a moment to Frank, then, it was as if the words fell out of his mouth. "Zane Grey Hotel, Catalina Island, that's what it is." Jonny looked back at the computer screen. "It's a blue- print. Tell me Frank, why would you need a blue print of a hotel?" He continued to press the scroll forward key.

"You got me, man."

"Depths of the water around the island." Jonny looked to Frank in question. "Their leader was speaking from a submarine, man." He looked back to the screen. "Schedules of Navy and Coastguard vessels," Jonny highlighted with his mouse.

"Man, looks like they got it all worked out, Jonny, departure time too," Frank said.

"1:00 am." Jonny said reading from the screen. "What's the date, Frank?"

"Twelfth, game was on the eleventh, man," Frank replied.

"Well, that's good. They haven't taken him yet. And look what that says," Jonny highlighted a sentence via his mouse on the screen, which Frank read.

"Eliminate Secret Service at Zane Grey, wait for signal. That doesn't sound too good."

"Should have read the fine print in between the lines fellas, where it says, when you're dealing with scum-balls, prepare for the shaft," Jonny said.

"Yeah, probably give 'em a nice meal, then a bullet between the eyes," Frank added.

"Right," Jonny agreed. "What do you say we take a trip to the island, bright and early, 001752," Jonny suggested.

"Sounds like a plan. I still have the keys to the in-laws boat, they won't miss it for a day or two. It's a tiny piece a crap, but it'll get us there," Frank offered.

"Right. I'll dump this file onto the F.B.I. menu, convert any non-believers," Jonny said as his fingers did a quick dance over the keys. His computer speakers chimed as he opened his email to send the contents of the disc and a little note, requesting some backup, then signed, Jonny Law at the end.

"That should do it," he placed the cursor over the send icon, then clicked on his mouse.

"You think they'll believe ya this time after our little foo-pah?" Frank questioned.

"Oh, probably not." Jonny pondered a brief moment all the times he had contacted the bureau in the past with information of suspiscious activities by evildoers that they had shrugged off. He looked Frank in the eye with new-found determination. "But, nobody said it was easy being a hero."

"Boy howdy, you said it, Jonny. This is like the night before the championship game, buddy, if you know what I mean," Frank paused. "And you know what they say?"

"Fat lady again, Frank?"

"Nope."

"Share it brother, I've never been in one of those locker room huddles?"

"Losin' ain't an option. We're either comin' back with our President, or we ain't comin' back, man," Frank said with a confidence Jonny had never realized.

"That's right, Frank, that is right," Jonny held out his hand for Frank to lock onto then twist over, tap on top, tap on bottom, then tap knuckles together.

"Time to get some sleep, tomorrow we start living Frank, really living," Jonny said with a growing fire in his heart. He shut down the computer and the two laid down to get some sleep.

It was quiet in the park and the hypnotic sounds of crickets were comforting, Jonny thought as his heavy head hit the pillow.

"Say, Jonny," Frank called out from his bench seat bed.

"Yeah."

"You think the public knows about the president?"

"Nope. And they never will, cause two of the biggest losers that ever walked the halls of Freemont High are gonna save him," Jonny said. And not two seconds had passed and Jonny could hear Frank sawing some big logs, and he too quickly dosed off after setting his watch for a 6:00 am wake-up.

Chapter 19

The next day, after sleeping through the early alarm, then retrieving the keys to Frank's inlaw's boat, Jonny followed Frank through the maze of expensive looking boats and yachts of every size that were moored at Marina Del Ray. The two appeared like typical boaters clad in bright colored summery attire, with sunglasses, and flops on their feet and who were weighted down with an assortment of bags. Bags strapped over their shoulders, around their necks, and one in each hand. Jonny continued walking as Frank tossed his golf bag into what appeared to be the smallest boat in the marina.

"Nothing like the smell of the sea, Frank!" Jonny called out for every boater in the marina to hear.

"Jonny! Where are you goin'?"

Jonny stopped, then turned around and reluctantly approached what appeared to be a lifeboat of one of the larger vessels.

"Is this it?" Jonny inquired with reservations.

"Yep, here she be," Frank replied.

Jonny's face appeared to be taken over by an assortment of looks from various feelings and concerns he was obviously having regarding the boat.

"Carpathia?" Jonny read the name that was written on its side and stern. "Is she seaworthy?" He inquired with a tone of trepidation.

"'Course she's seaworthy. We got lifejackets anyway, Jonny. Not to worry when you're with the captain." Frank affirmed.

They loaded up the boat, then Frank placed the key into the ignition and started the snappy Evinrude 150 engine. They made a slow departure through the collection of boats docked in the harbor, and when Frank saw the last of the signs that read GO SLOW, he gunned it.

The small boat bounced over the choppy ocean waters that lie between the mainland and Santa Catalina Island. Jonny was quick to find his sea legs and got drenched from head to toe as they pounded over wave after wave after wave enroute to their destination. He had decided to ride on the front of the fresh water- craft holding onto a mooring rope for stability. He appeared to be either surfing or riding a wild bull with one hand holding on for dear life, the other held up to the blue sky as the spray of the ocean periodically drenched his body.

"Ride it, Jonny, ride it!" Frank called out from behind the wheel.

Jonny knew this was an important mission and the cool ocean water and scent would peak his level of alertness by the time they arrived. His touristy looking Hawaiian shirt flopped over his orange colored t-shirt that he wore beneath it, as the spray of salty sea water drenched his entire body. He pointed to a school of jumping dolphins that reflected off his mirrored sunglasses and that appeared to guide them along their way.

"Frank! Sharks!" Frank acknowledged the sighting and nodded. And when the small island came into view the dolphins seemed to magically disappear into the vast ocean.

There must've been at least a hundred boats moored in the bay at Catalina, and the pier was busy with people arriving and departing from the island at around eleven thirty in the morning when they arrived. Frank had come in a little quick on his approach to the dock, which sprung Jonny from the front of the boat and onto the dock where he landed on his hands and feet then rolled to break his fall.

"I'm okay," he called out to the other boaters on the dock as he quickly sprung to his feet, then helped Frank tie down the small, black, fourteen foot, freshwater fishing boat. As Jonny was tying down the front, Frank was leaning over the edge of the boat getting the rubber bumpers in place.

Jonny looked up when he heard the splash. While Frank leaned over to fish for one of the rubber bumpers, that was slightly out of his reach, he had fallen over board. It was the fatigue factor. Jonny shook his head and realized people made stupid mistakes on little sleep, so he continued tying down the boat.

"Arggghh!" Frank gurggled out when his head momentarily popped up from the cold salty water with seaweed covering it, then went back under.

"Oh, Frank," Jonny casually called out after he finished tying down the boat. He stood up and called out to his buddy again as his eyes scanned the dark waters around the boat. "This is not the time to take a dip - Frank. We've got people to meet, places to go, buddy." Jonny appeared perplexed as his eyes darted around the immediate area searching for Frank. "If this is your idea of some sort of get even joke, you can stay under there all day if you like, cause I'm gonna head up, find a nice comfortable hotel room that's got some pay per view, kick off the shoes and relax ol' buddy. Frank?

Frank?" Jonny called out loud enough for the people on main street to hear as he stood there wondering if he swam under the dock, where he was catching his breath in the space underneath it, then would jump up when he bent over to look, and when he least expected it, surprise him. Should he lie down on the dock and put his face closer to the water and see if he could see him. No, he thought to himself, that's what he had seen in every horror movie he had ever watched. The killer then grabs his victim and pulls them under and they're never seen again. Not that Frank would do that he debated with himself as he scratched his head. This is not amusing. "Okay Frank, you win, alright." He called down to Frank. Nothing.

A well-dressed elderly woman, who was with her husband, tapped Jonny on the shoulder. "Young man?"

"Yeah," Jonny said taken off guard.

"Does your friend know how to swim?" The old woman kindly inquired.

"Why didn't I take those swimmin' lessons!" The comment Frank had made after the rig plunged into the ocean flashed through Jonny's mind.

"Frank!!!" he screamed and immediately dove into the cold water.

A small group of boaters quickly gathered around and watched in near silence as the waters grew still where Jonny dove in to rescue Frank.

"He's been under for nearly two-minutes, maybe someone should call the coastguard," one of the onlookers suggested.

"I just asked him if his friend knew how to swim," the elderly woman stated, now with her handkerchief out, fearing the worst as her distinguished looking husband, who wore a Yacht Club cap, consoled her.

"It's alright dear, there's nothing we can do," the elderly man said to his wife. And just at that moment, Jonny's head sprung from the water like he had been ejected from a cannon.

"Somebody help, for Godsakes!" he gasped.

Several of the onlookers applauded at the sight of Jonny who pulled his friend up by his brightly colored Hawaiian shirt.

A marina worker picked up a pole that was lying on the dock and held it out. Jonny reached for it with one hand while he still had a hold of Frank's bright colored shirt with the other. He had seen the bright colors in the murky waters, then pulled him up from the bottom.

Several men assisted in getting Frank onto the dock. They quickly rolled him over to get the water out of him. One of the men started pushing down onto Frank's back and he coughed up what appeared to be a gallon of water.

"He's coughing! He's coughing! That's a good sign, isn't it?" Jonny cried out.

"He'll be alright. You saved his life," another man, who wore a fisherman's vest on with a collection of lures attached to it, stated to Jonny before he walked away.

Jonny, a little chilled from the cold water, breathed a sigh of relief as Frank slowly came back to full consciousness.

"Whoa, what happened?" Frank inquired, then coughed up some more water, as Jonny remained hunched over looking down at his friend.

And the onlookers, knowing everything was alright, quickly dispersed and continued with their touristy business.

"You fell in, Frank. You okay?"

"Yeah, I think so. That's some salty water, man." Frank coughed up more of the salty water before he sat upright.

"Right. Swimming lessons for you when we get back, huh?" Jonny suggested.

"Oh yeah. And thanks for fishin' me out. I owe you one."

"No problemo." Jonny pulled seaweed from Frank's yellow t-shirt and flowered short pants that stuck to his plus sized body like glue as he got to his feet, then shook his head and body like somebody's pet lab.

"Okay. Stay right there, Frank. I'm gonna get into the boat, grab the bags, and hand 'em to you. No jumping in, okay. I'm just kiddin' ya man," Jonny said. He chuckled as he hopped back into the boat, then handed Frank the bags; His long, military green duffle bag, Frank's golf club bag, which he convinced Jonny would make them blend in to the locals carrying his clubs, two dark colored duffle bags, and two hand bags, which were all the bags in sight, then he stepped out of the boat.

"Ready?" Jonny still felt the up and down motion of the sea beneath his legs.

"Yeah," Frank said and they picked up the collection of bags and proceeded to walk the length of the long dock, dripping wet, to set foot on the island, then find out the location of the Zane Grey Hotel.

"Carpathia?" a voice called out, which Jonny and Frank paid no mind to as they continued walking.

"Carpathia! Hey you!" An old man on the dock, whose face was darkly tanned and appeared like old aged leather, called out to them.

The two turned around.

"You forgot to pay," the old man said.

Frank stammered. "Ah, yeah, geese, you know I think I lost my wallet in that little plunge I took and, well, we're only gonna be here for a little while," Frank explained hoping for some sympathy.

"Well, everyone pays, friend," the man said.

Jonny smiled at the man, then pulled out his drenched wallet and took out his last remaining, soggy five-dollar bill out and handed it to the man.

"Keep the change," Jonny said with a warm smile.

The old man laughed. "Ha ha, that's funny, nightly fees are twenty dollars per night for a small boat like yours," he said to them.

Jonny looked at the man distrustingly. "Seems a little high, don't you think?"

"No." The man shook his head.

"Come on, Frank, there's probably another island around here we can go to." Jonny sneered at the man.

"If you buy a can of gas maybe you can make it to Hawaii," the man said and laughed out loud.

Jonny and Frank walked back to their boat and placed their bags back into it and reboarded, then pulled away from the dock in search of something a little less pricey.

A couple miles down the coastline from the resort they found a secluded cove a short distance away and moored the boat to a small tree that stuck out from some rocks that led up an embankment. From there they hiked their way into the main street area that bustled with vacationers and tourists.

They had walked about a block down the main street where mainly vacationers and a few locals walked in every direction, then stopped to eye the terrain.

"This guy'll know where it's at." Jonny approached a distinguished looking man who had a goatee and wore a French barrette and who was looking into the viewfinder of a camera strapped around his neck.

"Excuse me, could you kindly direct us to the Zane Grey Hotel?" he said.

The man looked at Jonny blankly as if he didn't understand English and said what sounded like a "New," then quickly walked away from them.

"Locals are friendly," Frank said.

They both appeared like typical lost tourists. Each looked up and down each street in every direction. Jonny lifted up his patrolman-like shades a brief moment to see if that helped, as did Frank. It didn't.

"Thanks for the shades, man. Where'd you get these?"

"Army surplus. I buy 'em by the bag. I'm always losin' em. One of the hotels should have a map," Jonny said to Frank as his wondering eye caught a weathered looking sign down the street with the words Hideout Hotel written on it.

"Bingo," he said to Frank and then gave a quick hand gesture in the same direction and they began walking.

Jonny and Frank entered the old run down hotel and stood in the lobby and looked around for any signs of life. Not a soul. Jonny removed his sunglasses and studied the once, colorful, elegant looking wallpaper that had yellowed and begun to peel away from the old walls.

"They're probably cleaning the rooms," he casually said to Frank who had a finger in his ear trying to release some of the salt water that had entered from his plunge.

"Yeah." Frank agreed.

"Somebody'll be down in a minute." Jonny glanced up some stairs that led to rooms.

"Pretty scummy place," Frank commented with no reservations.

Jonny elevated his nose several degrees and took a whiff, "It's a toilet bowl, that's for sure. What a stench," he then stated as a staple point to the first comment. And just at that moment a noise could be heard coming from behind the front desk. Jonny looked to Frank, and Frank to Jonny. It was a dull thud, then another, and another.

"A pretty scummy place, huh, and a toilet bowl, you say?" the old curator of the run down hotel called out from behind the front desk while seated in his wheelchair. He reached for a concealable handgun that he placed under the blanket that covered his legs, then struggled to maneuver his wheel chair out from behind the front desk to confront the belligerent pair. The frail, salty bearded man had a striking similarity to Osama Bin Laden, so much so that he could be the man's twin if he wasn't in fact the terrorist himself. Frank immediately gave the man a second look. He recognized the face from somewhere, uncertain though from where, as he jogged his foggy memory. Jonny was more focused on getting the map so he paid no mind to the man's distinctive appearance.

The man eyed the two potential guests dripping attire as Jonny spoke. "No, no, no, I think you misunderstood," he warmly stated with the genuineness of a politician to the old man. "We were referring to the last establishment we were just at," Jonny tactfully explained, enunciating each word with a broad smile. "This is a wonderful place, isn't it, Frank?" Jonny smiled at

Frank to solicit some back up and all he got were some peculiar looks and motions of the head, which he merely brushed off as Frank still trying to jar the water from his ear.

"Yeah," Frank reticently agreed. "In fact we'll probably want to book the whole next month here for the family reunion," Frank said to the man as his eyes shifted about with the sincerity of a used car salesman. The old man's eyes widened an increment.

"If we could just obtain a map of the city with the directions to the Zane Grey Hotel," Jonny added.

"I have the map," the man stated with a distant accent. "How many people will be staying at the hotel?" he questioned the two with a quick, rythmic tongue.

Jonny looked to Frank, who shrugged his shoulders, then he smiled back at the old man. "Well," Jonny hem-hawed with a warm smile. "How many people will your lovely establishment accommodate?" he asked with the innocence of a puppy and with such a genuineness that could generate warmth in the coldest of hearts.

"With hide-a-beds, fifty-six-people, we can accommodate," the man said. Once again Jonny glanced to Frank, who stared at the man with a reluctant, questionable demeanor.

"Can you believe this luck, Frank? That's how many are in our family," he said to the man smiling and as if he was in total amazement at this serendipitous moment he was having. The man's eyes then appeared to roll back into his head briefly as he sat there almost in a trance.

Jonny looked to Frank, then back to the man. "You know you look kind of familiar." Jonny said as someone would who had a vague recollection of crossing paths somewhere, but couldn't pinpoint exactly where. "Does he look familiar to you, Frank?"

"Ah?," Frank stammered. "I don't know, ah, yeah a little I suppose," he hesitated.

The sly looking old man stroked his long grey beard with one hand, and slowly placed his other hand under his blanket, as he continued staring into space. "Many people say that, I do not know why. Let me get my book, do not go." He wheeled himself behind the front desk with the same bumping and thumping as occurred when he presented himself.

"Don't forget the map," Jonny reminded him. He peeked his head up a little in an attempt to see over the desk, then to Frank who silently mouthed the word "terrorist," to Jonny, who simply ignored whatever it was Frank was trying to say as they listened to the man fumbling around behind the desk for his book and a travel map.

Jonny read a small sign behind the front desk that read, WE RENT GOLF CARTS.

"Oh and sir, we'd like to rent one of your golf carts if that wouldn't be too much trouble for you," Jonny called out over the desk at the man.

"No trouble, no trouble," the man replied.

In no time Jonny and Frank were headed out the door with the map they had requested.

"Jonny, you know what I was thinkin' that guy reminds me of?" Frank paused while he glanced back at the old man through the large front window that had the name of the establishment written on it. "What's his name?" Frank paused to think a moment. "Terrorist guy, oh shoot, what's his name, Jonny?" he paused again.

"I don't know, Frank," Jonny impatiently replied while he wrestled to un-fold the large map.

"Osemma Ben Lowdin," Frank cried out as they proceeded onto the busy sidewalk. "That's his name."

Jonny continued looking down at the map. "If that guy's Osamma Bamma Slamma, then I'm Mother Teresa, Frank, come on, let's focus here." Jonny insisted.

"Well, sure looked like him to me," Frank countered.

"Zane Grey, Zane Grey." Jonny studied the map. "Okay, there it is right there," he stated to Frank with his finger on the location.

"Jonny are you listenin' to me, man?" Frank questioned.

Agitated, Jonny replied still focused on the map. "Yes Frank, I'm listen-ing…we take a right on that road, right there, go down two blocks, then" Jonny looked up a moment to view the street, "Take another right, then head up Chimes Tower Road, grab the President and get the hell out of here," Jonny matter of factly stated as if they were picking someone up for lunch, then leaving.

"Call me crazy, or call me crazy, but that guy was either Osemma Ben Lawdin, or his twin brother, for pete's sake."

"Frank, oh Frank." Jonny chuckled as he shook his head. "He's only been dead for probably five years." Jonny said in such a convincing manner that he even believed the statement himself.

"Huh?" Frank appeared perplexed.

"Yeah, man, in a bunker in Talaban, Afghanistan. They nailed his ass." Jonny said as they approached their golf cart.

"Are you sure?"

"Yes, I'm sure. They have this knew thing called DNA, Frank. Don't you watch the news, man?" Jonny insisted, more in an effort to calm Frank down, whom he figured to be merely under duress from breaking free from the evil clutches and the spell of booze and more recently nearly drowning to death.

"Come on, you want to drive?" Jonny said in a playful manner as he placed his bags into the cart. He held out the keys to Frank, and just when Frank reached for them, he tossed them into the air for him to catch, then hopped in the passenger seat of the last remaining cart parked on the side of the establishment.

"Yeah, sure," Frank replied. He sounded a little relieved from Jonny's reassuring comment regarding the terrorist as he tossed his bags on top of Jonny's, then hopped in the driver's seat and started up the two-seater and they proceeded out of the parking lot and passed the front of the hotel. The old man had mysteriously gotten up from his wheelchair and spied on them from the side of the window as they drove past.

A moment later Jonny reached for his cell phone and dialed a number. "Let's try this again," Jonny said.

"F.B.I.?" Frank questioned.

"Right." Jonny replied.

"Think they'll believe ya this time," Frank inquired.

"Oh, probably not," Jonny casually replied. "Hello," Jonny said then paused to listen to a recorded message at F.B.I. headquarters. "Machine again, man that is one long beep, must have a lot of messages," Jonny said to Frank. "Eddie?" Jonny paused to clear his throat, "It's me again, Jonny, say listen, real sorry about the, ah, you know mix up at the gas station there and the wrong limo, geeessssee, I wouldn't have a, well a Chinaman's chance in trying to explain that one to you, but anyway, got some good news. We've followed the kidnappers to Catalina Island. All the info is loaded onto the F.B.I.'s main menu. We're going to need some heavy-duty backup over here, pronto if you catch my drift. Hope you guys can make it. See your boys soon, over and out," Jonny then slapped shut his cell phone and looked out at the gorgeous view of the ocean and at least a hundred boats moored in the bay as he and Frank continued heading up Chimes Tower Road.

Jonny closed his eyes a moment and soaked up the warm sun and soft breeze and breathed in the scent of the ocean as the cart proceeded up

Chimes Tower Road. He couldn't help but think of Karen and wonder what she might be doing. And just as a clear picture of her pretty face and sexy smile filled his mind, Frank's voice snapped him to the present.

"What's this up ahead?"

Jonny opened his eyes. "Road block?" He observed the two, body builder types whose bodies were greased down and were clad in muscle shirts and shorts. A large cart filled with dead branches blocked the road not allowing them to pass.

One of the men stepped in front of the cart, while the other stood behind it as they approached.

"Hi fellas," Jonny warmly greeted the two, who starred coldly back at them. "You know, we're just a little lost and were wondering if you could help us find the Zane Grey Hotel?"

"It's closed," the man in front of the cart said.

"Closed?" Jonny questioned in a very perplexed manner, then glanced to Frank as if in total amazement.

"Remodeling," the man behind the cart called out who sounded American.

"That's not what the brochure said." Frank said.

The man came out from behind the cart after he pulled out a military style machine gun from under the branches and aimed it at them. Jonny smiled and raised a hand.

"That's okay, fellas. There must be some sort of a misprint, sorry to trouble you. We'll just turn this little buggy around." Jonny smiled at the two as Frank began to turn the cart around while the two starred coldly at them.

"Say is there any other place you guys would recommend to stay? You know some place clean without any… cockroaches, bedbugs, or other types of insects that can really get under your skin!" Jonny accentuated the last part in almost a mocking manner, as he had to turn around now to look back them. But the two just stood there and said nothing as they headed back down the same road they came up.

"Looks like they mean business," Frank said.

"Oh yes. It'll be dark soon enough, and that's when the party will begin," Jonny said in a scheming manner as they drove away.

Chapter 20

Night had fallen and the lights were still on at the J.Edgar Hoover building in Washington D.C. where Patricia Dire, Edward Goodman's secretary, hurried as she grabbed some last minute things before catching a flight to Los Angeles to meet with Goodman.

Call it fate, luck, or the simple fact that good will prevail over evil, but something gave her the inclination to retrieve one last message from her phone before leaving. She pressed a button on her phone and listened to the message.

"Jonny Law, Jonny Law?" she pondered after she had listened to Jonny's message. She recalled Goodman's comments, "He's a nut, a whacko." She scribbled down Catalina Island on a notepad, then clicked on her mouse to check the F.B.I.'s message page.

"Oh – my - God," she said as she paged through the startling information pertaining to Sphere and its members and the entire plan and abduction of the President. She wondered to herself how in God's name did this, Jonny Law character come up with it. It didn't matter. She knew Goodman's thoughts and also knew she would have to be discreet in revealing the information to him.

Her fingers flew over the keyboard. She deleted the address of the sender and in its place typed THE UNKNOWN SENDER, then copied the file, and emailed it directly to Goodman. She picked up her phone and dialed Goodman in L.A. The number didn't even ring, but went directly to a recorded message.

"This message box is full. Please try your call again later." A busy signal followed. "Oh," she said in frustration. "You have got to be kidding." She thought a moment as she slowly set down the phone. Her pulse began to race as she paused to examine the information on the computer. "He's on the phone," blurted from her mouth. She reached for the phone and dialed the operator.

"Operator."

"Operator, my name is Patricia Dire and I am with the F.B.I. I need you to interrupt a phone call. It involves national security." She glanced up at a clock in the office. 11:33 pm.

"What is the number?" the operator stated without hesitation.

She gave the operator the number and a moment later was speaking with Goodman.

"Mr. Goodman, I'm sorry to interrupt your call, but I just sent you a file I think you should look at immediately," she stated.

"What sort of a file?" Goodman fired back.

"It involves the President," she stated.

"Give me a moment Patricia, all hell is breaking loose over here," Goodman paused as Patricia sat there a good long moment waiting for a response.

"Can you see the file?" she impatiently questioned.

"Yes, I can see the information." He looked down at the screen of his laptop. "It would be nice to know the source of it. The unknown sender, who in the hell is that? I'm going to be a laughing stock if I send the whole damnable military machine on another wild goose chase from some anonymous computer nut," Goodman fumed.

"What are your options?" She asked throwing reality into his face.

"I don't have any!" he shouted. "I'm sorry, Patricia. I'll be lucky if I don't have a heart attack over this whole ordeal," he said.

"I understand," she replied. "If we were taking a vote," she paused, "I'd say it's legit."

"Hmnn," Goodman contemplated the playing field. "I'm going to have to go public with this thing if I don't get some answers, and quick," he said.

"Should I contact, Damon?" She inquired, nudging Goodman to act.

There was a brief silence. "No. I'm sure he must be aware of what's transpired. I'm starting to think that whole Secret Service is corrupt." He couldn't help but think of what it could do for the image of the F.B.I. if they handled this crisis on their own. And since the source is questionable, his reasons for not wanting to release any information out to anyone, including the Secret Service would be acceptable.

"I've got the vice President on hold, since this is all we've got, we're going to give it all we've got. Also, contact the Assistant Director for me, I want him over here along with several of his top Special Agents, and have them get me a Cyber Action Team as well. I want to know who and what we're dealing with here, and I also want to know who in the hell sent us this stuff," he demanded.

"Anything else?"

"Get out here as quick as you can," he said.

"Yes sir, Mr. Goodman," she agreed and Goodman hung up the phone.

Goodman ran the information by the Vice President, who agreed that if there were no other options before them, they had better move on it. He told Goodman he had total confidence in his abilities and gave the go-ahead to proceed.

A moment later Goodman was on the phone with commanding officer, General Gerome Powers at Miramar naval Base in San Diego. Powers, a hard-nosed, seasoned war veteran, devised a quick plan on paper and assured Goodman that nothing above or below the water within a hundred-mile perimeter would leave that island. Twelve specially trained navy Seals would be choppered in first, followed by a series of airdrops where roughly a hundred troops would secure the beaches and another hundred troops would arrive as a second wave from amphibious vessels launched from Miramar. One aircraft carrier and one destroyer in the vicinity would soon be there for backup along with a nuclear powered submarine that was presently enroute. Powers wanted to send a message that no one was going to mess with America, especially in their own backyard. He summed up their brief conversation by stating, "That island is going to look like Normandy beach on D-day in about ninety minutes."

"I don't care how the in the hell it looks, just get me back my president," Goodman ordered.

Even though there was a severe storm warning out in the Pacific with heavy winds, rain, and lightning forecast, General Powers promptly replied, "Yes sir," then hung up the phone.

Meanwhile, on the island, Jonny and Frank, dressed in black, and equipped with only their bulletproof vests and bullet deflecting pens, had begun their trek up to the old hotel in their rented golf cart. Upon seeing what appeared to be the same two good-sized figures still at the cart they had stopped at earlier that day, they opted to take an alternate route. It was probably an old donkey trail used by the original builders of the 1920's getaway that paralleled the newer Chimes Tower Road. The trail was narrow and slick from the rain, which forced them to abandon their small four-wheeler and continue on foot. They slowly maneuvered their way up the slick, rocky terrain through the rain accompanied by loud clangs of thunder and bolt lightning that struck down at various parts of the island. They had stumbled across several bandito-like dummies, wearing burlap shawls with sombreros and toy rifles that were set up to make it appear as if the perimeter around the old hotel was guarded to deter any possible intruders.

"We made it, man," Frank whispered to Jonny as the two crept up to the wall of the Hotel, and peeked into the kitchen area through a small back window. They could see Debbie, a.k.a. Starfield, alone in the large kitchen area dressed to entertain in a sexy, shoulderless, gold satin evening gown. They spied on her as she filled seven glasses with champagne, one for each agent, an extra if someone spilled, then took a plastic baggie from her hand bag that was filled with gel capsules and opened each one and dumped the contents into the drinks one by one, then placed each one on a silver tray.

"What do you think, vitamin supplements?" Jonny whispered to Frank as rain beaded off his black, greased face.

"Oh, I'm sure," Frank agreed. The two watched as Rhajneed entered. He was also dressed for entertaining, wearing a white suit and a dark blue turban with a large green emerald pinned to the front of it. The pair talked briefly, then Rhajneed left the room.

Jonny motioned to Frank and they headed around the building to get another glimpse into the lobby. Frank tugged on Jonny's arm as they made their way around the hotel.

"Jonny, check it out." Frank eyed the large fifty-foot antenna that interior lights from the hotel illuminated just enough to see.

Jonny looked through the pouring rain into the darkness. "What?" He asked paying no mind to the tall metal object with wire cables attached to it for support.

"Their antenna. You think we oughta clip the cord to that baby?" Frank suggested.

"Nah. My guess is that's probably their pay per view. We don't want to piss 'em off, Frank, not yet anyway." Frank nodded in agreement and they scrouched down and made their way around to the front area of the hotel to spy from a different vantage point. They poked their heads up just enough to see through a side window in the spacious lobby area, where guests could relax, and could see that all the agents were there. Each of them were nicely dressed, some in their usual dark suit attire, some more casual as they awaited their reward. However, the President was nowhere in sight.

It could've been a scene out of Casablanca. The nineteen-twenties décor with Norman Felder laying down some out of tune mood music at an old piano that looked like it could've been original from when the house was first built. Bob Cramer stood by blowing smoke rings from his Cuban cigar getting into the slow jazzy number, holding a near empty glass of whiskey. Bob Grossman, Herbert Dreyers and Thomas Randolf all drank as they talked about beachfront real estate, and David Banks starred blankly while seated in an old leather chair chain smoking cigarettes as if he pondered why he had been so foolish and done what he had done.

"No president," Frank quietly said.

"He's probably in an upstairs room." Jonny pulled his head away from the window just as the lightning flashed. He noticed an extended trellis with thick plant life that extended up to the roof and right next to the upper room windows.

"Feel like scaling a wall?" Jonny asked Frank. And before Frank could answer the sound of a door being closed hard could be heard.

"Shrubs," Jonny eeked out and the two made a beeline behind some large shrubs next to the hotel. They held their breath and listened through the spatters of rain that bounced off the cement walkways and flowed down from the rain gutters that extended away from the house into growing pools of water, and heard nothing as Rhajneed checked on the antenna.

They waited a long moment, then, when it felt as if the coast was clear, came out from the darkened hiding place.

Jonny looked at the trellis. "Think you can handle it, big guy?"

"Piece of cake, Jonny. We used to do a drill just like this at football practice all the time." Frank placed his hands onto the wooden structure then attempted to find a handle through the viney plant growth.

"See if he's up there. I'm gonna keep an eye on the festivities." Jonny then gave Frank one of his indecipherable hand gestures to proceed, then went back to the window. He could see Debbie who gracefully entered the room and with a phony smile greeted her guests. A moment later, she pretended to be surprised as Kaleeb, dressed in waiter's attire, had brought out the tray of drinks she had just doctored and approached each of the agents who gladly accepted their deadly concoction. And when she saw that they all were holding their drinks, she addressed the group. Then, one of the agents said something, which appeared to make Debbie blush. She looked to Kaleeb, who stood there with an empty tray and who appeared befuddled, not knowing what to do. As he was about to leave the room, she quickly reached for his arm for him to stay, more than likely she didn't trust him. She quickly left the room. A moment had passed and she was back, now holding a drink in her hand.

210

Jonny had seen enough. He pulled away from the window to check on Frank who had only made it a short ways up the trellis. "You okay, Frank?" he whispered.

"Yeah, gimmie a minute here," Frank struggled for each step as he attempted to make progress up the slippery trellis so he could see inside the upper floor window. "Urrrggghhh…this stuff is slippery, man!"

And at just that moment a loud exploding sound could be heard as lightning flashed up the sky and the grounds that surrounded the hotel, then another blast that appeared to strike somewhere behind the house. Jonny heard a voice from the rear of the hotel. Someone was yelling in a foreign tongue that he did not know from where on earth it originated from, but did know it was not English. He could see a flashlight darting around from the back of the hotel.

"Somebody's comin'!" he whispered up to Frank, who had elevated himself about six feet up the aged, flimsy wood structure. He sucked his body into the plant growth to hide himself as Jonny snuck behind the shrub.

Rhajneed's flashlight darted in front of him over the soupy terrain as he walked directly under Frank and close enough that Jonny could've reached out and touched him if he'd had the inclination. Another lightning flash lit up the entire area that revealed a large black mass that clung to the plant life, which was Frank.

When the coast was clear Jonny stepped out from behind the bush and looked up to see Frank's progress. He still had another fifteen feet to get near the upstairs window.

"Just a little farther, Frank," Jonny coached his buddy. "Frank?"

"Yeah." Frank struggled.

"You okay?"

"I think I'm stuck, Jonny. I'm gonna try'n pull myself free," Frank groaned.

Jonny looked up and knew it wasn't a good thing when he heard the sound of wood cracking. His eyes widened like a person who was about to witness an accident. The old trellis just couldn't hold all of Frank's two-hundred-and-forty pounds of weight. Jonny was so stunned that he didn't even move as he watched as Frank, who clutched onto the thin wood apparatus with the bean stock-like plant attached, began its' motion out and away from the house.

"Whoooooaaaaa!!!" Frank cried out. He clung like Velcro to the wood frame as it fell directly backwards and right on top of Jonny. Fortunately a four-inch pool of water had formed over a soft muddy portion of the grounds, which broke the fall rather than any bones in either Jonny or Frank.

Jonny lifted his head from the mud spitting the wet mucky debris from his mouth.

"Frank! What are tryin' to do, kill me?" he exclaimed in a hushed manner while still under the vine-laced trellis.

"Sorry, Jonny," Frank said concealed under the wall of green covering.

Jonny fished around through the pool of water for his black stocking cap. "I can't find my," and before he could finish the statement Frank held out his cap.

"Lookin' for this?"

Jonny plucked the soggy stocking cap from Frank's hand, rung it out, and placed it on his head, then lifted the light structure up from himself and peeked out to see if anyone had noticed. "Coast is clear," he said and the two got out from underneath the leafy covering just as another flash of lightning lit up the entire area as if it was daylight. A dim light emitted from a cellar window behind some bushes that caught Jonny's attention.

"Cellar window, Frank." Jonny pointed in the direction of the window. "Discreet and always a good choice. Let's do it." They both appeared like a couple lagoon creatures from the mud and earth matter that clung to their drenched bodies as they got up out of the good-sized mud pool that had recently formed and proceeded over to the cellar window.

Rhajneed had paused at the front door of the hotel. Was that the sound of wood cracking, he had just heard? He paused a moment to listen. As he did, he felt the water on his feet that had seeped through his expensive Italian shoes, which diverted his attention. "Arrrggg," he moaned, then shrugged off the sound as another blast of thunder, followed by a crackling bolt of lightning exploded directly overhead. He wiped his feet on an old door matt that had "Welcome" written on it, then reentered the hotel.

Inside the main living room, Starfield appeared warm and cordial with her champagne glass filled with water. She raised her glass to complete their toast. The agents, who all had been drinking earlier, were primed for slaughter and filled with a fools' elation that they were about to get their reward for their seemingly easy, but dirty deeds.

Norman held up his drink, then smiled at the sexy looking Starfield. "I'd just like to say, thank you, Starfield, without you this whole thing wouldn't have been possible. I really think it's too bad we couldn't have done a group photo - or something, -You know, to show our grandkids," he foolishly stated.

"Well, it's a nice idea that we can all drink to, Norman," Starfield warmly responded, then held up her glass in another attempt to toast.

"And now," she said to the group, but was interrupted again.

"Wait," Bob Cramer butted in as Starfield shot him a look with a subtle seethe brewing under her countenance.

"Before we do that," he loudly interjected. "I have something I'd like to share with the group," he held up his hand momentarily to pause the proceedings.

"Why don't we toast, first, Bob, then we'll share," she anxiously suggested, desperately wanting to finish her sinister goal of getting rid of all of them for good.

"No, no," he insisted shaking his head. He waved his arms about like he was calling time out at a sporting event. Starfield's eyes widened as she revealed a degree of concern that he might spill some of his deadly drink, then couldn't help from rolling her eyes back with annoyance as she lowered her glass, then listened to the drunk ramble.

"No, I'm afraid this can't wait. I need to make an apology to everyone here, especially to you Starfield, for running off after my ex today. It was stupid," he over emphasized the word stupid as he looked around the room to the others to make sure he held their attention. "It was stupid because I'm not in love with her anymore," and upon completing the statement his drooping eyes shifted about the room as if he had forgotten where she was standing, then his eyes wandered a moment until they accidentally fell upon the object of his affection. "You see, I'm in love with you, Starfeld," he stated barely able to properly pronounce her name, due to the alcohol he'd consumed. Starfield struggled not to appear nauseous from the comment. "That's very flattering, Bob." She began to raise her glass again with hopes the others, including Bob would follow.

Rhajneed, who had taken off his raincoat, began to make coughing sounds from the foyer to get Starfield's attention. When he began to sound like he might choke to death, she finally glanced over her shoulder at him, and then in a sherades like manner, he attempted to tell her the news of the fallen antenna.

She appeared perplexed and discreetly shook her head at him, not understanding his message, then focused her attention back to the group and to

Bob. "And it is certainly a wonderful gesture Bob, but let us all drink now," she reiterated.

Rhajneed startled Debbie as he approached her from behind and whispered into her ear.

"The antenna is down."

She appeared stunned at the revelation, then blurted out, "Yes, to love and victory." She held her glass outward and high, almost like a Third Reich gesture and waited for each of the agents to follow her misguided lead, then downed her tap water as an example for the others to follow, which they did.

Bob was the last to drink as he held out his glass one last time and gave her another one of his sexy, drunken looks, followed by a wink. "I feel like a school kid again, thanks to you, baby. You are beautiful," he slurred, then downed his poisonous drink as did the others.

Outside, heavy rains continued to pound down onto the small island as Jonny and Frank peered through a downstairs window and spied down upon Rushnad, who appeared to be dozing, while seated on a stool in front of a wooden door at the end of a hallway.

"I don't think he's guarding the wine," Jonny whispered to Frank.

"Boy, howdy, you said it, Jonny."

Jonny quickly devised a plan to get his attention where he and Frank would pretend that they had just arrived and were there to take him and the president to the submarine and flee from the island. Their goal was to get him curious enough to approach the window, then Frank, who had found a good-sized log-pole would wait and on Jonny's command, would charge the window and plant the log through the window and into Rushnad's belly, temporarily knocking him out of commission so they could recapture the president and take him to safety.

"Okay, probably need just a little trajectory Frank upon release, so it'll come down, get him right in the 'ol breadbasket," Jonny quietly instructed Frank as the two studied the situation.

"Got it," Frank agreed.

Jonny looked up and paused a moment. He heard something in the distance.

"Listen," Jonny said.

"Chopper?"

"Right, but whose side?"

"Good question."

"Why don't you get in the ready position Frank, and I'll see if I can draw him in." Frank walked over to the narrow log, picked it up and stood ready as the pouring rain drenched him to the bone.

Jonny tapped on the window and could see that he had gotten Rushnad's attention. The large man quickly snapped out of his dozing state and looked up at the window. He unholstered his gun as he stood up from his chair, then took a couple cautious steps towards it with his gun aimed up at the intruder.

"Open zi vindow, ve are here," Jonny sounded as much like a Russian comrad as he could, not knowing if it in fact was a Russian counterpart the group waited for. It was known as reaching into your bag of tricks for anything that might work, even if it was a trick you used to play on schoolmates growing up. It worked then, and it appeared to be working now, at least enough to get the bear-sized man's attention. Jonny heard Rushnad say something as he spied down upon him, while Frank stood ready as he waited for his cue.

"Velov?" Rushnad called up at Jonny.

"Da." Jonny answered, conversing to him with the one Russian word he had in his vocabulary. "Open zi vindow, you fool," he continued. And Jonny looked down and was surprised that the childish trick was working and thought to himself, that this is one big idiot as he watched Rushnad holster his gun.

"Frank?" Jonny kept his eye focused through the rain-speckled window on Rushnad.

"It's still raining, Jonny," Frank replied in an eerie tone just to let him know he was ready.

Jonny watched as Rushnad got closer and closer to the window. "Get ready, Frank," Jonny said in monotone still eyeing his subject through the window.

"On your mark," Jonny paused as Rushnad began to reach up to open the window. "Get set," he continued. Then there was a crash of thunder, followed by a long flash of lightning that lit up Jonny's face as if he was something ghost-like that put the fear of God or something into Rushnad as he nearly tripped as he stepped back and fumbled about, then frantically attempted to unholster his weapon.

"Now!" Jonny shouted as he moved away from the window.

Frank let out a battle cry as he charged the window towards the wild spray of gunshots that were drowned out by the crashes of thunder. He planted the six-foot log-pole through the window, but not into the big man's belly, but rather onto his head. Jonny looked down through the window and saw Rushnad unconscious and sprawled out on the cement floor.

"Beeeeeeautful, Frank!" Jonny exclaimed. "Let's do it, buddy, time's a wastin'" Jonny kicked out the remaining glass from the window and slipped through it and down into the damp and dimly lit cellar. He immediately grabbed Rushnad's gun that had fallen from his hand and lie on the floor next to him, and stuffed it into his pants. Frank followed him through the window. He tried to be as careful as he could not to get cut on any shards of glass as he eased his way down.

"Somethin' sharp, I feel," Frank said as he lowered himself slowly down, but then toppled down onto the floor next to Jonny's feet.

"Nice to see you could make it, 001752. Your buddy's got a little bump on his head, and he's not feelin' too sociable."

"Oh really," Frank eyed the big man flat on his back with the pole lying next to him.

"I'd say we've passed go." Jonny paused again a moment to listen. Machine gun fire could be heard in the distance.

"F.B.I.?" Frank questioned.

"It ain't Lawrence Welk, buddy," Jonny breathed in the musty air of the damp cellar and stood outside an old, thick, oak door to listen.

"Mr. President, are you in there?"

"Yes I am, who's out there?" The President called back and Jonny sighed a sigh of relief. He knew the President was alright, then gave the thumbs up to Frank who returned the gesture.

"The name is Law, Jonny Law, along with my partner, agent 001752, also known as Frank. We're going to get you out of here, Mr. President," Jonny confidently stated through the thick door, then stood back and surmised the situation.

"Think you can shoulder through it, Frank?"

"Looks pretty thick, maybe you oughta just shoot it open," Frank suggested seeing that Jonny had pocketed Rushnad's gun.

"And accidentally kill the President? I think not, Frank. Somebody would hear the shots anyway." Jonny quietly insisted.

"Okay, okay, I'll give it my best shot." Frank stepped back about ten feet away from the door.

"I'm going to have to ask you to stand away from the door, Mr. President," Jonny stated with his face next to the door, then gave Frank the go signal to charge and crash through the door.

"Ummmph," he groaned as the door knocked him backwards and right onto his behind.

Jonny shook his head, then bent over and looked down at Frank. "One more oughta do it, buddy," Jonny said with total optimism. He extended a hand down to Frank to help him up, and then once again stood back and gave the go ahead for Frank to charge the door again. This time he bounced back even farther and right onto his back again.

"Owwww," Frank moaned nearly unconscious. He continued lying on the floor.

"Frank? Frank? You okay?" Jonny tapped Frank's cheek to rouse him.

"Ewww, boy," Frank momentarily saw two of Jonny, then got his focus. "That's one thick door, Jonny," Frank said still on his back.

"Good work 001752." Jonny scratched his head for an idea, then his eyes fell upon the wood pole.

"Geeeeezzze, the wood pole, is that thick or what?" Jonny attempted to pick up the slick piece of old wood as Frank slowly got up.

"Find the key," the President called out from inside the room he was held.

Jonny paused and appeared to be a little annoyed at the President's impatient attitude and dropped the piece of wood onto the floor.

"That is exactly what we're looking for, Mr. President."

"The key!" Jonny mouthed to Frank. "Where is it?"

"You think he'd know?" Frank looked down at Rushnad.

"Your buddy?" Jonny lit up. "Well, I don't know, but I'm gonna find out." Jonny bent down and rummaged through Rushnad's pockets.

Another loud explosion of thunder, crashed overhead, then an extended flash of lightning added a burst of daylight to the small corridor, which temporarily knocked out the power. And it became so dark in the cellar you couldn't see your hand in front of your face.

"Oh great, just what we need." Jonny continued with the task at hand of finding the keys.

"Oh Frank," Jonny said.

"Right here, Jonny," Frank casually replied in the darkness.

"I know it can be scary in the dark, but you don't have to choke me for cryin' out loud, and I did find the kkk ee, " Jonny said, but the last word was choked off.

"I'm not chokin' you, man, I'm not even touchin' you. I'm over by the stairwell," Frank said in his defense.

"Well, if you're not," Jonny gasped through his constricted windpipe while he jingled the set of keys he had found, "Then whoooooo -" He exhaled the word. " -is? Ahhhh..." he gagged, then the small, dim, single, overhead light flickered, then popped back on. Jonny looked directly into Rushnad's taped up, angry face as he attempted to strangle him.

"Ahhhhhrrrrrgggggg," Rushnad growled.

"Fraaaaaaaaaaaank," Jonny barely squeaked out through his closed throat.

Rushnad had his back to Frank when the lights came back on and Frank reflexively delivered one sharp blow to the side of Rushnad's neck that dropped him to the ground like a sack of potatoes.

"001752, what was that?!" Jonny exclaimed.

"That's what Danno used to do all the time, you know on those old re-runs of that show Hawaii-Five-O." Frank replied.

"Oh yes. He was a master!" Jonny exclaimed massaging the blood flow back into his voice box. With the door key in hand, he approached the door the President was behind and inserted the key he obtained from Rushnad's pants pocket into the old cast-iron lock.

"What in the hell are you guys doing out there?" the President demanded. Jonny turned the key and opened the door to greet the President.

"Just wrestling with a gorilla, Mr. President," Jonny stated to the President, who was clad in boxers and a sleeveless under-shirt.

The President stood there a moment almost stunned at the two who greeted him. A tall lanky character and a shorter overweight fellow, who both appeared to have just rolled in a muddy grease pit.

"Are you alright, sir?"

"Yes, I'm fine," he replied. "Thanks for coming to my aid, and by the way, who are you guys? F.B.I.?"

"Well sir," Jonny was about to explain, then glanced to Frank who knew too well the story of Jonny and the F.B.I.

"You're pretty darn preceptive, Mr. President," Frank fired back.

"Perceptive, I think he means, Mr. President." Jonny nodded in agreement.

"You fellas wouldn't happen to have a spare pair of trousers, would you?" he questioned them.

"No, but he does," Jonny looked down to Rushnad, then to Frank as the two hurried and removed Rushnad's pants and shirt, then drug him, as he was waking from his brief state of unconsciousness, into the presidents former room and closed the thick oak door and locked it.

Jonny instructed Frank to assist the President with his new outfit, and he would wait at the bottom of the old wooden stairs that led up to the kitchen area and stand guard with Rushnad's gun. Please, God, don't let anyone come down those stairs. I don't want to shoot, but I will if I have to.

In less than a minute the President was ready. Jonny and Frank locked their hands together and had the President raise his foot, then lifted him through the window and out of the cellar. Frank put a knee down for Jonny to use for leverage and then stood there a moment trying to figure out something to use as a step.

"You jump up, Frank, and we'll pull," Jonny said as he and the President held their hands down through the window for Frank to be pulled up.

"Got it," Frank agreed. He did as he was told and jumped up as they pulled, but he was too heavy and slipped through their hands that were wet with rain. Frank fell backwards onto the cement floor.

"Umph," he groaned while on his back.

"Frank!" Jonny desperately called down to his buddy.

"Somebody's comin', Jonny! Get the President out of here!" Someone upstairs fumbled with a key to the door that led to the cellar. Frank quickly hid under the wood stairwell.

"See you at the transpo in five minutes," Jonny's whispered down to Frank just loud enough for him to hear, even though he couldn't see him.

"We better get moving," the President suggested.

"Right. Follow me," Jonny said and they crowched down low and headed down the same path they arrived to make their escape.

Chapter 21

Rushnad's large, designer-like jeans hung down low on the President and the shirt he had aquired was large and loose on him, making him appear more like a gangster rapper. He hurried along in a clumsy manner in the large, black steel-toed boots right behind Jonny, who led him through the darkness and rain over a rocky trail slick with mud. After several minutes Jonny began to wonder when this trail he had taken would begin to descend. He continued by feel and intuition along the path to get the President as far away from the Hotel as possible. He figured it wouldn't be long before Debbie and her Sphere counterparts would be in deadly pursuit.

"We've got some trans-po tucked in the brush about two-hundred yards away," Jonny informed the President. He felt a little uneasy that Frank was left to fend for himself, and also felt a subtle uneasiness that he may have followed the wrong path.

"Lead the way," the President stated. He followed Jonny over the darkened path he believed would lead them to safety.

Machine gun fire could be heard as it erupted from perhaps a mile away in the surrounding hills, but from whom? Jonny didn't know, perhaps the F.B.I. did get his message and were coming to the rescue. He could only hope, but couldn't be certain, and when you're dealing with the President of the United States, it's the one time he figured he would have to be, so they kept moving, slowly, and methodically over the rocky old trail that Jonny hoped and prayed headed towards the golf cart, which was well concealed behind some good-sized rock formations and covered with dead branches and brush they had gathered.

"I think we're just about there, Mr. President." Jonny attempted to reassure the President, but at the same time wondered to himself where the large bolders they hid the cart behind were?

"You think? I hope you're right. These clunkers on my feet sure don't feel like my Nike's." The President quietly replied to Jonny.

"Hold up a second, I need to get my bearings straight." Jonny nervously looked up into the cloud-covered sky.

"What are you looking at?" The President questioned as Jonny searched the sky.

"In a situation like this one, Mr. President, your stars are your best source of guidance." Jonny quoted from some survival manual he'd read when he earned his Weblow's patch during his tenure as a boy scout.

"I don't think you're going to find too many stars through this rain, kid," the President stated, then wondered who had sent this lanky, amateur to rescue him.

"It's letting up a little," Jonny said with a hint of desperation and an ounce of hope. He looked upwards into the rain that beaded and rolled off off his greased, blackened face. There was not a star in sight.

"It's a pretty small island, we'll probably run into something if we just keep moving," the President quietly urged, then decided to take the lead.

Jonny continued his upwards gaze at the black sky, unaware that the President had slipped away and begun the trek on his own. He felt his pulse increase as anxiousness began to cloud his mind with the fear that he was lost. His sense of direction was not that good and something just didn't feel right. No! He said in a demanding tone to himself. I'm not going to freak out. I am going to remain calm and get the President to safety.

"Not yet," Jonny whispered to the President who didn't hear the comment. He knew people made stupid mistakes from being impatient, so he continued to scour the sky for a peek of an opening. The falling rain had subsided to a sprinkle. Jonny felt his breathing increase. His lungs felt like an accordian getting a good work out at an Italian wedding. He licked a finger and held it up. He heard the President make a grunting sound that he assumed was a muffled sneeze. "Kazoontight." he responded. He hadn't realized, due to the darkness from the cloud covering, that the President had slipped over the edge they had mistakingly approached. He held on to dear life by a mere overhanging root and momentarily lost his breath.

"In case you're wondering, Mr. President, what I'm doing now is checking for wind. There's a slight breeze that I'm sure will blow these clouds away soon enough so we can get started again after we get some sort of bearings of where in the heck we're at," Jonny explained. "Cool air feels good, doesn't it?" Jonny took in a deep breath of the fresh ocean air. "To be honest, I'm not really overly concerned with Frank. If you knew him like I do. Mr. Smoosher, ha. That guy could talk his way out of a camp of cannibals, if you know what I mean, ha ha," Jonny nervously chuckled up at the darkened sky. "You're not too talkative are you? Might have to give you a little nickname after this excursion as "the quiet President," you know after we're all home safe and sound and tucked in bed in our jammies. You're probably just tired like me, been a long day, huh? Mr. President? Jonny paused. He looked in every direction. "Mr. President?" Jonny said again more concerned.

"Ahhh, Jonny? Over here." The President desperately pleaded.

And at just that moment a flare went off several hundred feet in the air that, slowly drifted down. It was followed by another barrage of machine gun fire, this time from a closer distance. The flare lit up the entire area. Jonny looked out over the cliff they had just approached down at the President who clung on for his life.

"Oh my God, Mr. President!" He cried out.

"Help." The President struggled with every ounce of energy to hold on to the root that felt as if it was about to give way.

Jonny got down on his belly and extended his hand down to the President.

"Get your footing if you can and reach for my wrist and I'll grab yours." It was another exercise Jonny recalled from his scouting days.

"I'll try," the President moaned. He surprised Jonny when his hand quickly locked around his wrist. It felt like a vice grip.

"Try to step up as I pull. Ready?"

"I'm ready," the President responded.

"Nooooow!" Jonny said. He grunted and groaned as his left arm clutched onto the earth, his right tugged on the President of the United States. Fortunately, by the grace of God, the President found a protruding rock to step onto and Jonny was able to pull him up to safety. The President panted out of breath as he crawled away from the ledge. Jonny breathed a sigh of relief as he stood up. "You alright?"

"Yeah. That was a little too close for comfort. Lead the way kid, you're in charge," he said winded to Jonny and they proceeded in the opposite direction. The light from the flare helped them find their way back down the rocky trail they had followed and from there they were able to find, what Jonny figured to be, the right path. As the flare extinguished itself the clouds began to separate and a handful of stars shined down from above.

In the Hotel, a short while later, Starfield had changed into dark clothing more conducive to traveling on foot. She had packed her bag and headed down the stairs to the main lobby. She could not recall a time when she felt so proud and elated - victory was so close, she could taste it. Little did she know that a highly trained group of Navy Seals quickly approached their location and several other transports filled with troops had landed on nearly every beach of the island.

And just as she casually walked down the stairs carrying her bag as if she was going on a long vacation, a crash of thunder bellowed from directly overhead, followed by an extended flash of lightning that struck a nearby power transformer and once again all the lights went out. She froze in her tracks half way down the stairs. There was silence. Her eyes darted around through the darkened room as she listened. Her eyes slowly grew accustomed to the blackness and all she could see were little specs of light out the large front window from distant boats moored in the harbor.

What was that gurgling sound? Are they all dead? She wondered of the agents as a wave of fear rushed over her. She called out in a very sweet sounding voice disguising her fear.

"Rhajneed?" No answer. "Rhajneed!" She called again, but sounded more insecure, still there was no answer. "Kaleeb?" She meekly called out, as her feet felt frozen to the step she stood on. Her voice echoed through the walls of the old haven. She was alone. She grabbed onto the railing and slowly headed down to the main lobby and once again the eerie thought that perhaps one of the agents wasn't dead and might jump out and grab her shot through her mind. The fear of that alone could be enough to kill someone, she thought as she tried to recall the positions of each one when they fell dead. It was all so foolish she thought to herself, of course they're all dead, she reassured herself? I'm such a worrywart she told herself.

Then, a moment later, she could see several flashlights darting around outside and two members from the awaiting SPHERE sub entered, accompanied by Kaleeb. She could see others also in black wetsuits outside, who combed the area around the hotel.

"Kaleeb?"

"Yes," Kaleeb replied in a hushed secretive manner.

"Comrades," she joyously greeted the pair, who wielded uzi's, and darted their flashlights around the room of apparent mayhem.

One of the men was bearded and appeared pear shaped from the wet suit he wore. His English was not authentic, but colored with an eastern accent. "Did you not get our signal?" he inquired with a dire sense of urgency.

"No, our antenna was struck by lightning."

"Where is the President?" Another member of SPHERE, who wore the same divers attire, asked as he shined his flashlight in her face.

And just as she was able to say, "He is,..." She was interrupted from a voice across the room. The flashlight darted over to Rhajneed as he finished the statement.

"He has been taken from us?"

Starfield looked over at Rhajneed and with a voice that could curl the hair of a corpse, cried out, "Whaaaaaattttt!"

Rushnad held his hand over the bump on his head, for sympathy perhaps, when he said. "The American imbeciles. They are not far," he reassured, hoping he would not be immediately shot by this volatile woman, who was driven to the level of madness to achieve her crowning accomplishment of capturing America's president.

"We must leave now! American Seals are everywhere!" The bearded man stated.

"No!" She seethed sounding satanic. "We are too close to leave now!" she belched out with a look of insanity in her eyes.

And just as she finished her statement another flare was shot up into the air directly over the lifeless appearing edifice, which briefly turned the night into day. It was as if judgment day was falling upon her where every deed in the end will be illuminated. She went into shock as she numbly walked towards the window to witness her own demise with the realization that her house of cards was about to collapse. And the light revealed her face, child-like, pale and innocent as it once was, but only for a brief moment, until her eyes fell upon something she could not even believe.

"Them, arrrgggg..." she groaned like a beast. The two American idiots, who festered at her like something deep beneath her skin that had become infected and oozing, were fleeing. She moaned and groaned like a wounded animal as she watched as they sped away in a golf cart.

And her innocent look quickly vanished which was replaced with a sour, wretched, evil look.

"Give me that!" She plucked the uzi from the hands of her comrad, then aimed the gun in the direction of Jonny, now accompanied by Frank, and fired the weapon wildly through the large front window of the hotel. It shattered it into a million pieces. The light from the flare faded and darkness once again fell upon the old hotel. She continued firing the machine gun hitting everything in God's creation, but Jonny and Frank as they fled.

224

"They're getting away!" She screamed at the others who also fired blindly into the darkness. A moment later they stopped. A smoke residue filled the air.

"It is over!" The pear shaped said. "We must go, out the back way! Now!" he insisted.

"Cowards!" She screamed with a vengeance. "I will finish our work, then!" And she ran out the front door and proceeded to the side of the hotel where several motor scooters were parked that guests normally used. Not having much experience firing the uzi, she was not used to the vibrating kick it had so it sprayed bullets like water from a garden hose turned on full blast and gone wild. She lost her footing as she ran around the corner and fell face first into a shallow mud pool that had recently formed. "Arrrrgg!!!" She cried out covered from head to toe in mud, then ran to a covering that extended from a garage and mounted one of the recreational scooters and turned the key to start it. It coughed and sputtered momentarily before it finally started. She revved the tiny engine at full throttle as if it might be stuck in that position.

Rhajneed had pried one of the uzis from one of the divers, slung it around his shoulder, and exited the hotel right behind her. He fired random shots from his large pistol into the darkness and followed Starfield to the side of the hotel where he also mounted another scooter and turned the key. He couldn't hear his scooter, from the loud-pitched sound from Starfield's. She appeared crazed as mud dripped from her face and drenched her body. She kicked the scooter in gear at full throttle and began her pursuit of the Americans. As she fled the area, soupy mud flung out from her back tire, spraying Rhajneed with mud as her scooter fishtailed wildly in a murderous pursuit. Rhajneed held the key in the on position as the little engine turned over and over, but failed to start. He wiped the mud from his eyes and spit it out of his mouth as he yelled something high pitched and indecipherable. He turned off the engine and tried again, still nothing. Then again, he held the key over in the start position. The tiny engine coughed and sputtered until it finally started. He grabbed the uzi drapped over his shoulder and sprayed a stream of machine gun bullets in the same manner as Starfield, like a wild garden hose in every direction as he fled. A bit of a kick he thought as he sped away on the scooter heading down Chimes Tower Road.

Meanwhile, Jonny was behind the wheel of the golf cart as they raced down the darkened road at a top speed of twenty-one-miles-per-hour to retrieve the President, who remained hidden in some brush behind the rock formation where they had concealed the cart. Frank had retrieved a flashlight from his duffle bag to light the way, along with several golf caps so the trio would appear like golfers who had perhaps got caught up in the storm and were just now heading back to God knows where. It was a crazy notion, but their bag of tricks was limited, so they took the role of vacationing golfers.

When they arrived at the designated hiding spot that was a short ways up a hilly slope, Jonny stopped the cart, got out from under its covered top and stood in the sprinkling rain and gave a signal whistle, then waited. It was dark and quiet with the exception of the intermittent machine gun fire that erupted from the area of the Hotel. He followed the beam of light that Frank shined up the embankment.

"This the right spot?" Frank questioned.

"Yes, it's the right spot," Jonny stepped up the dark slick embankment, then called up at the President.

"Mr. President, it's us!" he whispered loudly.

And a beat later the President waved a hand up from behind the rocks and he hurried down the slope and approached the cart.

"Thank You, Jesus," Jonny said like a Baptist minister. The President slowly made his way down the slick embankment and towards them.

"Frank, why don't you take the wheel," Jonny suggested in a casual manner, as if they were changing drivers while on vacation.

"Ten-four," Frank readily agreed.

"I was startin' to wonder if you boys were ever going to make it." The President stated as he approached the cart.

"Sorry to keep you waiting, Mr. President," Jonny announced, feeling like a five star general or any other high-ranking officer.

"Welcome aboard, Mr. President. We like to travel incognito. " Frank passed the President a golf cap, that read Golf Pro Ace written on the front of it, which he immediately put on, and also handed him the flashlight to light the way.

"Why don't you go ahead and take shotgun, Mr. President, I'll cover the rear," Jonny suggested to the President who took the passengers seat and they got situated to exit the area.

"Gladly," the President stated.

"Let's do it, Frank." Jonny said and Frank gladly obliged and put the cart in gear and proceeded down the rough road that was under construction for resurfacing.

Jonny began to relax a little and started to feel a chill from the cool night air as they drove away from what sounded like a war erupting at the top of the island. Members of Sphere were getting acquainted with American military personnel who had surrounded the old Hotel.

The road appeared rough in spots and water from newly formed puddles splashed around them as the flashlight the President held bounced along from the divots in the road.

Jonny casually looked behind them and noticed a small light that appeared to be slowly getting closer.

"Oh, Frank?"

"Yeah, Jonny."

"We've got company," Jonny looked back as the light that was trailing them appeared to be gaining ground.

"Friend or foe?" the President inquired. And not one moment after he completed the question, a spray of machine gun bullets whizzed up into the surrounding trees.

"I'd say that's a foe, Mr. President," Jonny casually replied. He immediately reached for his long military green, gun-toting bag, unzipped it and pulled out his bazooka. Frank started to zigzag the cart down the road in an attempt to avoid any stray lead.

"Gun, Jonny! Shoot his ass!" Frank said with a smidge of desperation knowing there was no bulletproof glass that would protect them.

"Ah, I don't think that's a him, Frank. I think it's your lovely neighbor. She is hot for you, man! " Jonny reached his hand down and rummaged through another duffle to retrieve a mortar shell.

"Oh, Frank?" Jonny questioned.

"Yeah?" Frank and the President quickly ducked their heads down as another spray of bullets whizzed through the air above and past them.

"I think your neighbor's dying for some of your tuna casserole." Jonny felt around inside the bag.

"Give her a message for me," Frank said.

"What's that 001752?"

"It ain't on the menu, baby." A low hanging leafy branch slapped down at Frank, who swerved the cart too late to avoid it.

"She's gaining on us, here, try this." The President pulled Rushnad's gun out from his pocket that Jonny had given him earlier and handed it back to him.

"I order you to shoot that bastard," he instructed. And Jonny turned around and took careful aim, and thought to himself, maybe if I just hit her headlight, or a tire, she'll get the hint. The thought of using the bazooka seemed more appealing to him, no mess with that. It would probably just disintegrate her, a cleaner way to wrap things up he thought. He never forgot the blood from his measles shot when he was a toddler. It was still fresh in his memory bank. It made him pass out. But the President gave him an order so he pulled the trigger. Nothing. He pulled it again. Nothing.

"Empty! Plan B!," Jonny called out, relieved as he tossed the weapon high up into the air behind them.

"Time for the big guns, Jonny!" Frank cried out.

"Oh yes, we do have a special treat for that special someone," Jonny sounded like an old, friendly, Irishman as he reached for his bazooka.

"And let's just see what we have on the menu." Jonny searched his bag. His eyes widened when his hand found one of the military green mortar shells.

"No casserole tonight, honey, how 'bout a baked potato instead," Jonny stated with a down home tone to his voice, then dropped the pod shaped shell down the long barrel of the weapon. He looked back at the wretched woman with a fire in his eye, but being in somewhat of an awkward position, and since he'd never actually fired the weapon, he realized it was on the wrong shoulder, or so it felt, so he laid the weapon onto his lap, turned to face the other way, and somehow in the process got the weapon turned around and so it faced the opposite direction. He had no realization of this fact as he took aim.

"Can this thing go any faster?" the President called out after another wild spirt from Starfield's machine gun.

"I got her punched," Frank replied.

Jonny aimed the bazooka in a direct trajectory that faced the ensuing Scooter and the little she devil that rode on it.

"Like a little sour cream, chives with your mortar shell, little miss tender heart?" Jonny pulled the trigger of the old WWII bazooka, which fired the shell that exploded a hundred yards in front of them. The blast singed the Presidents hair and blackened the side of his face with a sooty powder.

"Whoa!" Frank cried out as more machine gun bullets filled the air. "What was that?"

"Ooops," Jonny said.

"I think you singed my hair," the President exclaimed not realizing his face was now blackened like Jonny and Frank's.

"Sorry Mr. President," Jonny apologetically said.

"He singed my hair," the President repeated himself. Once again he gave Jonny the order. "Would you turn that thing around and shoot that bastard!"

"Yes sir, Mr. President." Jonny barked back like a newly enlisted soldier.

"And do not adjust your sets ladies and gentlemen that was just a test!" Jonny exclaimed. He looked back at the foulest of all women he had ever crossed paths with and the anger welled up inside him so that he began to growl like a badgered animal. His hand frantically rummaged through what he thought was his duffle bag, which began to feel somewhat unfamiliar. He felt his way through the contents trying to find another mortar shell as Starfield continued spraying machine gun bullets wildly in their general direction.

Jonny was not finding what he was looking for in the duffle bag. He lifted it up and put his face into the bag to get a closer look.

"Whew!" He pulled his face out of the bag, then pulled some of the contents out to examine. "What is this stuff?" He questioned as he retrieved socks, underwear, golf shoes, half of a pizza, a woman's plus sized bra and other miscellaneous things Frank thought were important to bring on the excursion.

"Oh for God's-sake, Frank, what are these?"

Frank looked over his shoulder briefly at Jonny.

"Those'd be my shorts, Jonny," Frank matter of factly stated. And Jonny tossed them up into the air. An ocean breeze must've caught onto them for they shot upwards from a gust just long enough to land directly in Starfield's face.

"Ewwwwww!!!!" She gagged and coughed as she nearly lost control of the scooter. Blinded by Frank's shorts, she plucked them from her face, then continued shooting sporadically and wild like a drunken sailor as she slowly gained on them.

"Would you like to tell me where the rest of my mortar shells are, Frank?" Jonny questioned in an agitated tone.

"Ah, I think they're in the other duffle bag, man," Frank confessed. He glanced back at Jonny with a sickly, childish, timid look that was given to elicit sympathy.

"Eyes up front," the President said to Frank. He grabbed the wheel and corrected the cart from driving off the road as they sped along their way over potholes and puddles as the rain began to fall harder.

"Other duffle bag?" Jonny sounded nauseous. "Just great, now what are we supposed to do?" Jonny questioned in frustration.

"Don't lose your head, kid," the President reassured Jonny as Starfield's bullets sprayed through the trees, into the hills, up to the rocks, and probably even hitting some of the boats in the bay.

"Fraaaaaaank!" Jonny hollered out to Frank in desperation for something.

Frank got a peculiar look over his face as he looked over at the President's sooty face, back to Jonny's blackened face, then to the golf clubs that were right next to him. He had it.

"I always say when the pressure's on, get out the golf clubs, Jonny. Do you mind takin' the wheel, Mr. President?"

"Oh, Frank," Jonny cried as if Frank had now completely lost his marbles once and for all. "A round of golf? That's funny man, that's really funny when we're about to get riddled with machine gun bullets any second, ha, haaaa," Jonny winced as if he was about to cry at the lunacy, then laugh, then cry and it was as if he thought he may lose his own faculties if they didn't come up with something, and quick. He turned and looked back and now saw another headlight following them about fifty yards back. Turban head? he wondered.

"Ah!" Jonny gasped, "Two on our tail now! Just great, another machine gun wielding bastard that wants to kill us!" Jonny bellowed out as the scooters drove under a remote light on the road and he could see that it was Starfield's cohort, who also fired as wild as a drunken sailor in their general direction.

And the President grabbed the wheel with one hand, then handed the flashlight to Frank who made the transition. And the cart weaved all over the road, which made them a difficult target for the two amateurish shooters, as they maneuvered themselves over Frank's clubs that were lying in between the two front seats.

And now the two champions of evil were driving side by side sporadically shooting at the fleeing golf cart that held "their president."

"Die you imbeciles!" Starfield belted out from the depths of her soul.

"Here, Jonny, try a driver." Frank handed Jonny one of his drivers from the bag.

Jonny grabbed the club just long enough to hurl it up into the air behind them.

"Oh, Frank, you know I don't golf!" Jonny cried out like a person who was about to admit defeat. "We'll get you some counseling if we make it out of this thing, man, okay?" Jonny said with all sincerity, then placed a hand on Frank's shoulder, as he winced again as if he could be crying, or laughing, or going mad himself for feeling he was the one responsible for Frank losing his mind.

Frank looked back following the trajectory of Jonny's hurled club.

"Good shot, Jonny! You just about got her!" Frank exclaimed.

"You mean the club as a weapon?" Jonny snapped out of his defeated mental state.

"Boy-howdy-right," Frank cried out as they sped down the old road.

"001752!" Jonny grinned ear to ear. "Yes!"

"What do you think, Mr. President?" Frank requested the President's input for the next shot as they drove through an extremely bumpy section of the road that was like driving over a vibrating machine.

"Well," the President pondered. "They're getting pretty close, terrain around here is fairly rough. I'd say go with a six, maybe a seven iron."

"Six iron it is, here you go Jonny," Frank handed Jonny another club from the bag.

Jonny, with new found confidence, grabbed the club and jabbed the head of it through the cloth-like top several times, then stood up and poked his head through the hole and looked back with a vengence in his eye.

"This one's for the championship!" He yelled with a hint of insanity. "His eye is on the ball!" Jonny looked back at the two gutless scooters, whose riders were having a difficult time driving with one hand while trying to shoot their weapons as the sporadic divots, veiled in darkness, jarred their aim.

"And he swings ladies and gentlemen!" He hurled another club.

"You pulled it a little, Jonny." Frank matter of factly said like the clubhouse pro trying to improve Jonny's game. Jonny pulled his head down through the hole in the top to address Frank.

"Well, gimmie the seven, Frank," Jonny said as if he was eager to improve his stroke.

"You got it. Now remember, follow through, Jonny, following through with golf is everything, okay," Frank stated. "Now try it again, you can do this, man!" Frank reassured him.

"Follow through, huh? Ouuuukay." Jonny popped his head back up through the newly formed tear in the top and looked back at the two little demons. He gritted his teeth then opened his palm.

"Club please," Jonny eyed the two pursuing scooters as he held out his hand.

Frank, acting as caddy, was quick to respond as he placed a seven iron into Jonny's palm.

"Feet planted and shoulders straight, son," the President added as he swerved the cart to avoid being shot.

"Hole in one, buddy," Frank added. Jonny focused as he rocked the head of the club back and forth as a warmup, like he'd seen many a professional do on television.

"Feet are planted, shoulders straight," Jonny said to himself as his grease blackened eyes focused on his target, and the rain droplets bounced up from the cloth-like top of the cart and into his face.

"And with a nice follow through." Jonny hurled another club towards the gun wielding pair.

"And he scores!" he exclaimed as he caught Rhajneed directly in the forehead with the club. He reflexively squeezed the trigger of his uzi as the scooter went wild and out of control before it went off the road and down an embankment as a flash of bullets streamed from his weapon.

"You got one of 'em!" Frank cried out in glory.

"Good work, son," the President added.

"Club please," Jonny nonchalantly said with a growing confidence.

"What do you think, Mr. President?" Frank inquired as to which club the President thought would be most appropriate.

"She is really close on our ass end, I'd have to say a chipper," the President suggested.

"Chipper it is," Frank agreed. Frank reached into the bag and pulled out a chipper from it and handed it back to Jonny.

"Thank you, Frank." Jonny said, now feeling like a golfpro, after his last score.

He looked back and focused intensely on his subject, then rocked the head of the club once again. "Eat your heart out Lee Travino!" He followed through with such velocity that the club made a very professional-sounding whoosh, as he sliced it through the air.

"Two for two. We have a bogey or a bingo or some damn thing!" Jonny cried out.

Frank watched Starfield get clobbered by the flying club. Her scooter went down in a mud bank off the side of the road.

"Good work, I knew you could do it!" the President said to Jonny who pulled his head back down through the cloth-like top, then half smiled as if it was nothing, but instantly felt puffed up with pride like an enormous hot air balloon at a carnival as he sat back down on his vinyl seat. He breathed in a good long breath of the cool fresh night air as he savored the feeling of accomplishment and power like a juicy steak.

"You F.B.I. boys are pretty sharp, real heroes, the both of you," the President added.

"Well, it's just a part of the job, you take the oath, then you just follow it, you know," Frank said as if he was a seasoned, twenty year man, and not revealing any unnecessary information as he looked back and smiled at Jonny.

"Couldn't have said it better myself, Frank." Jonny agreed in more of a competitive nature, making sure Frank didn't score more points with the President's favor. And he leaned back in his seat and continued relishing in his feelings of grand importance and a great sense of pride, so he continued.

"That old hypocritical oath we all take, ha," Jonny stated as if he was reminiscing to some imaginary time of his own oath. "You know when we commit to serve, to God first and foremost, and then of course this great nation of ours, Mr. President, just as Frank so gracefully exployli, ...ah, expoyliated on, I think that's the word I'm searching for, ah, I think you know what I mean," Jonny stammered as he attempted to sound noble and patriotic, while he shared his thoughts in a brief, yet concise manner so he wouldn't run the well of his limited vocabulary totally dry.

"I do know what you mean, son," the President added, also with a patriotic sentiment. And Jonny just nodded as if his deep intellectualism was understood by the greatest of minds.

"Me too, Jonny. I know just what you mean, man," Frank added that he understood Jonny's reiteration of his own thoughts.

"You might want to slow her down, Mr. President, there's a path right around here, we'll need to ditch the cart and hoof it down to the boat," Jonny said as Frank shifted the light from the road, then shined the flashlight up into the surrounding hilly area where they would hike a short distance up, then down a trail which led to the secluded cove where their boat was moored.

And the President slowed the cart down to a crawl as he veered off the road and stopped behind a large rock formation. The sound of distant helicopters approached.

"This looks like the spot, doesn't it, Frank?" Jonny questioned.

"Yeah, I think so," Frank reluctantly replied.

"Kill the light, Frank." Frank turned off the light as a number of helicopters flew directly overhead.

"Navy Seahawks, probably should've flashed them an S.O.S.," the President said.

"Yeah, Frank. Way to go," Jonny said, now siding with the President in an attempt to gain his favor.

"I thought you said to kill the light," Frank defended, then turned it back on so they could see.

"I know what I said, Frank," Jonny quickly reminded him.

"Well, ah?" Frank hem-hawed. "What about our orders, Jonny?"

"Orders?" Jonny sounded perplexed.

"Yeah, our orders from Goodman, to get the President back to the mainland safe and sound, or else," Frank said recalling the name Jonny used when he called the F.B.I.

"Right. How 'bout a little light, Frank." Frank aimed the light into the cart just long enough for Jonny to lift his duffle bag from the cart.

"I don't think it would be a wise to leave this bazooka out here for some young children to find. Somebody loses an eye and then they'll be fishing for its' owner from the registered serial number." Jonny exclaimed while looking to the President again for acknowledgement.

"That is a good idea," the President agreed. Jonny put the old bazooka back in its long green canvas carrying case and lifted it out from the cart, along with the rest of their bags that he handed to Frank.

"Ready?" Frank inquired so as not to get any further admonishment.

"Listen, kill the light, Frank, " Jonny said and Frank killed the light and they all fell silent. Someone, or more likely, a group of someones, could be heard running towards them from a short ways down the road. Heavy military boots pounded down onto the rough pavement.

"Wonder who?" Frank said.

"I don't want to know, let's get the hell out of here," Jonny whispered, then motioned for Frank to lead he way and they headed down the dark, narrow, overgrown path that was rarely traveled that led to the boat.

Roughly, twenty minutes had passed as they hiked a short ways up the terrain, then on a downward slope towards the water. Frank shined the light towards the ground directly in front of them just enough to stay on course and so they wouldn't be noticed. It felt as though the hilly area around them had eyes. The few stars that peeked through the storm clouds were starting to grow dim as signs of the early morning light began to reveal itself. They could now hear the water and Frank darted the light down to the area where he thought the boat to be, and there was - no boat, just the water lapping onto the small patch of beach.

"Say, Jonny?" Frank questioned in a whisper.

"What's up, Frank?" Jonny replied in the same hushed tone of voice.

"I don't see the boat, man." Frank said as he abruptly stopped and the President bumped into him and Jonny into the President.

"Huh? Very funny, Frank." Jonny said with a concerned tone of voice.

"I'm not jokin', man. Oh well, in-laws never liked me anyway," Frank surmised. He shined the flashlight down onto the small tree that they had tied it to.

"Did you drop your anchor?" the President inquired, thinking it was a much larger vessel.

"Well, not exactly, we were in kind of a hurry, so we just sort of, you know, tied her off," Frank said with some reluctance.

"In this storm, she could be anywhere," the President stated.

And they continued down the steep trail towards the sound of the water to get a closer look. When they approached the small tree, just above the water line on a very tiny portion of beach, the limb it was moored to had broken off.

"Let me see the light, Frank." Frank handed Jonny the light. He shined it, first in one direction where there was nothing, but steep rocks that went straight down into the water, then in the other direction. And down the beach fifty or sixty yards, there it was. If it wasn't for the name of the small boat being painted with a reflective type of lettering on its' sides and stern, the small, black boat would've blended into the dark surroundings and they would've never spotted it. But when the beam of light from the flashlight hit it, the good sized letters stuck out like a beacon - C A R P A T H I A.

"There she is," Jonny said with confidence.

"Good work, kid," the President said, which made Jonny feel as if he had just hit the jackpot of brown-nosing points with the President.

"Just part of the job, sir."

"Two hikes in one day. You guys are makin' me work," the President said.

"Light please, Jonny," Frank said.

"Lead the way, maestro," Jonny said. They picked up their bags and proceeded back up the trail a short distance, then traveled roughly the fifty or sixty yards diagonally so they would be in the vicinity of the boat, then descend back down to where the boat had landed.

By the time they approached the boat, they no longer needed the flashlight. The hint of daylight was enough so they could maneuver themselves down the steep slope to where the boat was. The branch it was originally moored to had snared itself between two good-sized rocks during the peak of the storm that prohibited the boat from going anywhere.

The President paused and scratched his head as he looked at the small boat. "Is this the right boat?" he questioned thinking there must be a mistake.

"Oh yes, this is it," Jonny proudly responded as if there were more under the hood of the boat than met the eye, which there was not. It was just your typical freshwater boat powered with an Evinrude 150 motor.

"You think they could've given you anything smaller?"

"Nope, this was the smallest one they had," Frank commented as he tossed the bags into the boat, then boarded. He thought it would be best not to divulge that the boat was stolen, or rather borrowed from his in-laws.

"We're just vacationing golfers, Mr. President, watch your step," Jonny instructed the President while he held the rear of the boat in place as the President climbed up the ladder at the rear of the boat and boarded. Jonny winked at Frank, who acknowledged the gesture, and also knew that what the President didn't know about the boat, that it was not some high-powered, official government craft, wouldn't hurt him.

"Incognito," Frank said.

Jonny was last to board and he took the rear seat. The President was seated in a side seat. Frank, who was up front in the drivers seat, started the engine.

"Let's do it, Frank," Jonny said with a hint of urgency that nothing else hinder them and their efforts of getting the hell out of harms way.

The night storm had blown over and the waters were now moderate as they gently lapped up to the rocky shoreline. Majestic cloud formations that had broken up across the sky were slowly revealed as the sun, which had not yet risen, began to paint subtle, beautiful hues onto them.

236

"Mission control, engines are running, and would everyone please hold onto your hats, here we go," Frank glanced back to see that his passengers were seated and in position for take-off.

"Aren't you going to? - " But before the President could complete his sentence, Frank had already turned around and gunned the boat.

They all heard the loud crack as the force from the power of the boat ripped off a good sized piece of fiberglass along with the short metal tie-down at the rear of the boat. They could see the fiberglass portion and rope still floating in the water, as it remained tightly fastened to the thick tree limb that remained anchored between two bolders.

"- Untie her," the President finished his statement.

"Ooops." Frank appeared wide-eyed, like a child who had just broke something as he glanced back to the damaged portion of the boat.

Jonny looked at Frank and shrugged his shoulders like it was no big deal and hand signaled him to keep on going. Getting the President back safe and sound was top priority, so they didn't look back as they hightailed it as fast as they could, heading towards the mainland with the most valuable cargo in the world.

Chapter 22

Goodman's penthouse suite at the Beverly Hills Hilton was buzzing with F.B.I. personnel. The assistant director Grant Bowman, along with several of his Special Agents were present, and four of the F.B.I.'s top computer geeks who headed the west coast Cyber Action Team had also arrived, all carrying supercomputers in leather brief cases. They ate pizza while they sifted through the data that was sent to the F.B.I.'s main page by an unknown source.

Goodman, feeling like a heart attack, reached into his pocket for his blood pressure pills, opened the bottle and dumped a couple pills into his slightly trembling hand, tossed them into his mouth and picked up his cup of luke-warm, strong, black coffee and downed them. After carefully evaluating the profiles of the members of SPHERE, he knew that anything was possible, including the assassination of the President.

"Would somebody get Powers on the phone for me," Goodman called out.

"Right away, sir," one of the Special Agents replied.

Goodman looked at his wristwatch – 3:47 am. "Why in the hell hasn't he called?"

Bowman shook his head. He didn't have an answer.

One of the lead geeks, who appeared young enough to be somebody's son and who looked like he just woke up and threw on some jeans, a wrinkled sweatshirt and tennis shoes, approached the two.

"Whoever sent this isn't too high-tech, got a snail speed dial up line, night-shift guy at his service provider is waiting for a phone call with the password to get into accounts. That'll tell us who sent it," he explained.

"Thank you, keep me posted," Goodman replied.

"You got it," the geek replied, then walked back into the other room where all of the computers were set up on a table and where the Cyber Team was huddled digging for information.

"Sir? General Powers," one of the agents called out from across the room and held out the phone for Goodman.

Goodman quickly stepped over and plucked the receiver from the agents' hand.

"This is Goodman?"

You didn't have to hear the other end of the conversation to know the news wasn't good. It looked as if someone had just let the air out Goodman who absorbed the unfavorable report.

"All dead? Good God," he flatly stated after he received news of the dead agents. "And no President? Well then where the hell is he?"

Bowman didn't have to ask for a progress report. He appeared as stunned as Goodman at the news.

"Alright, let me know if there's any new developments." Goodman said, then hung up the phone.

"Doesn't sound good," Bowman stated after evesdropping in on the conversation.

Goodman shook his head. "We won't need a firing squad - all the agents murdered, drugged with something." Goodman needed a moment alone. He stepped over and looked out the window at the fading city lights as morning approached. He could see his tired looking reflection in the window as he sipped his coffee and tried to remain positive, which became more difficult with each passing hour.

The same lead geek had just received a phone call. He hurried over to Goodman.

"Senders name is one J.L. Hoover, who goes by the name, Jonny Law," he said, then stood there waiting for a response.

At the sound of the name Goodman choked a little then went into a brief coughing fit, and it appeared that his legs nearly came out from beneath him as he quickly sat down.

"What did you say?" He inquired praying to God he didn't hear what he thought he heard.

"Jonny Law," the geek quickly fired back again.

"I thought that's what you said," he stated with a tone of naseousness.

"You know him?" the geek inquired.

And just at that moment Goodman's attention was turned to the door of the suite as Patricia Dire, who had just arrived from Washington D.C., entered the room.

"Patricia," he moaned from across the room.

"Mr. Goodman, I made it as quick as I could." She promptly approached Goodman and immediately noticed the peculiar look on his face.

"Mr. Goodman? Are you alright?" she inquired as she took off her light jacket.

"No, I'm not alright. I'm tired and I feel like shit," he stated.

"I brought some of your blood pressure medication if you're out," she kindly offered.

"Tell me one thing." He looked directly at her.

"Sure," she agreed appearing concerned at Goodman's shaky demeanor.

"Tell me you didn't know it was this, Jonny Law character, the nut, the wacko that has been pestering me for the past umpteen years for a job that sent this material, would you please, Patricia, would you please tell me that," he pleaded. He feared he would certainly become a laughing stock if he made two foolish blunders right in a row.

"Well, sir, at first when I received the message, I wasn't sure, uhm," she hem-hawed like a fearful child who was about to distort the truth.

"I can't tell you that," she then blurted out.

"What do you mean? - You can't tell me that. It was either from him or it wasn't! So which is it?" He demanded.

She paused for a good long moment.

"I'm waiting," He called out loud enough for the adjoining rooms to hear.

"It was from him," she confessed.

"Oh, dear God, Patricia. I'm going to be the laughing stock of every history book that will be written for the next thousand years!" He bellowed.

"Oh, Mr. Goodman, I am so sorry, I just felt that, we didn't have anything else, and, well, I just believed that the information was credible," she defended.

Goodman placed a hand over his face momentarily as if he wanted to hide in shame. "Oh no," he moaned wearily.

The room still buzzed with activity and amidst the chatter, someone's cell phone could be heard ringing from somewhere.

"Somebody's got a cell phone," Bowman called out to his L.A. people. They each shook their heads.

"Mr. Goodman, that's your cell phone," Patricia reminded him, knowing Goodman's ring-tone.

Goodman followed the sound as he searched around for his suit jacket located on the back of a chair in the room that was filled with computer apparatus. He reached for his cell phone from the inside pocket and flipped it open.

"Goodman."

240

"Eddie? Hi, it's me."

"What? Who is this?" He demanded.

"It's me, Jonny."

"Jonny Law?" Goodman asked as a puzzled look came over his face.

The agents all appeared frozen a moment as they looked to Goodman.

"It's him," Goodman mouthed to the rest of the room that fell silent.

"Yeah, how you doin'?" Jonny questioned.

"I've been better, why do you ask, and what's that noise?" Goodman rattled off, not wanting to reveal much information on what was transpiring, nor, to frighten Jonny into ending the call before he had any information that might be helpful.

"Boat motor. That's too bad you're not feeling too well, easy Frank!" Jonny called out, sensing the ride was getting a little rough for the likes of the President.

Goodman could hear Jonny speaking loudly to someone over some strange loud background sound.

"Boat motor? What are you up to?" Goodman firmly questioned.

"'Bout six feet, one or two inches, huh! I'm just joshin' with ya, man. Ha ha ha," Jonny chuckled as a cool morning ocean breeze blew across his face.

"Listen you, you've got about two seconds to get to the point or I'm ending this call!" Goodman shouted.

"Well then, if that's how you feel, I've got Damon's number too, Eddie, you see I'm friends with him as well. We're not as close as you and I are, but, that's okay, I'll just give him a little jingle, sounds like I caught you at a bad time anyway. We'll get everything worked out over there, with the President I mean. You take care now, bye…" and before Jonny could say his last goodbye, Goodman was screaming into the phone.

"Jonny! Jonny! Now don't go and do anything foolish like calling Damon!" Goodman shouted, "He could be on the take just like the rest of that bunch," Goodman pleaded in a hushed manner cupping the mouthpiece with his hand.

"You think so?" Jonny played along.

"Yes, of course," Goodman stated in a deep sincere tone and more composed manner.

"He seems nice enough to me," Jonny continued.

"Alright, alright, you win," Goodman gave in to Jonny.

"That's better."

"Now, what is it you want? I'm listening," Goodman stated.

"Well, I've got some news that I think will make you feel - a whole lot better." Jonny said the last portion of his statement like a mother to a toddler. "But you know the sad thing of it is, is that I'm running a little low on my minutes on this phone, they charge me an arm and a leg, Eddie. I sure hope I don't run out."

"Would you get to the point, I've got to keep this line open!" Goodman fumed.

"Alright, my point is this, - all of your agents have those really cool phones and all of their minutes are unlimited and FREE!!!!" Jonny sang out the last word.

"And?" Goodman prodded.

"And, if I, along with my partner, agent 001752, also known as Frank Miller, were agents right along side some of your boys, well, I wouldn't have to worry about a stupid little thing like my minutes when we're talking about national security and the safety concerns of the President of The United States," Jonny emphatically stated in one long breath.

"Well, are you saying you know where he's at Jonny? Is that what you're trying to tell me?" Goodman prodded.

"Nooooo o o o." Jonny elongated. "I've got a little more than that, Edward," Jonny stated using Eddie's birth name to signify the seriousness of the matter.

Jonny looked over at the President and to the hat he was still wearing. "I'm holding the Ace, Eddie, say we're in, I'll put him on the phone, the wrong answer and I swear on my great granddaddy's grave, you know who I'm talkin' about, you'll read all about it in tomorrow's paper, and probably wonder where you went wrong." Jonny surprised himself that he actually raised his voice to the head of the F.B.I. Now, the tables were turned in his favor.

"You're in, now put him on," Goodman gruffly demanded, then paused to listen to the mayhem in the background.

"Frank, who casually chatted with the President about the possibility of the trio heading to Denny's for breakfast when they got back, was shocked back to reality when he heard Jonny scream.

"Frank! Submarine!" he shouted as a huge hunk of iron emerged from the water directly in their path. Frank quickly whipped the boat hard starboard to miss the emerging black metal beast that nearly ejected all of them from the tiny boat.

Bowman, who eavesdropped on the call, couldn't take it any longer. "What did he say? Does he have him?" He questioned.

"I'm not sure. He was about to put him on the phone then it sounded like he screamed, submarine! Put this on the speaker," Goodman ordered as another voice came on the phone.

"Hello, hello, hello," a frantic cry could be heard on Goodman's speakerphone. The room grew silent and all eyes were on Goodman and the conversation he was having.

"Hello," Goodman replied.

"Hello," the voice at the other end continued.

"Hello, who is this?" Goodman demanded.

"Ah, we've got a little emergency," the voice on the other end stated, who sounded unconcerned with the conversation, and more on what sounded like a machine gun firing in the background.

"What the?" Goodman, along with the others, were aghast at the apparent mayhem.

"Grab the bazooka, and load that thing, Jonny!" the President cried out.

"Who is this?! Hello?" Goodman hollered.

"Hello," the voice responded again. "We're having an emergency out about ten miles off the coast. We're heading towards the mainland from Catalina Island, could you please notify the Coast Guard or somebody for Godsakes! We're about to get blasted out of the water from some nut on a sub with a machine gun," the President stated.

Goodman's eyes got buggy as he addressed the agents who were present. "Get Powers on the phone for me!" He ordered.

Immediately several of the agents were on the phones to get through to General Powers at Miramar Naval Base.

"Who in the hell is this!?" Goodman shouted.

"This is the President of the United States of America, we've got a Mayday ten miles out in the Pacific, we're being attacked by a submarine! Did you copy that?" the President exclaimed, then a loud BOOM was heard. Goodman appeared dumbfouned.

All Goodman could say was, "Good God!" as he and the others continued to listen.

"Frank - mortar shell would you please!" Jonny hollered out.

"Mr. President! Just keep zig-zaggin' it, I need to help Jonny!" Frank hollered, then assisted Jonny by feeding shells down the barrel of his bazooka.

"Mr. President? Mr. President!?" Goodman shouted into the phone that was tossed onto the dash of the boat so the President could direct his attention at avoiding being anhilated. He gave the boat full throttle and zigzagged the boat wildly in an attempt to elude the members of Sphere, who knew they had failed and now had decided to set their sites on killing their subject.

All Goodman could hear was the sound of a distant machine gun that burped loudly along with the rev of the Evinrude, then another BOOM from close proximity that made him and the others wince at what was transpiring.

"General Powers is on the phone," one of the Special Agents called out to Goodman.

"Tell him the President is on a boat in the Pacific, midway between the mainland and Catalina Island and under attack by a sub. Have him send everything he has to that location, now!" Goodman spewed out from across the room.

"Did you say sub, sir?" one of the agents questioned.

"Yes! As in submarine!"

"Mr. President! Mr. President!" Goodman shouted into the speakerphone. Another loud BOOM at the other end of the line belched out of the tiny speaker phone.

"Sounds like World War III going on out there," Bowman said in disbelief to the group of onlookers. BOOM! Again, he could hear a thunderous sound reverberating through the phone.

"Aim a little higher, Jonny!"

Goodman listened to what sounded like the President yelling orders to Jonny, who continued firing at the relentless sub.

"Did you say higher?" Jonny questioned back.

"Yes, higher!" the President shouted back.

"Frank! Shell please!"

"Come on, kid, you can do it." Goodman felt a tinge of shame for now supporting someone whom he referred to as a nut, a whacko, and a list of other adjectives that he used to describe Jonny.

"Jonny, I'm going to straighten out the boat for three seconds, when I do, let 'em have it, tell me when you're ready!" the President directed Jonny.

"Yes, sir!"

Goodman couldn't take it. He looked away from phone and out the window. Dear God, please give that idiot presence of mind for one moment, he thought not realizing he was holding his breath, as was everyone else in the hotel room.

"This one's gotta count, Jonny!" Frank yelled over the high pitch of the stressed little motor.

Jonny didn't say a word as Frank's words seemed to echo in his mind over and over again. He swallowed and it felt like his whole life was a kaleidoscope of pictures that flashed before him.

Jonny's eyes locked onto Frank's for a brief second. They appeared to realize in unison that this was it, a "do or die," circumstance. And all of a sudden something came over Jonny and things became quiet and the high-pitch of the engine disappeared, so did the machine gun fire, so did the fierce wind and mist of the ocean as he focused on the sub gunner. This was the kind of focus he thought that great athletes must feel when they get into the zone. It felt magical and almost dream-like. He carefully balanced the long awkward weapon on his shoulder and steadied himself as the boat bounced over the waves. When the boat rises on a wave – fire.

Frank dropped another shell into the smoking bazooka, then patted Jonny's shoulder.

There was a flash coming out from the sub's machine gun as the gunman stood in the conning tower of the sub firing at them. It seemed strange he couldn't hear the sound of it, then he saw the flash from the muzzle had momentarily stopped. Maybe his gun jammed. His own voice echoed back at him as he called out to the President.

"Ready!" he cried out and the President turned the wheel and straightened the boat for what seemed like a long moment. And for that brief moment in time the boat felt as if it glided on thin air and time magically stood still. He imagined himself to be like a large jungle cat on the hunt whose vision was acute and razor sharp. He took in a long deep breath and held it. He steadied the weapon and placed the crazed machine gunner in the cross hairs of his fold up site.

The tiny boat continued at full speed. It rose, then bounced down, rose and bounced down onto the water again, and as it rose again he timed it perfectly as he squeezed the trigger and watched the trail of smoke that followed the shell as it made a direct hit on the elevated portion of the sub where the gunner was located. He began breathing again and his face relaxed and all of a sudden he realized he could hear the revving motor again and the boat as it pounded down on each wave as he looked at the smoldering sub.

"You got him, Jonny, you got him, man! Way to go! Gimmie five, come on bro, gimmie five!" Frank hollered, barely able to get his words out he was in such a state of hysteria, and Jonny looked up stunned and in disbelief for a brief moment that he did it, he had hit his mark. He then reflexively complied by holding up his hand for a good swat from Frank, who felt like a Super-bowl champ.

"You got him, man, you got him!" Frank cried out.

"Yeah, it looks like I sunk their ship. That's what ya get for messin' with the big kids!" Jonny yelled out.

The hotel room of F.B.I. personell appeared to be resuscitated back to life with hoops and hollers, and high-fives upon hearing what transpired. Goodman sighed a sigh of relief and wiped his brow thinking they were home free.

And Jonny quickly sat down, feeling light headed from all the adrenalin rush and excitement. They could hear some yelling going on from the sub that was getting smaller and less threatening as they continued to hightail it home.

Jonny seemed unconcerned as he rested the old green bazooka on his lap and looked back in amazement as smoke billowed from the conning tower portion of the sub, as it appeared to slowly lower itself.

"Fellas, I don't know, but I wouldn't count your eggs before they're hatched. I don't think he's sinking. I think he's going under," the President stated, still apprehensive to premature elation from an enemy that was merely wounded.

"Not to worry, Mr. President, they're headed back to the lagoon or wherever they came from," Jonny confidently rallied, feeling like Patton, or some famous general still holding his big smoking gun that rested on his lap. He couldn't recall a time in his life when he felt so elated. They had rescued the President of The United States all by themselves. He smiled at Frank, who pulled up his pants and felt larger than life, just as Jonny did.

Jonny gave the thumbs up to Frank who stepped over and gave him another high-five slap.

"Man, that was the coolest thing I've ever seen in my entire life, Jonny. You nailed their asses to the wall, man!" Frank said, then glanced back at the sub, which was nearly submerged with the exception of the conning tower.

"Yeah, I'm getting' to be a pretty good shot with this ol' baby," Jonny said petting the relic of a weapon.

And even though the President had some reservations, both Jonny and Frank felt like they had finally won, and both realized it wouldn't matter if they got credit from the papers, the F.B.I., C.I.A., Secret Service, local police, or even their own grandmothers. This great endeavor would be forever etched in their hearts and in their minds that they had done something that most men wouldn't have dared to contemplate.

"He's looking like he's stalled - maybe you did get him," the President stated while eyeing the lifeless sub.

"You want me to take her in, Mr. President," Frank suggested.

"Sure, Frank," the President obliged and Frank took the wheel and once again it felt like they were on a pleasure cruise with the President. Frank reached for his mirrored sunglasses that were on the dash, put them on and breathed in the early morning revitalizing ocean wind.

And they were all inspired by the majestic sunrise.

"Let's keep it full steam," the President said with his eye on their wake in question.

"Jonny," Frank called out, then tossed his phone back to him.

Jonny caught the phone one handed and fastened it back onto his belt. He glanced back at their diminishing nemesis and the vast Pacific and felt a little more at ease as they sped over the mild waters of the Pacific. Relaxed, he set the bazooka down and savored the fresh cool ocean air.

"Frank?"

"Yeah, Jonny."

"Shades."

Frank reached for Jonny's mirrored sunglasses on the dash and tossed them back to him. He put them on and felt a grand feeling of importance. It was too bad he didn't have a pipe, he thought to himself. His pride became puffed up like a hot air balloon as he imagined himself to be near in rank to the President. He was after all in the same boat.

"All in a days work, Mr. President, all in a days work. Right Frank?" Jonny called out to Frank as if people attempting to murder them, was just your average, typical day at the office.

"Ten-four, buddy," Frank agreed as he, Jonny and the President looked up as a trio of F-16's flew over low enough to touch.

"That was quick," the President stated. He held onto his hat as the air support shot past them then split apart, one left, one right, one straight up.

The boat began straying off course in the direction of God only knew where as Frank's mind was now in the cockpit of one of the fighter planes looking at all the fancy gauges and dials. He felt like a top gun that could decipher the meanings of all of the controls, and numbers on all of them.

Man oh man, maybe I should join the Air Force when we get back, those things can't be that hard to fly, he told himself before Jonny snapped him back to reality.

"Oh, Frank? Let's try California, huh?"

"Ooops." Frank steered the boat back on course.

"Who was it you had me talking to on the phone?" the President questioned Jonny.

"Oh, yeah. That was..." Jonny began and Frank quickly interrupted.

"That was our boss, Eddie Goodman, Mr. F.B.I. himself," Frank firmly stated, then gave a look to Jonny that said don't dispute it.

"Like the man said, our boss," Jonny agreed,

"Well, he must've got on the horn to somebody, looks like we've got an escort," the President said. Out over the distant waters of the Pacific, a U.S. carrier seemed to magically appear. A Seahawk chopper was lifting off from its' deck.

Jonny breathed a sigh of relief that the U.S. Navy had decided to join them and felt a quiver run up his spine as patriotic goosebumps came over his entire being from the sight. "I don't see a problem," he said at the welcomed intrusion.

"Geez is that thing big!" Frank announced to the entire Pacific.

"Indeed it is, Frank. That right there is your typical Navy destroyer," Jonny stated to educate Frank on part of the Naval fleet.

"Well, not exactly, Jonny. That's an aircraft carrier is what that is," the President corrected.

"Right. It's a carrier, Frank, that's what I meant to say."

Frank, wanting to savor every minute of their military escort back home, slowed the boat to a more moderate speed as they made their way back home.

Jonny's mind also wandered as he lapsed into a daydream of being the admiral of that traveling city barking orders at all of his incompetent underlings until his phone rang.

"Hello," Jonny calmly said as his mind drifted back to reality.

"Jonny?" Goodman inquired.

"Yeah, it's me, how you guys doin'?"

"We're doing just fine, Jonny. Tell me, how is the President, is he alright?" Goodman inquired.

"Ah, he's okay. We had to sink the sub. It was either them, or us." Jonny matter of factly stated.

"Good. Good work, would you mind putting him on the phone?"

"Who, the President?"

"Yes, Jonny, the President."

Jonny turned his head away and spoke in a hushed manner. "We still got a deal?"

"Yes, we've still got a deal," Goodman agreed.

"We get sworn in as agents and an assignment with the Bureau," Jonny bartered in the same hushed manner.

"Yes, sworn in and an assignment with the bureau that's fine, now would you please put the President on the phone, Jonny," Goodman pleaded.

"You got it, here he is." Jonny handed the phone to the President, then gave the thumbs up to Frank and a subtle nod indicating they were in and all was good.

"Hello, Edward," the President stated, feeling a little more at ease.

"Mr. President. Is everything alright?"

And at just that moment the President's eyes locked onto an underwater wake created by something about fifty yards out and approaching at a good clip. "Torpedo!" He cried out.

"What?" Goodman replied in disbelief.

Jonny turned to look. A look of sheer horror painted over his face. "Yikes! Frank? Hit it!" Jonny yelled to Frank. He immediately realized that the fine underwater wake was from your typical torpedo that he had seen in so many war movies just before it blew to smithereens whatever it was aiming for.

Frank turned to see what the fuss was all about. He could see it heading straight for them. It wasn't rocket science. It was just what the President said – torpedo.

"Now that don't look good," he said as the explosive projectile was now about thirty yards away. He crammed the throttle lever full forward, knocking the President into the back seat as the tip of the tiny boat raised up as he yanked the wheel hard left, which threw Jonny into the President's lap as they headed towards the Navy carrier.

"Did I lose it?" Frank cried out too afraid to even look back.

Jonny pulled himself up and looked back. There it was still hot on their trail. "'Fraid not, Frank." He looked at the President. "Mr. President?" The president appeared to be semi-conscious. "It's gaining on us, Frank!"

The white of Jonny's teeth became more defined from the black grease that remained on his face. His upper fronts became prominent like an angry dog's. "Enough is enough, and I've had just about enough," he angrily groaned. He picked up the bazooka, reached around in the duffle bag fished around for a mortar shell, grabbed it and placed it down the barrel of the weapon.

"That's the last one, Jonny!" Frank reminded him, now wide eyed with fear.

"That's the last one, Jonny," Jonny repeated the statement like a child who had been taunted one time too many. He glanced upwards. A Seahawk helicopter hovered overhead.

"What do you want?" he barked. He was surprised at his fearlessness and burning desire to once and for all put an end to this unrelenting foe.

The boat continued bouncing about as he looked back into the water. He lifted the weapon onto his shoulder. His eyes scanned the waters behind them. Their wake was making it difficult to see anything within a hundred feet behind the boat.

"Where is it? Where is the damn thing?!!! Hard left, Frank!" Jonny screamed out to Frank knowing that would eliminate their long wake and reveal the trajectory of the warhead.

Jonny's eyes appeared to bug out when he saw the trail not more than twenty feet from them. He didn't have time to think, only to pull the trigger.

Whooosh!!!

He raised his eye away from the eyepiece.

CABOOM!!!

A cannonball splash as tall as a building erupted up into the air. They felt the spray of the cold saltwater fall like welcomed rain as they sped away.

Jonny sat back down in his seat and hardly felt the boat as it bounced over the somewhat choppy waters. He seemed dazed a moment as he stared out into the vast waters of the Pacific. All of a sudden he felt unusually calm. I did it, he thought to himself. I stopped the bastards.

"Two for two, the kid is hot!" Frank hollered, which snapped Jonny back to reality.

"Obviously a heat seaking projectile." Jonny said.

The hovering Seahawk fired two torpedo missiles into the water.

Two high-pitched sounds, SHEW!!! SHEW!!! A beat later and another eruption of the ocean occurred, this time it appeared like a volcano that could easily be seen from three hundred yards away.

"Oh yes, and you folks have a nice day," Jonny said knowing that this time would be the last time that they would have any surprises from their friends from SPHERE.

"Now that's what we're talkin' 'bout, givin' it to 'em, baby, yeah! Right on, Jonny! Right on, bro." Frank hollered in exitement knowing the enemy was once and for all defeated.

Cheers from the crew of the Navy carrier could be heard from a hundred yards away.

Jonny looked over at the President, who sat in his seat rubbing the back of his head, and tended to him.

"Mr. President, are you alright?"

"Yes, I'm fine." The President rubbed the back of his head and looked up to the chopper. "Frank, I think he wants us to stop."

"Yes, sir," Frank responded slowing the small boat to a crawl. The chopper hovered, then began to lower a rescue harness for the President to be air-lifted to the destroyer, but he waived it off.

"I'll ride along to the mainland with you fellas, if that's okay?"

The chopper remained overhead a short while longer to radio to his commander that the President didn't want to be taken aboard, then its' pilot gave a wave and proceeded to head back to the ship. The trio watched as it landed safely onto the football field sized deck.

Jonny just smiled and looked to Frank.

"Sorry for the sharp turn, Mr. President," Frank apologized.

"That's quite alright, Frank. Your quick thinking probably saved our lives," he said.

Frank gave Jonny a proud look. Jonny smiled and nodded.

"Jonny, I'd like to speak with your boss," the President said.

"My boss? Yeah right, the bossman. The guy who signs the checks, yes sir." Jonny pulled his phone from his pocket, opened it and dialed a number.

"Eddie, hi, it's me again. I've got someone that wants to speak with you," and Jonny handed the phone over to the President.

"Edward, yes, I'm alright, a bit chilled, and tired, but I'm just fine, thanks to two of your finest."

Jonny and Frank both beamed from the compliment.

"Well, we just had a little run in with a rabid torpedo, from that same damn sub that one of our Seahawks just put to rest," the President explained.

Goodman's demeanor came to life like a time lapsed flower blooming in the mornings' sun after he knew everything was going to be alright.

"Mr. President?" Frank called out.

The President pulled the phone away momentarily, "What is it, Frank?"

"Did you guys ever catch that guy, oh what's his name, Osemma Ben Loudin?"

"Osama bin Laden? No, we never did, Frank, why?"

"I told you, Jonny."

"Why, because we think we know where he's hiding Mr. President, that's why," Jonny quickly blurted out.

"Hold on a moment, Edward," the President pulled the phone from his ear to listen.

"The Hideout Hotel," Frank jumped in before Jonny could speak. Jonny retaliated with a sharp look to Frank.

"He's right Mr. President that's where we spotted him," Jonny stapled onto the last comment.

"Edward?" the President questioned.

"Yes, Mr. President."

"Did you catch any of that?"

"Osama bin Laden at the Hideout Hotel, yes, where's the Hideout Hotel?" Goodman questioned.

"Hold on, I'll ask," the President told Goodman.

"Where's the?"

And before the President could finish his question, it was as if it Jonny and Frank were both on Jeopardy as they raced to deliver the answer to win additional points with the President.

"Catalina Island," they stated in unison, then snarled at each other.

"Catalina Island," the President reiterated back to Goodman.

"I'll get right on it," Goodman said.

"Get Powers on the phone!" Goodman called out to the agents in the room.

And the agents once again scurried to the phones to connect with the Navy commander.

"Mr. President?"

"Yes, I'm still here."

"If you like we can have a chopper take you aboard the Nimitz," Goodman suggested.

"Yes, they just offered, but I told them I'd prefer to ride in with these two, fine, brave men who saved my life," the President stated.

Jonny and Frank beamed with pride.

"I'll be fine, Edward, see you shortly, oh, do you think you could have a pair of Nike's, size ten-and-a-half, for me when we arrive?" The President began to unstring the heavy boots he wore. "Thank you," he said, then handed the phone back to Jonny.

"We'll see you at Marina Del Rey in about? Frank?"

"Twenty minutes."

"'Bout twenty minutes, then we can talk, right Eddie?" Jonny warmly probed, then paused to listen. "Alright, Mr. Goodman," he corrected himself, then slapped his phone shut put it in his pocket and enjoyed the cool ocean breeze as they proceeded back to the mainland.

Chapter 23

Cackling seagulls floated upon a gentle summer breeze as small white caps rolled onto the miles of white, sandy, northern California beach where Jonny sat, relaxed in a lawn chair. He was wearing his usual attire of short pants, a Hawaiian shirt, untied sneakers, and his mirrored sunglasses. His nose was white with sunscreen while seated under a large umbrella at the remote location. Through binoculars, he looked out to the open sea carefully monitoring for any suspicious activity. Nothing, only whitecaps against a hazy horizon as far as the eye could see. It was the assignment that he and Frank were promised by Goodman - to guard the west coast.

Jonny let the binoculars hang around his neck. He looked down at his watch and read the date. "Two years, and six months, to the day, Frank," he called out.

Frank was behind the counter of their undercover, Dog To Go, hotdog stand preparing some lunch. "Are you sure? Has it been that long already?"

"'Fraid so." Jonny's feet sunk into the soft beach sand as he slowly got up and walked over and stood at the counter opposite Frank.

Frank placed a hotdog into a bun then set it onto a paper plate. He reached down into a cupboard and pulled out a stack of papers and shuffled through them until he found the dated picture the photographer had mistakingly sent to Jonny that was taken at Marina Del Rey the day they rescued the President.

"You're right, Jonny." Frank set the picture onto the counter and the two feasted upon their moment of glory. There was a moment of silence as a sense of great pride welled up inside both of them. It brought back memories of when Goodman, at the last minute, had them put on F.B.I. vests just before the picture was taken, making sure, just for the record, that if there ever were a leak everyone would know who was responsible for the rescue.

It was a proud moment for Jonny and Frank. They stood on each side of the President, patriotically posed in front of the Marine One chopper with the American flag and Presidential emblem plainly seen on its side. They appeared like two of the baddest, bad-asses the world had ever known. Their faces blackened with grease. Both wore mirrored sunglasses with tough-guy poses that could've made them poster material for any F.B.I. recruiting office. The President smiled and saluted the group of top military brass, who were present that memorable day.

Jonny felt deflated as he stared at the picture. "It was a long time ago, Frank."

"Hey, man, I can't find my badge, and I have looked everywhere." Frank said to change the subject, knowing that Jonny was right. They hadn't done a thing, other than eat hotdogs and fish, in the two and a half years they were assigned their position on the remote beach.

"Not good, Frank, but, it's to be expected when boredom sets in."

"Well, nobody's shootin' at us out here, anyway." Frank defended. Even though he agreed with Jonny that it was boring at times, it was safe and secure.

"Call Eddie, he'll get you another one." Jonny's shoulders drooped down with his mood. He felt like a carbonated drink that had lost all its fizz. There was no danger, no excitement, no feeling of doing anything substantial for the world while they were stuck out in the middle of nowhere on a beach mainly occupied by seagulls.

"You want to go fishin' today?" Frank suggested.

"I'm sick of fishin'."

"How 'bout a hotdog, Jonny?"

"I'm tired of hotdogs, Frank. I just wish they'd give us an assignment we could sink our teeth into. We might as well be on the dark side of the moon, out here in the middle of nowhere." Jonny gazed out at the vast Pacific.

"Yeah, I suppose," Frank agreed. "Maybe this place is like an old toxic waste site and we're the only ones that don't know it." Frank suggested.

"Right." Jonny agreed with Frank to pacify him more than anything until the severity of the thought sunk in. "My skin has felt kind of scratchy lately."

"Mine too." Frank paused to scratch. "Then the details of our big caper would be washed down the drain forever when we mysteriously get some sort of flesh eating virus that disinigrates us into nothin'."

Jonny quivered at the thought, then began to scratch at his arms and legs. He shifted his attention when his cell phone chimed.

"Hello." Jonny's eyes widened and his demeanor took on new life as he paraphrased the incoming information. "Top secret! Covert mission?" Jonny began to glow at the possibility of a new challenge.

"What is it?" Frank was dying from suspence.

Jonny was too captivated to respond. "Chicago? No, I've never been there, sir."

"Terrorist plot, Jonny?" Frank impatiently inquired while his eyes squinted and his face contorted as his mind painted a montage of pictures of disaster. He reached for the hotdog to suppress his desire for information, then stuffed a good portion of it into his mouth. "Somebody get kidnapped?"

Jonny was too focused to give Frank a morcel of information.

"Not the president, tell me it's not the president again, Jonny, please," Frank pleaded.

"Can we notify our families?" Jonny urgently inquired to the caller.

"Notify our families?" Frank winced as he cried out. "Oh for love of God, it is the President, isn't it Jonny? I knew it, I could feel it in my bones!" Frank worked himself into a near frenzy.

"They've been notified already?" Jonny's jaw dropped. "Yes sir," he replied to the caller. "Burbank airport?" Jonny pulled the phone away from his ear momentarily to address Frank. "Drive time to Burbank airport?"

"Headin' south with the flow of traffic, I'd say three and a half hours, give or take a few minutes."

"Three and a half hours, sir. Is there a problem in Chicago?" Jonny paused.

"What is it, man?" Frank pleaded, now with half a hot dog in his mouth.

"The President?" Jonny's chest slowly rose and he came to attention with the mere mention of the President.

"It is the President, I knew it, I knew it! You always told me to trust my gut, Jonny, and that's just what I did." Frank took another large bite of his hotdog.

"Sure, yes, well of course." Jonny said to the caller. "A speaking engagement?"

Frank stopped chewing.

"The President wants F.B.I.'s finest for security," Jonny reiterated to Frank with his hand over the receiver, then smiled a modest smile. "Thank you, sir."

"Ah haaaa, now we're getting'to the meat and potatoes," Frank stated.

"A private jet?" Jonny excitedly mouthed the words a second time back to Frank, once again with a hand over the mouthpiece of his cellphone. "Yes sir, oh yes, top secret, shouldn't be a problem. Mum's the word, hm hm," Jonny chuckled as if the notion of something as simple as keeping a secret would not be a problem. "Right. See you guys in a few hours. Yes sir, we can find Burbank. Bye bye." Jonny suavely said, then slapped his phone shut and attached it back to his belt.

"Security for a speaking engagement with the President?" Frank proudly surmised with a smile.

"Right, and some of the big chiefs in the F.B.I. too. This is top secret, Frank, not a soul is to know," Jonny emphasized the, "Top Secret." He exhaled a gasp of air and groaned to release all the pent up frustration he had accrued while feeling abandoned on the remote beach. He sounded as if he was near tears as he shifted his gaze out over the Pacific.

"I was at my wits' end, man." Jonny scrunched his eyes together and massaged them with his fingertips. He then quickly recomposed himself back to a state of over flowing joy from the news.

"Heck, I can keep a little ol' secret like that," Frank pretended to zip his lips shut.

"They want us, man! It's about time." Jonny used every ounce of breath to speak his mind and sounded totally rejuvenated. It was hard to tell if he was laughing or crying.

"We're back in business….Life in the fast lane!" Frank performed some air guitar as he sang a line from an old Eagles tune.

"Oh yes. It's about time! Let's blow this coup."

"You got it, bro. My Crown Victoria's got a full tank, Jonny," Frank suggested.

"Then you drive." Jonny matter of factly replied.

Hardly a word was spoken the whole time while enroute to Burbank. Each played out fantasies of their second meeting with the President. The white lines on the freeway became hypnotic, and blurred as Frank casually weaved through the eighty-mile-an hour traffic.

Frank was on autopilot as his mind painted the scene. He imagined himself in front of a large gathering of people outside a packed auditorium wearing a dark suit and tie with an earpiece that relayed every movement of the President directly to him. Feeling like a rockstar in sunglasses, he signed autographs for all the sexy, Presidential groupies. And then, through his earpiece, the message came to him – an assassin was present. The scene shifted to slow motion in his mind. He dropped his pen and pushed his way through the group of women who had circled him and charged past Jonny who was security at the entrance that led into the auditorium. He could hear Jonny's voice slowed down, "Frank, no!" he cried, but he charged through the entrance anyway and ran down the center aisle of the standing room only auditorium as he reached for his automatic weapon that was holstered on his side. He barked out orders to the gathering, "Get down and stay down!" The crowd complied. He then proceeded to have a shoot out with not one hooded assassin, but a half a dozen, killing them all, but not after taking some lead himself. After the carnage, he ripped open his shirt to reveal a bulletproof vest with the large white letters, F.B.I. printed across it. Then, after a thunderous standing ovation from a grateful audience, and Jonny, whose gun jammed during the mayhem, the President resumed his speech after thanking F.B.I's finest for saving his life again. He then walked through the crowd while the men, women and children high fived him as he went back out to the lobby to continue signing autographs.

"Say, Frank? Frank? Frank!" Jonny quickly reached for the wheel to swirve the car to avoid rear-ending a semi.

"Yeah, what, Jonny?"

"Could we try to avoid some of the other vehicles, please? You might want to keep it under a hundred, too." Jonny suggested.

"Yeah. Sorry, man. I don't know what I was thinkin'."

Jonny leaned back in his seat and looked out the tinted passenger window as they sped past the mile markers along the freeway. He closed his eyes and drifted into his own daydream.

He imagined himself wearing professional, business-like attire embellished with his trademark mirrored sunglasses to mask what his attention was focused on at any given moment, while on duty at a press conference in the rose garden of the White House. The President addressed the group. "And today I'd like to announce to everyone that the new head of the F.B.I. is a good and trusted friend of mine that has saved my life on more than one occasion, ladies and gentlemen, I'm going to appoint J.L. Hoover, also known around here as Jonny Law."

Jonny, appeared stunned and surprised as he walked over to the President and they wrapped their arms around each other for a lenthy embrace. Some of the press yawned as Jonny and the President continued to hold one another. Both wiped tears of joy from their faces, and then Jonny took questions from the press.

"Jonny, if you accept this position, are you planning on implementing any new policies when you take office?" A journalist from the back of the gathering called out.

"I will be accepting the position," he stated as flashbulbs popped throughout the room. He looked over to the President who stepped over to give him another lenthy hug. Jonny had to gently push him away. The President, who was consumed with emotion, wiped tears from his face, then stepped off to the side where he blew his nose.

While fielding questions, he noticed some movement behind a purple velvet curtain in the back of the crowded area, which he inconspicuously eyed while he slowly spoke to the group. "And as far as policies, my first assignment, I'll be personally, undertaking, is eliminating the, terrorist threat," he paused. His eyes darted around the gathering as he sized up the terrain. The press continued to talk amongst one another wondering what he was looking at.

"That has infiltrated the White House!" He shouted out, then ripped out his handgun from his suitjacket and emptied the weapon into the curtain.

A slender, bearded man clutching a semi-automatic weapon fell out from behind the curtain in plain sight.

The press applauded Jonny for his quick thinking then began to chant his name. "Jonny, Jonny, Jonny."

Jonny blew on his smoking barrel before he casually placed the weapon back into its holster under his suit jacket. Over the applause, he continued, "Thankyou, thankyou, and I'd just like to say that I'll be appointing agent, Frank Miller, who will be directly under me as second in command."

"Could you repeat that name, Mr. Law?" A woman's voice called out from the press.

"Agent, Frank Miller."

"Jonny, I'm right here, man, wake up, we're here," Frank had to nudge Jonny to wake him.

"Whew, I must've dozed off."

"Yeah, you did. We're flyin' in a Lear Jet, man, check it out."

Jonny slowly got out of the car and feasted his eyes upon the sleek machine that was parked at an angle, like an expensive show car, he thought. It all seemed surreal.

"Oh, yes. I like it, Frank, I like it a lot."

"Boy howdy, you said it."

A fellow agent, wearing a suit, approached them and introduced himself.

"Good morning, gentlemen. I'm agent Newmiller, I'll be accompanying you on your flight." He said then shook both of their hands.

"Agent Law, and my partner agent Miller," Jonny stated.

"I'm sure that you've been informed that this assignment is top secret." Newmiller said.

"Yes, sir," they both replied.

"Good. We're ready when you are." Newmiller stated.

"We're ready sir, but, we drove straight to the airport and didn't really get a chance to change and freshen up." Jonny responded, concerned that their beach attire would be inappropriate for a meeting with the President.

"Don't worry, we'll have a change of clothes for you when we arrive," Newmiller said smiling.

Jonny and Frank exchanged looks and went along, and before they knew it they were looking down on the greater Los Angeles area that continued to get smaller and smaller as they ramped up to thirty thousand feet enroute to Chicago.

Newmiller went up to the front of the plane and left Jonny and Frank alone in the rear. They each had a window seat and were inspired by the majestic cloud formations.

"Comfy seats, man."

"Real leather." Jonny rubbed his hand over the soft leather, then placed his nose against it. It still had the new smell in it. He bounced down in his seat to check the depth of the cushion. Frank performed the same maneuver and the two laughed uncontrollably as they bounced up and down in their seats like two hyperactive children, seeing who could bounce the highest.

A short while later, when they arrived at O'hare, a shiny new black stretch limo was parked and waiting for them. It was just like something out of a movie Jonny thought as they went from the plane and directly into the limo that promptly whisked them away. Jonny, Frank, and agent Newmiller sat comfortably in the roomy, black leather back seats. Newmiller faced the rear of the vehicle opposite Jonny and Frank, who both appeared more than a little fidgety as they drove off the runway, then headed into the heart of Chicago. There was a long silence as they headed to the unknown location and unknown assignment.

"You guys look a little nervous," Newmiller observed.

"Not really," Jonny said attempting to appear calm, cool and collected under the pressure of the unknown.

"There's a fully stocked bar, either one of you drink?" Newmiller inquired.

"Don't drink," Frank replied. Jonny shook his head.

"Well, don't be nervous. It'll all be over soon enough."

A concerned look came over Jonny's face. "What'll be over soon enough?"

"Yeah what?" Frank lit up.

Newmiller chuckled. "You'll see," he said then picked up a magazine that had a good-sized O on the front of it and began thumbing through the pages.

Jonny wasn't sure what to make of agent Newmiller. A middleaged man in fairly good shape with a touch of grey along his temples, who had a subtle smile on his face at all times. He wondered what he thought was so humorous. He looked out the window, then glanced back at him – there it was, a little smirk. He didn't trust him. He looked over at Frank, who shrugged his shoulders and shook his head. Neither of them had a clue as to what was about to take place.

Jonny quickly grew bored with the skyline of skyscrapers, and agitated at Newmillers methodical manner of licking his fingers, slowly lifting the page, then whipping it over to spend between three to six seconds viewing the next page, and then repeat the process.

"Are we going to be flying back out tonight?" Jonny inquired.

"I suppose," Newmiller calmly replied with a hint of a sneer.

"We'll be flying out tonight, - " Jonny said then looked over to see Frank's eyes closed, - "Frank."

Frank's head sprung up. "Huh," he said.

"Nothin'." Jonny turned his head to look out the window and enjoy the city view as the limo sped up, then slowed through the heavy traffic. He was totally unaware that in a few short hours this would turn out to be the biggest day of his life where his grandest dreams would be realized.

Chapter 24

Jonny's heart began to race when he noticed the big O that was mounted sideways on top of a brick structure with the words, Harpo Studios written on it. They pulled into the parking lot on Washington Street that was adjacent to the studio where guests entered through a back entrance, and parked.

"The Oprah show?" Jonny's jaw dropped and he appeared stunned and a little confused. He glanced over at Frank, then to Newmiller.

"You guessed it. The President will be speaking on the Oprah show and wanted some top notch security, and that's all I'm at liberty to say," Newmiller explained.

"Oprah Windfree? Heck, I'm her number one fan," Frank said.

"Right after me, and her name is Winfrey, Frank, not Windfree. She's not a hot air balloon." Jonny chuckled.

"That's what I said, Windfree."

Jonny nodded in agreement. "You think we might, you know, get a chance to meet her?" Jonny meekly inquired.

"It is a very good possibility," Newmiller said with a hint of a smile, then got out of the limo.

Jonny and Frank followed Newmiller into a rear entrance. It was a short walk down a hallway that led to security.

"Metal detectors, man," Frank said as they approached the security checkpoint that was similar to that found at any airport in the country.

"Did you forget who was on the show, Frank? The President of the United States, security is tight with a capital T, buddy. Right, Newmiller?" Jonny solicited support from their fellow agent.

"Yeah, right," Newmiller agreed, then addressed the two large black security guards who each tipped the scales at around three hundred pounds. "This is agent Law and agent Miller."

"How you guys doin'?" One of the security gaurds asked.

"Just great. It's an honor to be here, fellas," Jonny said.

"Yeah," Frank agreed.

262

"It's an honor to have you, would you place anything that you're carrying that's metal into the dish and please step through the metal detector," the other security man stated.

"Hope this isn't gonna turn into a strip search, Jonny," Frank stifled a giggle.

Jonny smiled. "No problemo." He emptied his pocket of keys, some pocket change, gum wrappers, a rabbits'foot and his cell phone, then proceeded through the detector. Frank did the same and they were cleared and then led by one of the show's female producers into one of the numerous green rooms. There, she showed them the clothes she wanted them to wear. Jonny was to be dressed in a dark suit and tie, and Frank, a more relaxed look, which consisted of khaki slacks, a nicely pressed Hawaiin shirt and some casual looking Italian leather shoes.

"Man, they thought of everything," Frank commented.

"Oh, and by the way, my name is Gloria, if you need anything let me know. The food tray is for you guys, so help yourself, and a makeup person will be in in about, oh, fifteen minutes." She stated then started to leave.

Jonny poked his head out the door and wondered where Newmiller had gone. "Ah, Gloria? Could you track down agent Newmiller for us please, that knucklehead forgot to brief us," Jonny chuckled then shook his head at the incompetency of some people.

"I'll try," she said, then quickly departed.

"Thank you."

"Make up person? What is that about?" Frank questioned.

"They want everyone to look their best around the president, kind of a no brainer, Frank," Jonny explained as if he'd done this sort of thing a million times before.

"Hey, don't they usually give the food trays to the guests?"

"In your dreams, man," Jonny chuckled.

"You know, we might just have to forget to change back into our regular clothes when we leave, Jonny." Frank began to pick at the fruit tray.

Jonny held up the suit for a closer look, felt the expensive material, then, smelled the fabric. "Tempting, but I don't particularly want a SWAT team kicking in my door, Frank."

A short while later, after an older man, named Reggie, applied some makeup to their faces and gel to their hair, to make them appear healthy under the bright lights. They were then instructed by Gloria to wait in the wings of the stage. Every seat in the studio quickly filled and the eager crowd sat and waited for Oprah to take the stage and then the President, or so they were told.

Once again Jonny gave the same request to Gloria. This time his plea was more urgent. "Gloria, would you please find that Newmiller for me and tell him to get his butt back here," he demanded. He was getting more nervous by the second wondering what they were supposed to do.

"I'll try," she said, before she hurried away again. People scurried about in every direction like little worker ants back stage as Jonny, now dressed in the new suit, and Frank, in his Hawaiian shirt and slacks, stood with racing hearts in the wings, waiting.

"There she is," Jonny peeked from behind the curtains as the crowd came to life when Oprah made her grand entrance.

"Man, does this even seem real?" Frank leaned over and whispered in Jonny's ear. They both were in awe as the applause from the audience seemed to go on forever. It was loud, exciting and electric.

Gloria approached them again. This time she carried with her the same type of mirrored sunglasses they wore the day they rescued the President, and, little did they know would become their trademark look in the minds of millions of Americans who would watch the show and witness the two, great American heroes.

"Clothes fit you guys okay?" she inquired as she straightened Jonny's tie and brushed a spec of lint off his suit jacket.

"Yeah," they both agreed.

"Do we get to keep 'em?" Frank inquired.

"Yeah, sure," she replied.

"Bingo, Jonny," Frank said.

"Hawaiin shirt looks great on you, Frank. A little more relaxed, fits your personality," she said.

"Here, put these on, would you?" she told them as she handed them the sunglasses.

"These for the bright lights?"

"Yeah."

"Is the President here yet?" Frank eagerly inquired.

"Not yet, get ready," she told them. Someone's frantic whisper was heard, "Gloria, I need you," and off she went leaving Jonny and Frank alone in the wings.

"Ready for what? He's not even here?" Jonny questioned a little perturbed from all the fuss and the President wasn't even in the building.

"Yeah, ready for what? That puke green room they had us held up in has got my head spinnin', Jonny."

"Deep breaths, Frank, deep breaths."

Frank started taking deep breaths in an attempt to calm himself down. They put on the sunglasses they were given, then patiently waited, for what, they hadn't a clue. They could hear the excited crowd, calm as Oprah began to speak.

"The President must be the main guest, huh Jonny?" Frank nervously inquired.

"Who knows," Jonny sounded perturbed from feeling left out of the big secret of why they were flown out to an Oprah show, to supposedly guard the President, and didn't even have an inkling as to where he was and what they were supposed to do.

"Thank you, thank you," they heard Oprah say over the backstage monitors as the audience grew quiet.

"Today on our show, we're going to be speaking with our President, but first, before we do that, we're going to introduce you to two, truly great American heroes. You see a couple of years ago, some of you might recall, there was a brief story in the news pertaining to the President of The United States, and the story stated that the President had gotten separated from the group of people he was with on Santa Catalina Island. And for those of you who aren't familiar, it's the little island that's about twenty miles off the coast of Southern California."

"Huh?" Frank said in a stunned manner, then the two looked at one another in shock.

"Sweaty palms and rapid pulse, Frank," Jonny sounded dazed at what he was hearing.

"What's goin' on, Jonny?"

"I dunno, but I think we're about to find out."

They continued listening.

"And, they told us he was mistakingly left behind, if you can believe that. Well, that wasn't the whole story, you see the President wasn't really left behind at all; he had in fact been kidnapped. You heard me right, kidnapped. And, at the time, and after the President was out of danger, roughly two and a half years ago, the security advisor, and some other top officials, thought it would be best, due to the nature of our times and with terrorist threats that the story be hushed for security reasons. Well, wouldn't you know it, there's been a book written about the ordeal - so you might say there was a little leak. And today on our show we have the author of that riveting book, titled "Mark of a Hero," written by former head of the F.B.I., Edward Goodman, and the two men who are responsible for saving him and more than likely saving his life."

"Holy hot tomollee, Jonny, who are they talkin' about?!" Frank cried out three octaves higher than his regular voice.

"Probably a couple brown nosers the agency wants to groom for God only knows what," Jonny explained.

"You think so?" Frank inquired, then unconsciously resumed taking deep breaths in an attempt to calm himself.

"We're not the type, Frank, trust me?"

"I don't know, Jonny."

"I can assure you, Frank – they don't mean us." They stood in disbelief as Oprah continued with her opening monologue.

"Ladies and gentlemen the two, young, brave men you are about to meet are in for a big surprise. You see, they thought that they were on a top-secret assignment to be security for the President today. And well, we didn't fully lie, the President will be speaking today, via satellite, and former head of the F.B.I., turned author, Edward Goodman is here today.along with the two heroes he has written about in his book, who are in for a big surprise today appearing for the first time on national TV, and the book I've mentioned will be on stands tomorrow.

"When did Eddie retire, Jonny?"

"For Pete sake, they don't tell us anything."

"But before we bring them out for the whole world to meet we wanted to show you a little picture that was taken of our special guests two and a half years ago."

"Well, let's just see who they got to play us, huh, Frank?" Jonny said with trepidation as the picture taken the day of the rescue of them with the President appeared.

After eyeing the photograph, Frank immediately leaned over and placed his hands on his knees to get some blood to the brain while he took in deep breaths. "Oh my God! I don't even believe this, man!" Frank's voice screeched like his windpipe was instantly constricted and choked off. He remained hunched over like he was in a huddle waiting for someone to call the play.

"Huh, and will you look at that, Frank, they look just like us, too." Jonny still didn't believe it.

Frank raised his head to take another reaffirming glance at the photo. "Looks like us?! That's us, man!" Frank gasped.

Jonny wasn't sure how to feel. A moment of dizziness came over him as he stared at the picture with his mouth hanging open. A transformation poured over his spirit at that moment. It was them. All of the knocks he'd received while growing up from being the kid that didn't get it, that stemmed from his dyslexia, and ADD disorder, and the label of "least likely to succeed," from highschool seemed to, in an instant, melt away. He stood there frozen, speechless, proud. His eyes watered up from what was about to take place.

"I stand corrected, Frank." It was Jonny that now sounded dazed as he looked down at his buddy who remained hunched over looking down at the floor.

"Frank? You okay?"

"Yeah, I think," Frank eaked out, still panting.

"Ahhhhhh," Jonny exhaled as he looked out at the kaleidoscope of people in the audience."Oprah's pretty friendly." He stated sounding as if he was holding his breath, then shifted his view back to his friend. "Frank?"

"I know," Frank moaned.

"It's the other hundred million people I'd worry about," Jonny nervously chuckled not knowing how to react to the situation.

"Did you say hundred million?"

"'Fraid so, buddy."

"Good Gawd almighty, Jonny. What have we got ourselves into, now?" Frank stood up. Jonny was surprised to see tears had run down his cheeks and before he could say anything, Frank wrapped his arms around him and squeezed him so tight that he could hardly take a breath.

"Thanks, man," Frank tried to compose himself as he held onto to his buddy.

Jonny was taken off guard by Frank's gesture of gratitude. "Thanks for what?" he inquired.

"You taught me to believe in myself, man. I'd a been a homeless drunk in the gutter if it weren't for you, Jonny," Frank's voice squeeked and cracked with emotion as he wiped the tears from his cheeks, then slowly released Jonny from his bear hug.

"You made the choice, buddy, not me." Jonny reminded him. "Are you ready to take the field, win one more game?" Jonny knew if he reminded Frank of the courage that he already possessed, he would be fine.

"Game day, yeah, I'm ready." Frank instantly became rejuvenated. He pulled off his sunglasses and quickly wiped away any remnants of emotion that had trickled down his face and felt a sense of pride and courage come over him.

It worked, Jonny thought. With one thought, Frank reached inside himself to find the courage that was always there waiting to be tapped, and in an instant he pulled himself together. He would do the same, he thought as he watched Frank prepare himself by pulling up his pants.

The life-sized picture of Jonny and Frank, who stood on each side of the President in front of the military green Marine One chopper adorned with the Presidential emblem and American flag, remained in plain sight for the whole world to see. A moment frozen forever in time, both were clad in black and wore their tradmark mirrored sunglasses and charcoaled colored faces with thick bulletproof vests with large white letters, F.B.I. on the front of each, as they appeared like the baddest of the baddest of tough guys the world had ever seen.

The applause from the audience seemed to go on forever after Oprah said, "There they are." When the applause subsided she continued. "It's an unbelievable story of luck, determination, courage, persistence, a philosophy where giving up wasn't an option, and of course a lot of guts. Ladies and gentlemen, without further ado, give a very warm welcome to two, truly great American Heroes, F.B.I. agents, Jonny Law, and his partner, Frank Miller," Oprah said as she applauded along with the audience who looked to the wings of the stage for the guests to come out.

Gloria, once again appeared out of nowhere, "Guys, you're on!"

Jonny patted Frank on the back. "Let's do it, buddy," he said.

Frank adjusted his sunglasses and took a deep breath and followed Jonny out onto the stage. The crowd came to their feet and warmly welcomed the two.

They stood out on the stage and smiled out to the audience, who were still on their feet, and like your typical famous persons, they pointed out to various unknown people as if they were old friends who had come to see them on the show.

Jonny put his hands to his side pushing his suitcoat back that revealed his shiny, gold, F.B.I. badge that was fastened to his belt.

Oprah continued to applaud them, and just when the applause began to subside she introduced another guest. "Ladies and gentlemen, former head of the F.B.I., Edward Goodman."

The audience erupted again with applause. Jonny and Frank both looked on as their old friend, Edward Goodman walked out onto the stage and centered himself between them. He firmly shook both of their hands.

"Hi, Eddie," Jonny said beaming.

"Jonny, Frank, I don't think I ever got the chance to thank you two for savin' my hide." Goodman said as the crowd continued applauding the trio. Jonny and Frank were speechless as Goodman put an arm around each of them and gave them a squeeze on the shoulder, which was all the thanks they needed.

Oprah gestured for them to come over and be seated. Goodman sat closest to Oprah, Jonny next to him, and Frank next to Jonny.

Oprah began by thoroughly questioning Goodman about what exactly transpired the day the President was abducted and how a thing like that could've occurred in the first place. She obviously had read his book because she seemed to know every detail of what transpired on that fateful day, from the abduction by a group of treasoness Secret Service personnel at the Laker game to the return of the President at Marina Del Ray, and even events that led up to it.

Jonny looked around the room at the people, the lights, the producer who stood in the wings, carrying something in her arms, the people behind the camera, the people giving Oprah cues for commercial breaks. He wanted to savor all of it up so he could recall every detail of it to share it with his grandkids. He watched as the show director gave Oprah the cue for commercial. That's when she informed them that they would get the spotlight next. And it seemed like the blink of an eye and the director was counting her back in to resume taping.

"Jonny, before I ask you about the details of what will probably go down in history as the greatest rescue ever documented in law enforcement – what is the story behind your name? Your birth name, I understand is Hoover. Are you related to J. Edgar Hoover?"

"Well, to be perfectly honest, no, but everyone thinks I am," he chuckled.

"I understand you tried quite a few times to get into the F.B.I." Oprah questioned.

"Yeah, it wasn't love at first sight," he chuckled again as he glanced over to Goodman, who politely smiled.

"How many times?"

"Oh, once a week or so I'd call Eddie, Mr. Goodman, I mean, to let him know I was still thinking of them and that went on for, several years."

"Did you feel it was your calling to do this kind of work?"

"Most definitely, wouldn't you say, Frank?"

"Most definitely, Jonny." Frank's wide-eyed nervous response came off comical and drew some laughter from the audience.

And just as Oprah left no stone unturned with Goodman, she did the same with Jonny and Frank. She wanted to know what made each of them think, or believe that they could thwart a kidnapping plot on the President of The United States, and where did that belief come from. She thought it was borderline miraculous that two young men, equipped with next to nothing as far as technology and weaponry could do what they did.

Jonny simply explained that it was his burning desire to do something great for God and for his country, even though others laughed at him and told him he couldn't. He always knew inside that he could become anything he wanted to be, no matter what anyone said all he had to do was to believe. It was something his mother had taught him at a very young age. The audience enthusiastically applauded the comment. And then he proceeded to explain that, even though at times, he and Frank had their doubts, they never stopped believing they could do it. It was a feeling that they had to step up and rise to the challenge of making the world a safer and better place and that those feelings were inside both of them and that's what gave them the inspiration to never give up.

And then she questioned Frank about his relationship with Jonny and his battle with alcoholism and how he was doing.

"Clean and sober for two and a half years." The crowd come to life and gave another round of applause. "And, I owe it all to this guy seated right here beside me. I told him before we came out, if it wasn't for him, I'd probably be livin' on the streets right now."

All Oprah could say was, "Amazing, absolutely amazing the difference one person can make in the life of another." She said in awe of the two.

Oprah's floor director was giving her some hand gestures, which prompted her into her next segment of the show.

"Ladies and gentlemen, I was just informed that we have the President connected, via satellite. Hello, Mr. President," she stated as an image of the President in the Oval Office instantly appeared on a screen behind them.

"Hello, Oprah," and the crowd again went wild with applause. "I have a couple of your old friends on the show today." She said.

"Yes. I was informed. Thank you. Hello, Jonny, hello, Frank," he began.

"Hello, Mr. President," they responded in unison.

"I thought I'd take this opportunity to personally thank you guys for your courage, and perseverance that you showed the day you rescued me and saved my life. It is something that every American should strive for, which is standing up for goodness and what is right in the face of evil." The President stated.

"Thank you, Mr. President," Jonny stated.

"Yeah, thank you, Mr. President," Frank followed.

"Oh and Jonny?"

"Right here, Mr. President," Jonny quickly replied.

"I understand Oprah has a little surprise for you today." The President sat silent for a moment.

"I'd like to ask the both of you, how you think your families will feel about you after this becomes known to the world, 'cause if you don't know it, a lot of people are going to know who you are after today."

The both of them stammered unsure who should speak first.

"Frank, how do you think your family will respond?" Oprah inquired.

"Ah, they'll probably find it a little hard to believe," he said, then laughed along with Jonny.

"Jonny, you've been married now for two years?"

"Right, to my beautiful wife, Karen. Hi, honey," he smiled and waived to the camera.

"How do you think she'll take your new found fame?"

"I'm sure she'll be happy when she sees the show and hears about – " and before Jonny could finish, he could see the director giving a cue to someone in the wings. He looked over and was stunned to see Karen carrying their one-year-old son, Jonny Jr. out onto the stage to join them. " - the book," he finished his thought.

"Ladies and gentlemen, Mrs. Jonny Law, and son," Oprah said over the applause.

"I don't even believe this," Jonny said with an ear-to-ear grin on his face. Goodman, Frank and Jonny, all stood up as Karen came out and sat between Jonny and Frank. Jonny gave Karen a little kiss on the lips, then his little baby boy on the forehead. As the others sat down, he proudly held up his toddler for the world to see. His son was wearing a baby blue t-shirt that read – F.B.I.'s # 1 MOST WANTED written on the front of it.

"Meet the future head of the F.B.I. right here. His name is Jonny, too," he said to the audience, then kissed his baby again. The crowd was eager to applause.

The President spoke again as the applause subsided. "Jonny, Frank, I thank you both from the bottom of my heart for saving my life, keep up the good work and God bless both of you and your families." he concluded.

Jonny and Frank were speechless.

"Thank you, Mr. President," Oprah added.

"Thank you, Oprah," the President concluded and the satellite picture of the President slowly dissolved back into the picture of the day he was rescued.

Oprah proceeded with a myriad of questions until they had shared almost every detail of the experience they could recall. She then asked Karen how it felt to be the wife of an American hero.

"I'm very proud of Jonny," she meekly said.

Goodman then sang the praises of Jonny and Frank like the head of the choir, or as if they were his own sons.

Both of them smiled along and felt like they were either in heaven or somewhere near it as they basked in the realization of the grandest of dreams anyone could imagine.

"One more question I'd like to ask both of you before we run out of time. How does it feel to be true, American heroes?"

Jonny looked to Frank who held out the thumbs up, then to Oprah.

"Ditto," he said, grinning ear to ear as he held up his thumb along side Frank's and then Goodman stood up to applaud them, and Oprah followed, then the entire audience was on their feet giving them a closing standing ovation.

And Jonny held Karen's hand as he looked into her eyes, knowing they would relish in the sweetness of this moment for a lifetime. Finally, Oprah came over and gave them all a hug and congratulated them once again. It was the grandest feeling he could ever remember having. He put his arm around Frank.

"Good work 001752," he said, then smiled.

"Thanks, Jonny." Frank said as this grand moment of recognition would be etched in their minds forever.

THE END